NADEZHDA

DIES

LAST

Dennis T. Cosgrove

DELENOVA
PUBLISHING

Library of Congress Control Number 2025920422

Paperback First Edition 2025

ISBN (print)   979-8-9985676-8-1
ISBN (ebook) 979-8-9985676-6-7

Published by Delenova Publishing, Fort Myers, Florida,
United States of America

AUTHOR'S NOTE

This book is a work of fiction inspired by my real experiences as a Special Agent with the FBI. While some characters also appeared in my previous book, which was rooted more directly in real cases, the events and scenarios in this story are fictional.

For continuity and storytelling purposes, I have retained the same character names and some biographical details. However, this book should be read as a fictional narrative. Any resemblance to actual events or persons, living or dead, is purely coincidental or the result of creative adaptation.

The characters will continue to evolve across the series. Each was inspired by real individuals I worked with, trained with, or relied on in high-stakes situations. Sometimes, the strongest support in the field came from the least expected places.

Chapter 1

"What did you get your mother for her last birthday?"

"Sharon, it's you?" I ask the familiar voice on the call, surprised she's even contacting me just days after saying goodbye in the San José FBI parking lot.

"Well, in 1931, the daughter of Marjorie Merriweather Post, Eleanor Barzin, gave her mother a Fabergé egg for her birthday. Now, that's quite a gift," she says.

"Yeah. I can't top that. Heck, I can't remember what I got my mother for any birthday but it wasn't a Fabergé egg, that's for sure. Where's this going, though, Sharon? Very enlightening, but I'm with my sister; we're in the car heading to Carmel for dinner. But I'm intrigued, naturally. You know me. And you've been doing more research on Fabergé, and on our mysterious and missing egg, so it seems."

"A lot of research, Odysseus, a lot. You think your odyssey is over, Special Agent Cosgrove? I think it's only begun. It would never be that easy. But you knew that all along, didn't you?"

"I'm sure going to miss you in Moscow, Sharon. A few days ago, during a courtesy visit to your office, you gave me that OSI lead. I sense you're far from done with me. Maybe toying with me a bit, perhaps?"

"Nope. I'm sending you more background on those eggs. You can pull up my full report once you're in Bureau space."

"But this isn't the real reason you're calling, is it?"

"Oh, I see you haven't forgotten the basic rules of the art of the interview, have you?"

She laughs.

"I'm not the sharpest investigator as you well know, but I have to give you credit. You've got my full attention, skipping the 'how are you doing' stuff, just like my sister here. She never bothers with the 'hi' and 'how are you doing' formalities either. You'll have to meet her someday. So, what's up? Why are you calling?"

"Yeah. You've got me there. Don called last night, told me to reach out to you. You need to go back to Washington. He didn't say why, just to tell you to get back there. He didn't sound upset or anything, but you know Don Pierce. He'll not show his hand, not to me anyway."

"OK. I was planning on leaving Monterey in a few days' time to fly to New York to meet up with family, so we can all return to Moscow together. Now, it seems I'm heading back to Washington. Regardless of the reason, can you tell me who I'm expected to meet?"

"Don said to call him as soon as you arrive, and he'll explain everything."

"Got it. Well, Sharon, since you've now revealed the actual reason for reaching out, give me the abbreviated version of your report on Fabergé eggs, and this Ms. Marjorie Merriweather Post and her daughter. My sister here's into this sort of thing, and it's not classified or law enforcement sensitive, so go ahead ... We might as well talk it through."

"OK, well, the Fabergé bejeweled egg gifted by Eleanor Barzin to her mother is known as the Catherine the Great egg, and it's on display at the Hillwood Estate Museum in Washington, along with many other items from the House of Fabergé."

"OK, so? I need to go there and steal it, photograph it, or what?"

"I'd have thought it was obvious," she says, chuckling. "You can hardly go looking for a missing Fabergé egg without having seen one up close, can you?" She leaves a timely pause for effect. "Oh, and while you're there, find the curator of the collection, introduce yourself, and let her or him educate you about this stuff, and about Ms. Post and her former husband, Joseph E. Davies. Now, Davies was the third husband of Ms. Post, heir to the Post cereal—General Mills—family fortune. While the two of them were working and living in Moscow in the 1930s, Stalin's regime was busy selling off the treasures of the Romanov family and former Russian aristocrats for hard currency. Davies and Post just happened to be there at the opportune time, buying everything they could get their hands on in the pre-war days, to include items from the House of Fabergé. And that included the bejeweled eggs, of course."

"And do I mention searching for the missing egg? Like you say, I'm not even sure what it looks like. But you know who told me she once glimpsed it? Heck, a part of me believes she's got her hands on that egg. Perhaps Nina gave it to her to hold for a while. Anything's possible."

"Dennis, we can talk about that another time. Just so you don't sound like a complete moron if you talk to the curator, based on my research, there are two prime candidates for the egg that Andrey Kozlenok likely has, or had: the 1909 Alexander III Commemorative egg, and the 1903 Royal Danish egg. As far as photos of them, well, that's another story but I've sent you detail in my report that you should find useful."

"Thanks, Sharon. We'll be talking again soon, I have a feeling … So many questions and issues remaining unresolved. Not sure where all of this is heading … the OSI lead you 'gifted' me, the missing Fabergé egg, and now this unexpected stop in Washington. But that's for another day. So, au revoir—or *dos-vee-dan-i-ye*—for now. The Romanovs spoke mostly French amongst themselves, you know."

I hang up the phone and look at my sister sitting in the car, looking straight out the windshield. I've seen that expression on her face before.

"OK, Jen. What's up? You heard most of that call. You look like you want to say something. What? It's my life, Jen. I'm just along for the ride," I tell her.

"Hmm. Give me a minute. I'm processing all of this. So, Sharon calls you out of the blue and tells you that you need to go to Washington, then gives you a briefing about that missing Fabergé egg. I have a feeling your life's about to get way more complicated, Dennis.

"Well, let's leave that all aside for now. Take me to that shop where you felt the presence of that poltergeist or whatever it was. Then we can have dinner at that Italian restaurant your Russian friends liked so much."

"Sure. Promise me one thing when we walk into that shop. Don't suddenly fall into some sort of hypnotic trance or start speaking in tongues," I tell her, only half joking.

"Yeah, I promise," she remarks. "Funny thing is that this will be the first time we're 'operational' together, taking on an otherworldly entity. Seems only fitting in a way, don't you think? Will be an excellent test for us as a team, right?"

I open the door to the quaint shop, full of an assortment of sundries ranging from pocket watches to knives and kitchen utensils. Some items look new, and some appear older and used, perhaps gained from an estate sale. We've barely set foot in the shop when an item—a wine bottle opener with some sort of emblem— tumbles off a shelf onto the floor a few feet in front of us. My sister and I exchange glances as I stoop to pick it up. The emblem is a double-headed eagle, the symbol from the days of the Russian Imperial Empire. I shake my head.

The sound of the item falling is probably what brings out the owner from behind the counter, peering around before his brows rise and his eyes light up. He seems to recognize me from my prior visit, the time when I asked him about his 'otherworldly' guest.

He takes the opener from my hand, returning it to its proper place on the shelf.

"He's letting us know he's here, and he's happy you're back," he tells me. "At least, I think he's happy. If he wasn't, you'd be picking up one of those knives, not this unique wine key bottle opener. Perhaps it's meant for you to buy?"

I want to chuckle; is he really hopeful of a sale? It would be rude to laugh if so.

"I'll take it," says Jennifer to my surprise, stepping forward and taking the opener back off the display shelf. "I could use one of these, and this one looks like it has a history. Besides, how can I not buy it when it comes with a rather unique recommendation?"

"For you, mademoiselle, it's yours for free," the owner tells her.

So, he wasn't angling for a sale after all.

My sister smiles, then leans forward, kissing the owner on both cheeks.

"Yeah, my brother told me about your mysterious friend, but you've no reason to be concerned. He's a harmless fellow, just wants to be acknowledged and appreciated sometimes."

"Yes? You think so?" the owner asks her.

"Absolutely. Merci, cher ami," she tells him in perfect French.

He's captivated, kissing her hand.

"OK, sis. Let's go. You can visit with your friends another time. I'm starving, and our table's waiting."

Julian Carrico, owner of La Trattoria de Napoli, greets us at the door. He nods to me and gives me that look, signaling that he remembers me from many months prior when I was at his restaurant one night with my Russian law enforcement partners.

At least that is how I process it.

He brings the menu over to our table once we settle in, describing the evening's specials.

"Good to see you back here so soon," he says, looking at my sister. His remark confuses me because he's blatantly addressing his words to her, not me.

She has never been to his restaurant before, has she?

Unless, of course, she's decided not to reveal it to me. For whatever reason, I can't imagine.

"You must mean my brother, Dennis, right? He recommended your restaurant to me and here I am, but I haven't been here before," she says.

"No? Sorry," he responds, searching for words to extract himself from a possibly embarrassing assumption.

I step in to bail him out. "Julian, I was here months ago with my Russian law enforcement partners. That night, you closed the restaurant for us."

"Oh, yes. I remember. How are they? Are they back in Russia?"

"Yes. Busier than ever. They really enjoyed your restaurant. Thank you for being such a wonderful host that evening. They all told me they'd never forget that night. This is my sister, Jennifer; she loves Italian food, so I just had to bring her. Jen tells me she's never been to your restaurant, but perhaps she's snuck in before somehow. I only returned to Monterey a few days ago. I'm working in Russia these days."

"Interesting. I guess I'm just getting old, but there was a young lady here a few days ago who looked just like you, Ms. Jennifer."

"Oh, yes? And did you talk to her at all? I know you have many customers, and it's impossible to recall every meeting, I suppose," she asks, and instantly, I see where my sister is going with this conversation. She's probing for information, likely suspecting that the young lady was none other than our mysterious 'friend' the LAX woman, the one who told me she lives in the Monterey area with her husband, studying Russian at the language school. I almost want to mention all this to Julian, to free him from his state of embarrassment at the mix-up.

But I don't, staying quiet. Sometimes, things are too peculiar to describe.

Anyway, he can't be that mortified by it since soon, he mentions it again himself.

"You know something? I'm pretty good with accents. In fact, I picked up your brother's accent, and remember telling him he was no stranger to the New York area if you know what I mean. But your accent, well, your voice, it's also not very different from that young lady I mistook you for. Well, no matter, I'm probably imagining things. You know how it is when we get older ..." He ponders on it, then promptly defends his position again as if unable to let it go. "Honestly, I'm good with accents. Might have something to do with being in the restaurant business and having clients from all around the world."

"Well, Julian, where was she from based on her accent?" Jennifer asks.

"Hard to say. Maybe Washington? I seem to recall her asking me about our local seafood and mentioning

Maryland crabs. She also named a couple of restaurants in the Washington D.C. area. I think she was with an older gentleman that evening. Much older, so it could have been a relative or a business associate. But I don't probe, you know; it's none of my business. The customers, they deserve their privacy ..."

And with this, he is pondering yet again, a quizzical look taking over his slightly distant expression. "But I noticed her jewelry. Her necklace, it looked Greek or Byzantine. Diamonds and sapphire, set in gold, really exquisite. Anyway, don't listen to me, rambling on! Enjoy your dinner. The waiter will come over and take your order. No rush tonight. We don't care about turning over tables, unlike many restaurants in the States. The table is yours for the evening."

With that, he smiles and wanders away with a slight wave of the hand, soon gone.

I turn to my sister, knowing exactly what she must be thinking, able to read her like a book.

"Jen, don't go there. Please don't. Let's just enjoy the evening," I tell her, anticipating she won't let this go. She told me many weeks ago that the LAX woman was no fluke, not a chance encounter. Now with this new and unexpected information from Julian Carrico, she is going to head down the rabbit hole again, losing herself in its tunnels. There will be no stopping her.

"You're the one who brought me here, don't forget that. And you want me to what, just forget it? Seriously? Aren't you wondering what's going on? I thought you were an investigator?"

"I am. So, the girl may have lied to me at LAX about her husband in the army. But so what? I can't blame her.

Just because I showed her my FBI credentials doesn't mean she's going to spill her guts about her whole life and everything she's doing in Monterey, right?"

"Stop. Let's back up. You spot her at LAX, thinking she's me. Then you hear her speak. Then you approach her and talk with her. She vanishes when you land at the airport in Monterey, and now she has surfaced right here in little old Carmel, at this restaurant with an older gentleman, wearing an exquisite necklace—no, an *unforgettable* necklace! Well, for Julian, that is.

"And oh, it just happens to be at the very same restaurant where you dined with your Russian partners. And you're telling me you're not even wondering or curious about what is going on here? Hmm." She pauses as she looks at the menu. "How is the veal?"

"What? You didn't just ask me about the veal, did you?"

"Yeah, so what? You have something against veal?"

I shrug, moving back to the awkward topic at hand.

"Never mind, long story. So, are we supposed to drop everything and start searching the Monterey peninsula for this mysterious woman? And if we find her, what then? Am I supposed to arrest her for bearing a resemblance to you?"

"We already know her taste in restaurants. Let's call her LAX, OK? And LAX probably enjoys shopping, window shopping, checking out the local jewelry stores and specialty boutiques. I'm going to be here for a few more days, anyway, so it's an easy decision.

"I'll walk around the downtown area and check out the upscale jewelry stores and boutiques. Perhaps she bought the necklace locally, and if so, a jeweler could recognize her, well, me. They might even think I'm her, then I'll use my 'gifts' to get them to tell me everything they remember. Heck, I may even get a name! They're salespeople after all, and if they think I'm there to buy something else for my exquisite collection … Plus, with a name, we might figure out who she is. If I spot her on the street, I won't approach her, only follow her to her car, home, whatever. Unless she approaches me instead, of course."

Jen never even stops for a breath, leaving me unable to interrupt her lengthy monologue.

She seems to have it all planned out in her head.

What she's just suggested—that the stranger may well approach her—is certainly a possibility; after all, which of us would not stop and speak to a stranger if they happen to be identical to us? It would be far more peculiar to walk on by, saying nothing.

But something tells me it's all a bad—no, a terrible—idea of Jen's.

And I need to stop her before she does something regrettable.

"Please don't do this, Jennifer. I think this is pure coincidence, a fluke, nothing more. It's a strange one, that's for sure. But it doesn't mean there's something nefarious going on with this LAX woman. I know I'll not succeed in changing your mind, and you're going to do whatever you think is right but be careful, okay? Odds are there's nothing here, but if by some remote chance you're on to something, things could take a dramatic turn.

"Remember, I'm heading for Washington tomorrow, then flying back to Russia."

"Yes, I know that," she says with a shrug as if she can't possibly imagine needing me.

"But I won't be able to help you, Jen," I reiterate with greater emphasis.

Whether she wants my help or not, I'm determined not to leave her in a potentially dangerous situation. "Before I leave, let me give you contact information for my old bureau friend, Paul Campo, and for my friend, Monterey County Sheriff Deputy Vance Stevens. Tell them you're my sister, and you need help. They'll respond, that much I can guarantee. Well, I hope it isn't necessary but these few days back here in California have brought a lot more drama than I expected, what with my 'OSI' lead, the developments in the search for the missing Fabergé egg, that South African woman on the beach— no, I actually didn't tell you about that one—the poltergeist in the shop, and now this LAX woman! I don't think I can take much more, frankly. So, let's just relax, try to have a nice quiet dinner, and enjoy the Frank Sinatra music."

I raise my glass of chilled vodka. "To us, the hunters."

Jen gives me a puzzled look.

"Yeah, to the hunters, why not?" she says as we clink glasses. "What is with that music, by the way, and those photos of Frank Sinatra?"

"No. Don't ask. Leave that alone. Please."

"OK, just curious. But what? You don't like Frank Sinatra or Hoboken? That Julian fellow sounds like he's from that part of the world."

"Yep. But not tonight. Your brother needs some downtime. OK?"

"Sure thing, brother. I'll give you a break, I promise …
For tonight."

Chapter 2

My mobile phone rings as soon as I enter my hotel room in Pentagon City. I've been here often; it's close to the Metro, but sufficiently distant from both the District and FBI headquarters.

"You're here, right?" the voice asks. I take a second or two before realizing it's Don Pierce, my former boss from the San José Organized Crime and Drug Squad.

"Yeah. So, you've got a tracker on me or what?"

"Yep. Well, Sharon sent me your flight details, and I figured you'd be at the hotel about now. Once you're settled, meet me in the lobby."

"Sure, Don." I try not to allow my mind to speculate what Don has to share with me, whether it's good or bad. I just need to accept it and deal with it.

He's sitting in a quiet corner of the lobby, with his usual cup of black coffee.

He starts as soon as I sit down. "Well, you're probably wondering why I asked you to return to Washington, but it's not that simple. Heck, I'm not thrilled about being here. I hate that place, FBIHQ. I'd rather be windsurfing, believe me. So, here's the deal. Remember your polygraph?"

"Yes, Don. The one I passed and put behind me. That one?"

I'm trying not to be sarcastic.

"The examiner told you that you passed. Well, it's unfortunately not that simple. Apparently, your results were inconclusive; it's the questions around foreign contacts that gave him the most trouble. I told him you had many foreign contacts. After all, you work in Russia, so what does he expect? I don't know if they want to retest you or interview you, or what their intentions are."

"So, I'm back here for what, Don? I don't want to sound paranoid, but are the counter-intelligence folks behind this? Are they still angry about my engagement with the San Francisco Russian Consulate and how I ignored that other agency's request to be their personal spy? What is this about? If they want to pull me and my family from our assignment in Moscow, then fine, pull me, or us, but this is crap, Don. You and I both know it."

"Look, Cos. Just let it play out. You need to go tomorrow morning to the assistant director for international operations. I honestly don't know if this is related to the polygraph. They only told me to reach out and make sure you don't head directly back to Moscow. I asked for details, but they wouldn't give me anything. The only reason I even know about the polygraph is because I know the examiner in that unit."

"Don, I'll be there tomorrow morning, but why are you here in Washington?" I ask.

Sharon told me that Don Pierce was on leave, and the fact he's in Washington seems odd.

"It's nothing to do with you. There's another issue I'm dealing with. It's just a coincidence, so let it go. Hey, and you might have to hold off on that lead I sent you from OSI."

"The Nazi war criminals, the ones I'm supposed to find and interview? It will have to wait? Seriously?" What other issue could take precedence over finding Nazi war criminals, still at loose? But with FBIHQ bureaucrats, you just never knew.

Logic and common sense didn't always apply.

"Yep. But they're not going anywhere, believe me."

"OK, Don. I understand. Some part of me thinks that these issues, hanging out there, seemingly unrelated, are in fact related. Maybe it's just creeping paranoia, something like that."

"You know I'm a man of few words, and I'm not a believer in conspiracy theories, but I'll tell you this," he says, taking a long sip of his coffee. "We're in a different world. Who would have thought we'd ever have an office in Russia and be working with Russian law enforcement? Not me. I once told you that everyone was corrupt in Russia, and I seem to recall saying your diamond case was a waste of time. Turns out I was wrong. I don't want to tell you you're just being paranoid about the issues floating around, from the missing Fabergé egg to the OSI lead, and you're being summoned back to FBIHQ. Just go with your gut, your instincts like you did during the Geschke kidnapping case, and it will all work out in the end. I suppose so, anyway."

I suppose so anyway does not sound all that convincing, but I smile.

"Don, you're sounding like my sister. That's a scary thought." I laugh it off.

"Hey, I have to get going, but I'm here if you ever need me. We'll stay in contact, yes? Sharon can always get in touch if you want to reach me urgently. Later, Cos."

Pierce and I shake hands, and he exits the hotel lobby.

Remaining seated at the small corner table, I stare into my coffee cup, trying not to let my mind wander. But the truth is there's been much to ponder these last few days.

It started with the beach run with my sister, when I encountered that mysterious woman from South Africa. Then there was the LAX woman and how she resurfaced at the Carmel restaurant.

Nothing seems to have closure or resolution. Everything drifts, constantly returning to mind.

The serial killer's likely out there too, stalking his next victim in Kansas City.

It's all in the past, and a distraction in some ways, or so I often tell my sister and myself.

Jen would tell me otherwise, insisting the past is always with us, even the past we don't know, such as our grandfather's cases from when he was an NYPD detective so many years ago.

I return to my room to change clothes.

There's still enough light to head for a run on the nearby Mount Vernon trail. While it's no beach, it will have to do for today as I need to clear my mind and reset.

Tomorrow, FBIHQ awaits.

I must accept the fates, good or bad.

Chapter 3

"Cos, come in, take a seat," Assistant Director Ben Nolan says in response to my knock on his office door. It's not yet eight a.m., but most of the HQ staff look as though they've been here for hours. Nolan stands, closing his door. "I know you weren't expecting to be back here before heading to Moscow. Thanks for coming in. I wouldn't have asked unless it was important."

"It's OK, Ben. I can catch up on some other items while I'm here. So, what's up?"

I just hope they can resolve this issue quickly. My gut is already telling me otherwise.

"Dennis, before we start with the main reason I've brought you in today, let's get the other issue on the table," Nolan says. He pauses and takes a long breath. "I got a visit a few days ago from the counter-intelligence directorate, this recently appointed Deputy Assistant Director Tiffany Ames. She got her hands on a copy of your polygraph results and was waving it in my face, claiming your results were inconclusive, and they need to resolve some 'issues' before you step back inside Russia. I pushed back on that idea, told her I needed you back there."

"So, Ben, she wants what from me? To resign because of inconclusive results? They're still upset about my interactions with the Russian diplomats in San Francisco. What's this about? Payback? They need to let it go. I don't like them, Ben, and frankly don't trust any of them. They have issues with agents like me on the criminal investigation side of the organization, dealing with Russian diplomats and foreign law enforcement. And now I'm in Russia, dealing with their intelligence agencies as well. They feel threatened. It's obvious, surely."

"Cos, I hear you, but they smell blood in the water. Your inconclusive results relate to your contacts with foreign nationals. I told them—well, I told this Tiffany Ames—that you're in regular contact with foreign nationals. What do they expect when you live and work in Russia?"

"Ben, they can retest me if they want. So, now this is going to hang over my head indefinitely? Well, it's their move. They can object to my returning there, or step aside and let me get back to doing my job."

Nolan reaches into his desk drawer, pulling out an envelope.

"It's for you," he says. "Before you read the contents, let me give you some background. Ames brought this over to me; she tells me the Director's Office gave it to them for their review before passing it on to my office, International Operations."

"Yes? And what does this have to do with me?"

"I'm getting there. Patience, Cos. She practically threw the envelope at me, telling me that 'your boy' had been mentioned in the Director's Office when the higher-ups were trying to figure out how to handle this one. She called it a 'gift' for me and my department, then stormed out in a huff. See how my life is here? You better stay out in the field, far away from this place."

I say, "I wouldn't last a day at headquarters. Beware of Greeks bearing gifts."

It just sounds right, given the circumstances. The C-I side of the Bureau notifying Nolan that they had a 'gift' for him … They're up to something, and whatever's in that envelope is no gift.

"Yeah. Funny you mention the Greeks. Well, go ahead, open it up, give it a read. It's from the Director's Office, passed through the C-I folks, and now it's yours. Take your time."

I slowly open the envelope and pull out the documents, immediately noticing Russian printed text, several pages of it, followed by what looks to be the English translation.

There are also some official-looking documents in Greek, or at least they appear to be in Greek, and what looks to be some sort of autopsy report with a sketch diagram of a body, perhaps a female. I flip back to the Russian documents.

On closer inspection, they look to be from the Russian embassy in Washington.

The attached cover page is from the Director's Office.

The note is brief, but to the point, so I read it aloud.

"Contact senior MVD representative at Russian Embassy in Athens. FBI to assist MVD to resolve. IOS to support as needed. NTK. Signed, Director."

'NTK' was the Director's personal touch, meaning 'need to know.' The investigation would remain confidential and if you knew about it, you had better have a good reason.

"Ben, what does this have to do with me? I'm in Moscow. This lead, well, my first read on it, looks to have something to do with Greece, not Russia. There's a Legal Attaché Office in Athens that's more than capable of dealing with this stuff, right?"

"It's not that simple. Believe me, if I could keep you out of it, I would. The documents in that envelope don't reveal everything. The Director's chief of staff called me; he told me to give you the lead, and you would have the Director's support, but keep everything on the down low.

"Reading between the lines, I think the Director liked how you dealt with the diamond case in San Francisco. Your star is rising, but you can crash and burn in a flash in this organization, as you well know."

"So, what's next? This is a murder investigation? I see the autopsy report. Well, the victim was killed. And her friend, missing or kidnapped."

"Take the file, head over to Athens. The Legal Attaché Office knows you're coming and will support you. Believe me, they won't mind you being there. They've already got plenty on their plate to deal with, unrelated to this. They're a regional office and cover several countries. You can read the file on your way across the pond. You've been to Greece before?"

"Yeah, many years ago, as a midshipman. No doubt a lot has changed since those days. I recall Greece was emerging from a period of martial law and practically no one spoke English. Anyway, despite all that, I liked the place back then. So much history, amazing food, and the Greeks were mostly friendly, with just a few exceptions."

"Cos, I don't want to put more pressure on you than you may already feel, but this assignment, straight from the Director, is a priority. It's also time sensitive and your only assignment for now. Resolve it as soon as you can. If you need anything, I'm here. Good luck."

I stand up to shake hands with Nolan.

He has a lot on his mind; I see it in his eyes. Whether he's holding back from revealing more, I can't say, but there's no point in pressing him. I'll review the file on the plane ride over to Athens. But first things first, I'll make a quick stop at the Hillwood Estate Museum to have a look at that genuine, one-of-a-kind Fabergé egg, the Catherine the Great egg.

***

"We're closing in fifteen minutes," says the young woman behind the ticket counter at the Hillwood Estate Museum.

"It's OK. I just want to take a walk through your collection of Fabergé pieces. Is that section open?" I ask. She looks as though she wants to close up for the day.

"Yes. But you have very little time," she says, handing me the ticket. "Here you go. It's complimentary for today. I wouldn't normally do this, so just don't tell anyone. Our secret."

"Thanks. I'm good at keeping secrets, believe me. You can count on it," I tell her.

She laughs.

I'm the only visitor left in the Fabergé room which is filled with an assortment of astonishingly beautiful pieces. But only one item interests me, the Catherine the Great egg.

It's a piece so unique and valuable that it must have its own display case, I figure. And there it is—the case is labeled—but it also isn't.

I have come all the way to the museum in this quiet suburban setting in a tree-lined street in the District of Columbia, and the piece I need to see, as Sharon has told me, isn't here.

I am left standing forlornly, looking at the empty case, contemplating what to do.

"You look disappointed. If you'd come a few minutes earlier, it would've still been there. We store it away in the evening, you see. It's our most valuable piece, as you might appreciate," the voice informs me. I turn to face the woman with the intriguing accent.

She sounds Germanic, but softer, perhaps influenced by other factors—by living abroad, speaking English, and perhaps other languages. It's difficult to say.

"I'm the curator," she goes on to say. "Normally, the staff are responsible for tidying up the place before closing, but we've been understaffed for the last few days, so I've stepped in. I don't mind; it's a privilege to handle such exquisite masterpieces."

"I came here specifically to see your Catherine the Great egg," I tell her.

"Oh? I suppose you're disappointed. Sorry. Can you come back tomorrow?" she asks.

"Unfortunately, I can't. I'm flying out first thing in the morning, and don't know when I'll return. It's OK. I understand a thing or two about security," I say, and pause. "Well, there are some who would disagree with that statement, but no matter. I'll try when I return."

"Why did you come so late, just before we close? You're not with anyone else, are you? Well, it doesn't appear so," she says, scanning the room.

A part of me wants to blurt out that I'm an FBI agent, searching for a missing Fabergé egg, and my sole reason for visiting is to see an actual egg up close, to acquaint myself with its fine details so I can spot a real one.

I know nothing about this woman, the one with the intriguing accent I can't quite identify.

She looks like a curator, everything about her physical appearance conveying it, from well-coiffed hair, the lab coat which fits perfectly, down to her plain but practical flat leather shoes.

I extend my hand to introduce myself. Why not? She's the curator, and it might be useful to know someone with an expertise on Fabergé eggs.

"Actually, I'm here on business in a way. Dennis Cosgrove, from the Bureau, the FBI. Nice to meet you," I tell her, figuring, *so what if she knows who I am, and that I've come to see their Fabergé egg just minutes before closing time. Nothing to lose, is there?*

"Dr. Hedwig Kiesler, the curator here. You can call me Heddy."

"Let me show you my credentials," I tell her as I reach into my jacket pocket.

"Why? I believe you. Follow me," she says as she opens the door to what looks to be a storeroom. "Wait here and I will bring it back out."

In a few minutes, the curator returns with a small wooden box. She places it on the worktable and carefully opens it. There it is, the Catherine the Great egg. It's smaller than I imagined, but its detail is far greater. A person could spend hours gazing at the piece, it's that intricate.

The stock photo that I once saw doesn't come close to revealing its unique artistry.

This is no ordinary work of art. I'm stunned, and left speechless, staring at the piece.

"Yes. This is the normal reaction when people first see this extraordinary piece, this piece of history. Quite normal. Does this satisfy your curiosity? Look, I need to lock up. Here's my card in case you need anything in the future. There are missing eggs out there. They are not all accounted for, but you already know that, don't you? It's why you've come, isn't it?"

She offers a slight smile. Her first smile.

Somehow, her accent sounds stronger and different. It's Germanic for sure, but she is not Swiss, perhaps Bavarian, or Austrian. I'm curious as to her background, but it would be rude to pose such a question to the cultured caretaker of such an important piece of history.

After all, she told me she didn't need to see my FBI credentials as proof of my identity. She's been more than accommodating, allowing me special access to the museum's Fabergé bejeweled egg once belonging to the Romanovs, the ruling family of the Russian Empire.

I'm about to ask if this same egg was ever on display at Ms. Marjorie Merriweather Post's Mar-a-Lago estate in Palm Beach, but that seems somewhat trivial now. Anyway, I've accomplished what I set out to do this late afternoon. Athens awaits.

"Yes, indeed. There's another reason for my visit. But I can't disclose those reasons to you, although I appreciate you accommodating me today. I won't forget this, Dr. Kiesler."

She gives me that look, one I've seen before, many times, during interviews. It's the look when someone is on the verge of revealing something, deciding whether to say aloud what is weighing on their mind or to keep it hidden away, unspoken, concealed.

"Heddy, you've been helpful to me today, but is there something else on your mind? I know you want to close up for the day, and I've got a plane to catch. It's too bad we don't have time for coffee. Not this time, anyway."

"There is something," she says, and sighs. "A woman was here a few days ago. It was near closing time, and she was alone, like you. The egg mesmerized her. I hadn't even removed it yet from the display case. So, anyway, I spoke briefly with her, and when she turned, I noticed what looked like a gun beneath her blazer. A pleasant woman, but a bit off, and she seemed edgy, distracted. Kind of rushed. I'm honestly not sure. She asked me about missing Fabergé eggs, how many there were, what they looked like, etc."

"Really? And what did this woman look like, if you can recall?"

"She was attractive, medium blonde hair, sort of like mine, perhaps late thirties, early forties, athletic looking.

Like someone who exercises and takes care of herself. She didn't say if she was police or from your agency, but I definitely saw a weapon."

"Thanks, Heddy. Can you do me a favor? If you see her again, please don't tell her I was here, OK?"

Kiesler nods. "I won't. Well, I need to close up but I hope you find whatever it is you're looking for, Special Agent Cosgrove," she says as we shake hands, and I walk out of the museum. Sharon was right. I needed to see one of those eggs up close.

I did just that. But now, I also know there's someone else out there, perhaps from the Bureau or from another agency, also interested in missing Fabergé eggs. I don't have the name of the woman, nor much of a physical description, but at least it's something.

I force myself to set it aside for now and focus on my mission. My next stop is Athens, to solve a murder and find a missing or kidnapped young Russian woman. The missing Fabergé egg, and the mysterious woman Dr. Hedwig Kiesler told me about, will have to wait.

Chapter 4

As soon as I settle into my window seat on the flight from Washington to Athens, I pull out the envelope from my carry-on bag. Fortunately, the middle seat is unoccupied, allowing me to review the documents without concern about the wandering eyes of the middle seat occupant.

I flip through the pages to find the protocol, the official autopsy report by the medical examiner. Normally, the protocol comprises an external and internal examination, along with an examination of the central nervous system focusing on the head and brain, and a discussion of any injuries found by the medical examiner. It concludes with the opinion of the examiner as to the cause and manner of death. This protocol, in Greek with the English translation attached, looks to be no different in format. For a homicide investigator, a thorough examination with a well-prepared report is critical since the investigator might have to rely—at least to a large degree—on the examiner's findings in fashioning an investigative plan and strategy.

I find I'll need a more thorough translation, since the one affixed to the document may not be entirely accurate and precise. The report describes the victim as a female, twenty to thirty years old, 175 cm, about 5' 9". Her weight is given as fifty-three kilograms—117 pounds.

Blue eyes, fair complexion, dyed blonde shoulder-length hair. I quickly skim to the end of the protocol, to the cause of death, revealed as excessive blood loss from a deep laceration across the neck with a sharp object, possibly a knife. The toxicology report notes traces of the drug best known by its street name, ecstasy. No apparent signs of sexual assault. Some defensive hand wounds. The attacker overpowered his victim rather quickly.

There are no photographs in the envelope. The Greek detectives no doubt have these. There's no mention of where the body was found, nor any statement as to its condition or state when initially discovered. The report omits all crime scene information, so it seems.

The file also contains a copy of the original Russian Embassy letter addressed to the FBI Director, requesting investigative help to find the girl's killer. The letter is light on details, although it describes the female victim as a Russian national from Moscow. She is Yelena Aleksandrovna Borodina, a fashion model working abroad. Seeking to locate Anastasia Nikolaievna Popova, a friend of the deceased, the letter asks for the Bureau's help.

According to the letter, the two girls were traveling together, on holiday in Greece from their recent modeling assignments in Milan and Paris. They suspect someone has kidnapped Popova but provide no further details of the grounds for that suspicion. I'm stunned at what I read next.

It transpires that this Anastasia Nikolaievna Popova is no ordinary Russian citizen, but the only daughter of Nikolai Popov, the deputy prime minister, a prominent member of the Russian President's administration, and a leading reformer in the Russian government.

He is a pro-Western-leaning politician, a rare and precious commodity in Russia of late. I met Popov several months earlier at a U.S. Embassy reception in Moscow.

We spoke only briefly, and I already knew of him since he had led his government efforts to allow the FBI and several other Western law enforcement agencies to establish permanent liaison offices on Russian soil. So, I find myself thinking back to my exchange with Popov that evening.

Although it was brief, his words stayed with me.

When we met, he spoke passionately about his belief that Russia could only become a truly democratic society with a free market economy by first establishing the rule of law, also undergoing deep reform of its most important government structures.

I was later told by one of the U.S. Embassy's political officers that Popov was a firm supporter of the Congressionally funded law enforcement training program, allowed Russian officers and investigators to receive highly specialized training from U.S. law enforcement agencies such as the FBI.

In other words, the same sort of training that none other than Aleksandr Fillipov received, ultimately leading to the unraveling of the Golden ADA conspiracy linked to Kremlin officials' scheme to loot the Russian treasury of millions in gold, diamonds, and precious commodities.

A cruel irony indeed. The leading Russian government supporter of the FBI's presence in Russia now desperately needs the help of the FBI to help find his only daughter.

Pondering on that irony, I slowly close the file, place it back into the envelope, and slip it into my carry-on bag beneath the seat in front of me.

I have seen enough for the moment. The situation looks bleak. Working a missing person or kidnapping case is hard enough within the relatively friendly environs of the United States where the tools and resources of the Bureau are easily accessible for an agent.

Working such matters virtually alone in a foreign— sometimes hostile—environment, with the victim's family in faraway Moscow, will be near impossible.

Certainly, it will be a far more complicated business. Is there more to it than Ben Nolan told me when he handed over the file? Probably. But what choice do I have?

He told me that the polygraph exam results were inconclusive, and that the C-I folks still wanted a piece of me, perhaps still somewhat ruffled from my outmaneuvering them during the Golden ADA investigation. This assignment comes straight from the Director's Office, according to Nolan, and I have their support. The Director green lighted my engagement with the Russian Consulate in San Francisco a few years prior. I just can't refuse this assignment, although the voice inside my head, the one that my sister Jennifer persistently tells me to stop ignoring, is already flashing a red warning sign for danger ahead.

There is no doubt much more here, behind the veiled curtain.

Perhaps this time, I'm really in over my head, out of my depth, set to crash and burn.

I push the dark thoughts out of my mind as the plane touches down on the runway in sunny Athens. The runway is so close to the crystal blue waters of the Aegean that it seems to blend into those waters. It's been years since my last visit here, to Hellas as the Greeks refer to their country. I can only hope their ancient and mysterious gods will favor me and not put me to the test, not yet, at least not on this first day back since my days as a young midshipman arriving by sea at the ancient port of Piraeus.

This time, I'm back with a tough assignment, aware of needing far more than luck to succeed. On this occasion, I may well need divine intervention from the Greek gods themselves.

***

The line for diplomats at the passport control moves quickly.

FBIHQ has expedited the issuance of my visa, glued to the pages of my diplomatic passport. I retrieve my checked bags and grab the first available taxi in the long line of vehicles waiting to pick up the arriving passengers. The drive from the airport to the Hilton Hotel, where the embassy has made reservations for me, usually takes under thirty minutes.

All of my senses are suddenly, all at once, under siege. The city itself has a gritty feel, something I can taste, whereas visually, it looks unkept and neglected, although oddly welcoming. It's been a long time since I was last here as a young midshipman.

The sun-bleached feeling of the place, with its neglected, tired old off-white marble buildings—some with scaffolding and rebar sticking out of rooftops—reminds me of the tree forts my brother and I would leave half-finished in the woods back in New York.

Graffiti scrawls are random, covering some buildings, while others remain untouched as if protected by the gods' intervention from on high. Exhaust from vehicles also seems to hang in the air, while eye-catching billboard signs advertise the latest cosmetics and suntan lotions via beautiful models scantily clad or topless, showing off their dark tans, and oh, so much more.

After all, this is Greece, with its countless spectacular beaches and crystal-clear waters. In this country of extremes and contradictions, people tolerate topless bathing; in fact, it's the norm.

I next glimpse the imposing Parthenon temple dedicated to Goddess Athena atop the Acropolis hill. It's an unforgettable image, striking and overpowering, seared into my memory, exactly as I remember it from my last visit to Athens so many years ago.

So many years have passed by since then, so how does it all still feel so familiar?

The city's assault on my senses takes me by surprise, in fact, yet it's the smell of the place that my brain has somehow permanently stored away in its memory banks —perhaps in anticipation of my eventual return to the captivating city, the birthplace of democracy, with its unique history—that surprises me most.

For me, every city seems to have its own distinct odor, and Athens is no exception. This time, I figure it's the mixture of vehicle exhaust, the nearby Mediterranean Sea, and the smell of grilled meats over coals from the many local tavernas that account for the intoxicating aroma in the air. Or who knows, maybe it's something more.

I cast the thought aside, suddenly famished but decide to first head out for a walk, and then I'll try to find that local taverna, the one I stumbled upon so many years ago.

Yes, I'll do that after checking into my hotel room.

No doubt the jet lag will soon overwhelm and seduce me, and I shouldn't be at all surprised if after the check-in, I find myself languishing on the bed, managing to walk nowhere at all.

Of course, I should not venture outside of my hotel room but should take a long-deserved rest. Over the years, I have realized that it's best to fight the overwhelming urge to sleep, taking on the challenge as a test of will. The only way to fight off the feeling is to go for a long walk, then dine with the locals according to the new time at my destination.

That's what I always try to convince my wife and children to do, to adjust to the new time, avoiding waking in the middle of the night for days on end. It isn't the easiest advice to give, and harder to follow. The body sometimes overpowers any logic, and you can easily find yourself unable and unwilling to fight sleep's most powerful urge.

The woman at the hotel reception greets me in the native language, switching into English once she realizes I speak little Greek. Does she take me for one of her countrymen?

I can't say. Perhaps my features are what confuse her, from my dark hair and brown eyes, passed down from my mother's Italian and Jewish roots.

She's absolutely stunning with her long, flowing black hair and green eyes. Yes, I'm in Greece, a country of contrasts in which beauty and decay exist side by side for eternity, in an irreconcilable, mysterious symmetry.

Chapter 5

The infernal ringing wakes me and I check my watch. Indeed, I have fallen asleep in the room, reclining on the chair. It's 8:00 p.m., Athens time, making me shocked to realize I've been asleep for nearly four hours. Washington is on the line.

"Hey, Cos, how was the flight? Just wanted to check in with you." It's Ben Nolan calling.

"I'm OK. I'm glad you called; you woke me up from the chair. I didn't want to sleep, but the body is weak, Ben. Sometimes, jet lag works that way, just overpowers your will. No matter. Like I say, I'm glad you called because I still need to go for a walk and eat something."

Nolan says, "Cos, don't worry about those C-I folks. This Tiffany Ames is a piece of work, between us. She's super ambitious and looking to make a name for herself. If your polygraph were such a problem, she would have complained and tried to block your travel. She's not that stupid to take on the Director's Office. So, just focus on your mission. The Legat Office will reach out to you tomorrow morning, but for tonight, go out, get some fresh air, find a wonderful restaurant. Can't be too hard, can it? It's Greece after all. If you need anything, let me know."

"Sure, Ben. Goodnight, or good afternoon, I should say. We're six—no, seven—hours ahead of Washington time, right?"

"Yep," I tell him, looking at my watch as I subtract the seven hours. "Talk later. Yassas, Ben." I end the call, returning the receiver to its cradle on the nightstand.

The phone looks retro-seventies, as is most of the hotel, as if it's 1978 all over again and I'm back in the navy once more.

The hotel makes lots of money and is nearly full, although crying out to be updated.

Its reputation is solid, boasting an exceptional staff, and being clean and comfortable.

Most importantly, it offers unique and unobstructed views of the Acropolis from those room balconies which are facing the ancient site.

Suddenly, I feel hunger pangs, having eaten nothing for over twelve hours; I didn't bother to eat on the flight, falling in and out of sleep during the long journey.

In fact, I'm still wearing a dress shirt and tie. Opening my luggage, I change into a pair of jeans and a summer-weight cotton shirt. It feels refreshing and freeing to change from the confining, stiff business suit attire to light summer clothing.

The evening air of Athens on this June night is warm and comforting, the city alive with cars, buses, cabs, pedestrians, tourists, and locals heading off to dinner and drinks. Oddly, in the crowded capital city, I feel alone as I head out toward the Plaka, the pedestrian area with its countless shops, restaurants, and smaller tavernas in the Acropolis's shadow, and with its Parthenon temple ruins looming above. Scattered around the base of the Acropolis hill are other ruins of the ancient city dating back to 500 BC or earlier, even before the time of Alexander the Great. It feels humbling to walk among such ruins but exhilarating at the same time.

I recall my middle-school ancient history teacher showing us his Kodak carousel slides from his summer travels to the sites of the ancient world.

It was then that I first imagined myself as an archeologist or historian, spending summers like my teacher, visiting and studying ancient sites around the world.

Soon, I come across a small taverna on the edge of Plaka neighborhood, the waiter leading me to a small outdoor corner table. I spot a few locals here, always a good sign, and some tourists. There are young German girls and a few couples, possibly newlyweds from France or somewhere in Europe. Four or five languages are being spoken at the surrounding tables.

Luckily, I knew enough Greek to order from the local menu, having studied the language in high school. Although Greek has different spelling and pronunciation rules, the similarities between the Russian and Greek alphabets help me sound out the words.

A Greek monk named Cyril developed the Russian Cyrillic alphabet in the 9th century, accounting for the similarities between the Russian and Greek alphabets.

The waiter soon brings me a carafe of a local red wine, some hard-crusted fresh bread, a dish of green olives, and a bottle of mineral water. I sip the wine one sip at a time, and tear off pieces of the bread, dipping them into the small pool of the vibrant green olive oil on my plate.

My mind soon drifts, thinking of the unknowns that await me tomorrow.

There's a killer out there somewhere in the shadows. Someone has brutally murdered a young girl, and her friend has possibly been kidnapped, or worse.

The waiter's arrival breaks the trance, balancing several small plates on each arm. There's the large Greek salad topped with the slab of feta cheese, a huge portion of souvlaki, traditional Greek potatoes fried in olive oil, and several small side dishes.

I take nearly one hour to finish the enormous meal. The salad alone would have been satisfying enough, but my hunger was so intense when I arrived at the taverna, I couldn't stop ordering. I decide to walk back to the hotel from the Plaka, frequently stopping to gaze at the Acropolis, impressively backlit at night for the tourists. It was not that way when I was last here so many years ago. There were only a few tourists in the city back then. Hardly any Greeks spoke English, and they were not very welcoming to foreigners, particularly to Americans.

The U.S. military base had closed a few years prior, never to reopen.

As for the magnificent Acropolis, a rusty, broken chain-link fence—which I easily climbed over with another midshipman—was its only protection, since we had unfortunately arrived after the Acropolis' official closing time. So, we wandered around the site, the only ones there on the ancient hilltop as dusk approached, until we heard the approaching Greek police with dogs.

They may have assumed we were there to loot the place, so we quickly climbed back over the fence, and ran down the street back to the Plaka, laughing all the way.

Later, we thought about the foolishness of what we had done, realizing we'd been lucky they hadn't shot at us. After all, martial law had only ended a few years prior, with democracy finally returning to the country after years of military rule. Incidents of isolated fighting and protests were still happening around the country. But the Plaka in those days was little more than a slum with broken windows, trash everywhere, and buildings in varying states of decay.

There'd been no tourist shops or tavernas back then. Since those times, it had somehow magically transformed to become a central hub for tourism in Athens, with shops, jewelry stores, and tavernas on every corner. A lot had changed in Greece since I'd last been there, a lot indeed.

Chapter 6

The morning call catches me still in a deep sleep. It's my wife, Lenore. She is in New York with our children and has delayed her return to Moscow until I finish whatever I'm doing in Greece.

"Just be careful, whatever you're doing there. Don't trust anyone and go with your instincts," she tells me. I've never heard her say such things before, to "go with your instincts."

Where does this suddenly come from? But I just nod, saying nothing.

I brush the comment aside, quickly dressing to head out for a run while the city is still relatively quiet so early in the morning. It's a crisp, cloudless morning in Athens. I decide to head for the old Olympic Stadium a few blocks down the street from my hotel since it feels as if it's been several days since I last exercised. The run will allow me to prepare mentally for the day ahead.

Somehow, exercise always makes the stress more manageable, and it has the added benefit of releasing hormones into my bloodstream to fight off jet lag.

While the locals typically eat dinner late, well past nine, they somehow drag themselves out of bed to start their workday as early as in the U.S.

The traffic is nearing its morning rush hour peak in Athens, yet it's barely seven o'clock yet.

Many Greeks are still in the habit of taking an afternoon siesta after a late lunch, for two to three hours, and they then return to work until evening. They have been doing so all of their lives, as have their parents and grandparents before them, in the days before air conditioning.

It's a hard practice to break, even in this fast-paced, modern world. The run from the hotel to the stadium entrance takes me less than ten minutes, darting around vehicles and pedestrians on their way to work. Some look at me in amazement. *Crazy foreigner,* they probably think.

The stadium was the site of the first Olympics in the modern era held in the late 1800s.

The track has a peculiar narrow oval shape, but the surface is forgiving under my feet, and surprisingly well maintained. Many centuries ago, when the city-state of Athens was at the height of its power, on this very site, there once stood a stadium for forty thousand spectators.

The Olympic Games were first hosted by the ancient Athenians over two thousand years ago, so explained my middle school teacher of ancient history, showing us photo slides from his summer excursions. Now, here I am on this crisp, clear morning, running on the same track that our globe-trotting history teacher shared with us in his slide show so many years ago.

The run invigorates me. I feel alive again.

It's likely the hormones beginning to circulate through my body.

I am alone in the stadium, not a single runner or walker in sight so early in the day.

The Acropolis is visible on the distant hill, such a magnificent sight, propelling me to run faster around the track, to face the ruins again as I round the turns. My mind drifts, my grandmother and great aunt unexpectedly popping into my head, just like that. They both passed on years ago, having spent their entire lives in New York, living simple but honest lives.

Both were strong Irish Catholic women who were close to me and my siblings throughout our lives. When I told them I was being transferred to Monterey to study Russian, they gasped in horror. Would that mean a transfer to Russia? I could barely contain my laughter and amusement. After all, the Bureau had no office beyond the iron curtain and never would.

FBI agents traveling to such closed countries were inconceivable and prohibited.

No one would want to go there either, even if they could.

As I continue my run, I reflect on the irony of it all. They were not so naïve. Perhaps they saw it coming: the fall of the Berlin Wall; the eventual collapse of the Soviet Union, and the end of the Cold War. For them, it was inevitable. They didn't need a government think tank to explain it. In the end, they were right, spot on in their prediction, which seemed so unlikely.

I decide to run a few more laps before heading back to the hotel, not bothering to count. Perhaps the Greek gods are pushing me, taking bets on whether I'll survive their test.

After all, the Greek gods were fond of doing things like that to mere mortals.

The footsteps of a runner quickly overtaking me from behind awaken me from my trance. I rarely get passed so effortlessly when running laps on a track. It's a middle-distance runner or a visiting professional athlete out for a morning run, and the figure blows by me with relative ease.

It's a woman, wearing a headband to keep her shoulder-length dark hair away from her face.

Obviously an athlete, I figure as she isn't jogging but appears to be doing interval speed work around the track. I catch her profile as she heads into the corner turn.

Her face appears relaxed, at peace. She has that Mediterranean look with her olive skin, but there's also something different about her, with her high cheekbones, a Slavic looking face.

Bulgarian, I figure. She fades quickly, lapping me twice before leaving the track, bounding effortlessly over the waist-high concrete wall, back through the parking lot. She is gone.

I soon spot another figure near the track, a woman dressed in heels, business attire, exiting her vehicle and making her way over to the track oval.

There is something familiar in her walk as she slowly makes her way toward the track where I'm finishing my run. Then I realize it's Georgia Kaye, the Athens FBI legal attaché. I first met her years ago, when we were both studying at the Monterey language institute.

"Kalimera, Georgia," I greet her as I approach her vehicle in the parking lot.

They've recently assigned her to the Legat job in Athens.

It's been several years since I've seen or spoken with her. I know only that this is her third overseas posting, following tours in Brussels and Paris. The Legat job in Athens is no picnic.

Terrorism, the emergence of Eastern European Mafia groups, the American peacekeeping presence in the Balkans, and the upcoming Summer Olympics all seem to converge in one place, her office. She is an attractive woman with her flowing dark brown hair, dark olive skin and emerald eyes, a gift from the gods, passed down to her from the fair-skinned ancient Greeks of Alexander the Great's era, so her mother tells her.

Kaye spent a few years in the Air Force, following in her father's footsteps, before entering the Bureau. The Bureau soon identified her aptitude for languages and sent her to the Monterey school for Russian language training. She already spoke fluent Greek from her mother's side.

We became friends since our language study overlapped for more than a year.

She says, "Nolan called me last night. Didn't say much, except that my office should support you as much as we can but not get in your way. I thought you might be here running around the track this morning. I figured right, huh? Reach out later to Mark; he's the assistant legal attaché, and you know each other from San Francisco, he tells me.

"That's if you need support. We have an overwhelming workload as you can imagine. Nolan's had some documents sent over, only for you."

She hands me the sealed envelope. "I don't know what they want you to do, and it's none of my business, but you better be on your toes here. We're targets in this country—from terrorists, mafia types, take your pick. Fortunately, the Greek government lets us carry weapons. Stop by the office later, to pick up yours. Between us, what is it they want you to do?"

"I have to find a missing girl, a Russian model who's disappeared. Her friend, who was also Russian, is dead," I respond.

"Oh? I think I read something about a young model's body being found a few days ago, and then nothing. Nothing in the papers or in the news. That's just how it is here sometimes. I don't think the Greeks like this sort of negative publicity for their tourism industry in particular. Well, I'm off. If you need anything, let me know, and stop by the office anytime. Remember to pick up your weapon. I hope you won't need it while you're here, but you never know. You want a lift back to the hotel?" She enters her vehicle.

"Thanks, but I think I'll run back. Would feel like cheating otherwise. Later, Georgia."

Georgia's casual response gives me pause, but I don't want to over-analyze or read too much into it. By rights, as the country's legal attaché, she should be keenly interested and curious about what I have just told her. So, the question in my head is: why isn't she?

There could be many reasons for her apparent lack of interest in my assignment. I'll see what she has to say in the coming days but I'm hoping there isn't something more to it.

The small café on the edge of the neighborhood park behind my hotel has the best pastries in the city, according to the Aphrodite lookalike at the hotel reception desk, the same striking woman who checked me into my room yesterday afternoon. I order a freshly squeezed orange juice and a still warm chocolate croissant. As I bite into the croissant, the warm chocolate spills out from the sides. It's heaven. I watch the locals ordering their iced frappes and fredo espressos.

The icy caffeine loaded drinks make sense in the warm summer climate. I decide to try one. The caffeine jolt is powerful and hits my jet-lagged body soon after the first sips. I set the frappe down, quickly finish what's left of the juice and croissant, then take my iced frappe in hand.

After this, I walk to an unoccupied park bench with my envelope, sitting on the secluded bench, opening the envelope to find the protocol with the report of the autopsy.

The contents of this new envelope, handed to me by Georgia Kaye, look to be a copy of the one given to me by Ben Nolan at FBIHQ. Here I am in faraway Athens, Greece, about to step into the investigation of the murder of a young woman, and the kidnapping of another.

Yet, there is still unfinished business from a previous assignment of mine, from my first Bureau office in Kansas City, Missouri. I left a serial killer out there on those streets.

He is likely still on the loose, yet here I am in Greece, about to embark on the search for another killer, and find or rescue a victim of a kidnapping or worse.

My advice to Bureau colleagues temporarily assigned to assist in Russia pops into my head. I would tell my temporary office colleagues not to be reluctant to share information or ask for help from Russian law enforcement just because they would share it with a Russian, our former foes from the Cold War days. But I would also tell them to never forget that absolutely nothing is as it first appears, particularly in the former Soviet Union. There's usually more, much more.

This case, handed to me in an envelope, is no gift, of that much I am certain.

As I look up from flipping through the documents, I hear the laughter of small children playing and gaze across the park. They look so happy, content, and innocent running around the small city park with its dilapidated, broken-down swings and slides. I watch them as they play and can see their mothers also watching from a safe distance.

An unsettling feeling of paranoia comes over me.

The feeling is familiar, not pleasant. I think the combination of jet lag, caffeine, and my task cause my foreboding melancholy—or perhaps it's something more. My sister would tell me not to ignore such feelings but the only person who seems out of place in the park with the happy children is a priest, dressed in his dark flowing robes, perhaps out for his morning stroll.

He glances briefly in my direction, a Greek Orthodox priest, I figure, who appears to be in a moving meditation. He is walking and praying, holding something, perhaps prayer beads.

Closing the envelope, I walk back to the hotel, needing to contact Mark Anadiplosis, the assistant legal attaché (A-LAT). I'll need his help to find the Russian Embassy in Athens, so that I can contact Russian MVD representative just as the note from the Director's Office has directed. I toss my empty paper cup into the broken-down trash bin.

So now, it begins.

Chapter 7

It's late morning by the time I find the apartment building in the Glyfada section of the city, near some beaches, not far from the city's airport. It's exactly as the A-LAT Mark Anadiplosis described it to me, a plain five-story building, blending in with the nearby apartment buildings of the neighborhood. The building's only distinguishing features include an array of antennas, and other boxlike metal structures of varying shapes and sizes on the rooftop.

The building has a high security wall around the entire complex. Anadiplosis has told me the building is the residence for most of the Russian Embassy's staff. Since it's midday, I hope to catch the MVD representative, Eugeniy Zhirov, at home on his lunch break.

I press the buzzer at the one entry door I find, looking for the security camera.

Russians are pretty good at hiding their cameras, having been doing this sort of thing for a long time. The voice on the speaker answers in Greek with a Russian accent. I respond in Russian, identifying myself as a diplomat from the American Embassy.

"Mr. Zhirov is expecting me," I claim, a small lie.

Then I press the door open upon hearing the buzzing sound releasing the lock.

I'm told to go to the fifth floor and decide to take the stairs. The place has the unique odor common to most residential buildings in Moscow. I have never been able to figure out exactly what the odor comes from. Perhaps it's a combination of many things, emanating from what they cook, perhaps, to what products they use to clean their apartment common areas—if ever.

The hallway and stairwell are dimly lit, and the paint seems to be peeling off the wall in some areas. It isn't dirty, just neglected. The public spaces in such buildings often are neglected, in contrast to the neat, sometimes lavishly furnished apartments hidden behind those drab exterior walls. I feel strangely at home. After all, I spent several years of my childhood living in one of those apartment 'projects' in New York City, a public housing complex not so different from the endless apartment blocks of the former Soviet Union.

Eugeniy Zhirov is already waiting for me in the hallway as I reach the fifth floor of the building. He is a large man with a square face and thick, stocky frame, a former wrestler.

I've worked with him several times in Russia, during my half-dozen or more trips to Saint Petersburg, the former imperial capital of the Russian Empire.

He previously told me he was hoping for a transfer to Greece, and now here he is.

Zhirov has been rewarded with the posting in Athens after nearly five years in the high-profile and high-stress position as the MVD's organized crime chief for the Saint Petersburg region.

The city's two violent organized crime groups had been practically running the city, holding several key city officials in their pockets. There had also been several contract murders of high-ranking public officials which Zhirov had been tasked to solve.

He took them all on, the mafia, the corrupt bureaucrats, and the elected officials.

At the end of his five years in the position, he's departed with his family, leaving the city in a much better standing. Corruption is under control by now, and the open feuding of the mafia groups has ceased, for the moment at least.

Zhirov embraces me in the hallway.

"I didn't know it would be you, but Moscow told me someone from the Bureau would reach out to me soon," he tells me in Russian. "I am thrilled they've chosen you. Come inside. I will make us some tea."

I take a seat at the small kitchen table.

"The Center has ordered me to oversee the investigation, work with the FBI and find the girl. If she is being held against her will, my orders are to rescue her and liquidate those responsible," he tells me as soon as he sits down at the small table.

Zhirov uses the Soviet term—Center—in referring to his Moscow superiors.

It's a term I haven't heard in a while.

Zhirov launches immediately into the task at hand, skipping small talk, revealing the urgent nature of the matter. Understandably so, with the deputy prime minister's only daughter missing, possibly kidnapped, or worse. He places his teacup on the saucer as he looks squarely at me.

"Dennis," he says, stressing the last syllable of my name in Russian pronunciation. "I called over to your office earlier, and they told me you were coming to see me today. I will not be your partner for this one, unfortunately; I don't have the skill set required, but I have found someone who does, someone I trust. She'll be here soon. I don't think you've ever met her.

"Her name is Oksana, Oksana Aleksandrovna Koslova. She is a graduate of your I-LEA, the International Law Enforcement Academy in Budapest. Her English is good, and most importantly, her Greek is excellent. Oksana Aleksandrovna worked in one unit I supervised in Saint Petersburg. She's twenty-seven years old, but she's a competent investigator, aggressive, but not reckless. She's not a bad shot either. At least, that was my experience in dealing with her. I don't know if you recall, but she was my lead investigator in that case against the corrupt judge who was laundering his pay-offs in the U.S. with the help of some relatives in New York," he tells me. "You must remember the case as your office in New York assisted us?"

I respond, "Sure. I remember. So, it was this same Oksana Aleksandrovna who led the investigation? I didn't know." I do recall the case, having heard the judge later cooperated with Zhirov's team, leading to a string of convictions of corrupt public officials in Saint Petersburg.

The fact that this Oksana Aleksandrovna not only speaks Russian but also fluent Greek could prove to be an asset. My preference would be to work with Zhirov, but he has someone else clearly in mind; that person has been chosen already, no doubt approved by the Center.

"She's on her way over now. I suppose it's possible that you have already met, after all. Mir tes-en," he tells me, adding, 'The world is tight,' the Russian equivalent of 'it's a small world.'

"I don't think so, Zhenya," I respond, addressing him in the diminutive of his first name. "Perhaps at I-LEA, or in passing in your office in Saint Petersburg. But her name is not familiar at all to me. Please tell me she is unattractive, overweight … something," I say jokingly. "What should I tell my wife? You know her fairly well, Zhenya. My wife won't be happy to hear that I have a young, attractive Russian woman as a partner."

Zhirov laughs. He rarely does, but when he gives into it, his whole body laughs along too.

"Tell Lenore not to worry. I am your friend, I will take care of you. Look, this is a serious matter. It will not be easy to find the daughter of the deputy prime minister, assuming she is alive. And if she's been kidnapped, they'll have moved her to another city or country by now."

The knock on the door is loud, interrupting Zhirov.

"It's her," he says as he stands up from the table, heading toward the apartment door.

His visitor walks into the kitchen behind Zhirov. I stand from the table to greet her.

"This is my good friend from the FBI. Call him Dennis, or Cos, or his last name, Cosgrove, FBI agents refer to each other using their family names. Don't ask me why; no one seems to know the reason. That's what I have been told."

I extend my hand as she is now standing in front of me. Customarily, Russian women rarely shake hands with men or women upon being introduced, but I have made it a habit of doing so, mostly to gauge their reaction. She immediately extends hers and grasps my hand firmly, without hesitation. Well, she's passed the first test. I look into her eyes, her green eyes, as I utter the standard Russian expression, "Ochen priyatna."

Have I met her somehow or somewhere before? I can't seem to recall when or where, but her face seems familiar. As she releases her grip, my mind flashes back to my run at the stadium track earlier this morning. But before I can comment, Oksana Aleksandrovna is well ahead of me, and she hasn't bothered responding to my greeting.

"How vas run this morning?" she asks in her slight but somewhat charming Russian-accented English. As she speaks, I can't help but notice her erect posture.

Her back is straight, arms comfortably extended along her sides, feet together with one foot angled out slightly, perhaps the result of ballet training in her youth.

She has caught me off guard. I answer her in Russian. "It was slow. For me, that is. But we may have to run together, much faster, before this is over, Oksana Aleksandrovna."

Zhirov interrupts. "I need to leave in a few minutes. You two can stay as long as you like." He pours the remaining tea into our cups and excuses himself from the table.

"Oksana, we can take my car, drive to a café to talk a bit, and I'll call my office at the embassy," I tell my new partner.

I have worked with female FBI agents before, but never with a female Russian MVD officer, besides Katerina from the Russian tax police.

Katerina was the first Russian law enforcement officer I met when she traveled from Moscow to San Francisco during the Golden ADA investigation.

How much Oksana knows about the murdered girl and her missing friend Anastasia, I don't know, and don't want to conjecture what she has been already told and allowed to share.

We are both going to trust one another for now, even though we have only met.

I know practically nothing about her background, except what Zhirov has just told me.

She knows nothing about me either, besides what Zhirov and others in Moscow may have mentioned to her about me, the American FBI agent who has worked with MVD colleagues in San Francisco, and more recently in Moscow.

We find a quiet corner table outside in the café's courtyard, ordering two icy frappes.

I call Mark Anadiplosis, the A-LAT from my cell phone.

He tells me he will come over as soon as he can break away. He arrives a few minutes later, as the café is a short walk up the hill in back of the U.S. Embassy.

He spots us quickly at our corner table.

Oksana stands up to introduce herself, speaking to him in Greek; Anadiplosis looks impressed. He sits down and orders a traditional Greek coffee from the server, turning back toward the two of us. "So, what do you need from our side? The car is OK, right?" he asks.

"Of course. It's the best Bureau vehicle I have ever driven. I have never even sat in a BMW before, and it's armored. Hey, how is the threat level here?"

"Not good. 17 November, 17-N, the terrorist group, is still active. We need to catch them before they strike again, and with the upcoming Olympics, our Greek partners are under pressure to find these guys and put an end to their organization. That's their number one priority right now, and ours as well. But tell me, how can I help? I will try. It's just the two of you working this case?" he asks.

"Yeah. And we're supposed to work in stealth mode, more or less. Don't get me started, Mark. But if you can, I need you to do something right away. Please reach out to your most reliable and trustworthy contact working homicide in Athens. Tell him you would like to see the file on the investigation of the recent murder of that Russian model."

Oksana chimes in. "They found her body at the construction site of the new Metro station."

I say, "Mark, tell him you're interested from a terrorism perspective. Frankly, I don't care what story you come up with, just don't tell him that the Bureau is actively working this case with Russians. It will either piss him off or make him curious, or both. I don't want any of us getting PNG'd for this."

Being PNG'd, to be declared *persona non grata,* was always a possibility for a diplomat, a part of life in any overseas posting. It would mean the loss of diplomatic status for the person, with the immediate effect of terminating their posting.

Normally, FBI agents operating outside of the territory of the United States work with host country approval, or request host country authorization to conduct any independent investigation.

This is one of those rare exceptions. At least, that is how I understand it in so many words from the powers at FBIHQ, although no one has specifically told me so.

"I'll do my best, but the Greeks aren't stupid. They may suspect other reasons," Anadiplosis says.

"Look, I don't want to drag you or Georgia into this, but let me tell you about the murdered girl and her friend. You're probably wondering why I, well, we, are here. The victim, Yelena Borodina, was a close friend of the missing girl, Anastasia Popova, daughter of the Russian Deputy Prime Minister Nikolai Popov. Neither the Bureau nor the Russian MVD want publicity at this phase, which could precipitate the death of Anastasia—known as Nastiya—or make it nearly impossible to find her. If she is still alive, that is."

Anadiplosis stares down at his coffee.

He looks as though he is in a trance or deep in thought, reading the swirls on the liquid's surface in his cup. He slowly raises his head. "I don't have experience with this sort of situation. A murder, yes, I have investigated several of those, but a missing girl, the daughter of a high-ranking Russian political figure, perhaps kidnapped, that's uncharted territory for me.

You two had better be careful. I'll do my best to get you a copy of the file, but the Greeks can be funny about this sort of thing. I'm an American diplomat here in Greece. The murdered girl is Russian, with no apparent connection to the U.S., none that we know about, anyway."

I tell him, "Mark, do what you can; don't push it. Heck, we don't know if the Greek police even know that there is a missing girl or they could look for her right now. We can't assume anything. I know only one thing from my prior experiences with missing persons, and with kidnappings; the clock is ticking, Mark. We don't have long. Nastiya, if she's still alive, could be far from Athens by now. Perhaps she escaped or wasn't even kidnapped. She could be in hiding, completely freaked out. Or she could be dead. Just do what you can to get that file."

"Yassas. OK. I'll reach out to you as soon as I can manage and get those items on the list you've asked for, to include the Glock pistol. Yassas to you both, or should I say dos-vi-dan-e-ya?" he asks as he stands up from the table. "The coffee is on me today."

He motions for the server to come to the table.

"Good luck to both of you," he adds, walking out of the café.

"Oksana, let's get out of here. We'll leave the car at the hotel and take the Metro. Is that OK with you?" I ask.

"I'm Russian; we grew up on trains, don't you know?" she says as we walk out of the café together. I decide to take the Metro out to Piraeus, the port area of Athens.

If we are being followed or tracked, we might pick up the surveillance.

They will have to follow us on foot. It will also give me an opportunity to get a better sense of Oksana. She doesn't ask me where we are going or why. I take it as a good sign.

I tell her, "Oksana, before I forget, can you ask Zhirov to get us some photos of the girls? We could also use more background information about the two of them. Where they grew up, their hobbies, stuff like that. The more we know, the better."

"Zhirov told me they were already working on that, but I'll reach out to him this evening and tell him we really need this information, as soon as possible," she says.

"Thanks. We're going to see a bit of Athens. Do you mind?" I ask.

"Stop asking for my permission. Just tell me. If I don't want to do something, I will let you know," she tells me firmly, but in her accent, it sounds charming.

I detect a faint smile on her face.

We soon board the train that will take us to the end of the line, to the port of Piraeus, where many passenger ships are docked, bound for countless Greek islands.

I glance briefly around the half-empty subway car.

There is something familiar in the face of the middle-aged man seated across from us. For an instant, our eyes meet. He wears a conservative button-down knit shirt, oddly buttoned to the collar on this warm summer afternoon. He is reading something. A novel—no, it has a black cover. A Bible, perhaps. I spot a young Greek girl, perhaps early twenties, carrying a backpack.

She is young but could be surveillance. But who would watch us? Perhaps someone from my agency, or a foreign intelligence service, or the Greeks, their police or intelligence service.

Maybe no one is surveilling us, and no one is interested in watching us and our movements. But my instinct tells me we are being watched; by whom, and to what end, I'm not sure.

Oksana appears to be glancing around as well. She comments quietly to me about the man reading across from where we are seated. "A priest on his day off?" she asks me.

"Maybe," I respond. We arrive in Piraeus after a dozen stops. "Let's walk around for a bit. I was last here as a midshipman years ago. Perhaps I'll remember some of it," I tell her.

She laughs. "I doubt it. That was when you were young, such a long time ago."

"I'm still young, Oksana, only slower, as you have seen for yourself," I respond. "Let's walk faster and see if we have company with us."

'Company' was the term we would use in the Bureau for surveillance.

If we were being surveilled, they were nowhere to be seen. It meant they were very good, or they weren't there, at least not for our brief outing.

"Oksana, I don't feel good. Let's take a cab back to Athens."

I had been feeling off for the past several days, attributing it to work stress, and to the travel that had finally caught up with me. The feeling of nausea was getting stronger.

"Oksana, I …" I try to speak as my voice trails off, but I feel so lightheaded that I can't finish the sentence, close to passing out. Oksana grabs me by the shoulder and arm so that I don't fall and helps me enter the cab, which stopped just moments earlier.

As soon as I'm seated in the cab, I feel less nauseous, but feverish.

The virus, or whatever it is, has seized control of me.

Oksana tells the driver in Greek to take shortcuts, directing him to her temporary quarters in Athens, an apartment building close to the Russian Embassy.

We arrive there in record time, despite the heavy traffic, according to the driver.

"Oksana, I can manage. I won't pass out. Promise," I tell her as she steadies me on the sidewalk in front of her apartment.

She nods, but grabs hold of my arm to lead me into the apartment just in case, then guiding me to the living room sofa.

"Sorry, Oksana. I haven't felt like myself for the past few days. I didn't see this coming, not so quickly, like it has," I say.

She says nothing in response as she leaves the room and returns from the kitchen with two drinking glasses and a bottle of vodka. Placing the glasses on the coffee table in front of the sofa, she pours a generous amount of the clear liquid into each glass. I know what is coming next.

"PAY-tye, do don-YA," she says in Russia. 'Drink it to the bottom.'

"Nye ma-GOO. I can't," I tell her, my voice crackling.

I feel weak and feverish, my entire body aching.

Oksana is insistent.

"You must. You need to kill these bacteria in your system. The vodka will work. You drink all the glass, right now," she orders. She reaches for her own glass, clinking mine.

"Naz-da-RO-vee-ya, Tavarish Kap-ee-TAN, to your health Comrade Captain."

I am in no shape to object, so I put the glass to my lips, tilt my head back and gulp down the firewater in one swallow. I've been ordered, forced, cajoled, or convinced to drink the powerful liquid before. This will probably not be the last time, either. As soon as the vodka hits my empty stomach, I can feel its effects, the numbness overtaking my entire body.

I wake on the couch, underneath a sheet and blanket. My watch reads nine a.m. I have slept for over twelve hours, and I find the fever gone and I'm groggy, but the body aches have left. Perhaps the vodka has indeed worked its magic and killed whatever bacteria or virus was in my system. I'm alone in the apartment, so it seems. I can't recall removing my shoes or shirt.

Oksana may have done that.

A few minutes later, I hear the apartment door opening. It's Oksana, wearing her running outfit; her face is flushed and dripping with perspiration from her run.

"Oh, you're awake. There is food on the table in the kitchen. Eat and drink something. I will make us some tea," she says as she fills the kettle from the kitchen faucet. "Moscow wanted to know what we have done so far. I stalled them. They provided a bit more background. We can talk about it later."

"Thanks. I owe you one," I tell her.

"You don't owe me anything. You look much better. Your cell phone was ringing earlier. It was Mark. I told him we were busy. He will come to the apartment. He said to give him an hour to get here."

From the once-over look Anadiplosis gives me on entering the apartment, he suspects that Oksana and I are romantically involved.

As Oksana heads to the kitchen, we are in the living room alone.

"We're not, Mark. If you're thinking that. I've been sick, and collapsed on the street yesterday from a virus, or whatever it was. I'm much better now."

"Good. Hey, it's not my business. I don't care. I've got some good news for you. My homicide detective friend will do whatever we ask and will keep quiet about it. You can look at the file. Cos, I had to promise him a lot. I promised him a slot at the next FBI National Academy class in Quantico and a one-on-one meeting with the director. The detective will let me know in the next day or so. I don't think you'll be able to just walk into their offices and the file will be there for you. This is Greece, after all. We'll have to be flexible and accept whatever scenario he comes up with. He understands the urgency. Nothing is going to happen today or tomorrow."

He finishes his tea and pulls out the small case from his bag.

"There are several magazines and a full box of ammo for the pistol. The Greeks aren't crazy about us carrying in their country, being foreigners, but they're accommodating.

"For the time being. Oh, one other thing: your sister, Jennifer, called our office. She was looking for you and mentioned something about needing to talk to you as soon as possible."

"Oh? She didn't say why?"

"No. She sounded a bit, well, intense."

"Yep. That's my sister. She's intense, that's for sure. Welcome to my world, Mark."

"Good luck to both of you. Call if you need anything. I'll reach out to you as soon as I hear from the detective," he says as he leaves the apartment.

Suddenly back to life, I say, "Oksana, are you hungry? I'm suddenly famished. Let's grab a taxi and pick up my vehicle from my hotel. My office told me about a small taverna near some secluded beaches not so far from the airport. You can brief me on what Moscow had to say, and we can strategize on our next move if there is one. We can't sit around waiting on some file from the Greeks. Who knows if it will be helpful or not? Let's get to work."

She nods. "Lad-na. OK. I'm ready. Give me a few minutes to shower and change."

She motions for me to wait for her in the living room.

I sit back down on the couch. Oksana walks into the bedroom and closes the door. My mind immediately wanders, wondering why my sister has called the office. I'll have to reach out to her, but later, when I'm alone. There's no telling why she has called Athens, telling the office that she needs to speak with me. If it's an emergency, she would surely have told the A-LAT as much. At least I hope so. But with my sister, Jennifer, you just never know.

***

I find the seaside taverna with relative ease, thanks to the directions provided by the receptionist at my hotel.

As soon as we sit down, Oksana begins. "I have some background information about the girls."

"Go ahead, Oksana. I'm listening. Details are important, even those that might seem irrelevant. I need to know everything that you know, everything you've been told."

Oksana reaches into her bag and passes me some photographs. "These are photos from their portfolios— their modeling portfolios. All models have photo albums like these," she says.

"Yeah, I know. My mother modeled before she was married. She explained all that to us when we were children. Don't ask me why. Long story but I know way too much about the modeling world. The women are pretty, but their world is ugly, Oksana."

"Oh, but I always thought it was so glamorous, going to photo shoots in exotic locations, getting on magazine covers, working with fashion designers. I suppose there's another side, huh?"

"Yes, and look at Yelena and Anastasia. Yelena is dead and Anastasia, well, who knows what has become of her?" I say.

"Moscow tells me the girls have been lifelong friends since they were small children. They're pretty and even look alike. At least judging by the photos which are likely touched up, right?"

"Yeah. I hope the photos at least resemble Anastasia. We may have to rely on them one day. What else, Oksana?" I ask.

"They apparently had a habit of sharing clothing, changing hair color, enough to confuse people who was who. They must have looked similar, and with the same body types. Not surprisingly, they both studied ballet as children, and were fair swimmers. They loved to dance and loved the beach. Of more interest, neither smoked, which is surprising to me, and they didn't drink excessively either. But this information is likely from their parents. Who knows the reality of it?"

"And what about drug use, Oksana? The autopsy report for Yelena showed traces of ecstasy."

She answers, "I know. It's not that uncommon considering that they were young, attractive models from Russia. Oh, Moscow also told me they have no sign that Anastasia's father, the deputy prime minister, is being blackmailed or extorted. That could be true, or maybe he doesn't want to share such information with us, with the MVD."

"Well, at least MVD is in communication with Popov, and he's talking to them. One never knows how someone will react when their loved one is missing or possibly kidnapped. It's a high-stress event, and everyone behaves differently in the circumstance. I know that from my experience investigating missing children and kidnapped people. But I'm no expert at this stuff, believe me. We can't assume anything. If the murder of Yelena was not a random killing, and planned, it's possible that Nastiya, if she's still alive, is being held against her will. Whoever has her may try to figure out how to deliver the ransom demand, and how much to ask for. If that is even the motive. We just don't know."

She nods, saying, "She may already be dead, and no one has found her body. Or she may be on the run. Perhaps she has stowed away on one of those ferries bound for one of the countless islands around Greece," she says with a casual, almost fatalistic tone.

"Let's finish eating and then we can examine the crime scene. Specifically, the area where they found Yelena's body," I propose to Oksana as I reach for the bowl of Greek salad.

Oksana puts down her fork and knife, then pushes away her plate.

"I'm done. Let's go." She stands up from her chair, leaves drachma on the table for the meal and walks out of the taverna, heading toward the vehicle.

I'm not yet finished with my meal. But with Oksana, there's no point in objecting.

I race to catch up.

Chapter 8

We reach the construction site at the metro station where Yelena's body was found late in the afternoon. It has been nearly one week since the workers discovered her body. Since then, the site has been fenced off, but it remains easily accessible because they've left the gate unlocked.

The workers have already left for the day.

Some yellow crime scene tape still clings to parts of the fence. We walk together, looking for any signs showing where the body may have been lying.

"Oksana, don't wander off. Stay close to me. Let's take this all in, together," I tell her.

My crime scene training from years ago, when I was a member of the Bureau's Evidence Response Team, kicks in. I first focus on what is located just outside of the fenced-in area.

There's some light pedestrian traffic near the site during the daylight hours, but at night, it might be difficult to notice movement inside the fenced-in construction area.

I judge the site to be poorly lit, and there would probably be some shadowing from the surrounding buildings and trees at night. There are several small retail shops in the area.

These would likely have been closed by eight or nine p.m.

Oksana points out the entrance to a nightclub near to the construction site, beginning to make some notes on her small pad as we stand there, trying to absorb and process the site and its surroundings. I'm thinking about potential witnesses who could have seen something that day.

Perhaps the file will have information concerning interviews of bystanders and the locals working near the site.

More recent construction activity and the Athens police have undoubtedly disturbed the crime scene significantly; they've probably removed any objects of interest near the body.

I catch the reflection of a small metallic object partially buried in the sand. *A stray nail* is my first thought. I bend down and pick up the object, finding it's a small plain silver cross, not Catholic or Greek Orthodox. It looks like a Russian Orthodox cross with its distinctively smaller angled cross beam below the larger cross beam. I discreetly pocket it. Oksana is looking elsewhere and doesn't see me pick up the object or at least doesn't let on that she does.

"Nothing here, Oksana. Let's ..." I say until I notice Georgia Kaye, the Athens legal attaché, standing just outside of the construction site, watching us through the chain-linked fence.

She wears Capri shorts and sandals. The gold and blonde highlights in her light brown hair look almost metallic, reflecting off of the setting Athenian sun. Kaye is more athletic and fit looking than I remember her from our time together at the Monterey language school.

We walk out through the unlocked gate to meet her.

"I figured you two would be here. Just a hunch. Did you find anything of interest? You must be Oksana? I'm Georgia Kaye, the FBI's legal attaché here," she says.

She extends her hand to Oksana.

Then she says, "Dennis, the homicide detective is ready to meet. Mark set it up, but I told him I'd deal with this. His name is Konstantinos Dimitropoulos. He's agreed to tell you what he knows but just remember that he doesn't know Anastasia is the daughter of the Russian deputy prime minister. Best to leave it alone for now. I'm here to help, as I told you. But as soon as I can step away from this, the better. I'm buried as it is."

I nod, quickly replying, "Georgia, you've probably thought of this, but the Greeks are going to wonder, if they haven't already, why the FBI is getting involved in the murder investigation of a Russian national, which occurred on Greek soil. So, I have an idea. Let's have Oksana meet with him, alone, without me or you. This way, we can say that our role was to arrange or facilitate the meeting between the Russian authorities and Greek police, since the Russians know that we have close relations with our Greek law enforcement counterparts."

"Do I have a say in this?" Oksana asks. "You are talking about me like I am not here. Please don't do that. We're supposed to be a team, right?"

"You're right, Oksana. I do not intend to cut you out. I'm just thinking aloud, that's all. Our goal is to get access to that file, nothing more. I've got orders to assist and support the investigation and find the girl. Unless my HQ tells me otherwise, that's what I intend to do."

"Look, I'll do the introduction and step away. Are you game, Oksana?" Kaye asks.

"Yes. Of course. And I won't mention the FBI. I will take what this Konstantinos gives me, steal what I can when he isn't looking, and get out of there as fast as I can."

Oksana speaks with a mischievous smile.

"I'll take you to him now. You'll have to find your own way back though. Khar-ra-SHOW?" Kaye asks, summoning her Russian language skills back from her days in Monterey.

I head off in my vehicle, back to the hotel.

Oksana jumps into Kaye's vehicle as they drive to their meeting with the Greek detective. No matter what information is in those files, the trail may already have turned cold. The chance of finding Anastasia alive decreases with each passing hour and day. Yet, there's no sense in dwelling upon such a possibility. Better to focus on our next move. We are going to need a lucky break and to be ready to respond as quickly as possible. I reach into my pocket and feel for the cross. Yes, we may need a miracle to find this girl alive. The receptionist, the Aphrodite lookalike, waves to me as I walk by.

She is holding an envelope. "This is for you. Your sister told me to give it to you when you returned," she tells me.

"What? My sister?" I ask.

"Yes. Ms. Jennifer. She said that she is your sister. And the name on her passport accords."

I take the envelope and tear it open.

Yes, it's Jennifer's handwriting. 'Yassas! I'm here. Knock on my door when you return. I may be asleep,' the note reads. I remember the A-LAT telling me she called, and I've forgotten to call her back. Now she's here, in Athens of all places, at the most inopportune time.

Why she has traveled to Greece, I don't know. But I'm soon to find out.

"Why?" I ask as she opens the hotel room door. It's apparent that I have woken her.

"No. Why are you here and not back in Russia? That's the real question," she counters, rubbing her eyes.

"Jennifer, how did you even know I was here? No, forget that. I can guess who's told you," I say, taking a seat on the chair in the room's corner.

"Didn't take much to get the information. I didn't even have to use my powers," she says, smiling.

"OK. You're here for a brief vacation? This is what I need to hear, Jen. My assignment will be brief, I hope, and it's very specific, and hypersensitive. But tell me, why have you flown all the way to Greece?"

She asks, "Seriously? So, you won't tell me what you're doing here, after all we've been through? Yet you expect me to unload everything now. I'm barely awake, and what is this feeling?" she asks as she massages the temples of her head. "Is this jet lag? It sucks."

"Welcome to my world, sis."

"Yeah, your world sucks. Anyway, I'm not going anywhere. My source told me you were here working alone, and he or she is worried about you. After what I went through after you left me in Monterey, chasing that LAX woman, I decided I need to get over here. It's all connected. Oh, excuse me, sorry! I forgot that you don't believe in any of that stuff. Not in apparitions or in UFOs —or do you?" she asks and gives me that look.

"I'm here investigating the murder of a young Russian model; her friend disappeared, possibly hiding, or maybe someone's kidnapped her. I've got a Russian MVD officer —Oksana—as my partner. She reminds me of you in more than one way."

"What does this have to do with the Bureau? They assigned you to work with this Russian woman. For what? Is an American involved or suspected? I don't get it. And you're in Greek territory. They may not be happy about that. There's more to it, isn't there?"

"Yeah. But we can catch up on all that later. You feel like going for a run? Then we can find a local taverna where we can eat afterwards. I know a good place with a running track close to the hotel. See you in ten minutes, OK?"

"Sure. No beaches close by? Too bad. Well, the track will have to suffice. Meet you in the lobby," she says and closes her hotel room door.

***

Jennifer is waiting outside of the lobby entrance. She seems oblivious to the attention she's already attracting, with Greek men gawking at her as they walk by. Greek men are that way.

"Let's not talk shop, Jen. Let's just run. We can catch up later. I need to hear about the LAX woman, but not now. Agreed?" I ask.

"OK. Agreed. But you're going to tell me everything. You don't know it yet, but you need me. You've got no one to bounce things off of, and no one to trust. It's not like the States. There's no backup here. And I need to meet this Russian partner of yours, soon."

"What? That's nuts, Jen. That's not a good idea. You aren't law enforcement, you are family, my sister. The Bureau's office here would freak if they found out you'd flown into Athens. They could report me to Washington."

"So what? You need me on this one. I can sense it. The feeling is strong this time, really strong. There's much more to this murder and disappearance than you realize," she says.

We finish the run and head back to her room.

The knock on the door freezes both of us.

I look through the peephole to see Oksana standing there.

"Jen, it's my Russian partner, Oksana. I'll introduce you and tell her you're here on vacation. You can leave for a while and we can catch up later. Agreed?" I ask.

"No. I'm staying. I'm not looking to get you jammed up with the Bureau. But you need to trust me. I'm blood. She's not."

"OK. Enough," I tell her, as I turn to open the door. "Come in Oksana. You can meet my sister, Jennifer. She's here on a vacation of sorts."

Oksana extends her hand to my sister. Now comes the hard part, to get my sister out of the room quickly, so Oksana can brief me on her meeting with the Greek detective.

But Jen gets in first, speaking to make clear this is her room and she's in charge.

"Please sit down, Oksana. My brother speaks highly of you. I've worked with him in the past. I don't know if he's told you anything about me, or our family, but we've got a long history in this business," she says as she turns and looks at me, waiting for my reaction.

"Yeah, a bit complicated. But most families are complicated, you know. Aren't they?" I respond, looking at my sister. It appears she's not moving. I realize this is her hotel room, not mine. Oksana's come knocking on my sister's door, looking for me. The front desk must have told her where I might be, since the knocks on my door would have gone unanswered.

"I think we got everything we are going to get from the Greeks. He was a gentleman. Charming, and a little too interested in me. But he gave me a complete copy of the autopsy protocol and copies of their investigative reports. The Greeks know little about Anastasia, and I let it be. They were concentrating on the homicide."

Oksana is speaking in English but switching back to Russian when she can't call up the word.

My sister is looking, listening, and absorbing. This could present the perfect opportunity to keep Jennifer out of our conversation. If Oksana takes the invitation ...

"Speak in Russian if you prefer," I tell her.

"LAD-na ... the detectives interviewed the manager of the nightclub near that construction site. They talked to some of the staff. The manager, from Ukraine, saw the two girls at least three, maybe four nights at the club. They mostly kept to themselves, danced a lot. He recalled seeing them that night but never saw them leave. They were supposed to head to one island the next day. Santorini, he told the detectives."

Oksana looks at me, realizing she is sharing sensitive details in front of my sister. She did not grasp the opportunity to switch languages, and now, it would be too obvious if I asked her again.

"Go ahead, Oksana. Jennifer knows to keep quiet and will not speak about this. I'm her brother, her older brother. Right, Jennifer?" I ask her.

Jennifer only nods in response with a slight smile.

"OK. Well, the manager admitted chatting with the girls several times, just small talk. I got the name of the hotel where they were staying. It's on Syntagma Square, Kempinski, I think it was. The Greek police went to that hotel and went through the girls' belongings. I think they are turning over some items to my embassy. Their case has stalled." She pauses. "You like to dance?" she asks with a yawn, looking at my sister, not at me.

"Yes. Love to," Jennifer responds. I can only shake my head. I know exactly where this is going. Oksana wants to get inside the nightclub, and my sister is pushing her way into the investigation. If I don't confront her soon, it will soon be difficult or impossible to stop her.

"You two go to dinner. I will rest here a little," Oksana says with a long yawn.

"Good idea, Oksana. You can rest on my bed. We'll be back in a couple of hours," Jennifer tells her. By the time we close the door, leaving Oksana in the room, she is already sound asleep.

I reach out for Georgia on the mobile phone. "Feel like working tonight?"

"Sure. What's the plan?" she asks. I brief her on the latest developments provided by Oksana.

"I'll bring the equipment to your hotel room. We'll need it once we're inside the club. So, it will be you, me, and Oksana, right?" Kaye asks.

"Yeah, and my sister, most likely."

"What? I heard she was here, but we will have to talk about that. Hey, it's your investigation. You call the shots. I'm here to support, that's all."

Jennifer and I find a small taverna near the hotel for dinner. It will be the best opportunity for me to shut her down and keep her out of the investigation.

"I understand where you're coming from and appreciate your concern, but this is a serious, deadly serious matter. You could get hurt or worse. I don't care about the Bureau. My concern is you, Jen."

"And my concern is you, brother. Step back and think about what's going on here. Washington sends you here alone. You do not know who this Oksana really is, her capabilities, background, not to mention the matter of trust. As far as the missing Russian girl, there's no ransom demand, none that you know of. This Anastasia could be dead, in hiding or being held against her will. Who knows where, and more importantly, why, and by whom?

"Someone could set you up. Think about it. You've got your share of enemies inside and outside of the Bureau. And do you think it's a coincidence that Andrey

Kozlenok, from your diamond case, was living here in hiding before the Russians grabbed him and took him back to Moscow for trial?"

"OK. Enough, Jen. We'll do it on my terms. Let's see how things go tonight inside the club. It's not about your capabilities or intuition—your special gifts. Can you at least agree to step away from this, if I ask you, after tonight?"

"Agreed. But you need me. You'll see. Now let's eat and enjoy the view of the Acropolis. It's so stunning. I never thought I'd be here."

"Neither did I. Yamas," I say as we clink our glasses.

"Jen, this is how it's going to work tonight, and I need your cooperation," I say, hoping she won't push back. "Georgia Kaye, the legal attaché assigned to Athens is going to bring us some equipment, mostly communication equipment for us to use inside the club. I haven't told her you may be participating."

"No. I will be participating. She can't stop me from going to the club tonight. It's a public place, and I'm free to go where I want."

"OK. Let me talk to her when she arrives at the hotel. I'll tell her you're a psychologist specializing in behavioral analysis, and you'll be there observing, watching, and won't take any action. Is that agreeable to you?"

"Sure. So, you won't tell her about my other gifts and talents, right?"

She offers a coy smile.

"No way. She'd have trouble processing that, I think. Besides, those special gifts aren't for sharing. Georgia is a good person and a solid investigator, but she's not blood.

Let's get back to the hotel." I motion for the server to bring the bill.

***

Oksana is still sound asleep when we enter the room. We leave her sleeping and head to my room down the hall. Minutes later, a soft knock sounds on the door. It's Georgia Kaye.

She wears a clinging jumpsuit with a plunging neckline.

"You sure don't look like a Legat," I say, before engaging my brain, immediately regretting my remark. "I didn't mean it that way. It's just that you look stunning this evening."

"Yeah, right," Georgia responds. She seems to shrug off my unwise choice of language. "We need a plan for tonight. I've brought the tech stuff that you asked Mark for, and some other things, just in case." She opens her carry-on-sized bag. Inside there are mobile phones, cameras, pepper spray, concealable transmitters with tiny earpiece receivers. Oksana suddenly appears in the room. Jennifer has apparently awoken her and sent her down the hall to my room.

"I think you've already met my sister, right?" I ask Georgia.

"Well, we've spoken several times on the phone. Are you joining us this evening?" Georgia asks. I can only look at her astonished, wondering if my sister has used some sort of Jedi mind trick on Georgia. On some level, I don't care. At least I won't have to have that uncomfortable talk with Georgia about Jennifer coming to the club with us. It's a relief, although it makes me wonder what my sister could have told Georgia during those telephone conversations.

Jennifer is quick to respond to the offer. "Of course. But only as an observer. I can absorb and remember a lot of detail, even in a crowded club. You'll see."

"Good. Well, this is what I know about this Aphrodite Nightclub," Georgia says as she briefs the group. The club has had a recent change in ownership, according to a reliable source. The new silent partners are members of one of the local Russian organized crime gangs.

A Vor-v-Zakonye—thief-in-law—the Russian underworld term for a high-ranking member of the Russian Mafia, was the actual force behind the change in ownership.

The crowd at the club is unusually mixed, made up of locals, tourists, Russians, Ukrainians, along with refugees and émigrés from Eastern Europe and the Western Balkans.

Georgia admits she hasn't been there for some time.

It used to be a classy upscale place before the change in ownership, with a few talented DJs spinning the latest dance tracks of artists from around the world.

I say, "Let's go in there in pairs, and try to stay in pairs —Georgia and I, and Jen and Oksana. This way, each of us will have the languages covered: Greek, English and Russian."

They nod in agreement.

Now, I ask, "And what about a rendezvous time, no later than 0300, back at the hotel? OK?" Again, nods of agreement. "Remember, we're just trying to get a sense of this place. We're not there to interview anyone. If staff, a bartender or a manager looks approachable, fine. Just keep the conversation light."

Oksana comments, "Between the four of us, we are bound to come away with something useful. But it's important to relax, dance, and enjoy the place, otherwise we'll stand out, and not in a good way. I know this club is involved in the murder and disappearance. The killer could be a regular, or on staff. Oh, and be careful about your drinks too. Better to order something out of a bottle, not a mixed drink."

Chapter 9

Oksana and Jennifer are already chatting away with one of the staff by the time Georgia and I enter the club. They've had a twenty-minute head start. Oksana is gently stroking the arm of the slight young man as they are talking, while Jennifer looks relaxed, simply absorbing it all.

Gyrating, sweaty bodies pack the nightclub dance floor, awash in strobe lights.

Many women wear scanty clothing, looking as though they've just left the beach.

The hypnotic Brazilian dance beat is blaring, conversation still just about possible if you lean in close enough to the other person. I order a club soda for Georgia and a beer for myself.

I find the local Greek beer is ice cold, light, and refreshing in the summer heat.

Georgia leans in to talk.

"I'm going to cruise this place, use my camera to get some photos, see if there's anyone I recognize. I'll be back soon. Oh, tell any working girls who hit on you that you're already taken," she teases. After this, Georgia soon fades into the crowd.

I order a second beer, but need a quick restroom stop.

Bathrooms in such places are best avoided, but my bladder is talking to me.

Fortunately, the men's room is nearly empty, unlike the line already forming for the women's room. I make my way back to the original spot near the bar where Georgia and I were standing.

The woman seated alone at the bar freezes me. *No, here we go again.* The resemblance to my wife, Lenore, is striking. The same build, hairstyle—a short, jagged cut, and dirty blonde.

She's not an exact copy but could be easily mistaken for Lenore.

It's not so shocking, since this woman appears to be Russian judging by her high cheekbones and fair skin, similar to my wife's with her Eastern European roots. Passing pedestrians frequently stopped Lenore in Moscow, mistaking her for a local to ask for directions.

The woman looks to be waiting on someone, gazing around the club as she nurses her drink. When the adjoining seat becomes free, I take it.

There's something odd about that female, sitting alone in the crowded club. I can't put my finger on it, but my sister would tell me to go with my instinct.

"Sorry, but you look so similar to someone I know," I tell the stranger.

As soon as the words are out of my mouth, I realize it sounds like some juvenile pickup line discarded long ago in my youth. "You remind me of my wife," I add. The stranger smiles. She turns back to her drink on the bar. I'm about to stand up and walk away from the clumsy attempt at conversation when she unexpectedly turns back to face me.

"You are American? Yes?" she asks.

"Yeah. Guess it's obvious, huh?"

"No, not really. But you're not a local, and you're not from my country, Russia. You are not a tourist, either. Nice to meet you. I am Victoria but call me Vika if you like."

"Conner, nice to meet you, Vika," I tell her in Russian, using an undercover name from a previous assignment. "Do you live here, Vika? Or are you on vacation?"

"No. I am here looking for someone."

"Oh? You are waiting for someone?"

"No. Unfortunately not. I've been coming here every evening for the past days. My daughter used to come with her friend. Now, she is missing," Victoria says, her voice crackling.

It can't be. This chance encounter would not surprise my sister.

"What is your daughter's name?" I ask.

"Anastasia."

I swallow hard. This makes little sense. Popov's wife would not be here in this club alone, surely! From what Oksana told me, I thought Popov's wife's name was Natasha, or Svetlana, certainly not Victoria. "And her friend's name?"

"Yelena. But she is dead."

My head throbs. I don't know if it's the loud music, the smoke-filled air, or the conversation with this Vika. Who is this woman? Did Oksana tell me that Anastasia was the adopted daughter of Popov? Is this Victoria, her biological mother? Or is this all some clever ruse?

There is no time for analysis.

I somehow need to identify this woman. There's nothing to prevent her from suddenly standing up and leaving the bar, and I have no authority or any right to stop her.

"Look, there are people at the U.S. Embassy who might help you find your daughter. Where are you staying?" I ask.

"I'm at the Astoria."

I exhale. If she is being truthful, I should be able to find her.

Victoria's eyes are moist. She looks close to tears. Perhaps I was too aggressive with her, too quickly. I try to ease my way out of the sensitive topic.

"It's amazing how people, seemingly unrelated, from different parts of the globe, can resemble one another. But my wife's ethnic background is Hungarian and Russian. Maybe you two are distant cousins or something. Mirtes-en; it's a small world," I say in Russian.

She nods, wiping the tear running down her face.

I look down to pick up my beer. It will give me a moment to think about what I'll next say to this mysterious woman on the verge of tears. Say the wrong thing, and I could be done.

She will stand up and leave. I casually survey my surroundings, not wanting Georgia to walk up and surprise us. Yet, Georgia, as an FBI agent, would or should instinctively know to stay away while I'm in conversation with a stranger.

I again turn away from Victoria for an instance, glancing to my left toward the dance floor. By the time I turn my head back around and face her, she is gone. I quickly scan the bar area. No sign. Searching for her would mean rudely pushing past too many people in the crowded club.

Did I say something to cause her to leave so suddenly? No, this woman was already on the edge. She seemed sincere, but it could all be an act. To what end, I do not know.

I casually survey my surroundings, spotting two young women laughing, seated at a corner table. Russian prostitutes, I conclude. There is also a man, perhaps late thirties, their pimp or client, no doubt. He has dark features, jet black shoulder length hair.

He's wearing an expensive looking dress shirt and dark pants, and he's well-groomed. The gold jewelry screams mafia. As they laugh, the well-dressed thug smiles back at them, his expression suddenly transforming. When he looks directly at me, I don't look away.

His dark eyes look empty, dead. He motions with his hand to each girl as if offering one of them to me. He most likely is, and they are oblivious to what he is doing.

He seems to mouth something to me. I look away. There's no point in provoking him; I'm not sure he is looking at me and not at someone else nearby. Where is Georgia? I suddenly feel someone's arm wrap around my waist from behind. I recognize the perfume. It's her.

"I've got some wonderful photos of these hoods. Relax. Oksana and Jennifer are fine. They are still over in the other corner, talking to one of the staff, maybe a manager. Let's dance," she says as she takes my hand and guides me to the dance floor. There's a techno pulsating dance beat. Gyrating bodies pack the floor. The DJ gets an enormous cheer as he introduces his next track, Frankie Goes to Hollywood's Relax, Don't Do It.

I check my watch. It's already three o'clock. Somehow, more than one hour has passed since Georgia took my hand to guide me to the dance floor. "Let's get out of here," she says.

"We're in the cab, heading back to the hotel," Oksana tells me as she answers the call from my mobile phone. "Let's brief once we're back in the hotel. See you in a few minutes."

And in a few minutes just as planned, that is what we do. She starts telling me her side.

"Jen and I found one of the assistant managers. We told him we worked for a modeling agency based in the U.S., and had heard about the two Russian sisters, the models Yelena and Anastasia. His eyes moistened immediately, and he nearly started crying right there. Jen calmed him and got him to spill his guts to us. She did a great job."

"Yes? And what did he reveal?" I ask.

"A lot. Well, for starters, his name is Dmitry, prefers to be called Dima. Effeminate, but charming. He told us he enjoyed the company of pretty women, and seemed to enjoy talking with us," Oksana says.

Given her own acknowledgment of her beauty and my sister's, I can't help but comment.

"Sure, guess that means you two aren't so bad looking, I suppose," I say.

Oksana laughs. "He befriended Yelena and Anastasia during the first of several visits to the club. I understand why. He was no threat to them and helped them deflect unwanted advances of those men eager for a quick score with the two Russian beauties. They talked about organizing an informal fashion show at the club during a future visit. Dima was excited about the prospect. He told us he loves women's fashion; his secret passion is to be a dress designer."

Jennifer cuts in, saying, "I don't know if it's relevant, but he says he noticed the girls wearing each other's outfits during the week, and on the night of Yelena's murder, he needed a second look to distinguish one from the other. They'd exchanged hair colors. Yelena had dyed hers blonde, very blonde, and Anastasia's was jet black. It was an interesting switch, but it worked for each girl. He said the girls danced practically nonstop at the club, with men coming up, asking to dance with them at scheduled intervals. They danced with some and turned down others. The men would fade away after a few minutes. The girls weren't interested in being picked up."

"So, what else? That's it? You spent a lot of time with this guy, and that's all?" I ask.

Jennifer responds, "Give us a break. We're not done. Dima spoke about the mafia—the Russian Mafia—using his country as a vacation getaway. Even their hired hitmen rest in Greece between contract killings, surrounded by young, beautiful Slavic women."

Jennifer is clearly annoyed at my impatience.

But doesn't she see the clock is ticking? Don't Oksana and Jennifer understand the need to extract everything this Dima might know about the fate of the two girls?

They aren't taking it seriously enough, not probing enough. As far as Jennifer goes, I understand; she's not an agent. Oksana, though, should have gleaned more than this by now.

I wonder if Oksana let Jen take the lead, and with Jennifer being inexperienced …

Oksana next steps in just in time to stop my chastising thoughts running away with me.

She offers, "Is Dima hiding something? Possibly. At least the door is open for us to go back to talk to him, perhaps alone, in a unique setting. But honestly, I don't see your problem. Jen and I did good job. Finding someone like Dima in nightclub, full of local patrons, thugs, and tourists, isn't easy. He may prove helpful to us in the future. So, give credit."

She tells me off in her disjointed English, smiling at Jennifer for validation.

It's three women and me. Three alpha women. I'm not in charge. My ego tries to convince me otherwise, but it has to be set aside for now. My mission is to find Anastasia.

I tell them about the mafia figure with the dead eyes. Perhaps he was one of those vacationing thugs Dima talked about.

"So, Georgia, it's your turn," I say.

"I took some photos inside the club, and outside," she says.

"Outside? How's that?" I ask.

"I positioned my vehicle in a location to use the hidden video system to capture images of patrons entering and leaving the club. Not sure about the quality, and it will be a lot to review, but may help us."

I decide not to share my chance encounter with the mysterious Victoria, known as Vika. My gut tells me to wait. Besides, there's nothing more to do for now. We are all exhausted, and the sun is soon to rise. I've never been a night person, unlike my sister.

I'll need a few hours of rest. We all will.

Chapter 10

The activity in the hotel room hallway wakes me, a good thing since it's already past noon.

I dress and head down to the lobby for some coffee, on the way slipping a note under Jennifer's door, letting her know I'm awake and downstairs waiting for her there.

My decision last night not to reveal my encounter with the mysterious Victoria—Vika—weighs on me. I'm going to have to discuss it eventually with Oksana.

She's done nothing to cause me to distrust her.

Oksana is Russian, working for MVD, so it appears, but the possibility that she works for Russian intelligence, or is at least cooperating with them, is very real.

"OK, we're ready," the familiar voice says.

I look up from my coffee. It's Jennifer and Oksana standing in front of me.

I suggest, "How about we head to the beach for a few hours? There's a nice one just outside the city; the embassy staff told me about it. We can strategize there, and I'm sure the salt water and fresh air will be good for us."

***

I grab my swim goggles and head to the water as soon as we find a secluded spot on the sand.

"Do you mind if I join you?" Oksana asks. She has brought her own goggles.

"You see the island out there?" I query. "It's about a kilometer, but swimmable. What do you think?"

I've no idea if she can swim that far in open water, but judging by her running ability, it wouldn't surprise me if she happened to be an excellent swimmer as well.

She doesn't answer, but dives into the calm, clear water, an answer in itself.

Her freestyle stroke is powerful and efficient, leaving me struggling to keep pace as I expected. We reach the rocky beach on the small island in less than thirty minutes.

"Oksana, let's rest here before heading back," I say, finding a rocky plateau on which we can sit and talk. "Tell me about yourself."

She responds in Russian.

"There's not much to say. I was married at twenty, divorced by twenty-two, no children, went through the MVD Academy about five years ago. I have one sister. She lives in Uzbekistan, in Tashkent. My parents live outside of Saint Petersburg. My father was a regional prosecutor when we lived in Uzbekistan until we left, when the Soviet Union dissolved. The Russians offered us citizenship since my father is an ethnic Russian. His grandparents were from Leningrad. They left after the Great Patriotic War, seeking a better life, a life that was promised to them. Part of Stalin's Virgin Lands program to populate Central Asia with European Russians. Our family suffered a lot, just like many Soviet families. We endured war, Stalin, communism, the gulags."

"What about your mother's parents? They were Greeks, right?"

"Yes. My grandfather fought on the side of the communists in the Greek Civil War. After their defeat, tens of thousands of Greek nationals fled, and Stalin, welcoming them to the Soviet Union, summarily shipped them off to faraway Uzbekistan and Kazakhstan."

"But why didn't your family emigrate to Greece?" I inquire. "I understand the Greeks have been accepting thousands from the Soyuz after the breakup."

"My father was against it. He was not a Greek; only my mother was. I suppose he wanted to return to his own native land. Perhaps he thought he would be an outsider in Greece. I can't blame him," she says as she stands and stretches her limbs, preparing for the return swim.

"My parents never could see the West," she tells me next. "That I, a young Russian girl—still their little girl in their eyes—can travel to the West and work outside of Russia still shocks them. They believed only high-ranking Communist Party members had the right to travel outside the Soviet Union. The way things are going with this case, it might also be my last trip." She sits back down next to me. "You don't remember me, do you?"

"No. We've met before?" I ask.

She responds, "I was in Budapest when you lectured there once, about two years ago. I thought you had a big ego, a typical American who thought he was something special just because he spoke Russian and was an FBI agent. I didn't like you much back then."

Oksana's openness in telling me about herself and her family is unexpected.

I'm uncertain what to make of it, but it all sounds plausible and believable.

If this is some made-up story, her legend, then it's convincing.

"I don't know what awaits us in this investigation, Oksana, but we need to trust each other completely. There's no time to work on our trust. It has to be there. I'm far from perfect and have made plenty of mistakes … in my personal life, and in my work life. Just ask my sister," I say. "She knows many of my faults, well, not all of them, but enough."

I decide it's a good time to tell her about my strange encounter with Victoria.

As I finish the story, waiting for Oksana to react, she just sits there strangely silent.

She seems to be processing what I've told her.

Finally, she begins to speak in Russian.

"Why you didn't tell me about this last night? You just didn't forget something so important. You don't trust me. How can we work together like this?"

She clenches her hands in frustration, so angry and speaking in Russian so fast that I can't follow what she is saying. Her eyes are tear-filled, which catches me unawares.

It's a relief for me to unload the details of last night's encounter with this mysterious Victoria—Vika. It's also revealing to me, seeing the emotion pouring out of Oksana.

I see she is trembling. She stands, wipes her eyes, and composes herself.

"Don't do that to me again, not ever," she says, staring into my eyes, wiping her tears with the back of her hands.

"I won't, Oksana. My mistake. I am sorry," I tell her.

I have just learned a lesson. My paranoia about the Bureau and this assignment was allowed to affect my better judgment and investigative instincts. I can't make this mistake again.

The possibility that Oksana is working for Russian intelligence, it doesn't even matter.

I need to let it go. I'm about to kiss her gently on the cheek but stop.

Yes, she's a woman, but she is first my work partner, not a lover or family member.

"Oksana, we need to go to Victoria's hotel, to find and talk to her, perhaps first follow or surveil her. Well, she is our best and only good lead for the moment. It may be the only break we get in this strange case."

I stand up to prepare for our reentry into the sea for the swim back to the beach.

"Looks like we're working tonight. Oksana, before I forget, we could use more background on Anastasia and Yelena. Moscow needs to interview both parents more thoroughly about their daughters' likes, dislikes, hobbies, friends, travel plans, and everything else. Even their vices ... Drug problems, eating disorders, anything like that. I don't want to hear that Moscow is sending reports soon. We need them now," I say, as I put my goggles on and enter the sea. I laugh. "Here we are in this beautiful place, where normal people come to relax and vacation. We are here trying to solve the grisly murder of a young girl and find her missing friend. Ironic, huh?"

She turns to me with her mirrored goggles concealing her eyes. "Life is cruel. Anastasia is alive. We will find her. Let's swim back before your sister gets worried," she says as she dives into the water. She is several lengths ahead of me in a matter of seconds as she turns and smiles briefly, diving again beneath the surface and reemerging. With her olive complexion and shimmering dark hair, she looks like a Greek goddess returning to her watery kingdom.

I follow.

***

"How was your swim? You were gone for almost an hour," Jennifer says, but her intonation makes clear it's a question, not a statement. She wants an explanation.

"Yeah, sorry about that. I'll hang here while you go for a swim, but take your time. Oksana went to get something to eat or walk around. I don't think she'll be back for a while."

I still don't give her the explanation of our lengthy time away.

"What happened out there? And don't tell me nothing," Jennifer asks a second time.

"It's all resolved," I answer.

"No. Not good enough. I have a suspicion about what you two were discussing out there, but I need you to tell me."

"Really? OK. Here goes." Jennifer listens attentively as I tell her about my encounter with the mysterious Vika. "So, there you have it. That's all."

"Oh, I saw you talking to that woman sitting at the bar. She looked like your wife? I wasn't close enough to judge just how much she resembled Lenore. I'm just glad Lenore wasn't there to witness it. Honestly, I first thought you were hitting on her. But I can understand why you approached her, or did she approach you?"

"Huh? What are you driving at, Jen?" I ask.

"If she isn't who she claims to be," she responds.

"What? So, she spots us—me—then positions herself at the bar, so I'm bound to notice her. And she bears a striking resemblance to Lenore not by chance? Please don't tell me this concerns our LAX friend."

"I'm not sure. I'm just not ruling anything out."

"So, what do you make of Oksana? She unloaded on me out there on the island, asserting that I don't trust her."

"I figured that. If I had any doubts about her, don't you think I would have told you by now? Seriously. I know you miss working with your task force from Golden ADA—your all-male task force—but that case is over, done. It's you, me and Oksana. That's it. Georgia and Mark are solid and will support, but that's all. You can't and shouldn't drag them into this. Even your HQ told you not to do that, right?"

"Yeah. So, sis, what's our next move? I think I need to get Sharon over here. She can't help much from California. What do you think?"

She replies, "I'm way ahead of you. She's already on the plane. I spoke with her several days ago; there's no way she's going to be left on the sidelines for this one."

I laugh. "Perhaps I've created a monster of sorts. Sharon Austin has been with me since I started working in San José, and from the start of the Golden ADA saga. Heck, she gave me that lead to cover when I stopped by her office, that lead from OSI."

"What's OSI?"

"No, don't go there. It's the section in the Department of Justice responsible for investigating and prosecuting Nazi war criminals. It has nothing to do with this case."

"Yeah? You sure about that?"

"No. I'm not sure about anything. I'm just along for the ride, sis. Trying to hold on tight and not fall into the abyss."

"I'm here, brother. Relax. Oksana's back."

"Hi," says Oksana as she saunters up to us. "I love this beach, full of its beautiful people. Women love the topless look here, huh? In Russia, we don't do that. Well, we don't have beaches like this either, except a few in Crimea, on the Black Sea. Still, funny how their conservative priests can walk around in this decadent environment. But the guy's eyes didn't wander, not once."

"What guy?"

"The priest."

"What did he look like, Oksana?"

"Like a priest."

"No, I'm serious. What was he wearing? Give me a complete description," I say.

"OK. All black. I mean, even his beard, long hair, olive complexion, rosary beads, perhaps late thirties, 180 centimeters. I could swear he looked at me and even smiled."

Jennifer stands up from the blanket. "Hey, he walked right in front of me when you two were swimming. I felt something but brushed the feeling aside. What is it, Dennis?"

It seems the priest walking by may have activated Jennifer's special gift.

"Not sure. When I was in the park a few days ago, near the hotel, there was a priest. He—no, I'm just getting paranoid; it's probably nothing. There are lots of priests in this country, no doubt. Oksana, did you bring the papers with you? The documents from the detective?"

"Yes. Let's review them together," she answers.

We spend the next hour reviewing copies of interview reports, crime scene sketches, and the autopsy protocol that Oksana got from her meeting with the Greek detective.

The documents were in Greek, of course, so Oksana translated everything into Russian.

I then translated her Russian into English for Jennifer's benefit.

"I'd like to get these into the hands of my one solid contact in the Bureau's Behavioral Analysis Unit, the BAU."

"You joking? For what, though? They were useless to you in Kansas City. Now, you intend to involve them in this case? You nuts?" Jennifer asks.

She's shaking her head, clearly agitated at my idea.

"I met the profiler, Adam Wheaton, in Moscow when he was there to help the Russians with several cases and conduct some training for their behavioral profiling unit. He's lectured at the International Law Enforcement Academy in Budapest. He's actually not an FBI agent. He retired from the Baltimore Police Department's Detective Bureau; they hired him as a profiler after his retirement. They've never done that before. He's a modest guy and would never boast, but a television series called Homicide on the Streets featured several of his cases. I trust this guy."

"OK, but we don't have weeks for him to work up a profile. I'm here. Did you forget the subject of my thesis? The clock is ticking, as you like to say. Time is running out for Anastasia," Jennifer says as if she feels she really could be a credible stand-in for Adam.

"Look, I'll send this express mail from the Legat Office tomorrow, or Georgia will, and meanwhile, we'll keep going here. Nothing changes. Agreed?" I ask.

I flip through the pages to the crime scene sketches and photos.

The positioning of Yelena's body strikes me as rather strange. She's on her back, hands across her chest, legs straight together, head facing up. The killer or killers obviously positioned her body this way, most likely post-mortem. The Greek police concluded Yelena died at the scene because of the amount of blood and I'm not convinced they're right; the protocol contained conflicting information suggesting a post-mortem movement of the body.

I figure Wheaton will have something to say about that possibility.

"Let's get out of here and head to Victoria's hotel. We can't barge in there and expect the staff to share personal information about their guests. We're not police, not in this country. Going through Greek law enforcement contacts will take time, and we'll have to come up with some logical sounding excuse if we do that."

"I speak Greek. I can do it. Alone," Oksana says.

It makes sense. She's also an attractive female, which could help her. We don't have a last name for Victoria, so Oksana will have to approach someone on the hotel staff directly to get the needed information. I decide it's best to let her come up with her own story line.

The closer her lie is to the truth, the more likely people will accept it.

Jennifer and I wait in the car a block away from Hotel Astoria. The hotel is in a quiet residential neighborhood, a small boutique hotel judging by its outer appearance.

"What do you think, Jen?" I ask.

She answers jokingly, "She's a woman. Oksana will give it her best shot. She understands the culture and speaks the language. Besides, what choice do we have? Victoria's our only lead at the moment. Lead. I like that term. I'm getting pretty good at using it, huh?"

"Yeah. I'm so impressed. You're becoming a real FBI special agent. Speaking of the Bureau, I've heard nothing from HQ. Guess that's a good thing, right?" I ask.

"Well, it's better than them wanting hourly updates," Jennifer says as she spots Oksana emerging from the hotel. "Game time, I hope," she says.

Oksana reports, "I did it. Victoria checked out this morning, according to the nice looking, naïve man at the reception desk. He confessed everything. I told him I was on vacation all alone and agreed to meet him later. I won't, naturally."

"So, what did he tell you?" I ask impatiently.

"She's heading to Santorini. Well, that is what she told him this morning," she says.

"How do we know if it's true?"

"How? Well, I've got her telephone records for all the calls made from her room."

"He gave them to you, just like that? Don't tell me what sort of ruse you used. I don't want to know."

She gazes over at Jennifer, smiling. "I stole them."

"No. You didn't do that, Oksana. Do me a favor. In future, just say something like you borrowed them, or have them on loan," I say, shaking my head in disbelief, but slightly amused.

She's hurt no one, and the records could prove useful.

They also provide the last name for this Victoria: Tarasova.

"Oksana, reach out to Moscow. They need to identify this Victoria for us now that we have a last name. I don't know where this is heading, if it's a dead end or some sort of game, but we don't have much choice, do we? Let me look at those phone records. The records list telephone numbers, towns, dates, and duration of each call. "Here's one for Santorini. Oksana …"

She grabs the pages from my hands.

"I will call them and speak in Greek," Oksana says, dialing the number from her cell phone.

"Yep. A hotel."

"Let's slow down and think this through," Jennifer says.

"What? We need to go there. You have another plan?" I ask.

"She may not be who you think she is. We don't know if she's some sort of courier, or representative from the bad guys. Victoria could be luring us into a trap."

"What? She was very emotional at the club that evening, nearly in tears. She didn't strike me as a criminal," I say.

"Why? Oh, right. Because only men are criminals? And all women are pure? Listen to yourself. She's pretty and looks a lot like Lenore, so in your mind, you've decided she's one of the good guys and she'll lead us straight to Anastasia, just like that? It won't be that easy."

"OK, Jen. Good points but we don't have time. We need to get over to Santorini, find this Victoria. She's not heading there on vacation. Something or someone is pushing her to travel there, and my bet is that this someone is Anastasia, her biological daughter. So, we need to get on the next flight. Maybe Victoria's going there by ferry. If so, we may get there ahead of her."

"I need Moscow—well, Eugeniy Zhirov in Athens, at least—to approve and fund my travel there. This will take time," Oksana says.

"Forget it, Oksana. The Bureau will pick up the costs. We can't sit here waiting for your center to respond when they get around to it. I'll pay for your travel with the Bureau credit card. Jen, you're on your own. My finance division will be screaming at me soon, but I don't care."

"You're not leaving me out. No way. I'm going. You need me. I'll buy my ticket," Jen says.

"Absolutely no way, Jen. You're out of this. You were good the other night at the Aphrodite, but this is a whole other level. We know nothing about this Vika woman. She could be a psycho and dangerous. You could wind up dead. Forget it, Jen; I mean it."

"No. I mean it as well! I'm part of your team now. You need to accept this reality, the reality that you need me. I know much more than you think I do," Jennifer counters.

"We know nothing about this Victoria other than what she told me that night at the club. Yeah, she looks a lot like Lenore, but so what? I'm sorry, Jen, but this is far too dangerous, and engaging with a woman like this, well, you don't have the training or experience."

"Really? She's a mother looking for her biological daughter, who she gave up for adoption a long time ago. We know something about those sorts of people, don't we? And no, I'm not referring to our LAX woman. That's a whole other issue we've yet to discuss."

"Jen, don't go there."

"Will you two please stop? I need her. In fact, I insist," Oksana says, jumping in.

Chapter 11

The honeycomb network of whitewashed stairs and staggered terraces clumped neatly together in one village along the coastline comes into view, our aircraft lining up for its final approach.

In 1500 BC, a volcanic eruption and earthquake wiped out some of the island.

Perhaps this was the origin of the mythical Atlantis legend, that of the lost civilization.

The ancient people and its culture may have been lost forever, but our task is to find but one person, somewhat less daunting and simpler—at least I hope so.

The hotel where Victoria is likely staying proves easy to find.

Oksana has booked us rooms at one of the smaller hotels nearby, and there are tourists everywhere. Pleasure craft and passenger ships offer the island a constant supply of newcomers to feed the local economy and keep the locals employed.

Once we settle into our rooms, we decide to send Oksana and Jennifer on a scouting mission to check out the area's cliffside hotels and the volcanic rock beaches below.

"Just keep the transmitter turned on. I'll monitor the two of you from a distance," I mandate.

But if we find this Victoria, it's better for me to approach her," Jennifer says.

"Why? Wouldn't it make more sense for it to be Oksana? She speaks Russian, after all," I say.

"No. She's right. She could freeze up on me. With Jennifer, as an American, she might be more open and friendlier. You experienced that at the club with her, didn't you?"

"OK. Then start with her hotel, the pool area, then check out the local tourist shops and the beach below. If you have any sign she's with someone, back off. Get photos and leave, and don't approach her. We don't even know why she's traveled here. Maybe her daughter's in hiding here and reached out to her. There are many possibilities. It's not for a vacation, that much we know for sure," I say, handing over the concealable transmitters. "Let's get started. Remember, don't approach her if you have any sign that she's with someone. In fact, it's better not to approach her at all. I'd prefer us to watch her for a while first. Oh, and I didn't use my real name when I met her, in case that somehow comes up. I told her my name's Conner, and I work at the U.S. Embassy in Athens. I didn't say what I did there, and she didn't ask me."

Tourists are everywhere, crowding the narrow whitewashed alleys and stairs.

There's no sign of Victoria at her hotel—the one where we suspect she could be staying based on the telephone records from Athens. I call Oksana, suggesting she and Jennifer should walk down the winding stairs to the beach below. It's a secluded spot, not easily reachable.

"Bingo," Jennifer practically screams into the transmitter. "She looks to be alone, sitting on the beach. There's no one near her as far as I can tell."

"Just find a seat close by, but not on top of her," I say into the transmitter.

"No shit," Jennifer responds. "She's on her phone. She's glanced over and smiled. Oh, she's just put down the phone! I'm going to talk to her," she says brightly as if speaking about a friend.

"No," I tell her through the transmitter. "Please don't do that."

But it's already too late. I hear static, but the conversation is hard to pick up. It's up to Oksana and Jennifer now. They are on their own. My cliffside position, high above the beach below, doesn't allow me to see what is transpiring far below on the beach.

My mind drifts back to other beaches in the past.

No, I need to stay focused on the present, on this beach. My sister is down there, alone with this woman. The woman who could be a dangerous killer, or could simply be, as she purports, a mother searching for her missing young daughter. *Jennifer's a grown woman; she can take care of herself,* I try to convince myself. Then in the next breath, my small inner voice says instead, *this can all end badly, and quickly. And I'll be too far away to help. This was a stupid idea.*

I make my way down the winding stairs slowly, closer to the beach as the transmitter connection comes back to life. The conversation is audible once more.

It's hard to pick up exactly what they're saying, but it's in English, that much I can tell. I stop on one of the observation platforms along the stairs, a few flights above the black volcanic rock beach below. Tourists also stop to gaze at the incredible view of sea, sun, and land rising dramatically out of the blue sea. The volcanic explosion must have been sudden and instantly deadly to the island's unsuspecting inhabitants.

They have all become dust, their lives, their dreams, and everything they possessed, all destroyed in an instant. I'm brought back to the present with the sight of Oksana and Jennifer climbing up the stairs toward me. They motion for me to walk with them, saying nothing.

"So, what the hell's gone on down there? Where is Vika?" I ask.

"Calm down, brother. Give us a chance to explain," Jennifer says as she motions for me to sit on the balcony chair of her hotel room.

Jennifer says, "You weren't wrong; she really does look like Lenore, a lot! Her nose, face structure, hair. It's a bit unsettling, really. It reminds me of some Hollywood horror film. An obsessed fan of a starlet gets carried away, has plastic surgery and a complete makeover to become a double of the object of her obsession," Jennifer says.

"Stop. You're freaking me out," I say.

"No, really. Even her nose. Lenore has a unique nose! She told me more than once someone stopped her and asked who did the surgery, and she would answer, God!"

This isn't the time for joking around. I need to get Jennifer to focus.

"OK. So, what did you talk about down there?"

"Vika doesn't like beaches," she says.

"What? That's what you learned?" I ask.

"Be patient. There's more. We had an interesting conversation about the beach. As she sat there looking out at the vast sea, she told me she doesn't like beaches, yet there she was sitting on this isolated beach, with its dark volcanic rocky pebbles! She said that despite her aversion, she finds the beaches in Santorini captivating, alluring, and mysterious.

"The beach is actually on the edge of an abyss, a deep abyss. When the volcano collapsed after the eruption, the sea filled in the vast crater that was created. That violent eruption long ago claimed many lives. I've been thinking about what she told me and I'm still processing it as a psychologist—well, a soon-to-be behavioral psychologist. Whether she understood what she was telling me, I'm not sure. Perhaps there was some underlying subliminal message or meaning. Anyway, I told her straight up that I was your sister, and her reaction was, well, it wasn't normal. She didn't freak out, scream, nothing. Almost as if she'd been expecting it."

"Come on, Jen. Really? That's weird," I say.

"Yeah. It made me think about your so-called 'chance encounter' with her at the nightclub in Athens. How chance that encounter was in reality, I'm not sure. But she also shared with me a bit about herself. Her work, her life, and how she wound up in Athens," Jennifer says.

Oksana is staring at her. She has taken out her notepad, now sitting quietly, taking notes.

"She works for a Hungarian-based cosmetics firm, head of their regional sales team. She says she travels all around Russia and parts of Eastern Europe. She divorced in her early twenties and never remarried. She says she's in her early forties now though you'd never think that, honestly.

"She looks at least ten years younger, so maybe she's using the stuff she's selling and it actually works, who knows? Anyway, a couple of years ago, she hired a private investigator to find her biological daughter, Anastasia. The PI tracked her down and told her that her daughter was modeling internationally. This is where it gets interesting. Vika then heads for Athens, but she's too late. By the time she arrives, Anastasia's missing, and Yelena's been murdered."

"I don't believe her story, Jen. It's too neat, too tight. Perhaps the girls themselves were involved in drug trafficking, or in the trafficking of young women; it's big business in the former Soviet Union. This Victoria may be someone else entirely," I say, shaking my head in disbelief.

So, I continue, "This woman, Victoria—Vika—is sitting there on the beach, unloading all of this on you, a complete stranger? I know you can be persuasive and charming, but seriously, sis, something is off. We could waste our time with this Victoria—if that's even her real name."

Oksana cuts in, "You have another option? I have no information back from Moscow about anyone with that name. She's our best lead for the moment. And our only lead."

I say, "I sent copies of everything through Georgia to my one reliable Quantico contact, from the Behavioral Analysis Unit. She told me an embassy courier flying back to Washington would hand-carry it. Adam Wheaton should have it by now. I wrote to him it was urgent. He'll work up a profile, at least I hope so, a profile we can use to move the case forward."

Jennifer shakes her head and throws up both hands in frustration.

"To the BAU? You kidding me? It didn't work out so well when you were in Kansas City. They were useless. Well, if this Adam Wheaton is a reliable contact of yours as you say, fine, but we still need to be proactive. Isn't that how you work? That's what you told me. We can't sit here and wait on this Adam Wheaton. The clock is ticking; isn't that right?" she asks.

"OK. Enough, Jen. We'll go with this Vika woman. What's our next move?" I ask.

"Next?" Jennifer asks. "Back to Athens, tonight. Vika told me she already checked the hotel that the girls were planning to stay at in Santorini, and there was no record, no information, nothing. So, she's returning on the evening ferry to Athens. We need to be on it with her."

"I can ask my Greek detective friend if they can get the phone records from Vika's hotel, maybe even the mobile phone calls as well," Oksana suggests.

"No, you can't, Oksana. Please don't do that. We're done with the Greek police. FBIHQ told me I was to work with you, your agency, no one else. That's how I understood it. Perhaps there are reasons they can't or won't share. Besides, we could put that Greek detective in a very awkward position, working with us and not informing his superiors. It's not about trust, or whether their agency is corrupt. Maybe it is. We've already seen their files, thanks to you."

"OK. I understand, but those phone records could be helpful to us," Oksana says.

"Forget it, Oksana. I've said it already that we're on our own. If the Greek police learn about our interest in Victoria, they could start their own parallel investigation. We would lose control and find ourselves in the dark. It's not worth the risk."

Jennifer jumps in.

"True, this Victoria may not be who she purports. No matter! I say we stick with her, and don't let her slip away, not yet." She pauses and sighs. "Besides, we've got no other promising leads. My senses are flat right now. I'm getting nothing. Absolutely nothing."

"Huh? Sorry, my English isn't so good. What did you say? I am not understanding what you are not getting," Oksana asks with a puzzled look.

"Oksana, let me explain. My sister here is a bit, well, different, let's say. She has certain gifts. I don't know how to explain it to you without sounding ridiculous. Perhaps you don't believe in such things."

As soon as my explanation is out, it seems Oksana grasps what I mean.

"Oh, I do. I've heard of such people but met no one with such abilities. In our country, particularly in these difficult economic times, many people are seeking advice and guidance from gypsies, fortune tellers. Some are genuine. Some are fake. They take money, nothing more. But there are some real ones out there, so I've heard. So yes, I have heard, and I know."

I become suddenly assertive, perhaps not even considering how it comes across.

"Oksana, believe me, Jennifer's gifts are real. But please, let's focus on the case and stop getting sidetracked. I'll tell you what you are going to do, you two. You two are going to find her on that ferry and corner her. You will do whatever it takes! Reserve a private cabin for the overnight journey back to Athens and use whatever gifts and talents you have to get everything from her: details about her life, family, likes, dislikes, everything. Clear?"

They are glum, looking from one to the other, their mouths downturned.

I carry on, not sure what the problem is.

"By the time we dock in Athens, this Victoria or Vika should no longer be the mystery that she is at this moment. If she is a fake, or is simply a crazy person, we will know."

As soon as the words are out of my mouth, by the look on the faces of Jennifer and Oksana, I regret it, but it's too late. I should have shut up sooner, when the glowering began.

Here it comes. Brace for impact.

"Never," Jennifer responds angrily. "Never talk to either of us in that tone again. We are one team, one mission. You make it sound like you're ordering us about, as if we're your minions."

Jennifer has a flushed face and clenches her hands into tight fists, ready to strike.

"It's insulting," Jennifer cries out, fuming.

Oksana backs Jennifer up, giving a nod. But she looks simultaneously confused, taken aback.

Jen carries on, "We're all under stress, but it doesn't give you any excuse to bark orders at us, like one of your submissive, subservient women. Those days are long gone. *Clear?*"

Her face and hands slowly relax. "You certainly know that, don't you?" Jennifer says.

She's still not smiling, but at least her face and hands have relaxed a bit.

Oksana looks at us in amazement, processing the exchange. "Yes, it was … bad," she agrees.

She's likely never seen a woman talk back to any man in the manner my sister just has done to me, not without being slapped across the face, or worse. She looks at Jen with greater respect, I believe. Jennifer has just shown that she is not willing to be subordinate to her brother— or to me, a man in a supposed position of leadership as far as this task goes. But never mind.

We do not need to be arguing at a time like this. It would only fragment us and cause errors.

I swallow hard before responding, "OK. You're right. Understood. I apologize."

But it's difficult for me to let go of my ego at that moment.

Oksana and Jennifer head for the ferry terminal to buy tickets for the return trip to Athens. They return with reservations for a small, private sleeping cabin, and a separate ticket for me.

"We'll find her on board. She will talk to us. After all, Oksana has bought all the tools necessary for our work. There will be no mysteries about this Victoria by the time the sun rises and our ferry docks back in Piraeus. I promise," Jennifer says.

She opens the grocery bags with several bottles of vodka along with an assortment of drinks, snacks and fresh fruits.

"Good. I will stay out of your way, let you two do your work, and find a quiet seat somewhere to crash for the night. Good luck to both of you. And again, I am sorry for how I spoke to you."

They both nod, and their smiles are back.

I soon feel myself drifting off to sleep, my head firmly resting against the bulkhead.

I have forgotten the intoxicating effect of the powerful sea upon a vessel, and upon me, from my days as a midshipman and a naval officer. The ferry is gently rocking me to sleep.

The hand on my shoulder shaking me awake brings me out of a deep and restful sleep phase. I look up to see my sister and Oksana both standing in front of me. The morning sun fills the entire ship. The vessel has docked and there's a long queue of passengers disembarking.

"She's gone. Victoria is gone. We spent the entire night with her in our cabin. When we awoke, she was gone," Oksana says, shaking her head in disbelief.

"It's OK, Oksana. We'll find her," I say reassuringly.

Jennifer says, "We talked to her for most of the night. I can't believe she's bolted on us. She seemed so relaxed. Guess I was wrong. I am sorry. I didn't see this coming."

I say, "You never know what's going on inside the head of a person like Victoria. We'll find her, but she's got a good head start on us, and she likely jumped in a taxi by now. She's somewhere in Athens. But like I say, we'll find her, for sure we will. For now, let's get back to our hotel, regroup, and you two will tell me everything—I mean everything that Victoria told the two of you about herself. She did open up to you, right?"

Jennifer says, "Yes. She told us a lot and it all sounded so sincere. But who knows? I didn't think she would leave us in that cabin like that. I feel so unsure now."

I say, "Well, she's not in our custody, not our prisoner. You couldn't handcuff her to a ship railing, could you? Don't be so hard on yourselves, and relax. We'll find her."

I surprise myself with my calm and equitable response, perhaps shocked into being doubly reasonable after their previous telling off for being dominant and bossy.

Scolding them for sleeping in after Victoria's escape would also not be well received.

It would serve no purpose, and no good could come from it. It would only provoke my sister, and perhaps this time, even Oksana would join in. As before, we need to stay on an even keel and not end up fractured by disagreements among our small team. We must be cohesive.

Besides, I'm not angry at them, not even disappointed, but I'm more determined than ever to find this Victoria who has eluded us more than once. Time to get back to the hotel and regroup.

Chapter 12

"Here, drink these," I say as I hand Oksana and Jennifer each a can of Mythos beer from my hotel room refrigerator. "You both look hungover. It will help. Now, start from the beginning. What exactly did you learn from this Victoria?"

Jennifer opens the beer, tilts her head back and guzzles half of the can in one swallow.

Oksana does the same. In fact, I rather suspect Oksana is developing a sort of crush on my sister, mirroring her behaviors. Whether that is a good thing, I can't say.

Jennifer places her beer down on the small table in front of her.

She begins, "Victoria grew up in a closed Soviet city in Siberia. Her father was a scientist. She herself was never sure what he was working on. But it's not so surprising that he didn't share that with his family. Would you? When she was a teenager, the father got a transfer to

Hungary. Again, she had no clue about his work, but it was a secret project at some nameless Hungarian institute or clinic. They lived in a small town outside of Budapest. She loved it there and felt so free and alive, compared to her cloistered life in that remote city in Siberia."

"OK, Jen. We don't have all day. Where's this going? Give me something we can use," I say.

"I'm getting there. She was about to enter a university in Hungary when her father received a transfer back to Moscow. She was barely eighteen and suddenly found herself pregnant. Her parents insisted on an abortion, but Victoria wanted to keep the child. Shortly after she gave birth to a baby girl, her father and mother took the newborn to a 'Detski Dom,' an orphanage outside of Moscow. Of course, you can guess that she never saw her daughter again. Really tragic.

"Victoria moved on with her life, studying at Moscow State University while vowing to find the daughter others forced her to give up. A year ago, she hired a private investigator to locate her. For a relatively modest sum of money, it turned out it was not so difficult for the PI to find the adoptive parents of Victoria's baby girl from the archives of the orphanage."

"So, what did this PI tell Victoria about her daughter and the adoptive parents?"

"Victoria's daughter won the lottery when a young Russian couple adopted her. Not just any young couple; just wait! The father was already a rising star in the communist party when Gorbachev came to power. As a young exchange student, he had spent time in the United States, and Gorbachev's reform efforts had attracted him.

Through luck and timing, he eventually wound up as deputy prime minister. The rest, as they say, is history."

Oksana is nodding in affirmation.

"And what about this Victoria, her work and her more recent life and travels? This is more relevant, I think," I ask, looking from one to the other.

Jennifer says, "Victoria struggled after graduating from MSU, but through some luck and family contacts, she eventually wound up working as a regional sales representative for a cosmetics company looking to expand to the recently opened markets in eastern Europe and the former Soviet Union, including Russia. There was a huge potential market for quality western cosmetics. Victoria seized the moment and became successful and modestly wealthy, even by Russian standards. She suffered through one failed marriage, no children.

"She threw herself into work, determined to transform the faces of Russian women, introducing an array of cosmetic products not previously available: eyeliners; face creams; mascaras; eyeshadows; foundations. And all affordable and accessible. Victoria understood the market and its vast potential to transform the Slavic face, with its high cheekbones, flawless complexion and entrancing Asiatic eyes. Victoria's father died a couple of years back, not surprisingly from alcohol. He had lost his job at the institute when the Soviet Union collapsed, and since then, he had been drinking heavily. Perhaps with the father gone, and with the confidence of her business successes behind her now, Victoria searched for her daughter."

"Jennifer, this is interesting, but there are a lot of unanswered questions. Anastasia's kidnapping—if it is in fact a kidnapping—might have nothing to do with her adoptive parents. It could all relate to Victoria, her business dealings, and her newfound wealth. Isn't that possible?"

"Yes, definitely," Oksana responds, breaking her long silence. "Victoria is hiding something. She shared a lot with us last night, but there's more, no doubt. My country is a complicated place. Nothing is ever as it first appears. You have to be patient."

"Yeah. I agree with that. I've experienced that riddle and mystery before, Oksana," I say. Churchill's enigma, riddle, and mystery saying pops into my head.

A knock sounds on the hotel room door.

I reach for my Glock pistol, slowly opening the door.

"So, did you remember what you gave your mother for her last birthday? You've had plenty of time to think about that," Sharon Austin says.

She is standing with her luggage in hand, smiling at me.

"Welcome to Greece. And no, I do not recall what I gave her. But it wasn't a Fabergé egg. That much I can tell you, Sharon. Anyway, what are you doing here?" I ask.

"I've come from the other side of the world, Odysseus. You're not going on this particular odyssey without me. You need me," she says.

"OK. Well, you already know my sister, Jennifer. Let me introduce you to Oksana, my Russian MVD partner."

"I won't ask who sent you here. I can guess. You're a long way from San José, California, Sharon. Let's brief you on what we've done so far, and what we're dealing with now," I tell her.

Sharon sits in the chair and takes notes as we share the events and details of the past days. When we finish, she opens her bag and pulls out a large envelope.

"These are the photos that Georgia took at the club when you were there. Look," she says as she hands me the envelope.

I flip through the photos.

"Oh, here's a photo of that thug sitting between the two Russian girls. Amazing how Georgia got that picture. I suspect he's Russian Mafia, perhaps a contract killer, who knows?"

"I'm already checking on that," says Sharon. "The Russian Mafia runs the nightclub as you suspect. It's also a clearing house of sorts for drug distribution—ecstasy and other drugs for Greece and elsewhere, according to my DEA contacts."

"Oh, you have contacts in DEA? I should have figured. Perhaps Yelena and Anastasia were involved or were becoming involved in trafficking this stuff? And things went sideways for them. We can't rule anything out, right?" I ask.

I reach into my briefcase to find the printed pages.

"Sharon, here's a copy of the phone records from this mysterious Victoria's hotel room when she was staying in Athens. She's likely somewhere in Athens, or could have traveled on to Budapest, or elsewhere. See if your databases or any of your contacts have anything on the numbers. We could use a break," I say.

Sharon responds, "Dennis, this case, the little I already know, is not just about a murder and a missing girl. But you realize that. In some respects, it's a lot like the Golden ADA case, full of mystery, the unknown, and danger where you don't expect it. Yet, there are also differences, plenty of them. But I need some sleep. My brain's been slowly shutting down since I landed from California. I went straight to the Legal Attaché Office. Georgia Kaye was helpful, but she seems distracted by other priorities, as you already know."

Sharon stands up from the chair, taking her luggage in hand. "My room's just down the hall. I'll sleep a bit and catch up with you later." She yawns, pauses and turns back. "What is this feeling? Is this what jet lag feels like? It's awful."

"Yeah, I hear you. You'll be fine tomorrow, Sharon," Jennifer says. "Can you imagine dealing with this regularly? This is the price we pay for dealing with my brother, huh? I think he's in a constant state of jet lag." She laughs loudly.

"Oh, one other thing. I nearly forgot," Sharon says as she turns to me. "'Cos, call your BAU contact because he needs to talk to you. He sent me a message on our system. I saw it when I accessed it in the Legal Attaché Office. You're dealing with BAU in this case? Seriously? I am a bit surprised. You once told me they were useless, right?"

"Yes, I probably did but not all of them fit that description. I'll reach out to my contact. He must have already received the package that Georgia sent through that state department courier. I'd completely forgotten about it."

"Are you listening?" asks the voice on the phone. I check my watch.

"Yes, Adam. It's the middle of the night here. But I'm listening," I respond.

"Sorry. I was never good with time zones," Wheaton says.

"Go ahead. Give me something I can work with, Adam. This case has stalled. I'm here spinning my wheels in Greece."

Wheaton responds, "Based on the limited information I received, I'd say the attacker knew his victim."

"Yeah. That much I figured, Adam."

"Be patient and hear me out. This was not a random thrill kill either, and it's not his first kill. As far as the positioning of the body in a peaceful repose, the killer might have positioned the body to mislead investigators. Don't ask me why. I just feel it. Second point—Lyon—Interpol, is checking on this Russian orthodox cross angle. A reliable contact of mine there can discreetly research prior cases they've received for analysis. She knows this is sensitive and promises not to disclose anything. She owes me, so I trust her."

"OK, Adam. But I would have preferred you share nothing about this with Interpol, but if your contact is trustworthy, fine. What else? I need something concrete that I can run with."

"Well, not sure if it means anything, but I profiled a homicide case out of Omaha, Nebraska, about two years ago. A young man, about twenty, was the victim of strangulation. I recall something about a Russian cross found at the scene."

"What? What else, Adam? Can you find your file, your notes on that case?" I ask.

The middle-of-the-night call has caught me in a deep sleep, but I start to awaken with the unexpected news.

"Calm down. I profile hundreds of cases. I'll find it when I'm back at the office and call you back. The cross you sketched in the notes you sent is distinctive. This may have no bearing or link. After all, you're in Greece, and I believe the murder of the young man, who I now recall was adopted from Russia, occurred in the midwestern United States."

"Adam, just find your file and call me as soon as you're in your office. Goodnight."

I hang up and stare at the ceiling. Then I remove the last beer from the refrigerator.

It's the middle of the night, and the call from Adam Wheaton has my brain racing. I open the balcony door; I'm fully awake now, but the city is asleep, at least for a few more hours. Athens will be fully awake soon. I finish my beer and lie back down on the bed, closing my eyes.

***

The ringing awakens me anew. It isn't Adam Wheaton this time, but the hotel reception, my wake-up call. I glance at my watch. It's nine o'clock and the sun's morning rays already fill my room. I forgot to close the curtains. I quickly shower and dress, running late for my meeting with Oksana. We agreed that I would pick her up in front of her apartment. Eugeniy Zhirov previously informed her that the case file from Moscow had arrived and was ready for her.

I can only hope it has something new that we can use.

Oksana is waiting on the sidewalk as I pull up. "You ran this morning, didn't you?" I ask.

"I wanted to. You didn't?" she asks.

"No, Oksana. I had a beer. You look refreshed. So, you have the file with you?" I ask.

"I took za-me-cha-nie, notes. They wouldn't release the file to me. Let's get some coffee, and I'll brief you, OK?"

We head for the quiet neighborhood café and find a corner table.

Oksana pulls out her notepad and begins.

"The investigators went back and re-interviewed the parents as you suggested. The interviews looked pretty thorough. Anastasia's parents confirmed the adoption from the Detski Dom outside of Moscow. What we didn't know before was how much time the family spent outside of Russia when she was a young girl. The father worked as a diplomat assigned to Budapest, Prague, and London for a time. So, Victoria's own biological daughter spent some time in Budapest. Interesting, right? Not sure if it means anything," she says, then stops speaking as the waiter brings us ice-cold frappes and two freshly squeezed orange juices.

"Anastasia's parents recall her telling them she wanted to go back to Hungary to catch up with childhood friends, something like that. But they aren't certain. Victoria's telephone records from the hotel do show calls to Hungary. You don't think?"

"Anything is possible, Oksana. Perhaps they're already in contact with one another. We can't rule any scenario out, can we? My sister would say it's all related.

But then again, she's sometimes too eager to jump down the rabbit hole."

"What rabbit's hole?"

"Never mind. It's an expression. Not sure how to translate it. We just need to be careful not to jump to conclusions quickly without a solid basis. We could become trapped or ensnared," I say.

"Oh. I understand now. I think," Oksana says. She looks preoccupied, pensive.

Is it exhaustion, frustration or something more? Perhaps she was hoping the file would be illuminating and contain clues to help us find this Anastasia.

"Look at me, Oksana. Let's back up from this case. The file contains nothing useful—well, practically nothing. OK, but so what? We have no ransom demand. Anastasia's missing, and so is Victoria. We need to back away from this case, to look at it from another angle. We're too close. There may be something obvious that we're missing, overlooking," I say.

Oksana is still not looking at me, her eyes moist. Is she holding back something or is it the mounting pressure from Moscow to solve the case and find the missing girl, to complete what seems to be an insurmountable task on her own? And if she fails? What will be the cost?

"Oksana, let's get out of here. Clear our heads and go for a run on the stadium track. We could both use a break," I say, as we leave the café. She says nothing as we enter the vehicle.

I somehow keep pace with Oksana as we run around and around the ancient stadium track, lap after lap, breaking into a long sprint as we end the run. We haven't solved the case with some epiphany coming to us, but we have reset, ready for the next chapter.

Oksana is about to say something when I hear my phone ringing as I open the car door.

"I found the case," the voice on the other end says. I press the speaker button, so Oksana can listen in. It's Adam Wheaton. "It was in the closed file section in the BAU cabinet. Fortunately, they hadn't yet shipped it to the main archives. When you mentioned that cross, the Russian Orthodox one, that triggered it. The victim was a young man around twenty, with a cross tattooed on his inside thigh. A strange location for a tattoo, and what struck me was that this tattoo was old," says Wheaton.

"So what, Adam. Who cares? He had a tattoo. Thousands of people could have such a tattoo, no?" I ask.

"Patience. Are you listening? This tattoo is old; he might have gotten it as a toddler or even younger. That's strange to me."

"OK. Still, Adam, so what? That's it. That is why you've called me?"

"No. This young man, found murdered in Omaha, Nebraska, wasn't born in the United States. He was born in Russia, adopted by an American couple. Not just any couple. You've heard of Jeff Gordon, the U.S. senator from California?"

"Yeah, of course. I lived in California long enough. He was actually from San Francisco. And his wife, Elizabeth Gordon came from an old money family from the Bay area, as I recall."

"Cos, Gordon's roots were midwestern; his family was from Nebraska. The pressure on Omaha PD to solve the case was enormous. You can imagine, right?" Wheaton says.

I look at Oksana. She focuses intently on Wheaton's words, but her expression seems strange.

I shake it off. "Go ahead, Adam. What else?"

"The adoption took place in Moscow, but the adoption house, this Detski Dom, was outside of Moscow. The Russians gave numbers to these houses. This one was fifty-seven, that's according to the file, anyway."

"It's the same number, the same," Oksana says.

She is now animated as she nearly screams into the speaker.

"OK. But Americans have adopted a lot of Russian children since the collapse of the Soviet Union. The same adoption house as our Anastasia. Not sure if it means anything. The adoption house is the same, and the Russian Orthodox cross tattoo—well, Anastasia doesn't have such a tattoo, at least, not to my knowledge," I say and turn to Oksana. She says nothing and looks away, long enough for it to register with me. I'm hoping there isn't more. Something that Oksana hasn't shared with me. "So, this murder was never solved, Adam?"

"No. It remains unsolved. Oh, and the thing that really got me was the crime scene sketches, photographs, and the positioning of the body. The same repose as Yelena. But someone strangled this young man. No laceration across the throat like Yelena."

"Adam, you've given me enough. I'm going to catch the next available flight to Washington. We'll meet in Quantico, in that cold, damp basement office of yours. I'll let you know once I have flight reservations. Thanks for this, Adam," I say as I end the call.

"What, Oksana? Did you follow the conversation? What's up?"

"I'm sorry. I should have told you. Yelena had a tattoo inside her thigh. Her parents told the investigators she got it recently, a symbol of her close friendship with her best friend Anastasia."

"What? I'm confused. The autopsy report doesn't mention it, but it's not that surprising that the Greek authorities didn't report that or think it relevant, perhaps. So, what is with this tattoo as a symbol?"

"Well, Anastasia has a tattoo on her inner thigh. She's had it from a very young age, apparently. When her adopted parents got her home, they noticed it, the Russian Orthodox cross; that's what they told MVD investigators when they interviewed the parents.

"The parents thought it was odd that a Detski Dom would tattoo an infant, but it's not that surprising in a way, perhaps as a permanent marker that the child was or will always remain Russian Orthodox. I should have told you. I just didn't think it would be relevant."

"Everything is relevant, Oksana, in a missing person or murder investigation. Details matter. Nothing is irrelevant, even minor details. I don't have time to be angry or upset with you. I never shared the cross I found at the crime scene that day, so we're even in a way. Let it go, agreed?"

"OK. Agreed. What's next?"

"No, Oksana. You tell me. What will be our next move or moves?" I ask.

"You go to your Quantico, and meet with Adam. I'll try to find this Victoria. She's still out there somewhere, likely in Athens."

"I don't know if that is a good idea, Oksana. Not on your own. Let me see if Georgia is around. If not, then my sister. You speak Greek, I know, but this Victoria could be dangerous. Not her, but perhaps someone in her circle. This may sound strange, but I feel there's some sort of evil at work, just below the surface. My sister more than once told me not to ignore such feelings." Oksana slowly and deliberately makes the sign of the cross in the Russian Orthodox way, in the opposite direction from the Roman Catholic—right hand first to the right shoulder, to Constantinople, the seat of the Eastern Pope from the Byzantine Empire.

I look at her as she makes the sign. She isn't smiling, only looking at me intensely.

"Oksana, I'll return to Athens as soon as I can. You need to stay here in case Victoria emerges. Besides, my sister's still here. She will not leave Greece until this is over. I know my sister well enough. Keep an eye out for her."

"No. I'm going to Quantico with you. I'm your partner. Victoria can wait. We will find her when we return."

"Fine," I say.

There's no point in arguing with Oksana.

She is, after all, my partner, my equal partner. But she will need a visa, quickly. "I have to get in touch with Georgia at the Legat Office. We'll need her support to expedite your visa. I don't enjoy using up a favor like this, but there's little choice."

The visa process goes surprisingly fast at the embassy's consulate section.

Georgia's colleagues at the embassy like and respect her, and she's cultivated good working relationships with most of them.

"Thanks, Georgia. I owe you one," I say as she hands me Oksana's Russian passport with the U.S. visa glued inside.

"You don't owe me anything. Good luck over there. I don't need to know what you're up to but be safe."

"I have one more favor, Georgia. Please try to keep tabs on Jennifer. She's staying put in Greece. I told her to enjoy the sites, and not to wander away from the tourist areas. And certainly do not go looking for that Victoria. We'll deal with that issue when we return."

"No problem. She'll be fine here with me and Sharon. In fact, I'll meet them both for dinner tonight. I have a sense about your sister. She just doesn't want to be left out. Now, get to the airport. Safe travels, Dennis," she says, turning to walk down the long corridor to her office.

Chapter 13

"We're not going to Quantico, Oksana," I tell her as we arrive at Athens Airport for the early morning flight. "There's nothing more to learn from Wheaton—unless he comes up with other cases, that is."

"Oh? So, where are we going? I told Zhirov I was going to Washington for a couple of days. He freaked out as the Center hasn't approved my travel. He won't tell them, but they'll pull him back to Moscow if they find out, believe me."

"Oksana, we're going to San Francisco, California. Sharon Austin's found the funding for your ticket. I owe her big time when we get back to Athens."

"What's the weather like in San Francisco?"

"Cold and foggy if we're lucky."

"Sounds like Saint Petersburg in winter," she says as she scans the airport lounge buffet area. "I need a drink. We need to toast before boarding the flight."

She stands up to head for the bar area of the lounge.

"It's morning, Oksana. Really? Vodka before seven?"

"It's our culture. Even our pilots toast before flying. At least one shot, maybe two."

On some level, it makes sense, at least for a passenger, not a pilot. A shot or two of vodka can relax someone if they are nervous about flying and can make it easier to fall asleep for at least a few hours. Besides, if the worst happens and the plane crashes, the impact won't feel as harsh, so the Russians jokingly tell each other. I always thought it was just another excuse to drink alcohol despite the hour, be it early morning, afternoon or evening.

It's too early to refuse so I rationalize, and comply.

We finish the second shot, and Oksana stands up. "One more for the road—well, for the air, lad-na?" she asks in Russian for my agreement, slightly slurring.

"Oksana, eat something. You shouldn't drink on an empty stomach. That's what one of my Russian friends told me once in San Francisco. Long story, Oksana."

She returns to our small table with an assortment of cut vegetables, fruits, breads, and cheeses. "Now, I am ready to tell you something," she says as she picks up a cucumber, bites into it and takes a long swallow of juice from her glass, wiping her lips with the back of her hand.

I look at her, amused at the effect of the alcohol on her speech.

I've never seen her drunk before.

She's charming for the moment, but that can change in an instant. Vodka is unpredictable and can transform the nicest person into a monster with too much of the powerful liquid.

"OK, Oksana. Go ahead. What is it you wish to tell me?" I ask, glancing over to the monitor to check the flight departure gate and time.

"Katerina, your friend from Moscow sends her best regards," she tells me matter-of-factly, waiting for my reaction.

"Oh? And how is it you know Katerina, my dear Oksana Aleksandrovna?" I ask.

"We're not just first cousins, but also friends. Katerina is the reason that I became an officer in the MVD. She's my mentor, in a way. When I told her I would work in Greece with American law enforcement—with the FBI— she told me not to accept the assignment, that there was too much danger and some tragedy could befall me. When I learned it was you, she said that destiny was bringing us together," she says, and pauses. "So, I accepted the assignment. What choice did I really have? I am young and expendable. I speak fluent Greek, Russian, and passable English, and I am a graduate of your I-LEA in Budapest. I am too young to have been corrupted. They don't own me, but they find me useful … for the time being," she says as she reaches for the glass of vodka on the table in front of her, raising it to her lips. "You and Katerina aren't my business, Dennis. It's none of my business, you understand. But now, you have me. We are partners. You're lucky to have me. I may just save your life before this is over."

She clinks my glass, still sitting untouched on the table. She tilts her head back, swallowing all the clear liquid, and places the empty glass firmly back on the table. Her slur is gone. I'm not sure how to respond to all that she has just shared with me. We have a long flight in front of us.

"Let's get on board, Oksana. We will have plenty of time to sleep, and to talk."

I pick up both of our carry-on bags and head to the gate. "Da-vay, Oksana. Destiny awaits."

***

"San Francisco, there it is," I tell Oksana as she stares out of the window. "There's the Golden Gate Bridge. You can make out the towers above the fog. Let's hope it soon burns off."

"I don't mind the fog. It will be like home," Oksana responds.

She stares out the window, and although fog is blanketing most of the city, it all seems new and exciting to her. I reflect on life and work in San Francisco and in northern California. But we are not going as tourists. I hope this trip will turn out worthwhile, but there are no guarantees.

Adam Wheaton is there waiting for us beside his vehicle at the curb after we fetch our bags.

"The senator's home. It wasn't easy to get the appointment with him, and I revealed nothing to his chief of staff. Only that an agent in our new office in Russia wants to speak with him. Fortunately, he's agreed and hasn't given me a hard time. You better go in alone," Wheaton says.

"No, Adam. Oksana's my partner and she's flown all this way from Athens. We'll be doing this together," I say, turning to her.

She is yawning but looks surprisingly rested after the long plane ride.

Wheaton nods, conceding the point. "I brought the file with me. We can review it together. I know a small café near the senator's residence in Pacific Heights. He sometimes works from home and has agreed to meet us there."

"Adam, there's practically nothing about the circumstances relating to their son's adoption in Russia. It's barely referenced as far as I can tell," I say, closing the file and passing it over to Oksana. "I suppose nobody found that information relevant because Corey was adopted from Russia at age two, many years ago. The focus was on solving his murder in Omaha. The detectives probably didn't give it a thought, and dismissed the adoption in Russia as irrelevant, since it occurred so long ago. I can't blame them."

"Yet you were paying attention, weren't you, Adam?" I ask.

"It's what I do. No detail, no fact is irrelevant in a homicide investigation. Omaha PD detectives contacted the BAU, and they assigned the matter to me. I just have a knack for remembering details. For whatever reason, the tattoo of the Russian Orthodox cross stayed with me. Now, we're here together in this café in San Francisco. What is with that?"

Wheaton is shaking his head.

"It's destiny, Adam," Oksana says as she looks up from the file. "Destiny."

"OK, you two," I say. "Enough. Look, we're short on time, and I've been down this road before, interviewing elected officials. It's never been easy, not for me."

My thoughts go back to the Golden ADA investigation and the interview of the former California State Senator with my partner, Rich Marino, from the U.S. Customs Service.

"We won't have time for rapport building with this Senator Jeff Gordon. We have one shot with this guy. I'll take the lead. It will be me and Oksana. Adam, thanks for everything, but three would be a crowd in there. It could get ugly and confrontational. The senator might pick up the phone and complain to the director, attorney general, whoever. Yeah, it could be like that. You understand what I'm talking about?"

"OK. Well, not really. What are you talking about?" he asks.

"Adam, the senator and his wife adopted their son from Russia during the Soviet Union. He was first an exchange student there, when there were only a handful of Americans involved in such programs. He wound up back there a few years later and adopted a Russian child. Yet, we know almost nothing about the adoption circumstances. I'm not saying that Soviet intelligence has compromised or recruited the senator, but nothing is off of the table, nothing."

"And you're taking Oksana, a Russian police officer, into this interview? Really?" Adam asks.

Oksana steps in. "Yes, Adam. He is taking me. The Soviet Union is gone, dead, finished. I am Russian, from Russia. Your senator will have to deal with it. It will be as Dennis says."

I can only look at her and Adam, speechless.

We haven't rehearsed our strategy for the interview. The plan will likely be useless, anyway.

We will both have to trust one another and go with our instincts.

I turn to Oksana, sitting next to me. "I'll start the interview, Oksana. There will be no note taking. Keep your pen and paper handy, but inside your bag. If I pause during the interview, it doesn't mean I want you to jump in. Maybe I want the senator to feel compelled to speak, to let him fill in the silence. Or maybe I'm not sure of my follow-up question. We haven't done this sort of thing together before. Don't let yourself be intimidated or starstruck. Just because he's a powerful person, we have to control the room—his room. Yes, we will be in his home and office, but we shouldn't be timid, and we also shouldn't be overbearing or too aggressive. It will only anger him and put him on the defensive."

"I understand. You'll see," Oksana says.

"Well, good luck to both of you. I hope it was worth the journey for you to come here. I'll drop you off near his home. Call me when you're done," Wheaton says as he picks up the check. "It's on me. I wish I could be of more help."

I ask Wheaton to park his vehicle a couple of blocks from the residence, an imposing estate home overlooking the city below.

"Oksana, slow down," I tell her, so we'll arrive together at the entrance gate. "Look, things may get weird in there. Just go with it, with me, that is. He's a U.S. senator. But that can't intimidate us, nor should we give him too much deference. I'm not saying we should be disrespectful, but we need to find the balance. Are you following me?"

"He's probably no different from the powerful in my country. I've had to deal with such people. I'll do my best," she responds flatly, in a slightly dismissive tone.

"OK. Showtime, Oksana. Here goes," I say as I press the buzzer on the exterior wall.

The place is more fortress than home.

But as he's a powerful U.S. senator married to a wealthy heiress, it's not so surprising.

"Please come in and take a seat," the voice from behind the massive corner desk commands. When we enter, the senator is sitting behind his desk. He rises to greet us. I flash back to the last time I interviewed a high public official during the Golden ADA investigation. I hope this interview will differ, justifying our long trip from Greece. Accepting the seating arrangement, we sit in the chairs the youthful-looking senator has placed in front of his desk.

"I want to know all about your investigation, Special Agent Cosgrove, and I have heard about you, Oksana Aleksandrovna. Adam said you were investigating a murder possibly connected to my son Corey's murder. I want the killer or killers caught. It's been a couple of years and nothing is happening, until you two appeared," he says. He pauses and looks down at some papers in his hand. Perhaps he is looking at a copy of the file from Omaha PD. I can't tell from where I'm sitting.

"I am ready. Please go ahead with your briefing," he adds, as he picks up his pen and looks at me. This is no way to start an interview. This senator is accustomed to being in charge and calling the shots. We are not there to brief him. He knows that. Is he playing with us, seeing if we will submit to his will? Difficult to say, but the clock is ticking, and I need to turn the tables on this senator, and quickly, or else we will walk out of his office with nothing, and head back to Greece having wasted two or more days, while Anastasia is still missing, possibly dead. I decide to ignore his request, his command. Politicians often ignore or deflect questions fired at them from reporters, and this senator has probably done the same on countless occasions during his press conferences.

"Senator, we have little time. Oksana Aleksandrovna is my partner, from the Russian MVD, working on the murder of a Russian citizen and a missing girl, possibly kidnapped from Greece. We are determined to find the killer or killers. We need to ask you some questions which you may find irrelevant or perhaps uncomfortable," I say and pause for a moment, but not long enough for the senator to interject. "Let's start. Are you aware of any tattoos your son Corey had?" I ask.

I can tell the senator dislikes my response. I've ignored his line of questioning, but for whatever reason, he isn't objecting to my question, so far at least.

He places his pen back down on the desk and looks at me. "Yes. Only one. On his inner thigh, a small cross. It was there when we adopted him from Russia. He was only two years old. We paid little attention to it and never asked about it. My wife and I figured that his birth mother may have done that, or perhaps someone at the orphanage. At least it wasn't a hammer and sickle."

"And please tell us about the circumstances of the adoption itself," I ask him. Oksana is sitting there. She has opened her bag, slowly taking out her pen and pad but she isn't writing anything. I asked her not to take notes during the interview, but to focus on the senator.

He explains how a New York agency arranged the adoption, their trip to Moscow, and the train ride to the village outside the capital city. He had spent several months in Russia as an undergraduate exchange student. The exchange program allowed him to attend classes at the prestigious Moscow State University.

"It was an exciting time, my time in Russia—the Soviet Union that is. Well, the Cold War was far from over, but there seemed to be small cracks in that impenetrable wall, that iron curtain. The Russian students that I interacted with wanted to know everything about life beyond that iron curtain. Sure, there were probably some KGB types watching us, but they didn't interfere. I wasn't there to spy on anyone. What did I know? I was young and naïve, a student, just like the students I was interacting with."

"Senator, I see your photo on the wall. Was that when you were a student there?" I ask. I'm drawn to the wall of photographs, wanting to pull the senator from his desk, but Oksana's writing catches my eye. Despite my request that she not take notes, she was doing just that.

"Oh, no. That's my son, Corey. Although we adopted him, God blessed us with a son who closely resembles us. Now he's gone."

The senator looks on the verge of tearing up as he speaks. My mind races. Could Corey be the biological son of the senator? Perhaps from a brief affair he had there when he was an exchange student. The possibility seems remote, but nothing is off the table.

"Senator, do you know Victoria, Vika Tarasova?"

I drop the loaded question to see if I can detect any reaction from the senator while he is on the verge of tears. It's a calculated move, cold in a way, but nothing to lose.

His response is weak, and delayed, slightly, but still delayed. "No. I don't know her," he says, looking away, then back to me. He's lying. I've hit a nerve. He doesn't ask me who she is and why I'm asking about this woman. The interview has now begun.

Oksana speaks up, for the first time since we stepped foot in his office. "Are you Catholic?" she asks. I do not know where this is going, and why Oksana has raised such a question. I'm close to cutting her off, but remain silent, to allow the senator to respond.

"Yes," he responds.

"I am Russian Orthodox. Was your son Catholic?" she asks. I have no clue why she's asking such a question, but I am no longer in control of this interview. Oksana has stepped in and taken charge.

"Yes. But a month before his death, he re-baptized himself in our city's largest Greek Orthodox Church."

Now we are on to something. I decide it's time to make a move, a proactive one. "Oksana, can you please step out of the office for a moment?" I ask her. She isn't pleased by the look on her face, but she stands up and walks out of the room. "And close the door," I ask her politely. She practically slams it. "I need to talk to the senator, alone," I add for dramatic effect.

I turn back from the door closing and lean in to the senator.

"Senator, I need your help. There's a dead girl, and another one missing, perhaps already dead, and possibly others in danger as well. I think Corey was your biological son. There's more to it than you've told us. Senator, there are only you and me now."

"OK," the senator says as he leans back in his chair. "I could have your job with one phone call. You know that."

"Senator, get in line. I've been told that before, more than once. We need to find the killer, this monster. You lived in Russia, you understand the complexities of life there, unlike most Americans. If you want Corey's killer caught, then tell me. Give me what I need to catch this monster."

The senator gives a long sigh.

"This isn't pretty. Yes, I knew Victoria—Vika. Her father was a biologist working at some secret institute. I never met him. One time, after having sex with my Russian girlfriend, I caught Vika doing something disgusting in the adjoining bathroom. She was searching through a trash container, and I caught her with my used condom. It was gross and disgusting. She told me that her father needed it for his experiments. I dismissed her comments and told her she was crazy. Thankfully, I never saw her again. My girlfriend at the time later told me that Victoria's father was dealing with genetics research, DNA stuff at that secret institute. She said that they were into cloning. Look, the Soviets were way behind in genetics research, so I dismissed it as pure nonsense," he says as he stands up from behind his desk, walks over to a cabinet, fills two glasses with whiskey, handing one to me as he sits down in the chair next to mine.

"That orphanage was a strange place. There were many rumors about it. Supposedly it was KGB run, connected to that secret institute. Look, my wife doesn't know any of this. We adopted from Russia, and that was all. It's best she doesn't know, never knows. She's been through a lot already."

"I understand, Senator. But do you suspect any of this is connected to the murder of your son? What was the number of the adoption home, the Detski Dom?"

"57," he responds. He pauses. "Yes, I am sure about that." He walks back to his desk.

I can't judge whether what is being revealed is the beginning of a full confession of sorts, with more to follow, or this senator, this powerful political figure, is unraveling, losing it, presenting an imminent danger to himself and to me.

He could pull out a pistol from the desk drawer, kill me, and then himself.

It would be over quickly, in an instant.

I stand up from my chair, walking slowly around the desk. If the senator pulls out a weapon, I want to be positioned to stop him. He slowly opens the locked drawer.

"Here, take these," he says as he hands me copies of wire transfer receipts.

I look at the papers which appear to be financial transfers from a U.S. account to offshore accounts in the Cayman Islands.

"Extortion? Senator, you are being extorted?"

I am standing only a few feet away from the senator.

"I had a telephone call a few years back, on my private line. The caller, speaking in Russian, threatened to expose everything unless I paid, so I paid. I was sending money as requested, the amounts weren't much frankly. For me, it was worth it. To keep this away from my wife, and from my son. I thought that one day I would tell them both the truth, when the time was right. I don't understand why someone killed my son. If they wanted more money, I would have given it to them." The senator slams his desk with both fists.

"Do you still receive phone calls?" I ask.

"No, not since the murder. Nothing. Well, now you know. Please leave me alone. There is nothing more I have to tell you. Find the killer or killers, and liquidate those responsible," he says, and pauses. "*Liquidate* … that term, I picked it up in Russia. For us as Americans, it sounds harsh, doesn't it? But this monster needs to be stopped, to be liquidated. Dos-vee-dan-i-ye, Special Agent," he says as he turns away from me, staring at the family photographs on the wall.

The senator has unloaded everything, practically everything, so it seems.

This interview is over. I walk out of the office and slowly close the door behind me. Oksana is sitting there in the hallway, waiting. I can't take the credit for having turned the interview around. She had written Victoria's name in bold lettering on her pad. The pad that I told her not to open during the interview. It was her signaling to me, and the timing of that signal that turned the interview around. I am about to thank her when she interrupts.

"Well, what now?" she asks.

"Hey, first, sorry about dismissing you from the interview. You understand why I needed to do that, right?" I ask.

Oksana nods and says nothing.

"What now? Let's go to church," I tell her.

We walk through the locked gate back onto the street.

Wheaton is in his vehicle down the street, waiting for us. It had been over two hours since he dropped us off. "How did it go?" he asks.

"Not sure, still processing it, Adam. Just take us to St. Nicolas, the Greek Orthodox Church." I give him directions as he drives. It was the largest Greek Orthodox Church in town, and the head pastor was the father of the assistant legal attaché, Mark Anadiplosis. I had met his father several times with Mark, who was assigned to the FBI's Organized Crime squad I worked with on the Golden ADA case. The Church was an impressive structure and sat majestically on one of the many hilltops of the city, built after the devastating 1906 earthquake and fire that destroyed much of San Francisco. I found Orthodox Christianity fascinating, with its elaborate rituals more elaborate than the Roman Catholics. It also felt much more mysterious to me as a religion. Father Theofylaktos, Father Theo, as everyone called him, is in the rectory when we arrive.

"Well, Dennis, I haven't seen you in a long time. I thought you were working in Russia, that's what Mark told me," he says as Oksana and I walk into the office. Father Theo had a knack for remembering names, instant recall. A wonderful talent considering the sizable number of parishioners that his church served.

"Let me introduce you to my partner from Russia, Oksana Aleksandrovna. She is a police officer. We're working on a case that might have ties to San Francisco and have a couple of questions for you. If you have a moment, your Excellency," I say.

"Sure. Don't go formal on me. How can I help you?"

"Do you recognize this person?" I ask as I hand him a photo of Corey Gordon.

"Yes. It's Corey, the slain son of the senator. It's so tragic. We recently baptized him into our church, our congregation—just before his death. You know they adopted him from Russia, right?"

"Yes, we know. What can you tell us about his baptism?" I ask.

"Not much, really. One of our visiting pastors handled it. A priest from Russia. The Russian Orthodox Church and Greek Orthodox Church are close. We have a lot of similarities, and we sometimes host visiting priests from Russia, Ukraine, and Eastern Europe. Most stay for a few weeks at most. Some return periodically and stay in our modest apartments on the grounds."

"What's his name, Father? He's not here now, by any chance?" I ask.

"No, I don't think so. Let me check our files. Give me a moment," he says as he steps into another room and soon returns. "No, he's definitely not here now, likely back in Russia, I suppose."

"His name, Father. His name?" I ask a second time.

"Nicolas, a common Russian name, right? But his last name struck me. It's a typical Greek name. It means cross in Greek, you know. Stavros. I never asked him why a Russian person, a priest no less, would have a Greek last name, but it stayed with me."

Oksana steps in. "Father, it's not so unusual. I have Greek roots, Father. Goes back to the Greek civil war."

"Oh? Yes, I know a bit about that history. So, you probably have connections to Central Asia, Oksana?"

"Yes. Yes, indeed."

"OK. Let's get back to the priest. What can you tell us about him? What do you remember?" I ask.

"I checked the files. There isn't much, but I do recall that he spoke several languages besides Russian. Greek for sure. He was distant in a way but had piercing blue eyes. I remember those. He was from Smolensk, a town outside of Moscow, I think. There was no photo in our files. That is odd, but not that unusual. It probably got displaced or something. And something else just came to mind. I remember that Father Nicolas was in San Francisco when they found Corey murdered in Omaha. He was very upset about it and returned soon afterwards to Russia."

"Did Father Nicolas talk about his ministry there in Russia?" I ask.

"I recall little, sorry. It's been a while. But I remember him saying that he was on a mission, a crusade. I suppose it's good for a priest to feel that way, especially in Russia, where the communists suppressed religion for so long. Sorry, but this is a large parish, and we have many visiting priests. It's about all I can remember, and our files aren't so detailed, not like your files in the Bureau, I suppose."

"That's OK, Father Theo. We won't take any more of your time. Say some prayers for us. We've got a lot of work to do."

"Trust in the Lord, Dennis," he says as he raises his hand and blesses us in the Orthodox style, holding three fingers together, a sign of the Trinity. Oksana makes the sign of the cross, in the Orthodox manner, upon receiving the blessing, and kneels deeply in front of Father Theo.

He turns and strolls back to his office in the rectory after escorting us off of the church grounds.

I brief Wheaton in the vehicle, as he drives us back to the hotel for the evening, hoping to catch the morning flight back to Athens.

"Adam, keep tabs on that senator if you can manage. There's probably more to his story than he has told us," I say.

"There always is. What's your next move? I think your trip here was worthwhile, no?" he asks.

"Adam, I'm not sure. We'll have time to talk about that on the flight back to Athens. There are some new twists for sure. See if you can stay out here for a few more days. I may need your help with this senator. He told us a lot, but he's still holding back. I can feel it. And if you can discreetly check with Interpol in Lyon for any unsolved homicides, well," I say.

I'm about to pull back the request just as Oksana interjects.

"I don't know if it is worth it to ask Interpol anything," she says.

"Yeah, you're right, Oksana," I say, realizing that she is indeed right. Better to keep everything compartmentalized and closed for the time being.

"Let's go for a run. Meet up in, say, ten minutes in the lobby. I'll show you the Golden Gate Bridge, up close. We need to clear our heads," I tell Oksana before heading to our rooms at the hotel. Wheaton had arranged rooms for us at the Fairmont, the same hotel that my Russian MVD partners stayed at during the Golden ADA investigation.

The next morning, Wheaton is there, right on time to take us back to the airport for the return flight to Athens.

I'm tempted to go back to talk to the senator again, but it's not a given that he will be more forthcoming and reveal anything useful during a second interview.

"Adam, if you can stay here for a day or two more, it might be worthwhile in case the senator unexpectedly reaches out to you. I doubt he would do that, but you never know. Do you think your boss at BAU would allow you to stay for a couple of extra days?" I ask.

"I have some leads to handle with several local PDs in the area, so I don't think it's a problem. I agree, the chance that the senator will reach out to add something more is remote, but you never know."

"We may have shaken things up with our interviews here, talking to the senator, and our stop at the church. Something is going to break, well, fall out, I can feel it. I hope we will be ready," I say, gazing over to Oksana sitting in the back seat with me.

"I was born ready," she replies.

"You see, Adam, a few days in the States and she's got attitude. California, no, more like a New York attitude, but I sort of like it," I say, laughing. We could all use a laugh. This investigation feels dark.

Chapter 14

It's late morning the next day in Athens by the time the plane touches down. The Aegean is a crystal blue, the sky a light shade of blue with a few cumulus clouds. Another perfect beach day in Greece.

Mark Anadiplosis, the A-LAT, is waiting at baggage claim for us. By the somber look on his face, I suspect that something has happened. I brace myself for what he is about to tell me.

"Cos, I have some bad, well, awful news. Georgia is in the hospital, in intensive care. Someone physically accosted her yesterday morning at the stadium. I don't know if they were intending to kidnap her, assault or kill her. Your sister, Jennifer, came upon them in the middle of the assault. She basically saved Georgia. So it appears," he says. I'm stunned, but not shocked.

"Mark, what's her condition?" I ask.

"It's hard to say. She got throttled badly. She's in and out of consciousness, but Georgia is one tough agent. I just know she will make it."

"And my sister?"

"You can talk to her later. She apparently was supposed to meet Georgia for a run, showed up a bit late, but saved Georgia's life. Jennifer has some cuts and bruises, but that sister of yours is something. Apparently, her hands and feet were kicking like crazy. The attackers, whoever they were, gave up and took off. Maybe they were looking to steal the vehicle. I just don't know," he says, shaking his head in disbelief. He looks as though he hasn't slept for several days.

"HQ is sending out a team to investigate. I think it is best for you guys to stay out of that mess. You don't want to get caught up in their investigation. They will come out, do some interviews and leave. Let's hope that's all they do."

"Nothing has changed for me, and for Oksana, Mark. We still have our mission. Unless the Director's Office pulls me off of this case, and I have heard nothing from them. Not yet."

"Look, I think it's best for you to stay away from the hotel. A friend of mine is away on home leave for the month, and he's given me access to his place. You, Oksana, Sharon, and Jennifer can all stay there. With that HQ team arriving soon, they will all stay at the hotel. It's better to stay out of there, out of their sight. I already canceled your reservations. Hope you don't mind," he says as he gives us a look, waiting for our reaction.

"It's fine, Mark."

"Oh, was my dad helpful?"

"Yes. Very much so."

"He didn't give me specifics, but told me you and Oksana had stopped by. I know it wasn't just to say hi, and can't imagine how my father, or the church figures, into your case, but it's your business. I'm here to help, and with Georgia in the hospital, and that HQ team on their way here, I'm pretty stressed, as you can imagine."

"I understand, Mark. We're fine. I'll try not to bother you, unless it's absolutely necessary." I say. He hands me two sets of keys for the apartment.

"Oh, I almost forgot. Georgia had this CD with your name, sitting on her desk. I might as well give it to you. I didn't open it, but I suspect it might have something useful. She was working with Sharon, your analyst, since you were away," he says.

As we approach the entry gate with the high concrete wall around the three-story building, with our luggage in hand, Mark stops.

"Look, here's the real deal," he begins. "This is a safe house. Don't ask me questions. You have the keys and the alarm code for entry. No one will bother you here. Park your vehicle down the street and walk; don't park in front of the building. Your license plate number is local. It's better to be safe. There's a desktop computer inside and you can use it. Don't hang out on the balcony. The building is clean, as far as I know. The two entry-floor units are unoccupied and remain vacant. It's pretty spacious, four bedrooms. Sharon and Jennifer are inside, waiting for you. Good luck, Cos, and Oksana."

He turns and walks away, then stops and turns back. "Oh, and your vehicle. Sharon knows where it is. Wish me luck with this HQ team. I just hope Georgia will be

OK. The Greek police are 24/7 protecting her room. So, if it's 17 November, they won't be able to get to her while she's recovering. So, she's safe for now. We're definitely targets. I'm pretty sure of it. Stay alert, don't trust anyone. Trust your instincts."

"Sounds like you've been spending some time with my sister lately, Mark. Don't worry, we'll be fine. And Georgia will recover. I'm sure she will. That HQ team will do their thing and be gone in a few days. We're here for you as well," I say, as we shake hands firmly.

"Oksana," I say, "that guy is really weighed down," as he disappears from view.

"Can you blame him? It's a lot for him to handle." She pauses. "Well, shall we?" she asks, as she inserts the key and opens the entry gate.

Sharon Austin opens the apartment door as I'm reaching for my key. The second-floor apartment is more than spacious, with high ceilings, exquisite tile work throughout. Someone had put a lot of money and care into the design and furnishing of the place.

"Where's my sister, Sharon?" I ask.

"She's in her room, sleeping. She's a bit banged up still, but she will be fine. Jennifer needs rest to recover. I need to show you something," Sharon says as she guides me to an adjoining room. "Can you give us a moment, Oksana? Make yourself at home. Your bedroom is up the stairs, first door on the left," Sharon says, pointing to the stairs off in the corner near the kitchen.

"Georgia and I did a lot of checking in our databases to identify some players at that nightclub. We found a lot, more than we had expected," she tells me, as she motions for me to sit next to her as she powers up the desktop computer. "That nightclub is nothing but a front for the Russian Mafia as you suspected, I think. It's a convenient place for meetings and transactions, ranging from drug deals to money laundering, trafficking in women. Take your pick."

"Sharon, this isn't surprising, but my mission, our mission's priority, is to find Anastasia, that's all," I say.

"Give me a break. I'm trying to brief you on what Georgia and I have been working on. I wouldn't waste your time if I didn't think this stuff was relevant. You know me well enough. Focus. Focus," Sharon says, looking into my eyes.

"OK. Sorry. Go ahead. I'm listening. Promise," I reply.

"That thug, the one with the two Ukrainian hookers that night, when you and Georgia were there. Well, he's an interesting character. We think he is Maksim Dudayev. Well, that is one name he goes by."

"Sounds Chechen."

"Yeah. He's a contract killer. Not any contract killer, but for big money. The reporting in the databases—our O-C databases and others that I have access to and you don't—claims he's behind several high-profile assassinations in Russia and elsewhere. His moniker is, *cher-na-ya mert*," she says, then pauses.

"Black death in Russian. I think I've heard of this guy in Moscow. Rumor has it he was killed, but that might not be true. Who knows?"

"Yeah, right? There's something else you don't know. Georgia went back to that nightclub several more times, alone. I suppose she was just curious and wanted to be helpful to you. Those Ukrainian hookers aggressively confronted her, obviously curious about her, perhaps, but who really knows? If the nightclub's a clearinghouse, meeting place, whatever for drug distribution, and if this Maksim Dudayev is involved, anything is possible.

"We've got no direct evidence that the Greek police are on the payroll, but it wouldn't be surprising. I told Georgia never to go back there, but she ignored my advice. At least your sister stayed away. Well, that's what she told me."

"With Jennifer, you never know, but Georgia knows better. What else? You said there was more. I've got to brief you as well, so finish what you need to tell me as the jet lag's already hitting me. And take this CD. Mark gave it to me. He said Georgia had it on her desk with my name on it."

"Thanks. But it's probably a copy of mine. I'll check it out later," she says as she takes the CD in her hand. "Now, what I am about to tell you will wake you up. To your friend, Victoria—Vika Tarasova. I ran her name through the databases, every database I had access to. Her father, who is deceased, and one of her father's close associates—a scientist named Pavel Sokolov—show up in one of the more sensitive databases of ours. But this Sokolov is also deceased. He died a few years back, mysterious circumstances."

"So what, Sharon. This is relevant? How?"

"Patience. The reporting in the database on this Pavel Sokolov struck me as odd. There were several documents relating to Sokolov, and to Victoria's father. I couldn't open all the documents and didn't want to try, as it might trigger alarm bells in the system. But I saw enough to conclude that their linked references were likely related to their work, perhaps to their travel outside of Russia—

the Soviet Union—to the West and to the U.S. Sometimes, you just get lucky if you dig far enough, but carefully."

"Yeah. We could use some luck. What? What did you find?" I ask. I'm growing impatient, and Sharon seems to talk in circles.

"When I ran Sokolov's name for all of his associates, I stumbled upon a code name, along with initials and numbers. You know what that means?"

"No, Sharon. No idea, but please tell me soon, or I'll jump off of that balcony, the one that we are not supposed to go on."

She ignores my dark humor. "That guy with the initials and number, he was likely a source, a bureau source. So, this source, a Bureau source who is—or at least was—reporting on none other than Sokolov and on Victoria's father. Here is where it gets interesting. I can't tell you how I do this. Believe me, you don't want to know, but sometimes this sort of reporting leaves a shadow, a digital shadow, or footprint on the uploaded file. Not all analysts understand that shadow ... how to see what is behind it, or rather, who uploaded the reporting or information. I know how to identify that person or persons. And I was keenly interested in who exactly from the Bureau—from our agency—was talking to or dealing with this guy."

"OK. I think I'm following. Keep going, Sharon, but please give me the shortest, most abbreviated version."

She says, "This mysterious individual with the code name, well, let's call him Q for now. This Q was being debriefed, likely handled by none other than the current deputy assistant director in counterintelligence, Tiffany Ames. Along with the current assistant director—Ames' boss then—and now by Kyle Davenport. Do you know them, or perhaps you've heard of them?"

"Unfortunately, yes, I know of Ames. I don't think I've ever met her, but she certainly knows me."

"Oh? Well. I suppose you are fully awake, and the jet lag is gone, at least temporarily. So, here's the kicker," she says and pauses.

"What? This is weird enough, Sharon. What more could there be? My head is spinning. I am jet lagged, and my brain is in a fog. What else?"

"I told you about digital shadows, footprints, remember? Or did you already forget?" she says.

"Yeah. I remember. What about it?" I ask.

"Ames and Davenport were all over your case, the Golden ADA case. In the case management system, there is, or was, a backdoor, a way to look at the files without leaving a digital trace. Certain folks at HQ have such access. Understandably so, for oversight, stuff like that. But Ames and Davenport had no such role or backdoor access rights. Regardless, they tried to erase evidence of their accessing the case files, but still left a shadow, an echo, whatever you want to call it. I wasn't really looking for it, but something told me to look. Besides, that case isn't really over, is it? There's still plenty of work to do, to include finding that missing Fabergé egg, right?"

"No. No, Sharon, forget the egg. And I have a suspicion what made you check the case management system. Go ahead, tell me. It's not what made you check it, it's who, isn't that so, my dear Sharon?"

"So, I suppose you're not such a bad investigator after all. Yeah, your sister Jennifer suggested it. I shared a little with her. I'm not supposed to do that. She's not in the

Bureau. But she likely saved Georgia's life from those two thugs trying to kidnap or kill her."

Sharon pushes her chair back from the computer screen, turning to face me. "Jennifer told me to check back into the Golden ADA case files. She said this stuff is all tied together, linked. Well, I'm not sure about everything being linked, but she may be right."

"Oh, no. Please don't go into that rabbit hole. I understand that there are plenty of unknowns, but Jennifer can go the conspiracy theory route on you, and you can fall into that thinking if you are not careful. Sharon, why do you think that Ames and Davenport would be interested in Golden ADA, beyond curiosity, in the first place?"

"Why? Well, you tell me. Why do you think they would be interested?" she asks.

"Could be they're working for the other side, but that's an enormous leap, Sharon. And I don't want to report any of this to our HQ, not to Internal Affairs, not to International Operations either. Not without more proof. Something solid," I say, as the flashback comes over me suddenly. My head throbs. I hadn't had one in a long time. The museum. "You remember you told me to visit the Hillwood Estate Museum before I left Washington, right?" I ask.

"Yeah. You stopped there, I hope?" she asks.

"Yes. I certainly did. I met, quite by chance, the curator, Dr. Hedwig Kiesler. Nice woman, at least I think so, or thought so. She showed me the egg and told me something I found interesting. Now it feels more than just interesting," I say.

"What? What did she tell you, my dear Odysseus? That you are lost in uncharted waters, far from home on a voyage that is becoming more treacherous with each passing day?"

"Yeah. Well, you haven't called me that name in a while. A woman approached Heddy (that's what she wanted me to call her) a few days before I visited the museum, just as it was closing. Well dressed, fit and athletic, late thirties, perhaps early forties, blonde hair as Heddy described her. This woman had a weapon concealed under her sport coat.

She asked about the museum's egg, and about missing Fabergé eggs per se.

Heddy gave it little thought. Before my visit, that is. Unfortunately, Heddy didn't manage to get her name, or a business card. I told her to call me if that woman appears again, and not to reveal anything about me to this stranger carrying the concealed weapon."

"You trust her?" Sharon asks.

"Yeah, I think so," I respond.

"So, you figure that woman is Tiffany Ames, don't you?" Sharon asks.

"Yep. Can you pull up her photo in the system?" I ask.

"I don't need to. I already did. Look," she says as she passes me the photo.

"Well, hard to say, could be her, but who knows. Too bad we can't show the photo to Dr. Kiesler. Yeah, she is blonde, looks fit, somewhat attractive, and I would take her for late 30s for sure," I say, and pause. I look up from the photo, and there is my sister, Jennifer, standing in the doorway, holding an ice pack to the side of her head.

"Nice of you to return to Athens. While I was getting my butt kicked here in Athens, you were having fun back in California. It was a pretty good rumble. I landed a few Mohammed Ali style kidney punches, and my kicks came in handy. What gifts have you brought me, dear brother?"

"Gifts? Yeah, I should have brought you back a nightstick baton or something similar, like the one our grandfather used in the NYPD. But you have your lethal hands and feet. They seem to have worked fine," I say, and laugh.

"The thing about growing up around so much violence, Sharon," Jennifer says as she turns toward her. "Is that you never forget. So, when the time comes, and when it's body on body with kicks and fists flying everywhere, giving everything you've got, it doesn't feel so strange. It almost feels good. Doesn't it, brother?" She's turning back toward me.

"Yeah. I suppose so. Enough, Jennifer. I don't want Sharon to think that we are animals from the jungle, or circus performers. It's good to see you in one piece. Thanks for stepping up, without hesitation. Like I taught you, speed and decisiveness is everything in a street fight. But we need to keep this quiet. There's a team from HQ soon to arrive here. Georgia won't say word one about what you did. I guarantee it. I don't want HQ pukes to be poking around, distracting us. I still have a mission, the only mission to find Anastasia. At least until I'm told otherwise."

"No. We still have a mission, our mission. You need me here. You see that by now. I'm going back to sleep.

We'll catch up tomorrow," Jennifer says, as she lowers the ice pack to reveal a shiner on her left eye.

"Looks pretty cool, sis. Like old times, huh?" I ask, instantly regretting my choice of words.

"He's an asshole, Sharon. And you see that by now. Goodnight, both of you," she says, shaking her head, and laughing as she turns and walks away, heading toward her room.

"I already know what your next question is. Well, I think I do. You're about to ask me about Victoria, aren't you?" Sharon asks.

"Yeah. But if you found something more, you would have already told me. So, any theories, Sharon? Who is this Victoria, really? No, the real question is who is she working for? Who is directing her and what is their aim?"

"You're thinking Ames and her boss, Davenport?" Sharon asks.

"Yep. If they're involved with Victoria, what are they up to, and the larger question is, how does this impact our mission? The mission to find Anastasia. Part of me thinks that this Victoria, and Ames based upon what you have uncovered, while it's disturbing, may be nothing more than an unrelated and distracting side show. But there's a part of me … Call it instinct, my gut, whatever that says there's more, much more."

"And what are you going to tell Oksana?" Sharon asks.

"I don't know, honestly. But I can't withhold information that could put us all in danger, that's for sure. She doesn't need to know every detail about your research, but I need to share the relevant stuff with her. Do you agree?"

"Sure. What's your next move? Are you back to the chess match rules that governed your actions during the Golden ADA case? Once you make the move and take your hand off of the chess piece, you can't redo it. The move is done; it's yours to own. Accept the consequences, right?" she asks.

"Yeah, and as my U.S. Customs Service partner, Rich Marino, used to say, you can't be frozen or afraid to act either."

"So, my dear Odysseus, your next move? Your ship's alternative course? Where are you bound?" she asks.

"Tonight, I'll go back to the Aphrodite nightclub, Sharon. One last time, just to check the box. Perhaps Victoria will be there, or I can try to find that assistant manager, the one Oksana and Jennifer befriended when we were last there. Feels so long ago, but it was days, not weeks. I'm losing hope we'll find Anastasia alive."

"Don't lose hope. Not yet. It's not game over; it's game on, Cos."

"You sound like Rich Marino. I'm glad you're here with me, Sharon. We'll solve this thing together if the fates will allow. This is Greece after all; the ancients are watching us. I know it."

"You taking Oksana with you? You should not go there alone."

"I'll be fine, Sharon. She needs to report to her own people in Athens and in Moscow. Maybe they can find that priest, the Russian Orthodox one who baptized Corey Gordon. I'm paranoid about Oksana asking Moscow for help at this stage. You understand?"

I'm hoping she will agree.

"Yes, but you can't control everything and everyone. What was the priest's name? You never told me?" Sharon asks.

"Stavros, Nicolas. Or Nikolai Stavros."

"Sounds Greek. He's Russian though, is he?"

"Yeah. Long story. Run his name, Sharon. Let me know if anything comes up. Hey, do you think this Tiffany Ames and Kyle Davenport can see your queries and work in our system? That would not be good."

"I doubt it. I already thought about that possibility. There's no footprint, shadow, echo … nothing there for them to track or monitor. It's as if I, rather, we don't exist. I'm no fool. Don't you know that by now?"

"Sorry. Just paranoid, Sharon. Let me talk to Oksana. Don't venture out tonight and try to convince my sister to stay put as well. She needs to sleep."

I find Oksana resting on the living room couch. The jet lag from the long trip has obviously kicked in. "Oksana," I say, gently shaking her shoulder. "Wake up. I need to talk to you."

And just like that, in a mere instant, she is awake.

"Oh. Sorry for falling asleep. I called Zhirov to report to him on the latest. He wants to meet me soon, maybe this evening. Is that OK?" She is rubbing her eyes.

"Sure. I'm thinking about going to Aphrodite tonight, just to revisit the place. We know much more than the last time we were there. I'll be careful not to get into trouble, and I'll bring a weapon this time. You know, I feel drawn back to that place. We may have missed something obvious from the last time we were there, and —" I say but Oksana interrupts me.

"No. You cannot go there without me. Look what happened to Georgia. She went there several times alone and almost died. Your sister saved her, don't forget. And now, you tell me you intend to go there alone? Are you stupid? And if you see Victoria, what will you do? Confront her? No, this is ridiculous. Like I said, you are acting stupid."

Suddenly, she catches herself, covering her mouth. "Sorry. I didn't mean it that way."

"It's OK, Oksana. I'm your partner, not your boss and I'm not offended. Yeah, there are times I'm stupid; just ask my wife, my sister, former partners. Well, there's a long line of people."

Her head nods, not even laughing.

Thanks for the vote of confidence in me, I think, having hoped she'd rebut my claim.

She says, "Then you go, just don't stay there long. If you see Victoria, call me right away and I will come."

"Look, Oksana. There's something I need to tell you." I pause, inhaling deeply. "Sharon's done some research on the names I gave her. I don't want to get into detail as I don't understand everything, but it's possible that Victoria, and several others connected to her and her father, are working with certain sections of my agency. To what end or for what reason, I'm not sure yet."

"I don't understand, Dennis. What does this mean?"

"It means we are in deep, treacherous waters, Oksana. We're not out of our depth, at least I don't think so. But the circle of those we can trust is getting smaller. There's no one else."

"I am ready. Thank you for telling me this. We are partners. We have to take care of one another. After all, isn't that what you are teaching me, my dear Odysseus?"

She asks the question with a mischievous smile.

"Oh, yeah? Odysseus, huh? Guess you've been talking to Jennifer and Sharon. Hey, I'm going to step out for a short drive. There's something I need to do, go see Zhirov. You should brief him. And don't worry about me; I'll be fine tonight, Oksana."

I secure my weapon in the holster inside of my pants, grab my car keys, and leave the apartment. *There's still time for a run.* I need to run alone, to clear my head and overcome the jet lag, and the relentless urge to sleep. The clock is ticking. *Anastasia is alive. I can feel it. Yes, Oksana, we are in treacherous waters, but this is Hellas, Greece. What else could we expect?*

As I arrive at the small parking area for the stadium, glancing around for any other vehicles that may have followed me here.

I decide to sit in the car for a few minutes, trying to detect anything odd.

Just days before, someone assaulted Georgia at this same stadium track, and my sister saved both Georgia and herself by fighting off the attackers.

Am I tempting fate, being here so soon after that incident?

It was an attack of an unknown nature, with the two thugs still out there. A part of me wishes to be confronted, right here, right now, in the open. The element of surprise for my attackers would be gone, and I'm ready for them if they want to come for me.

I open the vehicle door and head for the running track, hurdling over the concrete barrier. Technically, no one may run on this track, but no one enforces this rule.

The Greek police have better things to do, I suppose.

I begin the run slowly, more aware of my surroundings than normal, registering the barking of a few stray dogs, the movement of vehicles, walkers, and other runners.

Nothing stands out from the ordinary. Not yet at least. The interval sprints force me to focus on the present. I concentrate on form, breathing, head and hand positions, my forward lean into the turns around the oval track. The effect on my state of mind, my mood, is gradual.

By the time I decide I've pushed my body hard enough and fast enough, I already feel renewed and so different from when I began the run.

It has to be the endorphins. My sister would tell me that her runs had the same magical effect on her, taking her from a melancholy, depressed state to an overpowering feeling of euphoria.

Long ago, we had decided it was a genetic thing, not fully comprehensible, but a family trait. Jen traced it back to the athletes in our family tree. For me, it went much further back, to our warrior ancestors, perhaps to the days of the Roman Empire and Greek city-states.

As soon as I close the driver's side door, I check my mirrors for surveillance, or worse.

Someone likely violently confronted Georgia as she exited or entered her vehicle, just like right here, right now, in this parking lot.

The confrontation I've been wishing for isn't materializing, so it seems. Not for this day, at least as I drive safely out of the parking area, scanning my side and rearview mirrors.

There's no movement, except for a late model white BMW coupé.

The vehicle doesn't pose a threat either; there appears to be a sole woman driver behind the wheel. Regardless, it's a good idea to check for any surveillance that could be following.

Not wanting to lead anyone following me back to the safe house, I decide to make an abrupt turn into a quiet neighborhood street for a last scan. There are no cars behind me. I make another turn to double back to the main road and check my rearview mirror. There it is, the white BMW late model coupé with the woman driver, sunglasses and a kerchief.

She is close behind me now, closing on me, the same vehicle I spotted when leaving the parking area minutes earlier. But it has to be coincidence, nothing more, doesn't it?

I give her a longer look in my rearview mirror, attempting to scrutinize her but she's so far away. But still, I can see the woman looks too polished, too well dressed to be surveillance. Is it my bias that I'm quick to dismiss her as a potential threat?

Jen would have something to say about that.

The vehicle speeds up and comes close to colliding with my rear, her brakes screeching.

If she's surveillance, she's not very good at it. I continue down the narrow, exclusive one-way street, parked vehicles lining both sides. There's a space ahead on the right, and a stopped vehicle. A taxi discharging his fare blocks the road. It's decision time.

I speed up and swing into the space, barely missing the front bumper of the parked car. The taxi remains stopped a few yards ahead while the BMW is now next to me, waiting for the taxi to move as backing up on the one-way street would be difficult and impractical.

I grab my weapon from the locked glove box and slam my door shut as I leap from the car. The BMW passenger door window is more than halfway lowered, so I reach inside the window to unlock the door and jump in the passenger seat, aiming my weapon at the driver.

"Keep both hands on the wheel," I order the driver. "Don't make any sudden moves and look straight ahead." As I speak, I am scanning the vehicle for a weapon or any communication equipment, seeing none. If she is part of a surveillance or hit team, she could alert them to the fact I'm now in her vehicle. And if she is luring me into a trap to assassinate me, I may soon find myself surrounded. I am waiting for a motorcycle or someone on foot, their weapons drawn.

Finally, the irksome taxi pulls away, and the road is now open. "Drive. Do exactly as I say," I tell the driver, assuming she understands English. I keep my Glock low, pointed at her side.

"Stop shaking. Why were you following me?" I ask.

"Why? I thought it would be the best way to talk to you securely. You are making me very nervous. Can you please put the pistol away, Special Agent Cosgrove?"

Her hands are firmly on the wheel.

My mind is racing. Her face, the accent, her demeanor … Even in her heightened and jittery state, with my pistol practically pressed into her side, she feels familiar.

"You …" I say as she interrupts me.

"Yes, it's me. It's been a while. You didn't bring your rugby ball with you this time, did you?" she asks.

I put my weapon back into the waistband holster in the small of my back.

"No. No rugby ball. I could have shot you, you know. Pull over here," I say, directing the mysterious blonde to a near empty parking area at the end of a cul-de-sac. "Give me your keys," I tell her, and she turns off the vehicle and does exactly as instructed. "Take off your sunglasses," I say next. She slowly removes them, revealing crystal blue—Aegean blue—eyes.

Yes, it's the same woman, the Afrikaner from the beach in Monterey weeks ago.

"Is there anyone following us?" I ask.

"No. There is no one else. There is only you and me."

"I don't have time for mysteries, so who are you exactly? And don't lie to me."

"I would never. My name is Kandyse Brandt. I'm South African as you know, but you can call me Kandy. Here's my card. We never properly introduced ourselves, but I feel like I know you."

"OK. So, Ms. Kandyse Brandt, what is it you want? The Golden ADA case is over. The threat to your global consortium, to your diamond business, is done, isn't it? Your monopoly is safe."

"Yes. We are grateful to you for that. It was a masterful piece of investigation," Brandt says.

"Well, some would disagree with you on that assessment, Ms. Brandt. Besides, I didn't do it to save your monopoly over the diamond market. I was just doing my job as I told you that day on the beach, before you sped off from the beach parking lot. In a BMW, as I recall."

"I appreciate you are busy these days. We can meet when you have more time," she says, and pauses. "More time for us, that is. There is someone in my organization who would like to meet you. He has something to share."

"Seriously, what is with you people in this diamond business? So secretive and mysterious. It's exhausting, frankly."

"Oh. Listen to yourself. I'd imagine you're keeping more than one secret yourself, Special Agent Cosgrove, isn't that so?" she asks, pulling me into her translucent crystal blue eyes.

I'm close to drowning in that sea of blue.

I cannot allow this woman to manipulate and play with me, so I pull back from the brink. Kandyse Brandt is beautiful, no doubt, but dangerous. At that moment, she reminds me of one of my bureau sources. She has her own agenda, whatever that may be.

"Forget the Special Agent stuff. Just call me Dennis, or Cos. I think we are past formalities by now. But do yourself a favor, Kandy. Never follow me like that again. Here's my card. Call me on my phone, like a normal person. I could have shot you. I'm not here in Greece on vacation. But you know that already, don't you? And what's with your outfits from the 1960s? Even your kerchief. No matter, it's only an observation, not a critique, so please don't feel compelled to answer. It somehow works for you, I suppose."

I have no clue how she tracked me down in Greece but I never forgot her parting words to me as she sped off from the Monterey beach parking lot as the sun was setting, wishing me 'good hunting.' This Kandyse Brandt is striking in appearance, and mysterious but dangerous, so my instinct tells me. Sharon and Jennifer would caution me to stay well clear of such a woman.

I can only imagine what my wife would say.

With this Kandyse Brandt, it is difficult to judge how much is an act and how much is genuine. But her unusual demeanor isn't so surprising considering her work for the super secretive diamond consortium.

Brandt was on the periphery of the Golden ADA investigation for a long time.

I first noticed her sitting alone at the bar in the San Francisco restaurant a few years earlier, when Rich Marino and I were meeting with Dmitry from the Russian San Francisco consulate.

She was so striking in appearance, dressed like a Hollywood starlet from the 1960s, that I never forgot her. She drives me back to my vehicle parked on the narrow residential street.

"Kandy, I don't—" I begin, but catch myself. Closing the car door, I wish her a good evening. I have a full night ahead and need to put this strange encounter with the mysterious Kandyse Brandt, the Afrikaner from the Republic of South Africa, behind me. At least for now.

Jumping back into my vehicle, I head for our apartment, our temporary safe house.

"I don't think you should go, Dennis. It's a bad idea. There's no backup, and if things go sideways, you'll be on your own," Sharon says just as I'm about to head out the apartment door, headed for the nightclub.

"I'll be fine. I'm used to working alone, Sharon; you should know that by now. Anyway, I don't intend to stay long. If I spot Victoria, I'll step outside and call right away."

"I doubt she'll be there, but having more background about this woman, this disturbing woman, she could be there just to play with you, with us. She's an attractive creature, but she's also cunning, and dangerous. Don't underestimate her. Think of how she's strung all of you along and eluded you more than once."

"Relax. Just keep my sister here if she wakes up. I don't want her venturing out, not tonight. Promise me. OK?"

"I'll do my best. With Jennifer, you can only do so much as you well know. Jennifer's going to do what Jennifer wants to do. Convincing her of anything … Well, let's not go there. You already know this because you two are more alike than you realize."

"I'm going armed tonight," I tell Sharon as I tuck my Glock into the holster inside my belt. "Get some rest, Sharon. I'll be back in a few hours, at most."

***

The pulsating dance floor at the nightclub is even more crowded than when I was there with Georgia the last time, so the ventilation system is struggling to keep up with the cigarette smoke hanging in the air like a misty fog. I walk casually around the club which is more expansive than I remember from my last time here. I survey the crowd, seeing the ages range from early twenties to late forties. I order a double vodka martini from the attractive bartender.

She looks Slavic, perhaps a recent arrival from Ukraine or Moldova.

The dimmed lighting makes it difficult to scan the place. I think, *I hope Victoria doesn't walk up from behind and surprise me. That would not be good.*

The elevation of the bar area gives me a good vantage point to watch and observe, so I easily identify the locals, then the tourists, the foreign businessmen, even the hookers working on the dance floor. I can hear several languages being spoken at the nearby tables and by patrons as they walk past me to the bar. English, Greek, German, French, Russian, Ukrainian, Spanish, and Romanian. The nightclub appears to be ground zero for the beautiful people of Athens.

But there's a dark side to this happening nightspot as I see more than one drug deal taking place, with the exchange of small packets and cash hand to hand. It happens quickly, and you would never notice if you weren't looking for it. I have seen more than one hand-to-hand drug transaction in my life, so to echo Kandy's words of earlier, perhaps this is the 'good hunting' of which she spoke since I do feel more like a hunter than a passive observer this evening.

My mind wanders back to Georgia, still in the hospital recovering from the vicious assault. I can feel the emotion, the anger bubbling up and I try to suppress the rawness of how I feel.

It will serve me no purpose and could cloud my better judgment.

I need to remain calm, objective, and observant.

A young woman approaches just as I lift my glass for a sip. I take her for a prostitute, possibly Ukrainian, judging from her appearance and accented English. I respond to her direct advance in Russian, telling her to leave me alone for now. She abruptly turns and walks away. Now, I've insulted a working woman. I can only shake my head, disappointed in myself at that moment.

I need to do better. I should have engaged her in some light conversation instead of dismissing her so summarily. After all, the working women at the nightclub see, hear, and know everything.

She might have been a very useful source, and now, she is gone.

However, to persuade such women to give up information that may be useful to me is a whole other challenge. She is likely working for someone and perhaps is being watched over.

The vodka martini is strong, too strong for me to handle this night in my exhausted and jet-lagged state. I grab the bartender's attention, asking her in Russian for a bottle of the local Mythos beer instead as I slide the double martini away from me across the bar counter.

The bartender seems receptive to my speaking to her in Russian, smiling and handing me the ice-cold beer bottle as I push all of my remaining drachmas along the bar counter toward her.

She smiles again, thanking me in Russian for the generous tip.

I make one round through the crowded club but don't see Victoria.

It doesn't mean she isn't here tonight, of course. Maybe she's already spotted me and left or ducked into some dark corner. Regardless, I return to my original spot at the bar and am about to order another beer from the attractive bartender but decide to make a quick restroom stop before it gets too crowded. There's already a line forming for the women's room.

The men's restroom is virtually empty as I enter.

I walk up to the urinal, and shortly as I'm zipping up my pants, I notice him in my peripheral vision, standing two urinals away. It's him, cherny mert, the black death Russian hitman. *Guess everyone has to pee, eventually.* In the stark and dimly lit bathroom, he looks vulnerable.

There's only one working sink in there, so I motion for the hit man, this Maksim Dudayev, to use it first while I stand by and wait.

He washes his hands meticulously, as if he is a surgeon prepping for a surgical procedure.

Dudayev turns toward me as he finishes. "Your turn," he says in perfect Greek. "Do you like my girls?" he then asks in flawless, unaccented Russian. "They are the finest from Ukraine, Russia, from the entire 'soyuz,'" he finally adds in English, his language transition effortless.

I find the man charming and sinister all at once. His hair is jet black, pulled back in a tight ponytail while his eyes are black. If a contract killer could choose a face, this would be the one.

With his greased hair and two-day beard growth, he looks like a born killer, a thug.

"They are beautiful, but I'm not interested in your women," I say as I reach for the towels to dry my hands.

"Whatever you like is yours tonight. My pleasure," he says with a grin, a despicable grin which I find instantly repulsive. This hitman could have been responsible for Georgia's violent assault and I have the urge to throttle him with my fists. Whether he is responsible for the attack on Georgia, it doesn't matter. This guy is a killer, perhaps now retired, but no doubt responsible for many deaths. And now he is trafficking vulnerable, young and attractive women from the former Soviet Union and offering them to me as chattel, his property. He is playing with me, I'm sure. He's seen me at his club, and he probably knows I'm not from his world.

I need to maintain my composure and stay focused on the mission.

Throttling this thug with my fists may deliver to me momentary satisfaction, but it won't help me find Anastasia. I take a deep breath.

"Yes, they are beautiful, but I'm not interested," I say in Russian, reiterating.

"Whatever you like is yours, Mr. FBI," he responds in Spanish this time, and glares at me. I'm close to my breaking point and clench my fists as I fight the urge to pummel his face.

All my earlier admiration for his language mastery has abandoned me by now. I don't want to be here listening to this absurd talk, his propositions on the back of seedy trafficking activities.

But it's plain he has no intention of giving up, not yet. He is confident enough to push.

"Oh, I forgot you like black women also, Greek Black women," he adds.

I take it that the reference is to Georgia with her Greek and African American roots.

This hitman is egging me on, pushing me to my breaking point. He doesn't stop.

"When you're through with her, I would like her. Bring her to me, and then we swap, huh? You can have a lovely, fair Russian girl in exchange, maybe two."

At last, my patience snaps; I have heard enough.

"Go fuck yourself."

My left elbow lands hard under his chin, sending him flying back into the porcelain urinals. I move quickly forward into a boxer's stance, throwing a right cross, followed by a left uppercut, and an open palm directly into his face. All three blows find their mark.

His knees buckle, blood now flowing copiously from both nostrils.

Dudayev drags himself up to his feet again, still intent on continuing where he left off as if nothing has happened between us. He's staggering a bit from the blows as he wipes his nose with the back of his hand. Yet, he is laughing as if the beating hasn't even wounded his psyche.

"Don't be so offended. She is nothing."

He is snorting blood all over his shirt as he breathes.

I can't pull back. He's deliberately provoked me, but my adrenaline won't let me stop here, not yet. I move closer to his body, unloading my right knee as hard as I can manage into his groin, seeing him stagger and fall to the floor. He doesn't stand up, lying there prostrate on the bathroom tiles. I need to get out of this room before security shows up, or else it will be a free-for-all battle. I'm alone, without backup. My weapon is still secure in its holster inside my pants, but I may need to pull it out to get out of this place in one piece.

Dudayev motions with his hand for me to come closer to his bloody face. He wants to tell me something, coughing blood. I lean over toward his face, aware of having broken his nose.

But I feel no remorse or regret. In fact, it feels good.

"You are a piece of shit investigator. You are nothing. That girl is dead, and the other one is gone. Did you think you would find her here? You are, how is the expression? Out of your league, out of your depth."

The blow to the middle of my back at that moment staggers me.

The next blows to my kidneys bring me to the floor and I spin around onto my back, deflecting the kicks to my ribs. The two Russian goons now have the advantage, two on one.

I'm about to reach for my weapon when the second goon lands his kick in my groin. I scream out in agony, time slowing, and I feel close to passing out. To survive the night, I cannot lose consciousness so I shake my head, trying to regain my senses, still in the fight.

It's the old neighborhood where I grew up in which I find myself back again.

Fighting was an everyday occurrence, fists and feet flying everywhere.

Am I dreaming, losing consciousness, or is this some sort of drug-induced hallucination brought on by that vodka martini that tasted too strong?

It doesn't matter. I need to get back on my feet somehow and stay in the fight.

At this moment, the men's room door bursts open.

It's Oksana, standing in the doorway. "Oh, excuse me, but I need to use this bathroom," she tells the two goons in Russian.

They stare at her for a second, then the shorter one tells her, "Go ahead, bitch. Try."

Oksana walks directly toward the shorter goon with the shaved head and neck tattoos and brings him to his knees with a sidekick to his temple.

The second kick to his groin practically lifts him off the ground.

Just as the other man, the taller one, reacts and is about to strike her with his right hand, she spins and uncoils both feet powerfully into his chest.

The back of his head smashes into the sink. He collapses on the floor, where she promptly finishes him with a second powerful kick to his groin, making him moan in agony.

Her speed and power are impressive; someone has coached her well.

Dudayev is still there, watching everything as he lies on the floor, barely moving.

Oksana, even now, is not finished. She pulls her Makarov pistol from a holster on her thigh and thrusts it into the mouth of Dudayev.

"No. Oksana. He's not worth it," I hear myself saying.

I am now standing, coming back to my senses. My body is aching, and I feel bruised, but I am not bleeding and have no broken bones.

Dudayev slowly stands as Oksana holsters her pistol and unleashes a series of fist strikes to his already pummeled face.

The velocity of her fists is impressive and lightning fast, and I come close to commenting on her ability to throw combination punches but decide to keep quiet.

This isn't a boxing ring. This is a men's room in a nightclub.

The adrenaline is still flowing through my body, affecting my reasoning and judgment, the fight part of my brain still in control. I need to regain my composure and get us out of here.

Dudayev is leaning back against the wall, not laughing anymore.

His two goons are still on the floor, moaning and holding their groins. Her powerful kicks have debilitated and neutralized them, but not for much longer, so it appears.

"Oksana, we need to get out of here, now," I nearly scream at her.

It's only a matter of seconds before the nightclub's security bursts in.

We could soon find ourselves with no escape.

"No," she says, as she removes my arm from hers and turns back to Dudayev.

She takes her pistol in her hand and presses it forcefully against his temple; she pulls hard on his ponytail with her free hand. "Where is she? Tell me or you die."

She looks like a wild beast. More than that, she looks ready to pull the trigger and kill Dudayev. His eyes are wide open, fully aware he is about to die.

"Oksana, no, he isn't worth it. Don't do it," I scream at her, reaching for my pistol too.

We may have to shoot our way out of this place.

"Say your goodbyes. You will soon see your friends in hell."

Her finger begins to pull back on the trigger of the Makarov pistol, and the force of the gunshot will soon splatter Dudayev's brains all over us and the bathroom walls.

"Go check with God. God knows," is all Dudayev can say, gurgling blood out of his mouth.

He slowly raises his one good arm, pointing at something.

Perhaps he is hallucinating from all the blows. I don't understand what he is saying, nor what he is pointing at. I'm not sure if Dudayev himself knows what he is saying at this moment.

Suddenly, Oksana holsters her weapon, turning to glance at me, scanning me up and down, checking for any wounds or blood. Turning back toward the mirror, she calmly adjusts her skirt and blouse, slides back into her sandals, combs her hair, and takes a deep breath as if her little trip to the men's bathroom was all just routine for her.

She's ready. "Let's go. But quickly," she calmly says to me.

"Huh? Go where?" I ask.

"To the church."

"What church?"

We burst out of the nightclub in a full sprint, and I can see she's drawn her weapon. While sprinting, I'm drawing mine too, confused where we might head, but following as close as I can manage. She's just saved my life, so I might as well follow her wherever we are heading.

"The church. The one right next to the metro construction site," she screams out at me.

I can see it now. "Oh, shit. I never noticed it."

There it is, just around the corner from the construction site where investigators discovered Yelena's body over ten days ago. How we overlooked it, I just don't know.

The church is small and looks old, perhaps from Byzantine times.

Oksana is ahead of me. She tries the main door, finding it has a heavy chain and padlock.

"Oksana, there's a side door. Do you think—" I ask.

"Run back to the construction site. Find something to help us open the door," she says. Bingo, some luck finally as a careless worker has left his toolbox on the site. I grab a hammer, a long crowbar and screwdrivers. I have never been good at lock picking, unlike some of my childhood friends. But the application of some brute force might just work on that side door.

Oksana and I lean hard on the crowbar and the door pops open.

We're in! I glance around in the dead of night. No one seems to have heard us.

There's silence inside the church, several candles still burning, icons covering the walls. Their eyes appear to be watching us. I'm not sure what our next move is, looking at Oksana.

She finally turns to me, saying, "If my father is right, this is one of those churches built on top of an ancient Greek temple. Greek fighters used the ancient tunnel system to smuggle weapons during the Greek War of Independence in the early 1800s, against the Turks. There is an entrance. It's hidden and hard to find, but it is here, somewhere."

Her free hand begins tracing the walls while she holds her Makarov pistol. "Or maybe the entrance is on the floor."

She scans the flooring now, vigilant, willing to miss nothing.

In the dimly lit church, my eyes have finally adjusted, seeing no tunnel entrance, no door, no opening in the floor, only a simple wooden ladder in the corner. A worker, or perhaps a skilled artisan, has likely left it. The church looks temporarily closed and under renovation of some sort.

"What are you doing?" Oksana asks as I set off slowly climbing the ladder.

"I don't know," I respond. But there seems to be a ledge, a narrow walkway toward the top of the ladder. I holster my weapon and climb.

"Oksana," I practically shout at her. "There's a walkway up here. And there's a small door. Climb up! Bring the hammer and crowbar with you, and some candles." I tell her.

The locked wooden door opens after one powerful pull from the crowbar.

"Hey. You see it? A bit to the side, there's a set of stairs back down. This may be the entrance you were looking for," I tell her.

"I will go first. Greek freedom fighters did this. The Turks would never find this tunnel. It's clever, right?" she says.

Her focus is on the narrow stairs leading down.

There are lights strung in the passageway, only just enough to guide us to the bottom.

It's the tunnel entrance, just as Oksana suspected. The air is stale and old here; we are in an ancient place, carved out millennia ago, by an ancient people. This tunnel network is far older than this church, perhaps dating back to the Ancient Greeks. We follow it for over fifty yards and soon find ourselves in a larger room carved out of the limestone rock.

"Oksana," I whisper, and put my hand on her shoulder. "Stop. Quiet. Listen," I tell her. "Do you hear it?" A soft, moaning is coming from somewhere, perhaps close by. "It's behind us?"

"Here," she shouts at me. "It's here." She points as our eyes turn to the iron grate floor hatch in the far corner of the room. "What is this? A chamber below?" she asks.

"Step back, Oksana," I tell her, using the crowbar to spring the locked iron grate hatch open. "Bring that over." I point to the wooden ladder lying in the room's corner.

Oksana pulls the heavy ladder over to the opening in the tunnel floor and we slowly lower it through the open hatch before climbing down.

The ancient tunnel system is much more elaborate than I had realized, and more than one level. In the dim lighting, it's hard to see the contours of the area in which we are now standing, and we need to be mindful of our steps in case there's an open trapdoor leading to another tunnel. We are deep into the tunnel system, and I don't want to be surprised by attackers.

"There," I say and point to the darkened corner. "Look. What is it?"

We approach what looks to be a pile of rubble and debris.

"No. It's a person. A girl. She's alive." Oksana catches the outline of a body. There are blankets, pieces of debris, buckets, bottles strewn about. "What is your name?" Oksana asks.

The girl is groggy, barely moving.

"I am Nastiya. Anastasia. Who are you?" the girl asks.

She appears sedated and weak. But at least she is alive.

"Oksana, we need to get her out of here. Now," I tell her in Russian.

This won't be easy with Anastasia in such a weakened state, and we have to get her out using the ladder without her falling. "I'm going to have to carry her out, like a fireman's carry. It's the only way, Oksana," I say as I carefully hoist her over my shoulder and head for the ladder.

I just hope the old wooden ladder will support both of us without collapsing. My body is aching from the many blows at the nightclub. I ignore the pain, adrenaline pumping through my veins, giving me enough strength to get Anastasia up the ladder.

Slowly, she's regaining consciousness, perhaps realizing she's being rescued. We get her into the backseat of my vehicle and speed off in the dead air of the night to the safe house apartment.

***

Jennifer is standing at the front door as we approach. "Put her in my bedroom. Let's look at her. Did you check for the tattoo? It's Anastasia, right?" she asks.

In the rush to get to Anastasia, or the girl who we hope is indeed her, we didn't bother to check her identity.

Jennifer scans her body for any signs of trauma, bruising, cuts.

Thankfully, the tattoo is there. It's faint and small, but it's present nevertheless. We have confirmation it's Anastasia. Someone likely kept her sedated since her abduction that night.

"She needs fluid, but only water for now. She's been through a lot," I tell the group.

Sharon, Jennifer, and Oksana are in the room, looking intently at Anastasia as she is lying there on the bed. After nearly ten days, we've done it. She is alive, safe, and in our custody.

"Let's get her to a doctor," Oksana says.

"No, Oksana. She's not going anywhere. Not yet. You and Jennifer already checked her body for trauma, cuts, broken bones. She seems OK, overall. The kidnappers gave her something to keep her sedated. Anastasia will need some time to regain her strength. I don't want to turn her over to some doctor or hospital right now. No one, besides us, knows we have her. Let's keep it that way. We'll work in shifts at her bedside; when she's alert, we'll need to hear her story."

We agree that Oksana, Jennifer, and Sharon will keep a rotating bedside watch as Anastasia rests. "If she awakens and talks, wake Oksana," I instruct the other two. "If she wants food, give her light soup, nothing more for now as it will send her body into a crisis after her near starvation for such a prolonged time. I'm going to sleep. And don't make any phone calls, please."

"I'll take the first shift. The rest of you go to bed," Jennifer says.

"Before I crash for a few hours, something just struck me, Oksana," I say, turning to her. "How did you find me in the nightclub? How did you even know I was there? I thought you had to meet with Zhirov last night. Don't get me wrong, I'm grateful, but I didn't expect to see you just as I was getting pummeled in that men's room."

"How do you think?" she asks and pauses. "Jennifer called me." Oksana turns and smiles at my sister. "According to her, you were in danger and needed my help. I believed it when you first told me about her gift, and now it's certain, isn't it?"

"Yeah, OK. Please don't tell me more. Goodnight, ladies."

I close my bedroom door and set my alarm for four hours.

Completely exhausted, I collapse onto the bed.

Chapter 15

"Here. Take this," Oksana says, handing me the ice-cold frappe. "It's almost afternoon. I let you sleep after I heard your alarm. You weren't reacting, so I turned it off."

I take the frappe and sit up in bed, having slept so deeply I never heard the buzzing sound.

"How is she, Anastasia ...?" I ask her.

"She's in and out of sleep. I already spoke to her. Are you ready to hear?" Oksana asks.

"Sure. Go ahead."

"She's in an emotional state, so I had to let her talk, understandably. She's still freaked out, but those sedatives, whatever they were giving her, seem to finally be wearing off.

"Anastasia doesn't remember much, only that she stepped outside the club that night, looking for Yelena. They'd become separated, so she panicked but someone grabbed her from behind, and the next moment when she awoke, she was in that chamber, exactly where we found her.

"A person wearing a mask would bring her tiny portions of food and water and exchange the bucket, the one she used for a toilet. She tried screaming but was so weak, she eventually gave up, figuring the kidnappers were negotiating a ransom with her father for her release.

"Anastasia didn't know how long she was there. When I told her it had been ten days, she was shocked, saying it could not have been that long, there was just no way ..."

"Anything helpful about her kidnappers? How many? Descriptions? Maybe it was Dudayev and his thugs?" I ask.

"She's still in some sort of shock, still in and out of sleep. This will take time, maybe a few days, even. But I am going to have to inform Zhirov soon. He needs to know and will want to take her immediately. I know that, but—" Oksana says as I cut her off.

"Yep, and once Zhirov takes her, it's game over, Oksana. We won't be able to speak directly with Anastasia, to debrief her fully."

Oksana says, "I am an investigator, like you. There is much more going on. The killer—
killers—are out there, and we have solved nothing yet. With some luck and force, we rescued Anastasia. The Center may tell me to head home, Dennis, mission accomplished. But it's really not, is it? If I don't inform Zhirov, there is a risk to my future, my career. How about you? What will you do now? Are we still a team?" she asks, gazing intensely at me.

"OK. Oksana. I understand. Then let's wait a few days but we need to talk to Sharon and Jennifer. I don't want to get Sharon fired or suspended. For me, I'll take the risk; it's sort of my nature," I say as a knock sounds on my door. It's Sharon, clutching the phone.

"It's Nolan," Sharon whispers to me as she hands me the phone, and I nod. Whether Sharon called him already, or he's calling by chance, I'm not sure. Whatever the circumstances, I can't hang up and ignore Ben Nolan's call. FBIHQ will not simply go away.

"Ben, hi. Don't know if you heard yet, but we've got Anastasia and she's safe. We found her last night, Oksana and I. Long story, but she'll need a few days to recover. The poor girl has been through a lot, so we've only started to debrief her," I say in an effort to buy us some time, in anticipation of what Nolan's likely going to tell me—or order me.

"Congratulations, but that's enough, Cos. You're done there. I will recommend the director approve the formation of a special task force to follow up. And there's plenty to follow up on; Sharon's been providing me with daily updates. I want her out of there as well. You guys have done a tremendous job. The director will be pleased when I tell him Anastasia's safe and in our custody. He's pulling Georgia out of Athens. She's a target, and it won't get better; he just doesn't want her killed, but say nothing to her, not yet. She's going to Ramstein base in Germany to recuperate for a few weeks, then we'll see."

"Ben, what task force? This is nonsense, pure nonsense. You're going to send some pencil-pushing HQ pukes with no knowledge of this place, the streets, to work in this environment? And they're simply going to take over from us? That's nuts, Ben. Nuts."

I'm nearly shouting at him, Oksana motioning for me to lower my voice.

"Ben. We found the girl with our small group, operating independently. It wasn't easy, believe me, but we know what we're doing here. Give me one week more. There are leads we must follow up on and this thing isn't finished, far from it." I pause, only silence on the other end.

I'm not even sure if the call has dropped. "Ben? You there?" I ask. Silence. "Ben?"

"Yeah. I'm here. I'll give you three days, not more," Nolan finally says in response.

"Seven, Ben." Silence again.

"Five, and not one day, not one hour more. Cos, you're putting me on the hot seat. You realize I can't report any of this to the director, so my head will be on the chopping block with yours. Do what you need to do, but I want detailed and continuous updates from Sharon. I really can't believe I'm agreeing to this. And no extensions; I don't care what else you find, five days is all you're getting. Good luck."

The line goes dead.

Five days. Ben Nolan means it. Whether five days will be sufficient time to find Yelena's killer or killers and Anastasia's kidnappers plainly doesn't matter in Nolan's calculation.

He has to report to the Director's Office eventually. Oksana will have to convince Zhirov to hold off on reporting the rescue of Anastasia for a few more days.

Sooner or later, Anastasia will insist on reaching out to her family and want to go home, to Russia. We will have to convince her to wait, that we are searching for who is responsible for the killing of her dear friend, Yelena, and for those responsible for kidnapping her. I share the good news about the five-day extension with our group, our task force. No one suggests or even hints at the option of ending our involvement in the investigation, which will now focus on the search for Yelena's killers and Anastasia's kidnappers.

"There is someone I need to meet with before we do anything else," I tell the group.

"Oh, and who is that?" Jennifer asks.

"I don't want to say. It's someone from the past. I don't know if the person will be helpful, but I need to follow up," I say.

They all just look at me, three alpha women sizing me up, about to unleash their annoyance upon me. I brace for impact.

Sharon is the first to react. "Go. Do what you need to do. Check that box and don't waste time because the clock's really ticking now; every hour matters. Get back here as soon as you can. It's only a matter of time before Anastasia fully recovers and when she does, she'll want to reach out to the family. We'll have to convince her not to do that."

My instinct tells me I need to meet with this mysterious Kandyse Brandt from the diamond consortium. She told me there was someone in her organization who had something to share.

She's somehow tracked me to Greece, and I assume her presence relates to my reason for being here. I could be wrong but my gut tells me it's related.

I have never been to the Sounion Peninsula before. A short drive south of Athens, the sight of the Temple of

Poseidon's ruins as I drive the coast road high above the Aegean Sea tells me this area must have held a special significance for the Ancient Greeks.

The high vantage point gave the Athenians time to prepare for hostile ships approaching their waters, possibly endangering their city and its inhabitants. Brandt told me I would recognize the estate home by the high protective wall of limestone, with its huge iron entry gates bordered on each side by marble dolphin statutes.

The dolphins may be replicas, but they certainly look authentic.

I pull up to the gates and look for surveillance cameras, seeing nothing, the gates slowly opening. The home comes into view in the distance. This is no ordinary home, more like a palace or an ancient temple with its marble columns and white exterior facade.

I pull up to the front of the palace and park my vehicle. The residence looks like a temple, perhaps modeled after the ancient Temple of Poseidon nearby.

The front door slowly opens. It has to be at least ten feet high. A figure slowly emerges into brilliant light from the late afternoon sun; it's Kandyse Brandt, dressed in a white flowing Greek goddess tunic, embroidered with what looks like gold thread. Her gold Byzantine style necklace and bracelets adorned with emeralds and diamonds glisten in the sunlight. She is mesmerizing as she appears to be floating above the marble steps of the temple-like structure. I feel as though I'm caught in a powerful beam, pulling me away from my vehicle, up the steps toward her.

"Mr. Van der Wyk stays here when he is in Athens. I can give you a tour of the grounds and the home," she says as she escorts me inside. She is relaxed and poised as she speaks to me.

"Kandyse, thank you, but I'm rushed. I don't have time at the moment," I respond. I can't help but admire her beauty. She looks to be the personification of Aphrodite herself, without a single flaw, blemish, or wrinkle. I pull back from scanning her face and body, and turn my gaze to the impressive statutes and fountains in the interior courtyard. The place is more ornate and decorated than the J. Paul Getty Roman villa at the Getty Museum in Los Angeles.

She guides me to the conference room, asking me to take a seat and wait.

"Mr. Van der Wyk stays here when he visits Athens. He loves Greece, its history, culture, so full of mystery and intrigue," she says, and smiles.

The video screen slowly lowers on the far wall. Brandt is sitting behind a computer.

"Mr. Van der Wyk will speak to you now, by video link. His business obligations do not permit him to talk to you face to face. It's a pity. We hope you understand," she tells me from behind her desk as the image of an older man, dressed sharply in jacket and tie, appears.

"I know you are very busy these days, Special Agent Cosgrove, so let me get straight to the matter at hand," the man on the screen says. "Hopefully, my special assistant, Ms. Brandt, is providing you with excellent care. I would have preferred to speak with you face to face, but my schedule doesn't allow it at the moment. What I'm about to tell you is factual and true."

He pauses. I look around for a microphone and camera, wondering if Van der Wyk can see and hear me. I see nothing at first glance but have to assume they're somewhere in the room.

"I have gained an appreciation for your work, your perseverance and discretion. In case you are wondering why I wish to speak with you and share what I'm about to impart ..."

He pauses again but I'm remaining silent, having no patience for games with Mr. Van der Wyk. Nevertheless, I'm curious about his intentions. It's beyond my control.

"We have uncovered some troubling—let us say—*issues* relating to a certain deputy prime minister in Russia. He is being blackmailed and has been paying those criminals for several years. Kandyse will provide you with additional details. Naturally, I would like you to keep this matter strictly confidential. I hope the information is of some use to you. Good luck, Mr. Cosgrove." The screen goes dark.

Brandt stands up from behind the computer desk with a plain manila envelope in her hand, offering it. "It's for you," she tells me.

"What does Mr. Van der Wyk expect for this information?" I ask as I open the sealed envelope in front of Brandt who is standing next to me.

I remain seated at the conference table, glancing at the contents. It looks to be financial documents of some kind, perhaps copies of bank wire transfers.

Brandt gracefully and unexpectedly hoists herself on top of the conference table, crossing her legs in front of me. "Nothing, absolutely nothing. Mr. Van der Wyk wants to be helpful. He's a remarkable man, brilliant, a true visionary. I am sure he has his reasons."

There's no point in asking questions of Brandt. She is a trusted confidante, a messenger, nothing more. Intensely loyal to her boss, she obeys his orders.

I'll review the contents of the envelope later, alone.

"OK, Kandyse. I should leave now. Unless there's something else?" I ask as I slowly stand from the chair, ready to leave.

The room is probably wired, so someone will be monitoring my every word and movement.

"Let me show you the grounds. We designed it based on an ancient Greek villa, you know."

"I figured that, Kandyse. But I need to go," I say.

She looks at me with disappointment.

Then she escorts me through the open-air courtyard, and in the middle of it, I stop, turn, and face her. "Kandyse, this business of yours, so full of secrets and intrigue … Your life must be lonely. So many secrets, there's no one you can truly trust and confide in. In the end, you do what you are told. I suppose you are happy in this world but you surely realize they will dispose of you when you are no longer useful to them, to him. Don't think otherwise, Kandyse. And your beauty will fade one day. It's fleeting, after all."

Speaking to her so bluntly feels strange, yet something inside me says I'm finished with this mysterious, intriguing woman, no matter what's in the envelope she has just handed me.

She replies, "I am no different from you, with all your secrets. You also live a lonely life, don't you?" Her

Aegean blue eyes begin to moisten for an instant as she puts on her sunglasses.

"No, Kandyse, we're different. Get out of this business before it consumes you. It's intoxicating, so full of intrigue, mystery, and secrets, but it's empty and soulless. It's all about money, only money and those sparkling stones. You and I have both seen them up close in their rough, unpolished state. They are beautiful, but cold, inanimate, and dead. Yes, it's all so alluring, and you are no doubt well compensated. Kandyse, you are an intelligent and beautiful woman; go find some other profession. Well, goodbye, my fair Aphrodite. And you never did tell me why you attire yourself in those 1960s outfits. It's better you don't; I prefer not knowing anyway. Good luck to your Springboks; they are a great team, Ms. Brandt, but I'll stick with my New Zealand All Blacks."

She slowly closes the entrance door, laughing as she does so.

"See you one day on the rugby pitch, Special Agent, or perhaps on the beach. You never know," she says as she slowly closes the enormous and unwieldy door.

It's doubtful that Kandyse Brandt and I will ever cross paths again. And it's unlikely that anyone has ever spoken to her in such a blunt manner either.

I jump in my vehicle and race back to Athens, the clock ticking. There are fewer than five days left before FBIHQ pulls me off this investigation forever.

"Sharon, can you please look at these documents?" I ask, handing her the envelope containing the wire transfers taken from the hand of Kandyse.

She opens the envelope and flips through the documents inside.

Then she says, "I can tell you straight up the transactions look suspicious and will be difficult to trace … and even more difficult to identify the account holders behind these shell companies, for reasons that will take me a while to explain."

Sharon gives me a look, as if she is waiting for additional information.

"OK. I received them from a source, someone inside the diamond industry, let's say. I was only told the documents are genuine and connected to the Russian deputy PM, Popov."

"Oh, that Popov? The father of Anastasia? Look, this will take me a while, and so what? A lot of money is being transferred out of Russia, to Switzerland, it appears, and elsewhere. Do you have any idea how long it will take to trace these funds? Let me tell you, it could be days, weeks, even several months if we're lucky."

"Sharon, if you had to take an educated guess, what is behind these wire transfers?" I ask.

"I have no clue. There could be a thousand reasons, a thousand scenarios at play. Part of a money laundering scheme perhaps, but it could be extortion, blackmail. It's hard to say. There's huge corruption in the Russian government at all levels. We both know that and have experienced it firsthand. But you can't assume anything at all. Whoever gave you these documents could have ulterior motives to misguide, mislead you. You realize this, don't you?"

"I hear you, Sharon. Can we both agree there's something more at play behind the scenes with this

D.P.M. Popov? I'm just trying to figure out our next move. The clock is ticking, Sharon. The killer is still out there, perhaps stalking his next victim."

My gaze turns to the corner of the bedroom.

Jennifer is there. She's been sitting on the bed, quiet and listening the entire time I have been talking with Sharon. She stands up and walks over to us.

"Dennis, I'm no financial analyst as you know. But you need to look past these documents, not to overlook or discard them, but just to step back and think for a minute."

She pulls a chair over toward us.

"OK. I'm listening. Go ahead. I feel like things have stalled. Yes, we've rescued Anastasia, but so what? That monster's still out there and will strike again."

My sister says, "Stop. I know what you're thinking. You're thinking we ought to be proactive, aggressive, not in a waiting mode. You're also regretting Kansas City. I can't believe I'm saying this, but you need to put all that in the past for the time being. Yeah, that killer is still out there on the streets, but that is an unfamiliar creature, a different monster, let's assume."

"And your point, Jennifer?" I take a deep breath, anticipating my sister isn't done.

"Dennis, you want to catch this guy, right? And you have very little time, less than five days now. But he's in no rush, believe me. And it's not that Chechen, that's for sure. So, let's eliminate him. Dudayev may be a killer, albeit a retired contract killer, but he's a nobody.

"Yeah, he and his thugs knew or suspected Anastasia was alive and being held in that church, but don't think for a moment that he had anything to do with this. The guy is a criminal, a thug, but this thing is way too deep, far too complicated for someone like him."

"OK. Agreed," I say.

My mind is racing, and Victoria pops into my head. She's out there somewhere, perhaps in Athens, and now we have Anastasia with us in this safe house. Victoria may still be looking for her biological daughter, and we still don't have a complete picture of this strange woman.

Sharon interjects, "I'm not an investigator. I know that and I wouldn't want to be one either. Remember when you'd talk about making a move, a decision, in your Golden ADA case? You would tell your Customs Service partner, Rich Marino, that you shouldn't be fearful of being proactive, but once you move that chess piece, that's it, there's no putting it back into its original position. Live with that move, that decision."

"Yep. That's right, Sharon. So, do either of you have any moves in mind?" I ask.

Sharon responds, "This is our task force; take it or leave it. You, me, Jennifer, and Oksana. We can count on Mark, the A-LAT for support, and maybe some help from Oksana's boss, Zhirov, but that is a whole other discussion. The four of us will either solve this together, or we won't.

"It's that simple. Here's my proposal; you and Oksana head to Moscow, go meet with that deputy prime minister. You never know what he'll have to say, and what you may learn from him. The orphanage is there, outside of Moscow. Go find that priest."

She pauses, then adds, "Well, that leaves two of us, Jennifer and me, with Anastasia. She's safe for now, but we can't keep her here much longer. As she recovers, she'll become more restless and want to go home. She's young and likely not very mature. We can tell her it's only a few days more, so we can focus on finding Yelena's killer, but she may not understand or agree."

"Sharon, what about you and my sister taking Anastasia out of Athens, to Crete? Mark's family has a small place near Chania, the western part. I'm sure he wouldn't mind making it available to us. It's much safer than remaining here. I don't think we should hand Anastasia over to the Russians, not until this is over. Can you imagine releasing her, and she winds up dead, or kidnapped all over again?"

The Kansas City case comes into my head.

I left that serial killer on the streets and turned my attention to investigating the drug trafficking ring. I didn't catch the killer, and left him out there to stalk and to kill again.

"So, that blonde. What are you going to do with her?" Jennifer asks.

"What? Who? Katerina?" I ask. I haven't talked about Katerina from the Russian tax police with Jennifer for a long time, not since she claimed to have had a premonition about her.

She says with a sly smile, "You know exactly who I'm referring to, the one from the beach—Monterey beach. I saw her that day. You think I missed her? Well, I didn't. There's not much your little sis misses."

"No, I suppose not. Don't think I'll see her again, anyway. Those diamond folks have tentacles everywhere with their sources and contacts, but there's a limit to what they know, and what they're willing to share."

Jennifer says, "Don't underestimate them, brother. And don't underestimate that blonde either, just because she's a woman. You've gone down that road before, haven't you? And in case you've been wondering, our LAX friend ... Well, that affair's far from over, and not for sharing, not yet. That's for another day, when we finish this story, this case."

"Huh? Whatever are you two talking about? LAX? Los Angeles International Airport? You're talking in code?" Sharon asks, giving us both a confused look.

I say, "Sorry, Sharon. Just trying to keep you out of the rabbit hole ... *holes,* I should say. Let me talk to Oksana. We need to get on the next available flight to Moscow, and you guys need to get to Crete. I'll talk to Mark and just hope he'll agree. And I'm hoping he'll accompany you there. I suppose it will depend on how things are going in the office, whether that team from FBIHQ is still in town. I think Georgia's in Germany by now, recovering. At least I hope she is."

Sharon gives me that look as if she has something to share but is weighing her options. We can read one another well enough after working so closely for several years.

"Sharon? Go ahead. What is it?" I ask.

"Nothing. Just that your mention of rabbit holes sounded, well, desperate, or something else. I have this feeling you've become too focused, that you're no longer seeing the big picture. Sorry, but I'm with your sister on this. Look, no case—especially one of yours—is ever as simple as it may first appear, particularly when you're dealing with Russia and now, with Greece.

"I've been thinking about our old Golden ADA friend though, Andrey Kozlenok. It wasn't so long ago the MVD picked him up in Athens and took him back to Moscow in handcuffs. Now we are here in Athens, working on a seemingly totally unrelated matter. But is it? Some of our diamond friends are here in Greece, and don't assume that the missing Fabergé egg, and that OSI lead, are completely separate, unrelated matters. It could be a dangerous, misguided assumption.

"I'm not saying everything is connected, but don't assume the opposite," she says.

Sharon isn't done. I'm inclined to interrupt but decide to let her continue for a while longer. After all, Sharon Austin's research and spot-on analysis guided me through the twists and turns of the Golden ADA investigation, so I owe her plenty.

Finally, I decide it's enough. I will interrupt.

"OK, Sharon. So, what's your point? That I'm too focused, that I may miss clues or dismiss things that are relevant? Yeah, I'm not the best investigator in the Bureau, that's for sure. We both know that. Am I in over my head? Are we all in over our heads? Perhaps. But FBIHQ has given us a few more days to solve this thing, so let's give it our best shot. I don't want to look back and think we were so close. There's a dangerous killer out there; he'll not stop, not unless we stop him. We've come a long way together, Sharon. Let's not give up the ship, not yet."

She grins in response, saying, "Fair enough, Odysseus, and we're still with you. Fair winds and following seas to you and Oksana. Good luck in Russia."

I later pull Jennifer aside to talk separately as Oksana and I are about to leave for the airport.

Jennifer, Sharon, and Anastasia will depart for Crete the next day.

Fortunately, Mark Anadiplosis has agreed to accompany them to his parents' house and then return to Athens on the next day's flight.

"Keep a low profile. Stay out of town with Anastasia, especially in the evenings. There are a few nice beaches in the area with small tavernas. If anything looks out of the ordinary, leave, and don't go back. I mean it, Jen. And watch for surveillance in vehicles and on foot. Anastasia may still be in danger, and that means you and Sharon would be as well," I say, finding myself beginning to regret the decision to split us up and agreeing to send them off to Crete.

I pause, taking a deep breath. "I won't be able to help so far away in Moscow. Jen, you'll be on your own there. Still, better than staying here in Athens, in this apartment, I suppose," I tell her.

As she shuts the apartment door, Jennifer says, "Dennis, I know what I'm doing, and I wouldn't be doing it unless I felt confident, so please stop. I was there for Georgia and took care of things. Do what you need to do in Russia, and we will stay in Crete. Then when this is over, you can fly to Crete. Anastasia's going to be fine; she's improving daily. I've convinced her not to contact anyone, friends or family. As you know, I'm quite skilled at persuading people and getting them to do what I want. In fact, I think you and Oksana may be in far more danger than us. Brother, don't ignore your intuition, your gut. You have the gift as well. I've told you that many times. Dennis, you need to believe. Now get to the airport,"

Next stop, Russia.

Chapter 16

"Is that really necessary?" I ask Oksana as we set down our things next to the window table in the airport lounge. I can see she has spotted the drinks counter and heads off in that direction, returning with the ritual vodka shots before our flight to Moscow.

She lifts her glass, and I resign myself to lifting mine, figuring it's best to get the ritual done sooner rather than later. "To us, Oksana, to the hunters," I say in Russian as we clink glasses, and I throw the powerful liquid down the back of my throat.

"To what? Hunters? Yes, we are hunters. Who told you that?" she asks.

"One of your MVD colleagues," I respond. She laughs heartily.

I do not know what awaits us in Russia but we'll need to be at the top of our game, that much is certain. Sharon has made me copies of the wire transfer documents, so I flip through them, discreetly, at our small window table. Nearly two million dollars have been transferred during three years. How the diamond consortium came into possession of such documents, I'm not certain. Probably they have a source in the Kremlin, or someone at the bank in Switzerland.

The Greek immigration officer in the booth barely looks at our passports.

He just stamps them and hands them back to us.

From my seat, I scan the passengers' faces as they walk down the aisle to their assigned seats. There are families, business travelers, and tourists. The flight attendants, mostly young, attractive Russian women, smile as the passengers board. They can be exceedingly charming and captivating, but to cross them would be dangerous.

It feels as if I have been away from Russia for a long time but in reality, it's been a few weeks, not months, so hardly a long time at all.

The passengers continue boarding the plane slowly; no serial killers so far—as if they would be so obvious. I dismiss the ridiculous idea, slightly smiling to myself.

Oksana is surprisingly quiet by her usual standard, sitting in the window seat next to mine; she is staring out at the tarmac as the luggage is being loaded.

"You OK?" I ask.

She turns to me. "Da, yes. But I was thinking, I don't know if the MVD will allow me to continue this investigation once we land in Moscow. They may pull me off of this case. I'm only a junior officer, after all."

"We'll deal with that if it comes up, Oksana. Honestly, I don't see them doing that, reassigning this case to someone else. Sure, they can do it, and there isn't much I can do to change their minds if it comes to that, but my gut tells me they will leave us alone to continue our work. Think about it; who would want to step into this mess?"

She nods, though her expression remains serious and pensive.

I continue, "The Bureau hasn't stopped me. Yes, they put me on the clock—five days and no more. But they haven't shut me down, and they could have done so. Oksana, we are both expendable to our agencies. If we solve this thing, they'll take the full credit but so what? And if we don't, then Zhirov and Nolan can tell their superiors … Well, better if we don't go there. We need to put that thought out of our minds because I need you at the top of your game.

"Who knows what awaits us? Relax. Get some sleep."

She turns away and leans back in her seat, finally closing her eyes.

I lean back in my seat as well, closing my eyes too.

My thoughts wander back in time to the polygraph at FBIHQ.

I passed it, so the examiner told me, but Ben Nolan told me the results were inconclusive. Was he playing some sort of game with me? If so, to what end? I review the events of the past days chronologically. Is there more to this case? It's complicated enough, hunting for an elusive serial killer, but is FBIHQ withholding information deliberately? But why would they do that, and what clues have we missed or overlooked? Should we have stayed in Athens to find Victoria, perhaps to confront the Russian contract killer, the retired killer?

In the end, there's no way of resolving all or any of my doubts, my concerns.

In any case, I tell myself, *it doesn't really matter.*

We're three hours from touching down at Moscow's Sheremetovo Airport. Our task force has decided, and we've taken our hand off of the chess piece. It's our move, and we can't undo it.

My mind shifts next to Jennifer, and to Sharon.

The decision to allow them to travel with Anastasia to Crete is the right one, the only one, so I try to convince myself. Jennifer is not a law enforcement officer, not a special agent either, but she's tough and smart enough to be. Obsessing about things beyond my control won't help solve this case and could prove to be a dangerous distraction. Like I just told Oksana about herself, I too will need to be laser focused when we land in Russia.

I open my eyes and the flight attendant hands me a small bottle of vodka, matter-of-factly, as if she were passing me a complimentary bag of peanuts.

Then she asks if I would like a glass of juice or water. Yes, I am heading to Russia. It feels as if I'm already there. I close my eyes once more, soon drifting off into the vodka-induced sleep.

***

It feels like minutes since I dozed off, woken by the flight attendant announcement in Russian and English that we will land in a half hour.

Once inside the terminal, I look for the dedicated diplomat line for arriving passengers, and Oksana heads for the line for Russian nationals.

This airport looks dated now, frozen in time from the 1970s.

They built it for the 1980 Moscow Summer Olympic Games, later to be unceremoniously boycotted by the United States and other Western nations after the Soviet Union invaded Afghanistan. For the Soviet Union, it marked the beginning of the end of the Cold War, and the demise of their expansive empire. They just didn't know it at the time.

Lawrence Poinier, the FBI legal attaché for Russia—my boss in the country—is waiting in the baggage area as we retrieve our luggage. He has a concerned look as we approach.

I introduce Oksana in Russian, and his concerned look evaporates, replaced by a smile.

Poinier asks for a moment to speak with me separately.

Oksana steps away.

"I have to take you directly to the DPM's residence; he's waiting for you inside the Kremlin Dacha Complex, at his place. He's been driving me nuts, calling daily about a status update for his daughter. I don't know what's going on with your investigation, and don't like being kept out of the loop like this." When this case is over, he will still be my boss, and I don't want him to have sour grapes about being cut out. I figure I'd feel the same if I were in his shoes.

I say, "Lawrence, I didn't cut you out. It's been nonstop, and frankly, you're better off."

Instantly, I'm regretting my choice of words, suggesting he's better off not knowing.

"I'm the legal attaché here. It's up to me, not you, to decide what I should or should not know," he says.

"You're right. I misspoke," I tell him, trying to diffuse what I just said. "It's been pretty intense these past days in Greece. No vacation, Lawrence. I didn't ask for this assignment; it came straight from the Director's Office. I can brief you separately, afterwards. Is that OK?"

I need to remind him that our boss—the director, the head of our agency—was the one who assigned me this case, not Lawrence Poinier, the legal attaché for Russia.

We head out of the airport complex in Poinier's Bureau-assigned vehicle.

Oksana has a concerned look as she stares out the window.

Moscow is at its most beautiful this time of year, its trees in full bloom and the temperature pleasant, but the air is heavy and humid.

I tell her, recognizing the questioning in her gaze, "Relax, Oksana. You're not being pulled off the case. If you were, they would have done so at the airport, but believe me, no one wants to take your place in this one. Besides, I may need your fighting skills to save me again."

Poinier's eyes are visible in the rear-view mirror as he stares back at me in the rear seat. He's eavesdropped on our conversation but says nothing. I am sure my comment got his attention.

I hope the mention of fighting—of violence—will be enough to discourage him from involving himself or pressing for any details of the investigation. He's unlikely to be accustomed to or comfortable with such aggression; after all, he's not from New York and didn't grow up in my old neighborhood, where fighting was an everyday occurrence.

Poinier shifts his gaze back on the road ahead, away from the rear-view mirror. It's unlikely he'll glance back again, and unlikely he will ask me any probing questions, not today at least.

With the pleasant weather, there are pedestrians everywhere, and plenty of plastic tables and chairs on the sidewalks outside of cafés and restaurants.

The warm summer weather can end abruptly, at any moment, and the long, dark winter will eventually return, sometimes sooner than expected. No torn jeans and loose-fitting cotton T-shirts to be found in this country, in this land of contradictions and extremes.

It's a summer outdoor fashion show on the grandest of scales, however brief.

Russian women would never dare to appear outside in sloppy or casual attire. Hair, makeup, clothing are all to perfection, regardless of social status.

It isn't about impressing the opposite sex, so I conclude. Here, the women dress for themselves, taking pride in their appearance. With so much poverty and economic uncertainty in their world since the collapse of the Soviet Union, they cannot control much.

But they can take charge of how they present themselves, excelling at it.

So, even their gait, their manner of walking, is practiced, deliberate and graceful with the head upright, no slouching, all looking forward as if they have been ballet trained as children.

Many have been, and even their hand gestures are feminine and graceful. Pointing with one finger is considered rude here; full hand gestures are acceptable and the cultural norm.

Of course, there are exceptions to this too, but on the whole, the women are stunning and do their best to look that way. The men, well, that is another story entirely.

They are mostly brutish in appearance, and many suffering the long-term debilitating effects of alcoholism. Naturally, there are exceptions for the men as well but on the whole, no one smiles here, at least not in public. Not that everyone is miserable and unhappy although many must be, but smiles, laughs, and joking around are for friends and families, not for outsiders, certainly not for foreigners. If a Russian man or woman smiles at you, it means something. It has real meaning, unlike the mostly superficial smiles of strangers when greeting one another in the Western world. I find the Russians fascinating: their culture, their history, and beliefs.

I have done so since being a teenager. They were different, not so much in physical appearance, but in other ways. They were neither European nor Asian, outside influences having largely shaped their customs, beliefs, and traditions.

The invasion of the Mongols in the 12th century—the Tatars, as they were also known—brought with it a mystical belief system and values, with plenty of palace intrigue around its leaders, the so-called Tsars. The Golden Horde's control extended across a vast area encompassing Russia, Moscow, Kyiv, and surrounding territories, from eastern Europe to the Siberian steppes and the Pacific Ocean. Many Russian faces, especially those of women, still displayed the high cheekbones and exotic almond-shaped eyes characteristic of their Asian ancestry. Interestingly enough, the elongated face— Scandinavian features often depicted in ancient icons, on church walls—predated the time of the Mongol invasion and reflected the features of those Russians living in the far north, beyond the reach of the Mongol invaders.

Russians were justifiably xenophobic after having to repel a series of invasions, particularly the more recent ones that had attempted to dominate and control them. Napoleon's army in the early 19th century, and the Nazi invaders during the Great Patriotic War.

While the Nazis had killed millions, Stalin's own purges added millions more. Historians estimated the population of Russia alone would have reached 300 million if not for Stalin's brutal purges in the 1930s, and the two devastating world wars of the 20th century.

As I gaze out the window, I glimpse the recently opened 'Park Pobeda' or Victory Park, commemorating the Soviet people's victory against Nazi Germany.

Finally, we are nearing the center of town and will soon turn to the south toward the Kremlin Dacha Complex for our long-awaited meeting with the deputy prime minister.

"I think you and Oksana can manage from here," Poinier says as he stops the vehicle unexpectedly near an entrance to a Metro station. "Just bring the vehicle back when you're done. I'll use yours in the meantime."

"OK, Lawrence. Thanks. But you don't have to do that," I respond.

"It would be better if it were only you and Oksana interviewing the DPM. I don't know the case, and the three of us sitting there are ... Well, you understand," he says as he opens the driver's side door. "Good luck. I'll be in my office if you need anything."

Poinier has surprised me with his decision not to insert himself in the case. But it isn't so surprising a decision. He's an experienced investigator, and though excluding him might bruise his ego, his decision is correct; this lets me avoid convincing him to stay in the car while Oksana and I meet with the DPM. I jump into the driver's seat, and Oksana enters the passenger seat to guide me the rest of the way to the Kremlin Dacha Complex.

I tell her, "Oksana, listen to me. We need to be flexible in there. I don't want to be confrontational with this DPM, but if I get any sense he's holding back, or on the brink of admitting something, well, you know perhaps better than I do how to deal with that. We managed that fine line with the senator in California. I've no sense if we're going to learn anything from the DPM. Worst case, we'll learn nothing. But let's try not to anger him and at least leave the door open for follow-up."

I can't read her body language as I'm focused on the winding road ahead.

"I understand. But if, as you like to say, if he 'opens the door' on a sensitive topic, like blackmail or extortion, we should go for it. Oh, that is another expression you use a lot," she responds with a slight laugh.

I reply, "This interview could become emotionally charged. Emotional from his part, understandably so. As far as Popov knows, his daughter is still missing or worse. We can't tell him otherwise. I don't enjoy lying in an interview, but we have justification to do so at this point. I'm sure you've had to do this before, to lie deliberately or to withhold information during an interview of a perpetrator, even a victim, and so have I. Well, here we go," I say as the main gate comes into view. As soon as I stop in front of the gate, two security guards emerge from the booth and are standing beside the vehicle, their long guns at the ready position.

I can see what appears to be a two-story observation tower above the main gate, a wall surrounding the entire complex. They quickly clear our vehicle. The gate opens, and we slowly drive through, following the escort vehicle to the DPM's dacha inside the forested complex.

As we park our vehicle near the dacha, I feel strangely at ease.

Perhaps it's because Oksana looks so calm.

Nothing on her face shows she is nervous or anxious. I suppose she's accepted the possibility that the MVD could reassign her, remove her from the investigation, and transfer her to a remote MVD outpost in Siberia. She's been a solid partner for me, my first female MVD partner from Russia, and someone who likely saved my life in the nightclub.

Her instincts also took us to the church where we found Anastasia that night.

I force myself to focus on the present. We will both need to be at our best, regardless of what we will face when the door to the dacha opens.

He's standing there in the doorway, Nikolai Popov.

He's taller than I remember, but with the dark circles under his eyes, he looks like someone who hasn't slept for days. Popov greets us warmly and motions for us to enter the dacha.

Once we are clear of the threshold, he only then extends his hand, first to Oksana, and then to me. Russians have a custom of never shaking hands in a doorway.

It brings bad luck, so they told me the first time I attempted to extend my hand for a handshake in a passageway. I never made the mistake again.

It strikes me that this dacha is much bigger than I imagined from the outside.

Popov moves like someone destined for greatness as he leads us past exquisite Italian furniture pieces strewn about in the massive living room, its walls adorned with beautifully framed paintings depicting some of Russia's breathtaking and varied landscapes: wide rivers, birch forests, the Ural Mountains, deep valleys, and ancient churches.

We enter his private study and sit around a small table that looks to be made entirely of precious Baltic Sea amber. One of his staff soon brings us an assortment of biscuits and cookies and hot black tea poured from the nearby samovar, a Russian tea urn, standing at the ready in the far corner of the room. He says, "My wife and I appreciate your efforts to find our daughter, Anastasia. We call her Nastiya," he says in English.

His English is excellent, and his accent closer to British English than American. "Every second, every minute, every hour, and every day she is missing is an eternity for us. Nastiya is our only daughter, as you know," he says as he motions for us to drink our tea and try a 'biscuit.'

Even in his raw emotional state, he is still a host, and we are in his home as his guests, so he will continue to urge us to try his fresh-baked cookies in the way a doting mother might.

I explain to him, "We believe someone abducted Anastasia after the murder of her friend, Yelena. The nightclub where they were last seen together is owned and operated by Russian organized crime. Anastasia and Yelena may have stumbled upon something when they were there, and it cost Yelena her life. Someone may be holding your daughter for ransom, or for some other reason. Perhaps they are trying to figure out how to approach you without revealing themselves. Have you received anything? A letter, phone call, any sort of ransom demand?"

I ask him the question, careful not to touch the possibility the DPM is being blackmailed.

But the wire transfer documents which I received from Kandyse Brandt could be part of a blackmail scheme, or something else entirely.

My caution serves no purpose; I forgot I have a colleague with a different approach.

"Are you being blackmailed, Nikolai Ivanovich?" Oksana suddenly interjects. I'm taken aback by her question, but there's no point in trying to minimize what my partner has asked. It's out, and I can't rewind or undo the confrontational question from her.

I brace for his response.

"Nyet. No," he says as he looks at me.

I can't judge whether Oksana's question has struck a nerve, or if he is just an exhausted and emotionally drained father, hoping to get his daughter back. The thought comes to my mind to tell him we have rescued Anastasia. That would bring enormous relief to him and his wife, but I don't and won't reveal anything. They will learn soon enough that Anastasia is alive and safe. But not today. Oksana and I still have work to do, and this investigation is far from over.

"Oksana and I are heading to Smolensk to see if we can learn anything about the place where you adopted your daughter," I tell him. He puts the cup of tea down somewhat forcefully onto the table, obviously not pleased at what I have just told him.

"Why?" he asks, clearly frustrated, and has switched back to Russian. "That is a waste of time. It was a long time ago. What does her adoption as a child have to do with her abduction?"

Popov is furious, on the edge of losing his composure.

But it's the trigger reaction I'm looking for, to push him into a raw emotional state where he is more likely to say or reveal something he may not want to share with us.

It's an interview technique that doesn't always work, and not the best way to build rapport with an interviewee, but my instinct tells me to go for it. Besides, Oksana has already dropped the loaded question about blackmail earlier than I wish. She and I are obviously not on the same page for this interview, and I do not know why she's raised the possibility of blackmail with Popov so early in our interview. She has to sense something, at least I hope she does.

"We are looking at every possibility. It may have something to do with her birth mother, or her family. Do you have any adoption records? Have you ever heard from anyone claiming to be the birth mother of

Anastasia?" Oksana asks. She has now taken the lead in this interview.

"Nyet. They gave us no information about the birth mother or biological father. We didn't want to know. You are wasting your time here in Russia, and you came all of this way for nothing. Anastasia's abduction occurred in Greece. You should look there, not here."

Popov is clearly agitated, and Oksana's job could be in jeopardy.

One phone call from Popov could cause her to be dismissed or reassigned to some remote outpost in faraway Siberia. I glance over at Oksana, seeing her leaning in toward Popov.

She's not done. Somehow, this young female MVD investigator doesn't fear the senior Kremlin official who could instantly end her career. "We will find her. We have made some progress and will return to Greece as soon as we have finished our work here," she tells him as she stands from the table. "Thank you for your patience and understanding, Deputy Prime Minister. Please contact us immediately if you hear anything from your daughter or her kidnappers." She extends her hand. I take the clue and stand too; this interview is over, for now.

We shake hands outside the entrance door, jumping into our vehicle.

Oksana turns toward me in the car.

"They may pull me off this investigation," she says calmly. "I am a lowly captain. We just lied to him about the fate of his daughter. I feel like, how do you say—shit. But he lied to us. No deputy prime minister like him would ever admit to being blackmailed. Perhaps it's a matter of pride, ego, I don't know. Or perhaps your friends are wrong; those wire transfers reflect something else entirely. Still, he was holding back. I could sense it, and he would reveal nothing to us. Not in this first meeting, that's for sure."

Her confidence is back, it seems.

"Oksana, I'm impressed—no, proud of you. Sometimes, you go into an interview thinking you are going to say one thing, and the interviewee is going to respond in such a manner. But you never really know. You have to change course mid-stream. We can always go back there.

"If we had given him more, it might have had unintended consequences. We could have left there with the DPM learning more than we learned from him. Most of the time, that is not a good 'business' practice. But actually, putting him off balance, challenging him the way you did, we got him into an emotional state. He was in control of the interview at the start, but when we finished, it was us—well, you—in control of it. Well done, Oksana."

"Doesn't he understand that someone might have kidnapped his daughter to blackmail him? He must suspect that, no? Doesn't he want his daughter back?" she asks, sounding frustrated.

"Let it go, Oksana. We must head to Smolensk; a break may be possible there, and we can revisit him later. At least we didn't close the door with Popov. Perhaps he's not exactly pleased with us, but so what? He will call no one to complain, believe me. I just have a sense he won't."

The road to Smolensk is a three-lane highway with a single passing lane in the middle. It's a game of chicken with cars and trucks in each direction, almost challenging each other in the middle passing lane, testing fate. We drive through small villages along the way.

Life looks simple in those towns, but it's undeniably harsh, nothing like the idyllic scenes depicted in the paintings on the walls of the DPM's dacha. There are modest garden plots with villagers, mostly elderly, attending to them, trying their best to cultivate the rich black soil before the long winter sets in. Most of the younger families abandoned such villages long ago, fleeing to the bigger cities, leaving behind the elderly and disabled. It's a melancholy sight, repeated over and over, village after village as we head toward Smolensk.

The babushka is already standing outside the entrance to the Detski Dom as our vehicle approaches on the gravel road.

"When she sees our diplomatic license plate, she probably thinks we're interesting in adopting one of the children," I tell Oksana.

"Yes, we make a delightful couple, except …" she says and hesitates.

"Yeah. I'm too old for you," I say, finishing her sentence. It feels good to laugh after the interview with the deputy prime minister and the long drive to Smolensk.

Oksana tells me to wait in the car while she speaks with the babushka who reminds me of a tough elementary school teacher. I see Oksana show her MVD credentials.

The babushka looks closely at them. Regardless of her standing as a Russian law enforcement official, the babushka doesn't seem at all impressed and not intimidated.

To her, Oksana is a young woman, and this babushka is older, deserving of deference in this society where respect for elders is still the norm. She is in charge of the adoption house and responsible for the safety and welfare of the many children in her care.

I decide to step out of the vehicle and approach them before things become heated.

"Let me introduce myself," I tell the babushka in Russian, showing her my FBI credentials.

By her reaction, she has never met or seen anyone from the FBI before this day.

I tell her, "I appreciate that you, Natasha Constantinovna, have an important duty and great responsibility here, but Oksana Aleksandrovna and I will take only a few minutes of your time. We are interested in reviewing adoption files from the early 1980s for two children who lived here. We could use your help. This is a very urgent matter."

The head caretaker's—Natasha Constantinovna's—refusal to cooperate with Oksana has clearly annoyed her. Before I can say another word, Oksana interrupts me.

"We need to see those files. We will see them, or else I will have the MVD, FSB, and the tax police here, and they will examine all of your financial records. Who knows what irregularities they may find?" she tells the babushka.

It's not my style, but Oksana understands her people better than I do, and she's dealt with such babushkas before, I suppose.

I can hear the children playing in the distant playground. Natasha Constantinovna invites us inside. Like a switch, she is cordial, graciously offering us tea as we sit in her modest office.

The orphanage is spotless, and the children, ranging in age from newborn to teenagers, are all adorable, every one of them. They smile at us, several gazing curiously through the open office door. I suppose they are wondering if we are there to adopt one of them.

"You can look around, but the KGB removed all the adoption records from that period a long time ago," she says.

Nothing in her face or body language makes me doubt what she is telling us.

The news is not surprising, considering how threatening and omnipresent the KGB was in the daily lives of Soviet citizens.

"Was there a custom here at your orphanage, or have you heard of young children being marked—tattooed perhaps—with the Russian Orthodox cross?" Oksana asks.

"I recall something about it. But that was years ago. They kept it quiet as the communists were not believers. I'm a believer and most of my staff was or is.

"We had a wonderful young priest in those days. He would visit us periodically to baptize the children in the faith. Of course, the KGB harassed him in those days. He was an artist, as I recall, and would sometimes paint tattoos of the cross of our Savior on the children, to mark them as children of our Lord and Savior. The children were especially blessed in that way. It was a long time ago." She smiles and looks lost in thought or reflection.

"Babushka, the name? The name of this priest?" Oksana asks hurriedly.

"I don't remember. Such a long time ago. It was something like Aleksandr Nikolaievich, perhaps Nikolai. Something like that, but as I say, I cannot be sure now. There was something odd about his name, his family name, that much I can recall."

"In what way? You say there was something different?" I ask.

"Perhaps."

"Oksana Aleksandrovna, if I may ask—if you don't mind—were you born in Russia? You look, well, mixed, like that priest."

"I am half Greek."

"Yes, that's it," she exclaims as she loudly claps. "It was a Greek surname. Nikolai Aleksandrovich Stavros. So odd. But a charming person. It's been a few years since he was last here. I heard he got transferred to Leningrad."

I am stunned. Oksana sits next to me, speechless and frozen. It's the same priest who baptized Cory Gordon in San Francisco, before his brutal murder in Omaha.

"Natasha Constantinovna, are you sure? Leningrad? Saint Petersburg, correct?" I ask her for confirmation.

"I think that is what I heard, what he said. Yes, definitely. I remember it clearly. Leningrad. When I repeated the city name, he corrected me and told me Saint Petersburg. Leningrad was the name the communists gave the city in honor of Lenin. Well, he seemed thrilled about it. I think he has relatives there."

"Thank you for your time and help, Natasha," I tell her, dropping the patronymic.

She shrugs and smiles, no doubt trying to make sense of the odd couple she has encountered. Oksana from MVD, with this strange Russian-speaking FBI agent accompanying her.

This world no longer makes sense to this simple country woman who has survived Stalin, Hitler, and the communists, now in her older years and caring for so many orphaned children abandoned and left in her charge, with little financial support from the struggling government.

We jump in our vehicle to first race back to Moscow.

I turn to Oksana and explain to her we need to catch that midnight train from Moscow to Saint Petersburg. She looks flushed and is strangely silent.

"What's up, Oksana? You OK?"

"I have fever," she responds. And yes, she seems to; only now do I turn to her and see she is shivering. I reach my hand over to feel her forehead.

"Yes. You definitely have a fever. Let's find a hotel. You can rest and hopefully tomorrow you'll feel better."

"Nyet. Take me to banya," she insists. "We passed one on the way here."

The 'private' banya consists of a recently renovated one-story wooden structure, attached to the small hotel. It's a family run place. Anatoli and his wife, Marsha, greet me as I approach the reception desk. Oksana waits in the vehicle. For a modest fee, they agree to give us exclusive use of the banya for several hours. The banya includes two relaxation rooms, two dressing rooms, the banya itself, and a small outdoor pool filled with ice cold water to cool down after each session.

Anatoli gathers wood and lights the stove to heat the banya, while Marsha prepares fresh sheets, towels, snacks, and drinks and shows us around. I tell Marsha that my colleague isn't feeling well, that she believes the banya will help. Being Russians, they firmly believe in the therapeutic benefits of the banya, which I doubt, but I keep my opinion to myself.

Oksana changes out of her street clothing and wraps herself in the thin cotton sheet provided. I also change, figuring I'll closely monitor her periodically from outside, waiting in the relaxation room. To prevent her from passing out alone, I'll not leave her for too long in the dangerously hot and humid banya. I was never a fan of saunas, but if Oksana has convinced herself that the banya will cure her, there's no point in objecting. It's worth a try.

In under ten minutes, Anatoli appears and informs us the banya is ready but tells us to be careful not to stay inside for more than a few minutes for each session, and to hydrate constantly. He doesn't want his guests, and his American guest in particular, passing out from the high heat.

"There is a bucket of water inside, and plenty of birch leaves. I am sure you know how to use them. Knock on the door if you need anything. Otherwise, the place is yours. No one will bother you. We don't have many guests these days," he says as he closes the door.

He promptly heads back to the hotel's reception area.

"I go to pool first," Oksana tells me. Soon, she returns from the icy waters, shivering.

Her sheet isn't providing much concealment of her body but she doesn't seem to care, and I figure it best not to comment on that subject. Oksana opens the door to the banya, turns and looks at me, expecting me to enter. By her look, I can tell she will insist I step inside with her.

I don't bother trying to explain to her I don't like banyas.

As a Russian, that would not make any sense to her, and she'd likely have trouble understanding how anyone could feel that way. The interior of the banya is all fine wood made from aspen or spruce, with an array of raised platforms against the walls for sitting or lying on.

Oksana lies on her stomach on the lowest platform. The thin cotton sheet wrapped around her body is already drenched, again showing almost everything.

"Beat me," she whispers. "Bey men-ya," she says louder in Russian, motioning for me to use the birch branches. I have witnessed Russians beating each other furiously in the banya before.

To me, the practice is comical, even borderline sadistic in a way.

During such a 'beating,' water sprays everywhere off of the birch leaves into the super-heated air, adding to the unbearably high humidity of the intensely hot banya.

The Finnish dry sauna environment is nothing like this.

It offers a much more bearable and pleasant experience compared to the intensity of the typical Russian banya. I can only hope my body will somehow adapt to the extreme heat, and I won't pass out. I take the soaked branches from the bucket, lightly touching them on Oksana's exposed back, legs, and arms. She turns her head and looks at me in disappointment.

It's obvious this is not what she wants me to do with those branches.

"Nyet. Bis-tre-ye, ee seal-ne-ye," she commands, ordering me in Russian to whip her faster and harder with the branches. I can only shake my head in disbelief. I follow her commands.

What other choice do I have at that moment? She then lifts her body and flips over onto her back as I continue the bizarre ritual of beating my partner with the tree branches. It would be comical if she were not a woman, young and attractive. But she is my partner, who for whatever reason believes in the mystical power of the banya to help her overcome this fever and sickness.

I feel myself slowly becoming physically aroused.

Shaking off the feeling, I try my best to remain laser focused on the assigned task.

I dip the branches into the water bucket again and again, waiting for her return after the plunges into the ice-cold pool outside, so I can continue with another session of beating her with the branches. While I feel no embarrassment or reluctance in carrying out the task which I have to admit to myself is not an unpleasant one, I decide no good will ever come from disclosing to anyone about our otherworldly detour to this banya.

The whole thing feels intensely private somehow; it's between us as partners. I can only hope the 'treatment' will be effective and cure her of this fever and sickness.

I'm not so confident that I could manage another banya visit like the one I just experienced.

"Thank you. I already feel better," she says as she awakens on the lounge chair in the relaxation room. She has slept for more than an hour. Oddly enough, Oksana's fever has broken.

Her face is no longer flushed. She looks fresh, relaxed, and rested.

Perhaps there is something in the banya treatment after all, I reluctantly think.

"Let's eat and drink something, then we can get on the road to Moscow and try to catch that midnight train from Leningradsky Vokzal to Saint Petersburg," she tells me.

I'm relieved she has somehow recovered from whatever has been attacking her body, but I have no desire to ever again partake in the strange ritual, regardless of sickness.

There's symmetry to what has occurred, as I suddenly recall that days earlier when I became ill in Athens, Oksana took care of me. At least she didn't insist on a sauna or banya for me too.

The cure was vodka. My old Golden ADA Russian MVD partners would laugh but I decide that neither they, nor anyone else, will ever know what just took place inside the confines of that hot and humid place. I have safely stored the secret vodka ritual from the Golden ADA investigation and my time as a 'militsionaire' in my compartmentalized brain, and the banya episode now joins it there, permanently and secretly.

We arrive back at the U.S. Embassy in Moscow in time for me to drop off the Bureau vehicle and stop by my office. I need to call HQ. I haven't spoken with Ben Nolan from FBIHQ since he gave me the five-day extension. The legal attaché and staff have already left for the day and I find myself in the office alone. Oksana waits for me in a nearby café.

"I see you're calling me from the Moscow office," Nolan says as he picks up the secure phone in his office at FBIHQ, sounding more annoyed than surprised.

"Yes, Ben. We're close, really close to catching this guy. I'm heading to Saint Petersburg tonight to find a priest who's been in the shadows of this thing for a long time. Sharon's been keeping you updated, hasn't she?"

I instantly regret what I've just shared with him about the priest and my travel plans.

"It's quite enough. You've left me hanging out there and I gave you the extension. You want more time, don't you?" he asks.

"Ben, this guy works in the shadows. He's elusive, Ben. Cunning and dangerous. I am getting a sense about him. I'm nearly certain he's killed that senator's son, and that murder was on U.S. soil, Ben. There's a high probability there are other victims, U.S. citizens."

I pause, hoping his response will not signal the end of the investigation—for me, and for Oksana. Silence. I hear him breathing. He inhales and takes a deep breath, about to speak.

"What about this Victoria Tarasova? You gave up trying to find her? Where do you think she is? What is her game?" he asks, breaking the silence.

The questions surprise me, showing he is still reading the file at the very least.

If Ben Nolan intended to pull me off the case, he would not be asking about Victoria Tarasova, so I figure. I don't mention the analysis by Sharon, linking Victoria's late father Igor—and Pavel Sokolov, his deceased fellow scientist associate—with a Bureau source.

I cross my fingers, hoping Sharon has put none of that information in the file for Ben Nolan to see. If he weren't already skittish, that hyper-sensitive information linking Victoria Tarasova to a Bureau source would scare him and end my involvement in the case. I have to assume he doesn't know. I can't help but probe. Ben Nolan is a highly intelligent and experienced investigator, but I don't want to insult or anger him. I need to choose my next words carefully, but not so carefully as to arouse his suspicion, making him think I'm playing with him or withholding information.

"Ben, what about putting in for an Interpol red notice for Victoria? We have a sufficient basis with what the senator told us. I don't think the investigation's integrity would be compromised either. Might be worth a try, no?" I ask. There is again silence.

Ben Nolan knows something, something that he'll not, for whatever reason, disclose to me.

"No. I don't think so. If she doesn't want to be found, I doubt Interpol will find her. You've had a hard enough time tracking her." His answer is weak. He is holding back.

His response confirms it.

"OK. Agreed. But if possible, can you run Victoria's name through the databases on the other side? The C-I side. Sharon can't do that from Athens."

It's a small lie, but sometimes, as an investigator, you need to lie even to your own boss, which I seem to be making a habit of doing lately.

"And if anything comes up, anything odd, please send whatever you can—photos, background, etc. to Sharon. Victoria is a complicated woman, and we shouldn't write her off just because she's so complicated, and a handful. Yeah, she may be crazy, and a distraction in some ways, but you never know. She may also hold some sort of key to unraveling this case. Something tells me we shouldn't write her off."

I glance down at my watch. It's time to end this call. Oksana and I need to head to the train station if we are going to catch the train to Saint Petersburg.

"Cos, good luck. Keep me posted. I don't think I can grant you another extension of time. You realize that. Just finish this thing," he says as he hangs up.

At least Ben Nolan didn't order me to stop.

There is something more, something Ben Nolan knows and won't share with me.

He hasn't pulled me off the case. That is the bottom line. Nothing else matters.

There is time for one more secure telephone call from the Legat Office to Mark Anadiplosis in Athens. I asked him to keep close tabs on Jennifer and Sharon in Crete, since my calling them from an unsecured line in Russia would be too risky.

Anadiplosis answers on the first ring. "They're doing fine. Anastasia is also much better, Cos. But you have little time. Maybe a few days, certainly not a week. You need to end this thing, and soon. Anastasia's pressing them about going home, and once it's out there and known she's been rescued, I don't think you will continue in your stealth mode. The killer would go to ground, lying dormant for some time. Besides, you'd also be exposed, no?"

"Yeah. I suppose so. But please tell my sister and Sharon that I'm worried. No, forget that, Mark. Tell them

I have full confidence in them and their abilities, something like that. Just make it sound good but not over the top, OK?"

He says, "Sure. Well, you better get on that train. Hey, Georgia was asking for you. She's nearly recovered. She talks about your sister like she's a Greek warrior goddess —Athena, or some kind of Amazon warrior; it's extreme. But Jen saved her life in that parking lot. What a story, huh? She didn't tell you?"

"No, not really, Mark. But that's my sister. I told you she was intense when you first met her, remember? Thanks for everything and stay safe there. Yassas, Mark."

I end the call, locking the office and heading outside with my luggage.

Time to catch that midnight train.

I suddenly feel exhausted as I walk down the busy sidewalk to the café to meet up with Oksana, only imagining how exhausted she must also be feeling.

The banya stop unexpectedly pops into my head. I laugh and shake my head. It will be one of those stories I'll have to file away for good in my compartmentalized brain, the super-secret section. I can only hope my sister Jennifer doesn't sense something when I next see her.

With my sister and her 'gift,' you can never be sure.

Chapter 17

The embassy has reserved us the last first-class carriage on the midnight train.

We arrive on the platform as the conductor blows the warning whistle, and we run toward the last remaining door still open for boarding. We jump aboard with seconds to spare as the train pulls away from the station. Trains in Russia are usually on time, willing to wait for no one.

While the efficiency of the train system is not on the same level as during Soviet times, things are still functioning very well. Russians travel mostly by train since it's the most affordable means of travel for the average Russian, and relatively safe.

I always tell my family and friends that you have never truly experienced Russia until you take a train journey; the atmosphere on board is fascinating, with people playing cards, children running in the passageway. Some passengers read, while strangers talk with one another.

Others doze off to the gentle rocking of the moving train.

It's also not uncommon for passengers to sing or play musical instruments.

There is usually a dedicated dining car providing a limited choice of appetizers, entrees, and drinks. Oksana and I store our luggage in our first class coupé and head for the dining car. We haven't eaten for many hours. The conductor, responsible for keeping things orderly and safe, watches over each compartment, one conductor for each train car. If you want drinks or snacks, you can order them from the conductor, and they will provide them for a modest price.

We order traditional *pelmeni*—Russian dumplings, a pickled cucumber, and a carrot salad, along with two bottles of ice cold Baltica number seven, the best and most popular beer in the country. Swedish investors rescued the brewery after the collapse of the Soviet Union, and they are now operating successfully as a joint venture.

In fact, it's one of the few successful joint ventures in the entire country.

Oksana remains quiet during the meal since I'm sure we are both famished and exhausted.

We will sleep for most of the night as the train won't arrive in Saint Petersburg until eight o'clock in the morning. She raises her glass to toast. "Thanks God for banya and for birch branches," she says, and smiles at me. I smile back as we click glasses.

"Na zdrov-vee-ya," I say in Russian: to our health.

I gaze out the window, and although it's past midnight, it's still dusk. We will arrive in St Petersburg for white nights. Fortunately, there's a window darkener so we'll sleep.

But for this night, I don't think we'll need to use it at all as we are both that exhausted.

The gentle rocking of the train will no doubt put us both to sleep in a matter of minutes. I'm already having trouble keeping my eyes open as I finish my plate full of pelmeni.

***

I'm awakened by the conductor, a pleasant older woman, announcing the train's imminent arrival at the station. I glance at my watch. It's nearly eight.

So, it seems we both fell into a deep sleep.

During my assignment in Russia, I have always looked forward eagerly to my periodic work trips from Moscow to Saint Petersburg. The city fascinates me, so much so that I sometimes take my wife and children with me when there are school recesses.

Unlike Moscow, Saint Petersburg has a European feel.

It is a city which was planned and built by Peter the Great in the 1700s as his new capital, part of his vision to modernize Russia and bring it closer to the West.

With its strategic location on the Neva River, it was going to be accessible to the Baltic Sea for the new Russian Navy and the Russian merchant trading ships.

Its many canals and bridges have earned it the name 'the Venice of the North.' For many residents, the city is still known as Leningrad, its name during Soviet times.

This is understandable since its inhabitants have bravely withstood relentless bombing and a horrible famine during the Great Patriotic War, hundreds of thousands perishing during what became a three-year siege and blockade. After the victory over Nazi Germany, residents rebuilt their devastated city, particularly its churches and museums filled with priceless artwork safely stored underground or moved far away from the city by barge.

The residents took—and still take—great pride in their city, having painstakingly rebuilt all of it to exacting specifications from the pre-war time. Although the Bolsheviks moved the capital back to Moscow when they seized power in 1917, the city remains the cultural capital of Russia, with its museums and the most famous Marinski ballet.

The city's residents even dress differently, more western than their contemporaries from Moscow and elsewhere. Their manner of speaking sounds clearer too, at least for me and most of my colleagues from the language school. The best Russian language teachers in the language school in Monterey, California, hailed from Saint Petersburg.

Nearly all of my teachers seemed to have prior connections to the city, having studied or lived there. For me, it was also my favorite Russian city by far.

"Zhirov has got us a vehicle to use while we are here," Oksana says as we step out of the train onto the platform, now crowded with debarking and embarking passengers.

She tells me she called ahead last night, and it's all arranged.

"It's nothing fancy, not like your armored BMW in Athens, but it should work," she adds.

A plain-clothed MVD officer is standing there waiting for us, ready to pass us the car keys as we emerge from the train onto the platform. He tells us where to find the parked vehicle and then quickly vanishes, his task done. He likely has more important things to do at the start of this sunny workday, which already feels too hot and humid.

"I need to make a quick stop at my consulate, Oksana. Mark from Athens has reached out to me, but it's better to talk to him from the office," I tell her.

Several months ago, we convinced the consulate to provide us with a small, dedicated office, as the legal attaché and I seemed to be working in Saint Petersburg regularly. The office consists of two desks with a few pieces of furniture that were lying around unused. HQ's tech support has installed phones, computers, printers, fax machines, file cabinets, and two safes. The office has no windows, but it's adequate enough for our needs when working in the city.

"How's Moscow?" Mark says as he answers the phone.

I respond, "We're not in Moscow; we just arrived in Saint Petersburg. I'm calling you from our office at the consulate. Oksana's outside in the car, waiting for me. What's up?" I hold my breath, hoping he's not about to say something's happened to Anastasia, or worse, to my sister.

"Hey, I've some good news for a change. My father found a photo of that priest you asked him about. They misfiled the photo. I guess it bothered him that the file didn't have one, so he kept looking after you left, embarrassed by its absence. He unearthed it a couple of days ago and tells me he was praying when he found it! Sharon's had one of her contacts in the city pick it up from him and you can download it from the system. You do have a printer there, right?"

"Yes. We're heading to the small church outside the city where this priest was apparently last assigned. One of Oksana's MVD contacts in St Petersburg, where she works, did some discreet checking for her. Everyone's supposed to be registered in this country. The system doesn't function the way it did during Soviet times, but it still works—sometimes. But Mark, this feels too easy, and believe me, nothing's been straightforward in this investigation so far."

"You better be careful with that church. You've been looking for that priest for a while, so he may well know you're coming. Don't trust anyone at the church. It must sound weird to hear me saying that, coming from the son of a Greek Orthodox priest. But there's something else, Cos. Something concerning Anastasia and your sister."

"Go ahead, Mark. Tell me," I say, bracing myself for whatever's on his mind.

"It's not so surprising. Well, it's not so surprising to me, anyway. Anastasia's been pushing to go home for a while now. But she's got some heavy PTSD from the kidnapping, and it will take a long time to subside even with therapy, right? She's bonded with your sister, and now doesn't trust anyone else. I mean no one. They're flying back to Athens, then on to Moscow together."

"What? That's nuts, Mark. Please tell me Zhirov or someone from their embassy will escort them back to

Russia once they arrive in Athens. We're on the verge of finding this killer, so this is the last thing we need right now. To expose not only Anastasia, but also Jennifer. The DPM likely knows we have Anastasia, and others will find out. Not good, Mark. You understand what I'm saying, right?" I'm trying to maintain my composure as I speak.

But Mark isn't calling the shots. He's not at fault. I thank him for the help and hang up, activating the Bureau computer to download the photo and check for any new internal messages in the system. Next, I type out a quick message for Sharon to send me photos of the individuals she briefed me on days earlier. Hopefully, she will soon be back in the office in Athens.

I decide not to call her directly on an open and unsecured line, particularly as Anastasia and Jennifer are about to depart Crete. Closing the office, I head out of the consulate.

Oksana is standing near our vehicle, waiting.

"Are you OK?" she asks.

We've been working with each other long enough for her to sense when something is off with her partner. Whether it's a sort of feeling, hunch, or intuition, I can't say.

"Yeah. All good, more or less. Anastasia's bonded with Jen; no surprise there. So much so that Anastasia trusts her and no one else! It's PTSD related, I think. Anyway, they'll soon head back to Russia via Athens. I don't like it, Oksana. There's still a killer out there, and we could expose Anastasia and Jennifer to danger needlessly. It wasn't my call.

"Apparently, Anastasia was getting very anxious and wanted to go home. I wish she could have given us a few more days. Well, it's out of our hands. Let's go find that priest. You drive."

I jump into the passenger side and close the door.

I'm not driving, just sitting there, along for the ride and no longer in control.

Perhaps I never was. If we can somehow get through this, I promise myself to never involve my sister in anything related to my work again. As we drive past the Church of the Savior of the Spilled Blood, I make the sign of the cross, saying a silent prayer that God and the fates will spare my sister and bring her back safely from Russia.

Oksana notices me making the sign, doing the same in the Russian Orthodox manner.

"I've got a photo of that priest, Oksana. Mark's father, the Greek Orthodox priest from San Francisco, found it. Apparently, someone misplaced it. When we left, he kept looking, praying to locate it. I'll show it to you when we arrive at the church."

Oksana nods, saying, "Open the glove box. I forgot. You ever shot a Makarov pistol? There's two of them: one for you, and one for me. Just don't tell anyone. Now you're a real 'militsionaire.' How does it feel, tavarish Special Agent?"

She laughs, and I reply, "Here, take the photo. I'll stay in the car. You're a local, Oksana. There's no point in me talking to anyone there. But if you see anyone even remotely resembling the photograph, please don't approach. Just come back to the car. Can you promise me that?"

"Sure. But relax, I know this church," she says as we pull up to the parking lot. "I lived in this area years ago. Don't forget I am from Saint Petersburg. One or maybe two priests were there. I remember an older one, actually. Perhaps he's still here."

At that, she opens the door.

"Oksana, don't show anyone the photo immediately. I hope he is there still," I say, feeling I should accompany her. But it's only a simple church, and not a dangerous nightclub packed with gangsters and thugs like the one in Athens, so I rationalize to myself.

I sit impatiently in the vehicle. The wooden framed church looks to be very old, not updated, but also not run down. There's a small cemetery on one side, and what appears to be a walled vegetable garden on the other. I notice a handful of parishioners, mostly women, entering the church and leaving after a few minutes. Probably, they go to say some prayers, and light candles.

They continuously make the sign of the cross as they enter and leave, and it's a wonder how the Bolsheviks— all non-believers, atheists—ever took the reins of power in such a country.

"Your photo is no good," Oksana says, startling me as I don't notice her approaching. Like some rookie, I was people watching, looking at the parishioners outside the church's entrance.

I feel embarrassed, hoping she didn't notice my startled reaction.

"How's that, Oksana? Stavros wasn't there?"

No, I actually found the elderly priest. I remembered him from years ago, but don't think he recognized me. Well, he told me there was a priest named Nikolai

Stavros, one who served at the parish a few years ago, but left. The priest said it was all rather strange, that he just sort of vanished one day. He didn't have many belongings; none of them do. They live simple lives, serving their congregation. So, anyway, they thought he would eventually return and that perhaps he had a family emergency to deal with and would reappear, but he never did.

"I then showed him the photo. He told me Stavros had hazel eyes, not the piercing blue ones in the shot. Do you think they sent us the wrong one? I suppose we could show it to the babushka at the Detski Dom in Smolensk, but it would take a lot of time to travel back there."

Oksana is speaking fast, first in Russian, then switching to English.

She's talking so fast I'm having trouble following her.

I tell her, "Stop, Oksana. Let's talk this through, slowly. But assume the photo is correct. It is the image of the priest who baptized Corey Gordon, the same one who was there in San Francisco around the time of Corey's murder in Omaha. What does that tell you? Can you infer or draw any conclusion or theory? Don't talk yet, just think."

Her eyes close as she's processing what I've just said.

I have my theory, of course, but don't want to say or suggest anything to influence her thought processes. So, we sit in the vehicle in silence. Finally, after several minutes, she speaks.

She asks, "Assuming the photo is the right one, it's of the priest who was in San Francisco, the one who claimed to be Nikolai—well, in the U.S., Nicolas Stavros. On the assumption the elderly priest I just spoke with here isn't mistaken and his memory's accurate, it means the priest who baptized Corey isn't Nicolas Stavros. That priest may not be one at all, but an imposter; he could use the identity of Stavros. But where is the real Stavros? What has happened to him? And who is this imposter?" She pauses, waiting for my response.

"If we start from the assumption that the photo is accurate, it accurately depicts the priest who baptized Corey. And the elderly priest you just spoke with is correct that the one he knew was Nikolai Stavros ... Well, one of them must be an imposter. My gut tells me it's the one who baptized Corey, that he's the imposter, not the other. The real Stavros is gone, disappeared, perhaps dead, even. But we really don't know, do we? Do I think this alleged imposter had something to do with the murders of Yelena and Corey, and the abduction of Anastasia?"

She just looks at me and shrugs.

I have another theory, one I decide not to share with Oksana. It's that this imposter priest is connected to Victoria's deceased father, and possibly to the unnamed Bureau source Sharon Austin discovered in one of their sensitive databases.

The pressing question is what's the next step for us? If the elderly priest is right, then we have a new wrinkle in this investigation. But it could send us down a rabbit hole and lead us nowhere.

Oksana is still silent and I can sense she is processing it all.

We are peeling back the layers of the onion, but is it leading us anywhere?

Perhaps it's time to end this investigation; it just isn't solvable.

Maybe we missed something or the break I have been hoping for hasn't come and never will.

We are both now sitting on a small bench in the empty church parking lot, gazing up at the cross on the church's roof, hoping, praying. I eventually break the silence.

"Oksana, is it possible this imposter is a killer? Our killer? That he killed Corey, Yelena, the real Nikolai Stavros, and that he's been playing with us? He's one step ahead and could be out there somewhere in the shadows and might have changed his identity by now.

"Something else comes to mind. Did this imposter priest murder Yelena by accident? Did he intend to kill Anastasia? They looked and dressed alike, remember? And they had the same Russian cross tattoo but Yelena's was far more recent, of course, not from the adoption home.

"Yelena wasn't adopted. But who was behind Anastasia's abduction? Are the murders of Yelena and the abduction of Anastasia even related? Perhaps not. Did someone grab Anastasia that night for her eventual ransom, not necessarily for her rescue? How crazy would this be: a criminal saves the life of someone about to be killed, and then holds the person for ransom or as a bargaining chip? Sounds crazy, right? Or maybe not? But the thugs and that retired contract killer at the nightclub could have done precisely that."

She eyes me, slowly pondering my words.

I continue, "After all, Dudayev more or less confessed to knowing where Anastasia was being held, after you pummeled the living hell out of him. That's how it looked to me, that night, from my low vantage point on the floor of the men's room. Dudayev knew Anastasia was alive, and where she was being held in the bowels of that church. Oksana, why is this case, this investigation, linked to so many churches? Never mind, don't answer that," I tell her.

Oksana just looks at me. I'm not sure if she is following me, or if my Russian and English shifting back and forth is too much for her to process or make sense of.

I realize I'm rambling, talking in a stream-of-consciousness manner.

She calmly places her hand on my arm.

"Stop. Breathe. Let it go. Let it all go. The fates will decide. If it's your destiny—no, our destiny—to solve this case, we will. This is Russia. Nothing is easy, nothing is as it first appears. Don't you know that by now?" she asks, shaking her head.

Now, Oksana is the teacher, and I am the pupil—grasshopper, as my U.S. Customs Service partner, Rich Marino, would call me. The role change is not so surprising. I am working in her city, in her country, speaking her native tongue, not mine. My thoughts shift to Jennifer. I wish she were here with me, so I could bounce these new theories off of her. She's much more comfortable, and experienced, jumping in and out of rabbit holes. I wouldn't dare mention rabbit holes in her presence, as she would not find the comment amusing, more likely insulting. Another thought comes to mind. I hadn't reached out to Adam Wheaton for some time. He was my only and most reliable contact in the BAU. I need to brief him and get his take on what we have since learned, and see if he has any theories, updates or other news from his side. If our theory — that is, one of our theories — is correct, the killer is posing as a priest, a Russian Orthodox priest. The killer may have also learned that Anastasia is alive and well, and will soon return to Russia, where he may already lie in wait for her, stalking her and my sister.

They could both be in grave danger.

The thought sends a chill down my spine. I am not in control. Oksana may be right; it's up to the fates, not us, to decide as we are mere mortals. I push the dark thoughts out of my head.

"Oksana, we need to get back to Moscow. I don't think there's much more we can do here in Saint Petersburg," I tell her. She agrees and we soon head for the train station.

We reserve our own first-class carriage for the return trip to Moscow.

After we settle in, I call Wheaton, and brief him on the latest developments, and our shifting theories, sharing the earpiece with Oksana so she can listen in and take part.

"So, neither of you have mentioned your theory as to the motive, the why. These aren't sexual gratification, spontaneous thrill kills, Cos and Oksana. I think we can all agree on that. This guy may be a serial killer, but there may also be a motive behind the murders you've uncovered so far. I don't know if finding the motive—the why—will lead you to him. OK, enough on that topic for now. Let's step back for a moment. Let's assume he meant to kill Anastasia, but mistook her for Yelena, and she became his victim. By accident, bad timing, bad luck, whatever you want to call it. They switched hair colors, remember? I saw their photos. Yelena and Anastasia bear a striking physical resemblance to one another. So, he could have been confused."

"Adam, Anastasia is heading back to Moscow. If she was the intended target, then she is still in grave danger, isn't she?" I ask. I don't tell Wheaton that my sister is accompanying Anastasia all the way back to Russia from Crete.

"It's difficult to say, Cos. He's not the sort of person to panic, and act emotionally or irrationally, but there is a good possibility that he knows by now you are tracking —hunting—him. And don't forget how he spoke to the San Francisco priest, Mark's father, about his so-called mission, his obsession, I submit," Wheaton says, and pauses. "The guy's committed." His wheels are turning.

We both remain silent, not wanting to interrupt his stream-of-consciousness analysis.

"The adoption home, and perhaps the tattoo of the cross, are the most important commonalities between the victims. Those victims we know. But we need to be careful not to draw conclusions prematurely. The tattoos could be purely coincidental. But the victims being from same the adoption home, well, that's no coincidence for me as a profiler."

"OK, Adam, so he's committed to his mission. What exactly is his mission, Adam? To kill adopted children from Detski Dom 57 because they have tattoos of a Russian Orthodox Cross? That sounds bizarre, even ridiculous, Adam. What do those victims have in common besides Detski Dom 57, and the tattoos?" I ask, turning to Oksana. She is silent.

"I don't know, Cos. I honestly don't. Look, I am in Lyon, at Interpol HQ for a few more days, working here on some unrelated stuff, but I sent a message out to several of my Interpol contacts, the ones I know. Several of them work in Western and Eastern Europe. I kept the message vague, asking if they knew of any murder victims who had a Russian Orthodox style cross on their inner thigh. It won't compromise anything, so relax, keep breathing. Hey, I heard from my contact in Hungary earlier today, but he wants me to call him. He probably didn't understand my email request. The guy is a talented investigator. His English is improving but needs a lot of work. When we hang up, I will call him. You'll be traveling on the train for a few more hours, right?" he asks.

"Yeah. We've got another four or five hours, Adam. The afternoon train makes several more stops along the way back to Moscow. We're just hanging out here with the *na-road,* the people. More or less. After all, I'm a spoiled American, and we're sitting here in a first-class carriage."

"While you two are sitting there looking out your first class window, and dozing off, think about motive -motives. You've been tracking or trying to track this guy for some time. What does he want? What does he need? Which motives can we rule out? If any. Revenge, money, lust, power, etc. Anastasia's father is a powerful figure in Russia. The same goes for the father of Corey Gordon. That's likely not coincidental, but what does it mean? Well, it's too bad you can't ask Father Stavros why he gave those particular children in the adoption home the tattoo. That might answer a lot of questions. But if this maniac—the term the Russians use for a serial killer—is an imposter, and killed the real Father Stavros, we'll never know, not from the real priest. But this maniac knows; he knows the why. He could even have a list he is working from. Who is next on the list? We don't know. Only he knows. Well, I take that back. Someone else could have given him the list, and he is carrying out his assignment, for whatever reason."

Oksana cuts in. "Adam, you're giving me a headache. But we will catch him. You helped profile several other cases in Russia, so I heard. We will solve this one together," Oksana tells him. I do not know why she is now feeling more confident.

After our phone call with Wheaton, I'm feeling less optimistic about our chances.

Perhaps it's because my sister is soon to accompany Anastasia back to Russia to this land of riddles, puzzles, and enigmas, most of which are neither understandable nor solvable.

I feel no closer to finding the magic key to unraveling, to unlocking this case than I was when Ben Nolan at FBIHQ first handed me the file in his office days ago.

Chapter 18

"Your phone," Oksana says as she shakes my shoulder to awaken me. With the rocking of the train, I had fallen asleep staring out of the coupé's window. "It's ringing."

"Hey, this may be your lucky day. You listening?" Wheaton asks. I had fallen into a deep sleep since the phone call with Wheaton a couple of hours ago.

"Yes, Adam. I'm awake and listening. What is it?" I ask.

"I finally got hold of Atilla, Atilla Orosz, from Budapest. He's Interpol's liaison representative for Hungary, the one I told you about."

"OK. So. What, Adam?"

"He told me the police, this special task force dealing with serious crime, are investigating a murder. The murder of a young woman. She and her family had emigrated from Russia a few years ago and were living quietly outside of Budapest," he tells me, as I attach the ear plugs so Oksana can listen.

"Adam, it's interesting, but we can't involve ourselves in such an investigation, however tragic it may be, of a person just because they were from Russia," I tell him.

"No. You don't understand. Give me a second. You are so impatient. I feel for Oksana. This poor young lady, Natasha, I think that is what Attila said was her first name. Well, she had a tattoo on her inner thigh. Although faded and almost invisible, the tattoo was a Russian Orthodox Cross. Her killer strangled her to death. The Hungarian investigators did a marvelous job processing the body and the entire crime scene. Perhaps the Academy, the International Law Enforcement Academy in Budapest, is paying dividends after all. No matter. It's something, right?" He asks.

"Yes, Adam. Go ahead," Oksana responds. She has a pen in hand and is taking notes as Adam speaks.

"There's more. Much more."

"OK. Yes, Adam. Tell us already. We are listening. What else?" I ask. I want him to hurry as our train is slowing down; we are close to the station in Moscow, and we will have to disembark in a matter of minutes.

"Atilla told me something else. I had asked him to query border and customs for any entries and exits for Victoria. Well, I asked all of my contacts to do the same. I know you didn't specifically ask, but I figured you wouldn't be too angry with me for doing that. Not surprising, Victoria arrived at Ferihegy Airport in Budapest a few days ago. Probably she is still in Hungary..." he tells us.

I can feel my pulse quickening, and Oksana is now gazing at the phone at hearing this fresh development.

"Adam, we're going to Budapest," I say, cutting him off. "We'll get on the next available flight out of Moscow. Can you come over to Budapest? If your supervisor at BAU pushes back, I can have Ben Nolan intervene."

"No. Please don't do that. I'll get permission, without having someone at FBIHQ intervene. That doesn't always go well, as you know," Wheaton says.

"It would be good for you to be there, to introduce us to this Atilla Orosz. Strange last name. You know what it means in Hungarian?" I ask.

"No. No idea. I don't speak Hungarian," he responds.

"Neither do I. But having spent some time at I-LEA, I noticed the word being used, well, interestingly. Long story, but the name Orosz is fairly common as a family name. But it also has a meaning: it means Russian. You can't make this stuff up, Adam. See you in Hungary. Let's all stay at the Marriott, the one on the river," I tell him as we end the phone call. It's time to pack up our belongings and leave the train, which has just reached its final destination.

As we walk along the train platform, I turn to Oksana.

"We need to find this Victoria. Can you convince your superiors to allow you to stay with the investigation? They should be pleased, no? After all, the DPM will soon have his daughter back. I can't imagine them pulling you off the investigation now. But, on second thought, I take that back. They could—" I say just as Oksana interrupts.

"I will handle it. I am not going anywhere except to Hungary, with you. Travel there doesn't require a visa for me. Can you cover my ticket again? Sorry, but our agency does not have funding like yours."

"Sure. I'll take care of it. It seems only fitting to be heading to Hungary. But this won't be some training exercise at I-LEA. Let's hope this is the break we've been looking for. And this time, we'll find this Victoria and not allow her to slip away. I'm so tired of this woman and her games."

The next morning, we arrive at the newly remodeled Ferihegy Airport. The country had undergone a dramatic transformation in recent years with the parting of the Iron Curtain.

A new generation of reform-minded leaders took control and tossed out the communists in a matter of days, moving the Lenin statutes and Soviet era monuments to a park well outside of the city's limits. Hungarians rejected communism and fully embraced capitalism.

There were new restaurants and businesses opening everywhere.

Their language was another matter.

While I had several short-term assignments as an instructor at the Budapest I-LEA, I had couldn't manage more than a few simple phrases in Hungarian. I had concluded the language was beyond my brain's ability and capacity. Russian had been a difficult enough challenge for me, with its six case endings; Hungarian had over twenty. The Hungarian people were welcoming and friendly to Americans and to foreigners. They tolerated their Russian visitors but were a fiercely independent people. Moscow's oppressive orbit and its long, dark days of management were now a relic of the past. Hungary's establishment of the International Law Enforcement Academy (I-LEA) in Budapest signaled its transition to a full-fledged democracy governed by democratic principles and the rule of law. The FBI had the primary responsibility for organizing trainings at I-LEA, for the countries of Eastern Europe and the former Soviet Republics. The Bureau had even opened a new office, a legal attaché office, to help support the Hungarians in confronting the growing threats from transnational organized crime, Eastern European and Russian predominantly. I had met the new legal attaché, Mitch Boyton, during my previous trips teaching at I-LEA. Boyton is waiting patiently for us as we clear border control. He was a gifted linguist who had somehow mastered Hungarian, along with several other languages, to include German, Spanish, and French. They assigned him to Vienna, Austria, and he accepted the assignment to Hungary as a challenge. I heard his family wasn't thrilled about the transfer. The Bureau was fortunate to have such talented and motivated people and families, willing to live and work overseas and transfer according to the needs of the Bureau.

"Welcome to Hungary, Cos, and nice to meet you, Oksana," he says as we embrace. He knew some Russian, and didn't hesitate to use it, introducing himself to Oksana in her native language.

"Please don't speak Greek to him, Oksana. He probably knows Greek more than I. I hear Wheaton is already here. What's our schedule?" I ask.

"You can first check in at the Marriott, and then I'll drive you to the meeting with Atilla. I can stay and interpret for you, if you would like. It's your call."

"Mitch, that would be great. Adam said Atilla speaks some English, but you never know. Besides, it might be good for you to have another contact inside Hungarian law enforcement, right?" I ask. I hope we can keep Boyton, and that some other pressing matter doesn't pull him away—many such matters undoubtedly exist.

Boyton tells us we'll have a couple of hours to kill before our planned meeting with the gumshoe detective, as he drops us off at the entrance to the Marriott Hotel, on the banks of the majestic Danube, walking distance from the heart of the rebuilt shopping area. The hotel had been renovated, but its dark gray exterior still reflected the drab and dreary days of communist domination. Guest rooms overlooking Buda's scenic riverfront were the hotel's nicest feature. The Pest side of the city had taken quite a beating during the Second World War as the advancing Soviet Red Army shelled the entrenched Nazi occupiers from their high vantage points across the river on the Buda side. The 'Freedom Statue' on Gellert Hill was visible from most of the city, as it stood on the highest vantage point. It was one of the few monuments left standing from the era of Soviet domination after World War II. We use the downtime to stretch our legs and stroll through the pedestrian area, which is still in the process of transformation and reconstruction after World War II. It's as though the Second World War ended a few months ago, not so many decades earlier. The communists didn't see the reconstruction of the shops and cafés as a priority and left the place unattended and neglected.

It was only now showing signs of new life.

We stop at the world famous Gerbeaud Café, known for its fine pastries and refined coffees of another era when Hungary was part of the Austro-Hungarian Empire.

It was one of the few buildings left intact after the relentless shelling of the city.

The two hours of downtime help to refresh and energize us.

We will need to be at our best, ready and focused for whatever awaits. Boyton is right on time to pick us up from the hotel entrance, and we quickly set off to meet with the detective.

Boyton gives me a quick backgrounder on Atilla Orosz as we walk up the stairs to his third-floor office at the Budapest Police HQ. "Atilla can be moody, so let me try to first break the ice with him in Hungarian," Boyton tells me. He then turns to me, lowers his voice and adds, "He's not too keen about Russians. They killed his father and uncle in the '56 uprising against the Soviets. They were both arrested, tried, and summarily executed. I think he's unhappy about our working with Russians. Just for you to be aware, OK?"

Atilla seems preoccupied with other matters as we enter his office. A mass of files and loose papers covers his desk. It's chaos. The office itself is a dreary place with old broken-down furniture and stained walls looking as though they haven't seen a fresh coat of paint for many years. Atilla Orosz strikes me as the Hungarian version of a typical NYPD homicide detective: grizzled; chain smoking; coffee drinking; and—of course—overweight.

This guy has seen more than one cold dead body in his career. He immediately fixates on Oksana, giving her the once-over several times, from head to toe.

Boyton introduces all of us and then switches into Hungarian. Their discussion is a mystery to me; however, their body language reveals things aren't going well. I wait for Boyton to translate the issue, whatever it is, into English for us, so we can address it.

Their heated discussion might well be about our access to his homicide file.

Finally, Boyton turns to the three of us sitting there, waiting—Adam Wheaton, Oksana and me—to explain what they've been arguing about for the past ten minutes.

"Colonel Orosz isn't sure he has the authority to grant us access to the case file. He may need authorization from his superiors, and perhaps from the prosecutor as well. He wants to know when we will submit our formal request for legal assistance to the Foreign Ministry," Boyton tells us.

Before Boyton can continue, Oksana cuts him off. "Please tell the Colonel I would like a drink," Oksana says, smiling at Orosz.

Boyton looks at me, confused. I think I know what Oksana is up to. In fact, I'm pretty sure I understand what she is doing. We are both on the same page, so it seems. This Detective Colonel is in one of his moods. He doesn't want to hand over his case file to us simply, especially not to a female Russian MVD officer. That Oksana collaborates with us, the FBI, doesn't matter to him.

He doesn't see it that way.

To him, she's an attractive woman, but foremost, she is a Russian. Russians killed his father and uncle. In the end, he may cooperate with us, but it will be on his terms, not ours. We don't have the luxury of time to come back later, or in a few days, when his mood improves.

"Go ahead, Mitch. Tell him. Tell him we'd all like a drink. I know it's morning. Just do it. Translate it," I say.

Whether Boyton understands the nature of our request, I am doubtful, but there's no point in arguing. Oksana is right to call for time out, for a drink. Why not? It just might work.

The colonel smiles. He stands up from behind his desk, walks over to a wall cabinet, and pulls out a bottle along with four glasses. His secretary, a striking brunette with long legs squeezed into her short skirt, soon enters the room carrying a tray of cookies and candies.

Orosz sits down in the empty chair around the table with us. "First, we toast," he says in English, as he pours the mysterious dark liquid into the four glasses and passes them to us. It is the one and only Hungarian herbal liqueur, 'Unicum,' created in 1790 and made from a secret formula of over forty herbs, produced by the Zwack family.

I immediately recognize the bottle from my previous time in Hungary.

"Don't touch glasses," Boyton hurriedly tells us in English, the three of us lifting our glasses for a toast.

"And do any of you know why?" Orosz asks, in English, as he raises his glass.

"Of course," Oksana immediately responds as she turns toward Orosz. "Hungarians vowed to abstain from clinking glasses for 150 years from 1849, when Austrian generals clinked their glasses to celebrate their victory against Hungarian warriors who died fighting valiantly for their country's independence."

How Oksana knows this obscure piece of Hungarian history is a mystery to me, but she's a graduate of I-LEA in Budapest. It's possible she heard about the custom during her time there.

Orosz nods and smiles. He looks pleased. "To the brave warriors," he says as he makes eye contact with each of us, before throwing the dark, powerful liquid down the back of his throat. We each do the same.

"Now, let's go eat. The café is around the corner. You will be my guests. We will have authentic Hungarian food, and discuss our future cooperation," Orosz tells us in Hungarian, with Boyton translating. Orosz stands up, returns the bottle of Unicum to its rightful place in the cabinet, and we walk out of his office, heading to the café. Oksana just looks at me. I am speechless. With her simple request for a drink, she's turned the tables on what looked to be a 'waste of time' meeting with this street smart, hardened Hungarian homicide detective. I realize Oksana is way smarter than I ever imagined, this Russian MVD partner of mine.

They have already set the food out on the table in the small separate room, which the Colonel must have reserved ahead of time. There's an assortment of sausages, meats, and more meat, to include plenty of goose liver, a Hungarian favorite. This is no country for cholesterol level watchers. Atilla takes his seat in the middle of the table. He is no stranger to this sort of food and insists we drink beer while he stays with his sparkling water. He tells us his doctor insisted he lose some weight, so this was the compromise.

No more beer, but everything else is acceptable.

Boyton takes a seat next to Atilla on his right side, so he can interpret, and Oksana takes the empty seat on his left. She will not leave this café without knowing everything this grizzled homicide detective knows about the murder of the young Russian girl.

Without us having to probe him, he begins.

"The victim was the adopted daughter of a wealthy Russian couple, Peter and Anna Zakharov. They settled in Hungary and were investors in several new business ventures here. No suspects, but the father likely had several enemies from his past. My sources tell me he made his fortune during the privatization days after the collapse of the Soviet Union," Orosz says and pauses as he reaches for a large piece of sausage with his fork.

"Colonel, is the family cooperating with you and your team?" I ask.

"Yes. We've got access to emails, cellular phone records, voice mails. My analysts are going through everything," Orosz says as I hear my phone ringing. I stand up and step outside to take the call.

It's Sharon Austin calling. "Is it a bad time? I've got some news for you. Mark's father confirmed the photo of the priest is accurate. Well, that is what Mark told me anyway."

"OK, good. What else, Sharon? I'm in the middle of a meeting with the Hungarian detective."

"Don't scream at me, please, but Jennifer's heading to Budapest. She accompanied Anastasia all the way back to Moscow, and the Russian MVD met them at the airport on arrival. Anastasia is no longer our problem; I guess that's a good thing. As soon as Jen heard you were in Hungary, she found a direct flight and is arriving there soon. She'll stay at the Marriott with you. I know you're probably not thrilled to hear this, but I think you're stuck with her until this is over."

"OK. I'll deal with my sister later. It's not your fault, Sharon. My sister isn't the easiest person to handle. Jennifer is going to do what Jennifer wants; forget about convincing her of anything, not when she's got her mind set," I tell her, as I end the call. I need to return to the café to hear what else Colonel Orosz has to say about his investigation. As soon as I enter the room, I notice Orosz speaking on his phone in Hungarian. He finishes the call and reaches for the full glass of beer the waiter has just placed on the table in front of Oksana. He takes the large glass in his hand, puts it to his lips, draining the entire contents in one long swallow. I guess he couldn't resist the cold beer after all, despite the doctor's advice.

"Let's go," he says in Russian, as he wipes his mouth with the back of his hand. "They're pulling a body out of the river. It may interest you." We follow him as he hurries through the restaurant, nods to the waiter, who nods back. I can only assume the Colonel has an open account at the café. In front of the café, we jump into two waiting vehicles and speed off, racing through the narrow winding streets of the city, blue lights flashing, sirens blasting, as we barely avoid unsuspecting pedestrians crossing the busy streets. Orosz's driver is laser focused on the road, with Atilla not bothering to use his seat belt, as he turns to speak with Oksana and me sitting in the back seat. I reach for the seat belt and realize there aren't any. I hope we won't need them.

"I am glad you two made a stop in my quiet territory," he tells us sarcastically as the vehicle spins hard right, tires screeching. I can smell the burning rubber. Laughing, he says, "Hopefully, you aren't bored in my city. I think seat belts are overrated. I've never used one. They aren't trustworthy." I can see several police vehicles and an ambulance stopped in the distance along the riverbank. We're close to the scene. The partially nude, bloated body is being pulled out of the river as we walk down the grassy embankment along the river. A small boy who looks to be only eight or nine is being interviewed by one detective at the scene.

Apparently, the boy was fishing along the bank and noticed the body tangled among some branches. The uniformed police and detectives all turn in unison toward Orosz as he barks out orders in Hungarian at them, now in charge at the scene.

"You've been looking for her for a while, and here she is," Orosz says as he leans over to examine her face as the body is on its back, with its distorted limbs.

Oksana and I are standing close to Orosz. Boyton and Wheaton are further back. Sadly, it's Victoria. She is barely recognizable, her body bruised and battered by the strong river currents that swept her downstream, rudely depositing her onto the rocky shoreline. If not for the tree branches, she may have drifted downstream much further, perhaps never to be found. I look at her body for any obvious signs as to the cause of death. We are standing there silent, perhaps waiting for Victoria herself to explain what caused her untimely death. I had seen dead bodies at crime scenes before, but water does strange things to submerged bodies. Water sometimes preserves the bodies surprisingly well, and other times, it leaves them completely unrecognizable and decayed. The body looked as though it could have been in water for a few days, the skin mostly intact but stretched to the point of bursting. The unforgettable odor of decaying flesh hits me as they lift and place her remains in the bag. They carry the body to the coroner's office waiting vehicle.

I turn to Boyton. "Tell Atilla we would like to have a look at the body in the coroner's examination room before they do an autopsy. Victoria was our best chance to unravel this case. Now she's dead. She may still lead us to the killer. This was no accidental drowning or suicide jumping off a bridge into the river. She knew too much. Someone killed her for a reason. This feels personal now." Boyton gives me a puzzled look.

"What part of that do I translate?" he asks.

"I, rather, Oksana and I need a few minutes with the body before the medical examiner. But be polite and deferential; it's Atilla's call. We can't push this on him. Just tell him whatever you think will work." Boyton walks over to Orosz, who is busy barking out orders. It looks as though Boyton has interrupted the processing of the scene. I can see them talking back and forth. Attila appears to be nodding.

"He said it's OK. He'll meet us at the coroner's office once they're done with their interviews, photographs of the area. Let's go. He told me his driver will take us there."

They recently renovated and equipped the examination room, making it surprisingly clean. One of the staff leads us to her body laid out on the examination table. Oksana and I put on gloves, and I slowly unzip the body bag.

"Oksana, try not to touch her, but let's go slowly from the top of her head. We've got a few minutes." I look at her eyes for signs of strangulation, but the submersion of her body in the murky water makes it impossible for me to see the usual telltale sign of strangulation, red spots in the eyes, known as petechiae. There is some bruising on the neck area. But I am no medical examiner. They could be post-mortem, of course.

"What is that?" Oksana asks, pointing at the body's upper leg. "Is it bruising or a tattoo?"

"It's a tattoo, Oksana," I say, as I stare at the mark on the thigh. "Yes, the cross, the Russian Orthodox cross. Not so surprising, given what we know or think we know about Victoria. She may have gotten the tattoo as a young adult. But we can't draw any conclusions," I say as I photograph the tattoo using the camera that Boyton lent me from his office. "I'll remind Atilla about blood samples, vaginal swabbing, the works."

"Cos, this isn't the U.S.," Oksana reminds me. "This is Hungary. I wouldn't say or suggest anything to Atilla. He's an experienced homicide investigator. We'll have to rely on him and the medical examiner. He won't react well to your recommendations or advice."

"Yeah. You're right," I respond. "The Bureau has already provided a lot of equipment to their forensic lab, along with training. Let's hope it will pay off." I continue with the visual examination, looking for any entry and exit wounds from a bullet. "What is that?" I ask, pointing at the piece of string in her groin area.

"It's nothing. Loose twine that got caught up in her pubic hairs as her body floated downstream, right?" Oksana suggests.

"Not sure," I respond as I look closer.

"Sorry, Dennis. It's how to say, *sal-vet-ka*. A sanitary napkin most likely, I think," Oksana tells me.

"Can you pull it out?" I ask Oksana.

"What? Why? You said we shouldn't touch the body, right?" she asks, looking annoyed, perplexed, and a bit disgusted at my request.

"I know, Oksana. Can you just do it, please? It doesn't feel right, as a man, for me to do that. I'm not sure what it is. Just do it, OK?" I am pushing the bounds, not only asking Oksana to remove what maybe nothing more than a tampon, but to tamper with the body, removing something that could have evidentiary value. Oksana slowly pulls on the cord, as an object slowly emerges. She gasps.

"What is this?" she asks. A small metallic cylinder a few centimeters emerges. Oksana looks at the object, fascinated, but confused.

"It's, I don't know the English word, Oksana. It's a *plan*. That's the French term. Prisoners used to hide these things in their, well, you can imagine where. In the U.S., incarcerated gang members would use them to hide cash, valuables, encrypted codes, anything that would fit inside the tiny container."

"And can you tell me—" Oksana asks.

I cut her off. "How I know this? Well, it's from a movie, Papillon, that I watched as a kid. The French prisoners in Guyana used them. Years later, during my time at the Bureau in Kansas City, I learned that several

U.S. prisoners in Leavenworth, Kansas's federal penitentiary had such objects hidden in their rectums. They were more sophisticated, in a way. The containers, the *plans*, were made of plastic, not metal. It was harder for the prison staff to detect them by X-ray."

I find a sealable plastic bag on a counter and quickly place the plan inside, stuffing it into my pocket without the attendant noticing. Oksana just looks at me.

"OK. We're finished here," I say louder so that Boyton and Wheaton can hear. They've been waiting patiently for us in the next room. We toss our gloves into the trash, wash our hands, as the technician zips up the body bag. The medical examiner is already on his way to the office to conduct the autopsy.

"What were you two doing in there?" Boyton asks. I can tell by the tone of his voice he is curious, perhaps suspicious. I doubt he could have seen me take the plan but might have overheard Oksana's gasp at seeing the strange cylindrical object emerge from the body.

"Nothing. Really, nothing. Mitch, please keep in contact with Atilla. I'm sure the coroner will brief him about the autopsy once it's done. Toxicology results will take a while. But the cause of death—even the preliminary finding from the coroner—it's important for us to know. OK?" I ask. He nods.

"Look, I'm happy to help. Just don't get me fired."

"Relax, Mitch. You'll be fine. Just have the driver take us back to the Marriott. You can get on with your day. Thanks for your help, Mitch. I owe you one."

Oksana and I sit quietly in the vehicle as we head back to the hotel. Victoria is dead. Was it suicide or murder? We may never know. The strange object, the plan, may hold the clue, but with Victoria, nothing was a given. This woman, now deceased, was a mystery from the moment I spotted her in the Athens nightclub, the double of my wife. I hope the plan contains something useful to help us unravel the reason for her death and guide us to the killer.

There may be nothing inside, nothing of evidentiary value. Oksana stares out the window, in thought. There is plenty to reflect upon on this strange day, which is far from over.

We still need to open the plan.

I do not know what might be inside and prevent myself from drifting down the rabbit hole, considering the endless possibilities: did the killer insert the plan for us to find?

"Oksana, let's go back to that café, Gerbeaud. We can get a quiet corner table, and..." I tell her, as she interrupts.

"Find our next clue, our last clue? No. It won't be that easy. We both know that. Don't we?" she asks as she continues to look aimlessly out of the car window. "But what choice do we have? Now, to open that plan, as you call it? When does this end? How does it end?" she asks, turning toward me in the back seat. She looks exhausted.

"Like you told me, Oksana, more than once: if it's our destiny to solve this thing, we will. It's not up to us, is it?" I ask.

She looks at me, smiles, and nods.

I need her focused and ready. This case, and this day, are far from over.

Chapter 19

"I am starting with cake. The dark chocolate one," Oksana tells the waiter, as she points to the strikingly dark looking layered cake in the display case.

"I'll take the same. And two cappuccinos to start," I add. It just seems like the right way to begin or to end such a day, still our first day in Hungary.

It feels as though we've already been here for a week.

I head to the restroom to first clean the plan, and my hands. Oksana is looking intensely at me when I sit down. She knows what I'll do next, as I slowly and discreetly unscrew the metallic cylinder. Inside is a small cloth. I pull out the cloth and look inside. Something's there, or it may be my own eyes deceiving me in the soft and flickering café light.

I try to shake loose whatever's inside, and it's what I suspect.

Diamonds, or what appear to be diamonds, several of them.

Some stones look fully polished, but several appear unfinished, still in a rough state.

I had seen such stones before, during the Golden ADA investigation. These were similar in size, two to four carats, I estimate. "They're not all the same, Oksana," I tell her, as I don't know if she's ever seen loose stones before. "The café light might be affecting them, but some of these stones have a slight yellow tint," I add.

From my prior experience in the Golden ADA case, I knew natural stones were superior to their lab-grown competitors. The yellow color of synthetic stones was because of nitrogen remaining inside. Nature took much more time to produce diamonds and did a better job than any lab could manage. Still, naturally occurring yellow diamonds existed, and were quite rare. Depending upon the color and clarity, the value of such stones could range dramatically. Despite all I had learned during the Golden ADA investigation, the stones and the secretive diamond business remained largely a mystery to me.

"Why?" I ask Oksana before she can pose the question. "Well, why not? The stones are small, easily concealable, and are extremely valuable. I'm no expert, Oksana, but this tiny amount of stones could be worth well over $200,000, perhaps much more. And how did Victoria come to possess such stones? That is a mystery we may never understand. I'll hand these over to the Bureau, all of them. They're cursed, Oksana. We don't want these. Oh, and I don't think the killer inserted this plan. He would have taken the diamonds, no? If he knew." I'm disappointed the plan doesn't contain the clue or clues I'd hoped it would.

Victoria likely kept the stones as insurance, using them if she got into trouble or needed money—they were valuable and easily converted into cash.

Or was Victoria nothing more than a courier transporting the stones for someone else? And was our discovery leading us nowhere, down yet another dead-end rabbit hole?

Oksana extends her hand toward the opened plan. "Can I see it, please?" she asks. I screw it back together and hand it over to her. "It's evidence, Oksana. And so are its contents. We will together turn everything over to the Legat Office here in Budapest. They'll package it up and send it off to our lab for analysis, the plan, along with the diamonds. Not sure their examination—their analysis—will lead to anything, but we'll be done with it, at least from our side. I'll probably get polygraphed again. It's not every day the FBI's laboratory receives loose diamonds. Hey, no big deal, I'm used to polygraphs," I tell her, laughing, though only slightly.

She looks up at me, then turns her attention back to the plan.

Her fingers are slender, and she reaches her index finger deep inside.

"Sorry, no secret compartment in there, Oksana. That's all. No magic, nothing. Another dead end," I say. I try not to feel deflated but can't help it. The plan is nothing more than a useless rabbit hole, a distraction, and a waste of our time.

"Really, are you sure?" she asks, as her long, slender finger has grabbed hold of something inside. Paper neatly rolled up. I had missed it entirely. She carefully pulls the paper out and slowly unrolls it. It's likely a liner to help cushion the stones. Nothing more, I tell myself.

"There is writing on this paper," she tells me as she hands it to me. "In Russian, and look who's shown up, just in time, I suppose," she adds as she is discreetly signaling them to come to our corner table.

"You've got to be kidding me," I comment as I look up to see Jennifer and Sharon approach our table. They pull up two chairs from a nearby table.

Jennifer is quick in response, glancing towards Sharon, as she asks, "How? It's a straightforward decision. First, there is no way I'm leaving Sharon behind in Athens; there's a perfectly good office here in Budapest if she needs that. And you're not exactly hard to find. All I had to do after we checked in to the hotel was to ask them where the best pastries and coffees were within walking distance, oh, and the most luxurious, where a spoiled American, my brother, might go. Gerbeaud Café was the response in unison from the reception staff. They thought I was hysterically funny. I think they knew I was talking about you; after all, we do have the same last name."

Sharon jumps in and asks, "What are you two up to? The only person we're missing is Georgia, but don't count that woman out. I wouldn't be surprised if she appeared. So, tell us, my dear Odysseus, what are you two looking at so attentively that you barely noticed us walking up to your table?"

After they order cakes and coffees, I quietly brief Jennifer and Sharon on the events of our fateful day, a tragic day for Victoria. "Look at this paper. It's delicate and thin, so please handle it with care. It's in Russian,

Sharon, so you may need help in translation. The print is tiny but clear. Can I borrow your reading glasses, Sharon?" I ask, as she digs into her purse and hands me the glasses. They seem to work as magnifying glasses. Oksana pulls her chair closer as I unfold the paper.

"There are several columns," I say, as my eyes slowly adjust to the tiny Cyrillic lettering. "It's some sort of list. I think the column on the left contains dates, well, days and months. OK, the next column: names, first and patronymic, and family names. There's yet another column squeezed in here, cities and years." I pull back from the list.

The print is so small it's straining my eyes.

Oksana moves the paper in front of her chair. Her head is nearly touching the table.

"I can see it better this way. Yes, it's a list of names. Not just any names. I recognize several. Anastasia is here, so are her father, and Corey Gordon as well," she says and pauses. "Nyet," she nearly screams and covers her mouth. "Natasha, Natasha Zakharova, and her father, Peter, are on the list." She pushes the list back in front of me.

Sharon moves her chair next to mine. "I need to take this list to the office and run these names. Or at least I'll need you to translate everything into English. Are there names you don't recognize?" Sharon asks.

"Yes, several. There has to be what...OK, let me count," I tell her, as I silently count out each name. "Yes, twelve names in the same column as Anastasia, Corey, and Natasha. I do not know what the years on the right-hand side mean: 1980, 1981, 1982, and these cities. But it fits.

"Natasha, Budapest; Corey, San Francisco; and Anastasia, Athens. Although someone murdered Corey in Omaha, far from San Francisco," I tell them. My mind is now racing, trying to make sense of the names, dates, and cities listed on this small piece of paper I would never have found if not for Oksana.

Sharon places her hand firmly on my shoulder. "Stop. I know what you're doing. I know what you're thinking. You're not the analyst; I am. If this is a death list, a list of victims, then who's next? That's the real question. It's the only question, isn't it?"

Sharon is looking at all of us around the table.

Everyone nods in unison.

Jennifer looks intensely at me as she speaks.

"She's right, you know. The why, the how; none of that matters at the moment. We don't know who's next, nor do we know who else on that list this maniac priest may have already eliminated. Yes, there are many unanswered questions, plenty of them. And lots of theories, none of which can be proved. Leave all that aside for now. And as far as Victoria, while her death is tragic and very sad, she could have known the killer, perhaps even been involved with him, this imposter priest. It's possible she had a relationship with him. Was she trying to stop him? She could have been assisting him to find the victims on that list? We don't know. Perhaps it was a Faustian pact with the devil himself, to spare her biological daughter, Anastasia, in return for her help in locating others. Not saying that was the case, but we can't rule out anything, any scenario."

Jennifer raises the coffee cup to her lips and places it back down on the saucer without taking a sip. "So, the real question for us, for our task force sitting here in this stunningly beautiful café in the middle of Budapest, is who is his next victim and can we save that person and capture this killer before he strikes? That is the real question, the only question."

I've had enough. My head is aching. Jennifer and Sharon have raised valid points but I need time to think, alone. The diamonds, the missing Fabergé egg, Detski Dom 57, and its links to the secret KGB institute and the information from that sensitive database discovered by Sharon.

LAX pops into my mind. Is all of this linked in some alternative universe, somewhere in space, or is none of it related?

Oksana stands up and suddenly sits back down. She's so focused, it strikes me she's forgotten she's in a café, not in a classroom or office setting. "I have an idea. Please don't dismiss it, and don't laugh," she says as she looks around the table.

"No, Oksana. I respect you. We all respect you, so tell us about your idea. I'm spent, Oksana. It's been a long day. Go ahead," I tell her.

"We've got how many … Nine names on that list. Different cities, and these names in columns that make little sense to us. It will take a long time to locate everyone on the list, and we risk one or more of them being killed in the meantime. I will write out the nine names on a piece of paper. I want each of you to look at the names, only the names. Clear your minds of everything else. You following me?" she asks.

"Yes, Oksana. I think so. Go ahead, the floor is yours," I tell her. I do not know what she has in mind. Whether she's joking, I'm not sure. She looks quite serious.

"Focus. Read the names to yourselves. Allow your senses to speak to you. When you've decided upon the name, the one name, and write it down on this separate piece of paper."

She hands each of us small pieces of paper torn from Sharon's notebook.

This is nuts. But I keep the opinion to myself as my task force colleagues aren't smiling but staring at the list and concentrating. I want to laugh aloud, as this has to be a joke, some dark humor or a game to lighten things up, but it isn't. Oksana is deadly serious.

I figure Jennifer may have had private discussions with her about her own special 'gifts' and Oksana has now gone down that same path. My eyes scan the list. I write the name that first comes to mind. Why not? What other choice do I have at that moment?

"Give me your choices. I will not look at them tonight. It's late. We all need to rest. Tomorrow, we go to the Szechenyi thermal baths. We will know then what the fates have decided for us," Oksana says as she motions the waiter for the bill. We stroll back to the hotel.

Sharon says, "I'm skipping the baths tomorrow, Cos. I'll go to the office and see what I can find in our databases about these names. While you are relaxing and exercising at your baths, I'll be working as usual. Nothing really changes. No, seriously, Oksana's idea isn't that crazy. It's not so far from some of the stuff you've done in your own past, is it?" She laughs.

I figure she's referring to our exploits during the Golden ADA investigation or perhaps further back to the Geschke kidnapping case.

"Yeah, I suppose not. Goodnight, Sharon. Let's keep in touch. If you change your mind about the baths, let me know. We could all use a break. Well, it's the fates that will decide, huh?" I tell her as I close my hotel room door.

Sharon stops me from closing the door. "Wait. I need to talk to you for a couple of minutes. This was something I didn't want to discuss with others. First thing; your wife and daughter are heading to Rome. For whatever reason, and I think it's related to your daughter's studies, they are going to visit Pompeii and some other sites. They reached out to me a while ago. They want to surprise you in Athens. I think that was the plan. Your son, DJ, is still in New York with his cousins. Your wife told me not to say anything, but I thought you needed to know. The second item, this list you found on, well, inside Victoria. I'll check all of those names in every database I can access, but there's another issue here. I'm not sure why you didn't raise it with the others at the café …" Sharon says as I cut her off.

"Yeah. I know what you're going to say. That we have a duty to find everyone on that list and inform them, regardless of the possibility this list is a fake, nothing more than a figment of Victoria's own imagination. No matter, we have a strict obligation, a moral duty. They could face death, all of them, by them being on that list. So, for argument's sake, Sharon, say we identify and find all nine individuals, then we notify them they could be in imminent danger from an individual we have yet to identify, and for an unknown reason, beyond the fact these individuals were likely all adopted from Detski Dom 57 in Russia ... then what? We provide them with 24/7 protection until we find the killer? We know from investigation that several of the individuals on that list have a bit of baggage themselves. Look at Victoria; we still have no clue what she was really doing, nor why. This case is close to unsolvable. I hate to say that. And let's say we find everyone and notify them. This killer is patient and committed to his mission, whatever that is. He'll just go to ground, disappear, and emerge later, at a time of his choosing. Meanwhile, he could target and kill others, others not even on that list," I tell her.

Sharon is just sitting there, looking at me. She finally speaks. "I'm the intelligence analyst, Dennis. Your analyst. We've been through a lot together, and had some success despite overwhelming odds. Listen to me. I suspect this killer could be that Bureau source, the guy I referred to as Q; you remember our talk? My God, it feels like months ago since we had that conversation. If it's not that source, then it's someone in the circle around Victoria's deceased father, perhaps another scientist, biologist, someone like that."

"Sharon, it doesn't matter. We don't even have a photo of this source, and there is no way to get one either. Even if you could get your hands on those files, often there is no photo. I've never taken a photo of my sources. It's something we just don't do in the Bureau. The Bureau rarely takes photos of sensitive sources and files the pictures. That would be exceptional. And if you're thinking about putting out a notice through Interpol channels, forget it. That would be a waste of time. It will lead nowhere. We just need a break, a lucky break. Look, at least we rescued Anastasia. That is something, right?" I ask.

Sharon stands up from her chair. "OK. Enough for tonight. Get some rest. Go to your thermal baths. I'll head to the Budapest office tomorrow morning to run all of those names through every single database I can get access to. Let's not give up the ship, Odysseus, not yet. This voyage of yours is far from over. The gods will decide when this ends—how it ends, not us," she says as she closes my hotel door.

Chapter 20

The knock on my door jolts me awake. I look at my watch. It's already past nine a.m.

"Get ready, and bring all of your swim stuff. We're in the dining area, waiting for you," Jennifer tells me.

I was hoping to have a leisurely breakfast and head to the thermal baths in the afternoon but should have known better. My sister doesn't roll like that. She's one of those unique individuals who requires only a few hours of sleep each night.

"OK, Jen. But can you at least give me a few minutes to dress and come downstairs? The buffet breakfast at this hotel is amazing, the best yogurt and pastries in the world."

After breakfast, Oksana, Jen, and I walk to the metro station, Deak Ferenc Ter, to board the Metro Line 1 train, the oldest below ground metro line in all of continental Europe, which will take us directly to the Szechenyi thermal baths. A feeling of guilt washes over me as we sit in the restored 1890s train car, a moving museum heading to the baths. I push the feeling out of my head. After all, today is Sunday. We could all use some fresh air, exercise, and rest for a few hours. The metro stops close to the bath's ornate entrance gates. The Romans had discovered the heated springs centuries earlier, and the occupying Ottoman Turks later built a huge bath complex over the naturally occurring springs. Like the Russians, the Hungarians were true believers in the restorative powers of their spring waters for rheumatoid arthritis and an array of other ailments. The bath complex comprised several outdoor and indoor pools of varying temperatures. Large fountains and Roman statutes adorned several of the pools. They recently renovated the main building. They constructed the complex during Budapest's golden age at the turn of the twentieth century. There were separate changing rooms and private areas for massages. Hungarians of all ages frequented the baths, from small children to the elderly. The Hungarians welcomed visitors to their complex and were exceedingly polite and reserved. The complex is surprisingly quiet on this Sunday morning, but the crowds will no doubt arrive by early afternoon. There is no rough playing or running around the grounds allowed. It's just what we all need today. I soon spot several swimmers in the largest of the pools, swimming laps inside the dedicated swim lanes.

Oksana and Jennifer soon emerge from the changing room wearing fluffy white bathrobes. They will first have massages before swimming.

"After our massages, I am going to show Jennifer how to do banya—sauna. Your sister has never been to a sauna before," Oksana tells me, shaking her head in disbelief.

I just look at them both, hoping Oksana will not share any details from that time she and I were in the Russian banya. But it would be out of character for Oksana to share something so personal, even if it's with my sister.

"Go, enjoy the massage and the sauna. Take your time. I'll keep these chairs for us here by the pool, and swim some laps before the crowds arrive," I tell them. They smile and walk back toward the main building. I notice the Hungarians, men and women alike, staring at them as they stroll by. It's only human nature, so I figure.

After all, Oksana and Jennifer are both physically attractive young women, despite the puffy white bath robes they are wearing, concealing their trim physiques.

I grab my swim goggles and jump into the closest lane. The water is much colder than I had expected. It feels as though I have jumped into a bottle of salty mineral water and tastes like it. There are a few swimmers in the other lanes. They look like locals, taking their time, swimming at a leisurely pace. After three or four lengths, my body adjusts to the cold water, and my breathing settles down. It's been a while since I swam, the last time being the long swim with Oksana at the beach in Athens.

I decide not to count laps or keep time on my watch. There's no clock on the nearby wall; this is a spa meant for relaxation and rejuvenation, not for athletic competition. I spot the wall to prepare for a flip turn, when I realize this is not that sort of pool. It would be rude and look ridiculous to execute a flip turn in such a pool meant only for relaxation. Instead, I slow down, touch the wall, and slowly push off for the next lap. I look down my swim lane, which had been empty, and see another swimmer entering the lane at the far end. She's wearing mirrored goggles and a swim cap, a strict requirement for all swimmers at the complex. Since I'm not familiar with the swim lane etiquette at this pool, I wait to see if the swimmer will stay to the right side of the lane, so we can both swim in a counterclockwise direction, anticipating that other swimmers may soon arrive and join us. To my relief, she stays to the right, and I decide it's safe for me to continue with my laps. I let my mind focus on technique and breathing, blocking out all other thoughts. It's all in my mind that the spring water has a therapeutic effect. The Hungarians fervently believe in the healing power of their spring waters, and for that reason alone, it works. It's mind over matter, I convince myself.

The swimmer sharing the lane is moving faster than I first thought. After deciding to execute a flip turn, I push off the wall with force to create distance between us. I'd rather not allow this Hungarian woman who comes for her weekly therapeutic swim to overtake me in this relaxation pool. I find it hard to maintain this pace, which I know I can't sustain much longer, but the swimmer is still catching up to me. Perhaps she is a professional athlete who has come to the thermal baths as a break from her normal training routine on this pleasant, summery Sunday.

The swimmer continues to gain on me, lap after lap. I execute flip turns, lap after lap. She is gaining. She will soon pass me, mid lap. *Let it go, let her go*, a voice inside tells me. I almost feel embarrassed as I decide to stop at the wall for a break, and move to the side, allowing the swimmer to execute her turn to continue. I'm spent. She's a far better swimmer. Unexpectedly, she pulls up and stops at the wall. I can't help but look at her. Her body glistens and her figure is flawless, partially submerged in the water. She politely smiles at me. I take a few deep breaths, assuming she will continue her laps, and I'll continue with mine, once she is well ahead of me down the swim lane. She's made her point, and I've set my ego aside. This woman is obviously a far better swimmer than I'll ever be, at a level I'll never come close to reaching.

"It's a small world; what do your Russian friends like to say? *Mir tes-en?* The world is tight," she says, and laughs. The accent, the face, even behind the mirrored goggles covering her eyes. It's her, Kandyse Brandt. She has left me not only breathless, but speechless. Before I can respond, she places both her hands up on the side of the pool and effortlessly lifts her body up on to the pool deck. I am still in the water, looking up at her standing on the pool deck above. My breathing is slowing, but my heart is still racing, the blood flowing to replenish my oxygen starved muscles.

"Will you join me when you're finished? I see your things over at that table. I will be there, waiting for you," Brandt tells me. Nodding is all I can manage, still trying to catch my breath. I push off the wall and resume my swim, this time at a slow pace. How Kandyse Brandt could have found me here at these thermal baths in Budapest isn't so surprising. The question that comes to mind is why. Why is Kandyse Brandt here in Budapest, and what does she want, or rather, what have her handlers told her to pass to me? She is a courier, nothing more as I told her back in Athens at the temple-like estate of her boss. I had hoped to have a single day of rest and relaxation, to allow my mind and body to reset. Even that no longer seems possible. As I walk toward the table, I can see the eyes of the Hungarians fixated on Brandt. In this country full of beautiful women, Kandyse Brandt's beauty is still remarkable.

"They don't have your favorite beer … Baltica Seven, isn't it? But I ordered one I think you might enjoy," she says as she gazes at the name on the bottles set before us.

"Sopron?" I ask. "Fitting, Kandyse. You're too much for me sometimes," I tell her, as I pour the Sopron beer into our glasses. "Sopron, the border town where it all began. Well, the beginning of the end of the Cold War, that is. During that summer in 1989, where the East German tourists crossed from Hungary to Austria, to their freedom."

"Oh? Is that right? How interesting. I did not know," she says, lowering her sunglasses, pulling me into her trance inducing Aegean Sea-blue eyes.

"Kandyse, what is it you want to tell me, or have been instructed to tell me? Please do what you've been told to do and leave me be. I'm in no mood. I'm not alone here today. My colleagues will soon return from their massage treatments. I would prefer not to introduce you. You understand, I hope," I say, as I raise my glass in a halfhearted toasting gesture.

"Oh, please don't touch my glass. Not here. And as far as your sister and your Russian girlfriend, don't worry. I won't interfere. They will not know I was ever here. So, relax. Let's enjoy each other's company for a few moments, OK?"

"Kandyse, she's not my girlfriend. You know exactly who she is, don't you?"

"It's not my business. You're really easy to find. You want to know why I am here? Ask me anything. I am ready," she says as she shifts her lounge chair closer to mine and leans in, as if she expects me to whisper my deepest secret or desire into her ear.

"Tell me, Ms. Brandt, tell me about those synthetic stones—diamonds. But I'm in no mood for games. I don't care about your secretive diamond trade. Just tell me about synthetic diamonds, Kandyse."

Brandt leans back in her lounge chair, turns her head as if surveying the surrounding area for any eavesdroppers. She then looks back at me. "OK," she says with a deep sigh. "You really want to know. The Russians are close to perfecting a synthetic diamond on a large scale. They've been at this for a long time. For now, it's still far cheaper to mine them from the ground the old-fashioned way, but they can't help themselves, their scientists and KGB types. They think they will succeed and dominate the global market one day. They won't. Trust me."

"And Victoria? What is her role in all of this? Kandyse, please don't pretend you don't know who I'm talking about; that would be insulting," I tell her.

I'm done playing games with this woman.

Besides, there's nothing to lose. My intuition tells me to press her and press her hard.

"Victoria has a lot of … you Americans like to call it 'baggage?' Her father was involved in several secret projects, most of them failures. His passion was DNA research, but he had little support, and when the Soviet Union collapsed, so did the funding for his research. He was involved in some very messy things, Dennis. Ugly stuff. Some of it was related to that orphanage. Victoria is nothing more than a courier, a messenger, a go-between. Her business interests allow her to travel freely between East and West and make a lot of money. In the end, she is a broken woman, a sad figure in a way."

"She's dead, Kandyse. I don't know if she committed suicide, jumping off a bridge to her death, or if someone killed her. We may never know. Help me find this killer, Kandyse," I tell her. She doesn't gasp in shock, cover her mouth, nothing, no reaction. Did Brandt already know Victoria was dead? Possibly, but it's highly unlikely she had any role in her demise. At least my senses—my intuition—tell me she didn't.

Her head turns slowly, discreetly, casually surveying our surroundings. I only hope no one is watching us, or her. I'm in no mood to deal with surveillance or worse.

"We last heard Victoria was involved in fundraising related to developing the technology for the large-scale manufacturing of synthetic diamonds in a more cost effective manner. This sort of research takes a lot of capital. Perhaps that got her killed? She got sideways with an investor or defrauded one; who knows? This killer of yours, we don't know who he is, but probably he's connected to the synthetic diamond business."

"And you, Kandyse, what are you doing in this mess? What is your role?"

"My job is to monitor ... track this, among other potential problems so that one day, when the time is right, we can buy them out and shut down the research. Dennis, we don't kill our competitors; we buy them out. You understand that, don't you?"

"Well, Kandyse, you really don't know all that much. You should go home. I may be in over my head, but so are you. I once told you they would discard you when you were no longer useful to them, your diamond consortium. You've now come to Budapest, sitting with me in this beautiful and serene place at these ancient thermal baths. It's so peaceful here, but it's an illusion, Kandyse. We're probably being watched. By whom, I do not know. You have many talents and possess extreme beauty, but it comes at a price. So, tell me, Kandyse, before you depart, how do I catch this guy? We found a list of names on Victoria's body. It may be a list of his potential victims, but we don't know for sure. We want to save the next victim but do not know who that next victim might be. We still don't know what is driving this killer, this maniac, the Russian term for a serial killer. Is it revenge, lunacy, something else?" I ask her.

"It's always money, the love of money, isn't it? Perhaps he chooses his victims according to wealth or status or gets his enjoyment, his satisfaction from destroying lives, the lives of the victims' families. Purely sadistic in a way, isn't it?" she asks.

"Yeah. You might be right, Kandyse. But listen to me. I don't want you to wind up dead, his next victim. You need to keep a distance from me and my colleagues. I fear you may not be long for this world, Ms. Kandyse Brandt," I tell her.

She just looks at me, plainly, serenely, without expression. Her face is close to perfection, nearly as flawless as her body. But she is flesh and blood and could wind up dead, as broken and distorted as Victoria, brutally discharged onto the rocky shore of the Danube River.

Despite the open talk we've just had, this woman remains a complete enigma to me, the same as when I first spotted her in that San Francisco restaurant, sitting alone at the bar, while my U.S. Customs Service partner, Rich Marino, and I were meeting with the KGB resident from the Russian Consulate so long ago. She stands up and extends her hand. I extend mine.

"Farewell, Special Agent. May the gods be with you. It's been a pleasure, a genuine pleasure. I mean that, sincerely. No one has ever spoken to me in the manner you have. I appreciate that more than you can imagine. You'll catch him. Believe in yourself and in your team. Oh, and about my 1960s fashion style, well, would you like to know? Do you really want to know?" she says as she releases her firm grasp on my hand, turns, and slowly walks away. I'm left sitting on the lounge chair, speechless and breathless. I don't know women. I don't understand them, not one.

I have lost track of the time. I look over at the pool and think about jumping back in to swim a few more lengths when I spot Jennifer and Oksana approaching. They are glowing, and look refreshed, having finished their massage and sauna sessions.

"How was your swim? Were you bored without us?" Jennifer asks. She glances over at the table with the two empty beer glasses and looks back at me. I had forgotten to ask the waiter to remove the empty glasses and bottles.

"It was great. I was thirsty afterwards. I'll have the waiter take those glasses. He's busy and left everything on the table."

"I can see that. And the extra towels on the other lounge chair. Oh, those were for us, I suppose," Jennifer adds.

"We had such a wonderful massage, and I showed Jennifer how to take sauna. Too bad they don't have birch branches here, like in Russia," Oksana remarks, with a slight smile. "Women here are so casual about nudity. It's refreshing in a way. They have a separate section only for women. Hungarian women are beautiful, but there was one woman in particular. She looked like a goddess, so stunning. I never pay much attention to other women's figures, but her body was flawless. Funny thing is, she gave me and your sister the once over, then nodded politely to us and disappeared. Every eye in the place was on her. She looked like a starlet, one of your classic 1960s Hollywood movie stars, the way she carried herself, and moved."

"Oh? Well, they are making films here, and in Prague. Perhaps she's here for that? I've ordered a local Hungarian beer for you both, and mineral water. Go for a swim, if you like, and when you are both ready, we'll deal with our list," I say.

Jennifer just looks at me. I suspect she knows, and has thankfully stayed quiet, about my friend from the Republic of South Africa. I expect she will talk to me soon enough once we're alone. The lingering look she gives me says as much, and her comment about the two empty beer glasses confirms it. I'm not sure if Oksana suspects anything. But with Oksana, anything is possible.

"So, shall we?" I ask them as they emerge from the pool. I pour the cold beer into their glasses. We toast and they take their first sips of Sopron Hungarian beer. "Before we start, let's think about this for a moment. If this imposter priest had no part in Victoria's death, he may not yet be aware she is dead. Perhaps we can use that to our advantage? Just a thought," I suggest, but I can see they aren't biting.

"Nyet. We have our plan, our agreement," Oksana says as she removes the torn notebook pages from her bag. "We need Sharon here. She told me she would come as soon as she finished her work in the office," Oksana adds, as she scans the area for any sign of her.

Jennifer says, "I agree with Oksana. We talked and agreed about this last night. Nothing has changed. Or has it? Did you learn something new you wish to share with us?" she asks me, as she smiles coyly.

"No, not really. Go ahead. We've got nothing to lose," I respond.

Oksana slowly unfolds each paper until there are four torn pieces of paper on the table. She turns the first paper over to reveal the chosen name. "Nadezhda Aleksandrovna Kazakova," she says, reading the name aloud. "I think that is Sharon's writing. It's definitely not mine."

"Not mine, either," Jennifer says.

Oksana turns the remaining three papers over to reveal each chosen name. "Well, what are the chances?" she asks, looking down at the revealed torn papers on the table.

"Nadezhda, Nadezhda, Nadezhda, and lastly, Nadezhda," I say, slowly reading the same name written on the four separate pieces of torn paper. "What are the odds? I would have never guessed." I shake my head in disbelief.

"It's not a game of chance, Dennis. It's sud-e-ba, destiny," Oksana says. She pulls out the list and traces slowly the columns with her finger. "Yes. Rome, Rome, Italy. She's in Rome."

"Oksana, no. We're not heading off to Rome based on a turn of the roulette wheel. Don't even think about that. Let's wait for Sharon and see if she's found anything in those databases, something concrete that we can use to guide us like real investigators would do. If there's nothing, well, then we can talk about going to Rome. How does that sound?" I ask. Jennifer and Oksana are both looking at me. I can sense they don't like my dismissive attitude.

I sigh. "OK. So, Rome it is, the eternal city. Fitting in a way, isn't it? The Pope, head of the Roman Catholic Church, sits in Rome. This killer, this imposter priest, masquerading as a Russian Orthodox priest, there's a cruel irony here. Let's hope this ends in Rome, and Nadezhda is still alive. That's we're not too late," I tell them with resignation. I look up from my glass on the table to catch Sharon Austin approaching. It's good to see her, and I hope she will have discovered something in those databases that will set us on the right course to our next destination, beyond the one ordained through this absurd game of chance.

"So, Sharon, what gifts have you brought us?" Jennifer asks. It's the same question my sister asked me when I returned to Athens from San Francisco.

"Gifts? No Fabergé egg, that's for sure. That's the correct response, right? I went through every name on that list. With the help of a few analysts I know, I called in some favors. I couldn't help but reach out to one of my closest friends posted in the Legal Attaché Office in Rome. Even though I'm uncertain if any of you did, I selected Nadezhda. I've got an address in the eternal city." Sharon looks at the three of us, silently staring at her.

"What? I said something wrong? Sorry, but that was my choice. None of you chose her? Well, I suppose you didn't. A funny thing … I don't speak Russian as you know, but I like languages and I checked the etymology of the name, Nadezhda. It means hope. Oksana and Dennis, you both know that already, don't you, sorry for being…" Sharon says, as Oksana cuts her off.

"Yes, Hope, Sharon. You have an address for this woman in Rome?" she asks.

Sharon says, "Several addresses in different cities: Rome; Milan; Venice; and Naples. I think the family's principal home is in Rome. Nadezhda's family is extremely wealthy. They own several businesses in Italy. And what names did you all choose?"

I respond, "Only one, Sharon. Nadezhda—Hope. Fitting in a way. We've nothing else to go on; there's only hope. I guess we should plan on flying there tomorrow, do you think? To Rome, the Eternal City." I lift my glass and make eye contact with each member of our task force.

They all lift their glasses as the waiter appears carrying several more bottles of Sopron beer. I set my glass back down on the table and pour Sharon's beer into her glass, so she can join us in our toast to the Eternal City.

"Sopron? What's with the name? It has a familiar ring. You know this beer?" Sharon asks.

I say, "Yeah, but that's for another day, Sharon." I lift my glass. "To us, the hunters. The chase is on. We'll catch this killer," I tell them, my mind drifting back to Vasily's toast at that Italian restaurant in Carmel that special evening; it feels like so long ago.

Oksana and Jennifer finish their beers and set off to explore some of the complex's other pools. It leave Sharon and me alone, to catch up for a few minutes.

"So, anything else you need to share with me while we're on our own?" I ask.

Sharon gives one quick glance around us to make sure we're alone.

It seems there is no one else.

"Ben Nolan is close to pulling the plug on our investigation. I spoke to him earlier. He's a bit freaked out about the death of Victoria, and he's thinking about flying over to Budapest and will use an I-LEA visit as the official justification," she tells me as she takes another swallow of her Sopron beer. "Not bad, not bad."

"We need a break, Sharon. Either we stop him in Rome, or we gather our belongings and head home. But we're on the verge of catching this guy. I can feel it."

"There's something else. You just can't make this stuff up," she says, taking a deep breath.

"Go ahead, Sharon. I'm ready … I think."

"That curator from the Hillwood Estate Museum, Dr. Hedwig Kiesler."

"OK," I say, as I raise both hands to cover my face in anticipation. "Please don't tell me she's dead or missing. I don't think I can take much more."

She says, "No. She's very much alive. Thank goodness. She called FBIHQ, the International Operations Department. She was trying to get in touch with you. I got hold of her. You were right; it was the Deputy Assistant Director Tiffany Ames, and get this, she went back to the museum, this time with a vengeance. Kiesler said Ames grilled her, threatened her, apparently.

"Ames told her she was certain another FBI agent had been there, one who was also interested in Fabergé eggs. Kiesler never gave you up; that woman's got guts. What exactly did you say to her when you were there?"

"I told her not to disclose my visit to anyone, particularly that woman with the concealed weapon under her jacket if she showed up. Guess I owe her that coffee I promised?"

"You owe her a lot more than a coffee. Ames has been snooping around International Operations on the fifth floor, and braced several staff, trying to get a handle on your latest whereabouts. Fortunately, no one had a clue where you actually were. They told her you were probably back in Moscow. Nolan later found out she was snooping around. He's furious but keeping quiet for now. I thought we were done with three-dimensional chess matches. Guess not," she says, shaking her head. "Get me another beer. I'd rather drink than swim. Funny thing is, I don't normally even drink beer. I wish this would end, Cos. And I'm still so jet lagged."

"It will end, Sharon. Your jet lag—and this case—it will all end, I promise. Ames is dirty. She's deep in this mess. How? I'm not so sure. No matter, we're going to have to tell Nolan. I don't think we can keep this stuff from him much longer."

"I already took care of that. When I heard about Ames going back to the museum, and her snooping around International Operations, that was enough for me. I told Nolan our suspicions that the imposter priest is, or was, a Bureau source run by Ames and her boss. Funny thing is, he didn't sound that shocked. Maybe I'm just 'over-analyzing' things, huh?"

I say, "I'd kill—no, not kill, I take that back. Rather, I'd just love to get a photo of this source. Any chance? Now that Nolan knows, maybe he can discreetly find one for us if there is such a photo? By the way, Kandyse Brandt, the South African, is here—well, she was here, Sharon."

"What? You're joking? You saw her here in Budapest?" Sharon asks.

She looks as shocked as I've ever seen her. I nod.

"Yep. Look, Kandyse Brandt is a complicated woman, with her own agenda, but there's a part of her I believe is redeemable, sincere and authentic."

"Really? You're not joking, are you? I hope you didn't share too much with her. She's not trustworthy," Sharon says.

"Relax, Sharon. It's OK. I know what I'm doing. So, Kandyse thinks this whole thing is about love, the love of money. And it's all connected to the development and manufacturing of synthetic diamonds on a large scale. Something tells me she's right.

"Wow, I'm starting to sound a bit like Jennifer. Please don't tell me I'm heading down a rabbit hole," I tell her, scanning our surroundings to see if Jennifer and Oksana are anywhere nearby.

"Once Oksana and Jennifer return, let's get back to the hotel, have dinner there, and you can work on reserving us tickets for that early morning flight to Rome. We could all use some rest tonight for whatever awaits tomorrow," I tell her. "Come on, join me in the pool for one last swim. It will refresh you more than that Sopron beer and help cure you of your lingering jet lag. The Hungarians believe in the restorative powers of their waters. Maybe they're right," I say.

I extend my hand to Sharon's, to coax her out of the lounge chair.

It will be our last swim in the captivating Széchenyi thermal bath complex.

Chapter 21

After a quick dinner at the hotel, we retreat to our rooms. It feels so good to be back in my hotel room alone with my thoughts. I slowly organize my belongings as we'll need to leave for the airport tomorrow before six. My mobile phone is ringing, breaking the quiet.

"Dad? There's someone here who wants to speak with you," says the voice on the other end. I realize it's my daughter, Kristen. She must have arrived in Italy by now with my wife.

Sharon told me they intended to later surprise me in Athens.

"Go ahead, put Mom on the phone," I tell her. "We can talk later, after I catch up with Mom."

"Well, it's so nice to speak with you," the male voice on the phone line tells me. "Your wife and I had a lovely chat during one tour. Did she mention that to you?"

I still don't recognize the voice; the accent isn't identifiable.

It must be someone working at the embassy in Moscow, I figure.

"I'm sorry, I don't recognize your voice," I say, confused as to why my daughter didn't pass the phone to my wife instead of to a person I don't recognize, with an accent I can't identify.

"I know you, Special Agent. Well, I feel like I know you and your lovely family." No, it can't be. I fall back into my chair, the blood rushes to my head. I feel as though a truck has hit me.

"Put my daughter back on the phone. Put her on the phone, now," I scream into the speaker.

"Be patient. She is fine. I am taking care of her, since you obviously couldn't. You were too busy traveling, enjoying the sights on holiday with your friends."

"I'll tear your head off if you touch her. She is not part of this."

I struggle to keep my emotions from overwhelming me.

Somehow, I need to remain calm and rational.

If this is the killer, if I'm speaking with the imposter priest and he's taken my daughter, I need to keep talking to him as long as possible, gathering as much information as I can.

The caller ventures, "Kristen was on a class trip. I was there on business, and now we are in Venice. We've had the nicest conversations. Her Russian is quite good, barely an accent. I'll get to the point. I want to trade. Anastasia, for your daughter. Bring Anastasia from Athens to Venice, and you can have your daughter back.

Don't involve any of your comrades. It's just you and me. I need to get on with my mission, the one you have been interfering with. I will call you tomorrow. That should give you plenty of time. This is all so exciting, isn't it?"

The phone line goes dead.

I hear a knock at my door.

Oksana, Jennifer, and Sharon are standing there, all looking to be in shock.

"Lenore's just called me. Kristen's missing. They were touring Rome on that class trip, and she vanished. Lenore is heading to the Legal Attaché Office in Rome. She's waiting for your call. She tried to phone you, but your line was busy," Sharon tells me.

"Come in and close the door. Sit down, all of you." I tell them about the phone call. "Sharon, call Lenore, and tell her to get to Venice the fastest way possible. She's got a mobile phone, so try to get through and stop her from going to the Legal Attaché Office in Rome. I don't want the Bureau knowing what's happened. Not yet. Do exactly as I say, Sharon. I'm serious. And don't call Nolan. It's my daughter. If we cross him, he'll kill her, Sharon."

Sharon heads out the door, back to her room.

Oksana and Jennifer are sitting there, both looking at me.

"OK. We need to get to Venice. He said he'll call again tomorrow. He thinks Anastasia is still in Athens. That's a good thing. We obviously can't do a trade. I'm not sure he really wants her.

"Maybe it's me he wants. It doesn't matter. Give me something ... Your ideas. I'm in shock. I just didn't see this coming but I should have."

"Obviously, we'll not trade Anastasia for Kristen even if we could somehow get her to Venice. That's off the table." Jennifer is right. It's not an option.

"OK. I think we can all agree on that. But he thinks Anastasia is still in Athens in our care. Let him continue to think it. So, what's our plan?" I ask them.

Despite my efforts to stay focused, I can't help but worry about my daughter and what she might be experiencing right now. I can't allow it to cloud my judgment, and the intense emotions are impacting my ability to think with any clarity.

Oksana steps in. "We've been in a reactive mode for a long time. He acts; we react. We need to turn the tables. We act, and he reacts."

"OK, Oksana. I understand the need to be proactive more than anyone, but he's holding all the cards. Isn't he? And if he thinks otherwise, well, I don't want to even speculate about such things. Give me something concrete, a plan. How do we make such an exchange if we don't have Anastasia to trade?"

"I'll be Anastasia. We will exchange me—as Anastasia —for Kristen," Jennifer says with conviction.

"No. He'll kill you. He'll kill you both," I say, dismissing her idea. "I'll have a dead daughter and a dead sister. No way. This won't work. I'm serious, Jen."

"But she is right," Oksana says, nodding. "To a degree. There is a way. Think about it. Yelena and Anastasia confused him that evening in Athens, when they changed hair colors and clothing. He's not the perfect assassin. He blundered that night. But you're also right. It should not be Jennifer. It should be me; it will be me. I will be Anastasia. I speak Russian and Greek.

"We will use clothing, makeup, hair color, hairstyle, jewelry, everything we can find to make me look like Anastasia. She's slightly taller than I am, but he'll be laser focused on her face, on my face. If we can somehow distract him from examining me too closely, he'll never know.

"I will kill him. But for now, excuse me. I need to contact someone in Moscow, someone I trust absolutely. Someone who has the right connections to get us weapons, the disguises we will need, and do it quickly, with no outside interference."

Oksana stands up and heads back to her room.

Jennifer and I are now alone in mine.

I don't like the silence in my state of doubt and dread.

I say, "So, we'll need to be flexible once in Venice. He will probably run us around town for a while before setting the location for the actual exchange. Venice is a city of canals and bridges.

"This will play a role in the exchange, no doubt. He knows the city, and that's why he's chosen Venice with its canals, bridges and gondolas."

"Dennis, I've been thinking about the exchange. I recognize my limitations. Yeah, I'm not law enforcement trained, but I'm a psychologist and soon, a behavioral psychologist. He's blundered before, this imposter priest. He's far from perfect, although he thinks he is on his so-called mission. Here's my proposal. As you say, he may not know Victoria's dead, although he may have killed her; we don't know. He certainly knows Yelena's dead; he killed her that night."

"Jennifer, I know where you're going with this. No. No way. This isn't a game; it's real life."

"Exactly. When Lenore gets to Venice, she will be ready. I guarantee it; she's not just your wife, she's the mother to Kristen. So, we've got Oksana as Anastasia. I will become Yelena, and Lenore will be Victoria. He will have a hard time processing what he is looking at when he sees us, real-life ghosts. Actually, two ghosts, apparitions returned from the grave to take their revenge. This guy is close to unraveling. We need to put him off balance, to make him doubt himself and what he is seeing—will see—just as the exchange is being made.

"If Oksana can somehow get us the right experts in Venice to make our disguises convincing enough and get us into the right clothing … You and I both know the people possessing such unique expertise in Russia. You more than me, I suppose. Well, the three of us will rock his world and put him back on his heels, distracting him long enough for us—for you—to end this, to end him, and to free Kristen."

"I need some time to think about this. A part of me just wants to step aside, call in the cavalry and let the Bureau's Hostage Rescue Team take the lead. I can't believe I'm saying this, but your proposal, well, it's the best option. Will it work? Who knows? We can only hope it does. You and Oksana have both been in the arena from the start, not just mentally and emotionally, but in a real, physical way. So, for me, it's not about any lack of confidence in your abilities, your commitment, from either of you. You'll be there when the time comes, I know it.

"I'm thinking back to that kidnapping case, the Geschke one. At the end, it came down to a handful of us street agents and investigators including my partner,

Paul Campo, Sgt. Vance Stevens and me. SWAT moved too slowly, too cautious in the end.

"They weren't entirely ineffective, but I learned a lot during those intense days, about myself, about following one's instinct, working alone, seizing the initiative. This kidnapping, so intensely personal, is different in many respects, but still, it's a kidnapping. This will be our plan until someone or something convinces us otherwise."

Sharon's contact at the Legal Attaché Office in Rome arranges for our airport pick up and makes hotel reservations without asking questions.

The hotel is a former private villa next to one of the countless pedestrian bridges.

Lenore is scheduled to arrive in the afternoon, a few hours after our flight. We haven't seen one another for several weeks, not since we were both in New York on leave.

"So, tell me about Venice, Sharon. You've been here before. I know it's full of tourists and beautiful churches and museums with lots of treasures. Oh, and plenty of bridges and canals. The guy is pretty smart to choose a city like this. Too bad he chose the original Venice, not Oksana's hometown St. Petersburg. We're at a real disadvantage here. We'll just have to deal with it."

"You can't control everything. I thought about asking the Bureau for technical support, to geolocate his phone at least. But forget it. We couldn't get their help in time, and it would take too long to get the Italians on board. We're really on our own. Just so you know, I didn't contact anyone at FBIHQ, but if Nolan shows up in Budapest and we're not there, he'll want to know why. I hope you will have an answer for him. I certainly don't."

The knock on the door startles me. In my heightened emotional state, even a simple knock on the door triggers an overreaction. It's not a good sign. I need to regain control of my body, my mind and my senses for what is coming. It's Oksana.

She enters the room and motions for us to sit. There is obviously news she wants to share.

"They'll arrive this evening. I hope it's soon enough," she tells us.

"Who, Oksana? Who is coming?" I ask, in no mood for twenty questions.

"The people who do this for a living, disguises, and other things. I am not sure where they will stay. They don't share a lot. They will call me when they're ready for us."

"So, you can trust them? I don't want them taking over this operation, Oksana. Providing communication equipment, disguises, weapons, is all fine, but no tactical ops folks. This is my daughter's life on the line," I tell her.

"They guaranteed me they won't do that. It's our operation. They will be here to support us, nothing more. Unless we ask them for help, and I told them it's unlikely. This comes from someone I trust, like family, Dennis. I think you know who I am referring to?" she asks.

Sharon and Jennifer are sitting there, quietly listening.

"OK, Oksana. So, they'll contact us when they're ready? We'll also need weapons, reliable ones. They'll bring those, right?" I ask.

I can't quite believe I'm asking such a question, requesting weapons from Oksana's Russian contacts. But what choice do I have? The telephone call could come at any time.

I suspect he will call deep into the night when the streets are empty.

"This is a secluded, quiet hotel. It's highly unlikely the priest knows where we are staying. Remember, he needs to stay in the shadows as well. I don't doubt he has his own apartment, somewhere in town. You guys can go outside, not far, to get something to eat, to stretch your legs. But don't venture out for long. Better to stay in your rooms and order room service.

"We need to react swiftly. Once things start, they will move quick, believe me."

Sharon speaks up first. "I don't get it. How does this guy think we'll convince Anastasia to cooperate with us, travel to Venice, and allow herself to be exchanged? It makes little sense."

"I hear you, Sharon. But you're thinking like a normal, rational person, a human being with empathy. This guy is a cunning killer, a psychopath, and a narcissist. In a world of his own, he dwells, a world filled with lies, deceit, misrepresentation, and fraud. He has given no thought as to the how, not for an instant. If he were in our place, how would he convince Anastasia to take part willingly in such an exchange? Think about it. Through lies, deceit, whatever it takes.

"Let's step into his world for a moment. I prefer not to stay too long. So, we could drug her, threaten her, or tell her we need her help to stop a killer, that she will be part of a special operation, and will be the star actress. Or through some elaborate deception, convince her we are going to do a photo shoot when the city is quiet, and the streets and canals are empty in the dead of night to revitalize her stalled modeling career. There are many ploys or scenarios we could invent to deceive Anastasia. Remember, she already trusts us. Well, she trusts Jennifer implicitly.

"Frankly, he doesn't care about how we get her here, how we convince her to cooperate. And he's certainly not going to offer us any suggestions. He knows I'll do whatever it takes to get my daughter back, even if it means sacrificing another human being. Anastasia, in this case."

"OK. I get it. I think," Sharon says, shaking her head. "Oh, I forgot to tell you. I told Lenore to call me on my phone, not yours. So, I'll know when she's landed, and she'll get picked up and brought here. She told me she's ready to do whatever it takes."

"Good thinking, Sharon. Thanks. Look, we all need to get some rest. I have a feeling it's going to be a long night. If you decide to step out, don't go alone," I tell them. "Stay hydrated and don't forget to eat, even if not hungry. We need to be strong and rested as much as possible."

"I'll stay here in your room and crash on the sofa. We can sleep in shifts," Jennifer tells me. "You shouldn't be alone in case he calls."

"Yeah, you're right. Sleep a bit. I'll order room service. Lenore will arrive in an hour. I don't expect him to call me, not until much later. He's likely not very mobile, so he probably can't wander around the city unless he's incapacitated Kristen or locked her in a room, which is entirely possible. But he's no fool. He won't call more than he has to. He doesn't want us tracing his calls.

We've had no indications that he has an accomplice working with him.

"But we can't say with absolute certainty. Victoria comes to mind; perhaps she was an accomplice. Of what sort, who knows? No matter, my gut tells me. Well, Jennifer, my senses tell me, he'll call; it will be a one-time phone call, and it will be dead of night, perhaps early morning while it's still dark. He'll give me one chance to make the exchange on his terms.

"If he thinks I've double crossed or deceived him, he'll go to ground, vanish. I don't want to go there, to think what that might mean."

Jennifer says, "Yes, please don't go there. He wants you to be on edge, to doubt yourself. He lives for this, to be in control and dominate. I'm getting a sense about this guy, about how he thinks. His inflated ego and sense of superiority will be his downfall. Have faith, brother."

Jennifer closes her eyes on the couch.

She looks to be sound asleep in a matter of seconds.

I can only stare out the hotel room window with my thoughts. We will need a concrete, detailed plan, a plan which will need to be executed perfectly. I hope Oksana's trusted unnamed contact, who I suspect is none other than Katerina, her cousin and close friend, will come through and deliver what we need. From my past interactions with Katerina, my gut tells me she'll do whatever necessary to get us the help, the expertise we will need.

"They'll be here in a few hours. They told me they will contact me when they're ready for us," Oksana says as she enters the room.

"What do they need from our side? Photos, clothing, makeup? I'm not familiar with this sort of stuff," I ask.

"Nothing. They are professionals. You'll see. I was told they will need a couple of hours to prepare us."

"Huh? Who's us? I'm not comfortable about this, Oksana, involving Jennifer and Lenore. You and me, well, that's one thing. We're both law enforcement and trained. But …"

Jennifer wakes, interrupting me.

"Stop. Stop right there. This is not open for discussion. Lenore will soon be here, and can speak for herself, but I'm certain she'll feel the same as me. We're all in, end of discussion."

"OK. But we're going to have a plan and walk through it step by step—together—an agreed-upon and detailed plan. Is that OK?" I ask, hoping Oksana and Jennifer will agree.

"Sure. We'll discuss everything. Sharon also gets a say in this, even though she will not be operational with us. We need her input," Oksana says. "I'll be in my room. I am going to sleep. They will call when they're ready for us. Wake me up if you need anything."

She closes the door, leaving Jennifer and me alone.

"Dennis, how did this guy find Kristen?" Jennifer asks, staring at me. "You must have some ideas or theories about it. I mean, he didn't just stumble upon her, did he? Is there something you don't want to tell me? I need to know. I deserve to know."

"How? I have only theories, Jen. I suspect he could know someone inside the Bureau who has access to our travel records. But his source could also work at the embassy in Moscow, a local hire, or even an American."

"So, this priest has an accomplice or source for that kind of access? To such sensitive information? That's a scary thought."

"Jen, he could also have direct access to travel records at the embassy, or perhaps he has a connection who works for a travel agency the embassy in Moscow uses. There are multiple possibilities. We travel using our true names. They haven't classified or hidden the records. It doesn't really matter, Jen. The fact is, he's got her, your niece, and my daughter. How he happened to find her isn't relevant, is it?"

"OK. Sorry, but it's been weighing on me. I'm going back to sleep. When I wake up, I'll then let you get some rest. It's going to be a long night for all of us," she says as she lies down on the couch and closes her eyes, leaving me alone again with my thoughts.

***

The knock on the door startles me.

I fell asleep in the chair. It's Lenore, and we embrace in the doorway.

"Come inside and sit down," I whisper to her as Jennifer is still sound asleep in the room's corner on the couch. "I can't imagine what you've been through since Kristen disappeared. We'll get her back. I promise. But I'm going to need you to be laser focused and as unemotional as you can manage. I don't mean to sound clinical or uncaring, but we're on our own, Lenore. It's you, me, Jen, Oksana—who you haven't yet met—and Sharon, who you know from San José. That's it. There's no cavalry coming to the rescue."

I hand her a glass of ice water, beginning to brief her on what's occurred since I received the telephone call from the imposter priest and tell her about our tentative plans to rescue Kristen.

"What is this? Water? Get me some vodka," she says. "I need something to calm me down." I reach into the minibar, take out two bottles, and pour the clear liquid into her glass and mine.

"Do you think you can handle a pistol? I know you haven't shot one in a while, and we can go over how to use it once Oksana returns. She'll bring the weapons for us."

"I'll do what is necessary. Whatever it takes," Lenore tells me. The vodka has taken effect and seems to have calmed her nerves. "So, what's the plan?" she asks.

"Oksana will let us know when her people arrive and are ready to meet with us. They should be here soon. I expect to receive the call from the priest instructing us where we'll have to go for the exchange much later tonight."

"Stop calling him a priest. He's no priest."

"Lenore, I know that, believe me. But it's the most convenient way to refer to him, for now."

"Catch me up on things. I know you don't like to discuss your Bureau cases with me, ever, but you need to make an exception. Go ahead, brief me. I don't need to know every detail, but don't skip any important stuff. I mean it, even if it's not pleasant. You understand what I mean?"

"OK. Here goes, Lenore. I'll give you all the important highlights, starting from Athens. It feels so long ago."

I begin with Yelena's murder, Anastasia's disappearance, and her eventual rescue.

She gasps, then smiles as I describe Oksana's impressive fighting skills that night in the men's room, and Jennifer's flying fists of fury in the parking lot, which likely saved Georgia Kaye's life. She just shakes her head. Lenore knows my sister.

I decide to skip the Russian banya detour with Oksana, along with my series of encounters with the mysterious Kandyse Brandt.

It's something she doesn't need to know, and I'm not keen to share, never. No good would come of disclosing those episodes. Lenore gives me a puzzled look as I tell her about Victoria, the striking physical resemblance, and Victoria's eventual sad and tragic demise in Budapest.

The briefing takes longer than I imagined, nearly an hour by the time I'm finished.

"Well, that's about it. Those are the highlights. There's food on the counter. Please eat something. I doubt you've slept much. Try to get some rest. We all need to be ready when the time comes."

I hear a gentle knock on the door. It's already past eleven p.m. as I check my watch.

Oksana is there with Sharon.

"They're ready for us, upstairs. You and Sharon will stay here in the room. We'll only be a few hours. Just two, they promised," Oksana says as she walks over to the couch to wake Jennifer. "That's your wife, Lenore? Even sleeping, I see she resembles Victoria. Interesting."

"Hi Oksana. Nice to meet you. And it's good to see you again, Sharon. Been a while," Lenore says as she sits up in bed. I'm glad she's gotten some sleep.

"I've heard a lot about you, Lenore. Sorry to meet you in these circumstances, but—" she says as Lenore cuts her off.

"And Dennis told me all about you. We'll have plenty of time to talk once this is over, and I have my daughter back."

"We need to get ready. Let's go upstairs," Oksana says, turning to Jennifer and Lenore. They're out the door in minutes. Jennifer has barely woken, only nodding to Lenore as she gathers up her things.

I say, "It's just you and me, Sharon, for a few hours. You haven't heard anything from Nolan, have you? I don't want him landing in Budapest, and wondering where we've disappeared to. That could be an enormous distraction, right?"

"It's the least of our worries. What are your thoughts about this operation? Just interested to hear your views. We have to talk about something for the next few hours while we're waiting for them to return," Sharon says.

I respond, "The priest will call and direct us to a location for the exchange. It will be one of his choosing. Somewhere, he is comfortable and feels like he has the advantage. Then, he'll do something unexpected, to set us off balance, distract us. He may send us to a second location and set a near impossible time limit for us to reach that location. I've been thinking about Anastasia— well, Oksana. Do I tell him we drugged her so she'll be compliant, or just leave that alone? Maybe it doesn't matter to him; he just wants to make his point, to kill one of us. He may suspect we don't have the real Anastasia for the exchange. He's mission focused, or has been for a long time. Who knows, he may sense the game is up.

Perhaps he'll go to ground when this is over and disappear. Anything is—"

Sharon raises her hand to cut me off.

"Stop," she mandates, interrupting. "He wants you to second guess yourself. We will have our plan, and if we need to adapt the plan, we will. All your experience, your life and Bureau experiences, your training, intellect, all of it, will come to bear. You'll be fine. Our team has been through a lot already. We'll get through this, together."

"I'm glad you're here with me, with us, Sharon. Wouldn't have it any other way. We'll get through this and emerge stronger and wiser, I hope. I'm going to close my eyes for a bit. Can you stay here in the room with me in case I doze off?" I ask Sharon.

And she nods.

***

I don't hear the door open, but there they are. I rub my eyes. It's been over two hours since they left. "This is incredible. What did they do to you three?" I ask.

The transformation is stunning.

The three stand before me as I continue to rub my eyes to make sure I'm not dreaming: Anastasia, Victoria, and Yelena. "How, how did they do this?" I turn to Oksana—Anastasia.

"They are experts at this. They meticulously consider every detail: hair color; style; cut; makeup; facial features; eye color; and dress. Taking all factors into account, they even consider body shape and height. Impressive, right?"

"Sorry, I'm a bit freaked out right now. I've seen plenty of photos of Anastasia and Yelena, but even Victoria, they got her. Well, they got Lenore, spot on. I don't think we have this sort of expertise in the Bureau or in any other agency. Although, I'm not one hundred percent sure we don't. No matter, it's impressive. Sit down; we need to plan. He'll call sometime tonight. The city is going to sleep soon, and once that happens, he will call. I'm sure of it."

For the next hour, we sit in the hotel room and discuss the plan.

Who will have what role, and what we will do if the unexpected occurs? What if the priest changes the location for the exchange? We'll have to be ready for that and react swiftly.

"OK, so let me summarize so we're all in agreement, and so each of us understands each other's role. I think Jennifer's right; with this city of canals and bridges, there's a good chance the exchange will involve a bridge. Lenore, as Victoria, will take Anastasia—Oksana—by the hand and proceed toward the exchange location, walking slowly and deliberately.

"I'll inform the priest that we sedated Anastasia and administered something to make her compliant and controllable. That will be the justification for the slow and deliberate walk which will be to our advantage. Anastasia will have to behave like someone under the influence of such a drug. But Oksana," I say, turning to address her. "The tricky part is that you—as Anastasia— will have to be laser focused, even while acting the opposite. Oh, so we're all in agreement; even if he insists I bring Anastasia to him, we'll not do it. It will be Victoria and Anastasia, alone, for the psychological impact, just like Jennifer says, right? I'll stay in the shadows, away, but not too far that I can't react quickly. I'm not thrilled about this approach, but I've been outvoted, so that's how it will be. Tactically, it makes sense. It will allow Oksana to focus on neutralizing the priest, and my priority will be to rescue Kristen. We assume he'll be armed at least with a knife, perhaps with a sidearm. I don't see a guy like this using an explosive device; it would somehow be beneath him, but we can't discount anything."

Oksana stands from her chair, clearly wanting to say something.

It's stunning to see how her experts have transformed her to look just like Anastasia.

Her hair color, facial features, even her skin tone ... It freaks me out to look at her.

"I know how to act, to pretend. We already talked about that many times. Lenore may have to guide me, perhaps push me a bit as part of our pretense. We'll have to react to the situation as it unfolds. And, I agree, Jennifer—as the ghost of Yelena—might serve as a useful distraction when the time is right, returned from the dead but only if needed.

"It's up to you, Jen, your call. Otherwise, stay far away, safe in the shadows. No one shoots at this priest, not until we have Kristen safely with one of us. I don't want him to escape, but our primary mission is to rescue Kristen. We'll catch this guy another day, if we have to."

Chapter 22

"Dennis, wake up." Lenore nudges me awake. "It's almost three. He hasn't called. Your phone is definitely working, right?"

I look at the mobile phone.

"Yes, there's good coverage, and the battery is fully charged."

Sharon is sitting at the table, looking at her street maps of Venice.

We may need her advice to navigate soon. Jennifer appears to be dozing on the couch and Oksana is sitting calmly, looking out the window.

Finally. I hear ringing. It's my phone. "Rialto Bridge. Thirty minutes," the voice on the line says. The call ends, the line going dead before I can respond.

"It's time. Rialto Bridge, thirty minutes. Can we walk there that fast, Sharon?" I ask, putting the transmitter into my ear. I can feel the adrenaline kicking in already.

It's not a good sign. I take several slow, even breaths to calm myself. We surround the map on the table as Sharon shows us the fastest route, handing us each smaller maps to carry in case our comms go out.

"Oh, no," Sharon says, covering her mouth. "It's one of those covered bridges. Once you enter it, you'll be in a sort of tunnel. Not good."

"We don't have a choice, Sharon. I'm not surprised he chose this bridge. It gives him a tactical advantage. From now on, use your stage names, Anastasia, Victoria, and Yelena. Agreed?" I ask.

They all nod. Anastasia and Victoria leave first. Yelena and I walk well behind, giving them as much distance as possible without losing sight of them.

I turn to my sister. "Once the bridge is in sight, stay as far away as you can, but try not to lose sight of me and the other two. If you see anything odd, let us know. You just have to hold that button down on your sleeve to transmit."

"I know. We went over this." She gives me that look.

"OK, sorry, just making sure. I don't know about involving Lenore like this. Tell me I'm doing the right thing, Jen."

"Stop. We decided and agreed. She will be fine."

I hear static through my earpiece, then a voice. "We're here. There's no sign of life on this bridge. We are going to walk across slowly, then back. We're a few minutes early."

I see them enter the covered bridge.

I'm thirty to forty meters behind, using a building's shadow for concealment.

There is no movement, not on the street, and not in the canal, although there are several moored gondolas making creaking noises as the movement of water through the canal bangs them against the pilings, enough to make a noticeable sound in the dead of night.

"What are we supposed to do? He's not here. No one is here," says Oksana's voice through my earpiece.

"Don't leave. Assume he's watching you both. He may call me. Keep acting and don't forget," I whisper into my transmitter.

"We know. We know. Wait. What is this? There's something hanging down from the ceiling. It's a cross. Strange. It doesn't belong."

"What sort of cross?"

"Orthodox."

"Can you reach it? Is it just hanging? Try to grab hold of it," I tell her.

"Got it. It's nothing. Sorry."

"No, Oksana, I mean, Anastasia; look at it. There's nothing attached, it's just a cross. Are you sure?"

"Wait. There's writing on the back. It's in Russian: Ponte dei Pugni, now. Huh?"

I can hear static. It's Sharon.

"It's a bridge. Look at your maps. It's a twenty-minute walk, max. The Bridge of Fists; I know it. It was the scene of brawls centuries ago between two warring families."

"Enough, Sharon. This is no time for a history lesson. Oksana, I can't lead you there. Look at your map. If I think you're off course, I'll let you know. Otherwise, go now. Stay in character. He may be watching, and it's no surprise he's changed locations. He's not calling my phone, and I don't think he will. Let's just hope he doesn't run us all around the city from bridge to bridge. Sharon, is this Bridge of Fists a covered bridge?"

"No. It's not," Sharon answers.

"Good. That's a relief," I tell Sharon as I then turn to Jennifer. "See if you can find a good vantage point once we're close to the bridge. Let's try to stay in close range of one another so we have good comms. Only one hundred meters apart, line of sight if possible. OK?"

"Roger that," she whispers back, and salutes.

I almost laugh. My sister still has her sense of humor, even at this intense moment.

"I can see the bridge now. There's no one around. We'll walk toward it," Oksana says quietly through her transmitter.

"Stop, everyone. Don't move. He's calling me."

I hear, "Go to the middle of the bridge. There's a rope ladder. Toss it down. Tell Anastasia to climb down to the lowest rung. Do it now or Kristen dies."

The connection is gone before I can respond.

"Did you all hear that?" I ask. I've kept my microphone open so they can listen in.

Oksana asks, "Found it. I tossed it over the railing. He wants me to do what now? Jump into the canal?" She sounds nervous, tentative, and confused.

I can barely make out the silhouettes of Oksana and Lenore.

Still no priest, no movement, except for a slow-moving gondola in the distance.

It's already past four. Some of the gondola taxis are likely getting into position for the start of the day. It will be light soon. With Oksana hanging suspended on the rope ladder under the bridge, the gondola driver will soon notice her, and a loud commotion may erupt.

The priest will probably call off the exchange and vanish with the noise. Lenore is now alone on the bridge, vulnerable, with Oksana suspended below it, hanging on the rope ladder.

The priest could appear at any moment out of the shadows and grab my wife before I have time to react. Perhaps this was his plan all along, anticipating we'd try to use a ruse to deceive him. He's been one step ahead of us for a long time, and now, he's about to take my wife.

I race toward the bridge, reaching into the small of my back for my weapon, the Makarov given to me by Oksana from her expert friends. The unsuspecting gondola is closing on the bridge, and the driver will soon notice a woman—Oksana—dangling on the rope ladder.

I only hope she can climb up before the gondola driver spots her. My adrenaline is pumping through my veins, and my heart is racing as I sprint toward the bridge. If I spot the priest, I'll shoot him before he can snatch my wife off the bridge and disappear with her.

"Lenore," I scream. "Get off the bridge. Run toward me, now!" She looks at me, confused.

I lose sight of the gondola as it passes below the bridge. There are muffled screams and noises. They sound Russian, not Italian. In the next instance, I hear a loud splash in the water next to the moving gondola. I see a body. It's Oksana. No, it's Kristen.

I can tell by her swim technique and pace, her legs kicking furiously, heading away from the gondola, toward the edge of the canal. I look to my right and see my sister, standing on the very top of the bridge railing, yelling at the gondola as it continues speeding away.

"Nastiya, po-ma-gee-min-ye! po-ma-gee-min-ye! Nastiya, Nastiya!" My sister is screaming at the gondola and suddenly jumps into the dark water below.

I look down the canal at the gondola as it's moving farther and farther away.

I don't see Oksana anywhere. Perhaps she's already dead lying in that boat. It has to be him, the priest. This priest must be in the gondola, escaping with Oksana.

He's likely killed her or has somehow incapacitated her.

A figure in dark robes emerges on the boat, leaning out over the stern. My sister must have surprised him, gotten his attention, screaming in Russian for Nastiya to help her, using Russian words I didn't know my sister even knew or could pronounce so perfectly and dramatically.

I drop into a prone position on the bridge. Twenty meters, twenty-five. The gondola continues to move farther away down the canal, and away from my position on the bridge.

God, please give me one good sight picture.

I focus my weapon on his torso. *Hail Mary, full of grace, the Lord is with thee.*

The figure stands up in the boat, facing the stern.

He's slowly making the sign of the cross, yet again convinced he has emerged victorious and is now escaping. He may be right. It's over, he's got Oksana, and he will soon be out of my sight and range once the boat makes the turn down the twisting canal.

I don't want to let him go, to let Oksana go. She may already be dead. No. I won't lose my partner to this maniac. I repeat the prayer: *Hail Mary, full of grace, the Lord is with thee.*

Focus on his body mass and squeeze the trigger slowly, I tell myself.

This is a difficult but not impossible shot, thirty meters from the moving target.

I take a deep breath and squeeze one round, then another three in rapid succession.

I lower the pistol to see if any of my rounds have hit their mark.

There's sudden movement in the boat. It's Oksana, her hands appearing tied together.

She lands a kick squarely on his back, and the dark figure loses balance and tumbles overboard. The electric propeller blades at the stern of the boat instantly entangle his robes as it moves erratically across the canal, smashing into a small pier before coming to a stop.

I look over to where I first spotted a figure I thought was Kristen, furiously swimming away from the gondola. I spot her in the distance, now close to the opposite side of the canal. She's reaching her hands toward a wooden piling to climb up from the banks of the canal.

Yes, it's definitely Kristen, thank God.

As I holster my weapon, I turn to my wife.

"Go, run across the bridge to the other side, and get our daughter out of the canal," I scream at her, pointing to the location on the other side. "I have to find my sister. She's jumped in the canal." I don't see Jen anywhere, only hoping she hasn't drowned or gotten herself trapped between wood pilings on the side of the canal.

Or worse, that she's trapped underneath the framing of the bridge.

I hear sirens in the distance, getting closer. These, and flashing lights are closing in all around us. It's the Italian carabinieri, the police. In the commotion and echoing gunshots, someone must have called them since they are everywhere. Several of their officers are in the distance, securing the gondola while others are already working to untangle the body of the priest from the propeller blades. He is lifeless, dead. His robes have become tangled in the moving propeller blades, pulling him underwater. I spot Oksana, alive and talking to the officers.

But where is my sister? Running along the promenade, I frantically scan the canal.

I flash back, far back to my younger brother's disappearance on that fateful day on the desolate beach and to the dilapidated bungalow, when I grabbed my uncle's service revolver from his holster. I shove the dark memory from my thoughts.

Where is Jen? I'll find her.

I scream out her name as I frantically run up and down the canal's promenade, looking along the canal for any sign of her or for her body in the murky waters.

"Dennis. I'm here. It's over," I hear the voice telling me.

I turn. She's standing behind me. It's Jennifer.

"I found a good vantage point, and stayed away, but not too far, like you told me. What's the matter with you?" she asks with a puzzled, confused look. She still looks like Yelena at this moment. I think about telling her to wipe off the heavy makeup but let it go.

"Why did you do that, Jen? Why did you jump into the canal, screaming for Anastasia in Russian? What was that? I didn't even realize you knew that much Russian but it sounded authentic, not even an accent. You're truly crazy, but I'm so relieved you're OK. Well, you distracted the priest long enough for me to take those shots, and for Oksana to react, kicking him over the side. Good timing. No, impeccable timing, Jen."

She stands there, looking at me, rendered speechless.

"What? What are you talking about? Who jumped? Kristen? She's safe now. It's over, brother," she says.

"You. You jumped." I grab her shoulders, about to embrace her, but step back. "You're not even wet? How's that?"

"I didn't jump. I was thinking how to distract him once I realized it was him in the gondola. But I was too far away, so it was over before I could do anything. You saw someone jump into the canal and scream something in Russian? Really? You sure about that? It wasn't me."

"Yeah," I say calmly, the adrenaline having finally stopped coursing through my body. "Keep this between us. We both know what happened, don't we, Jen? Yelena must've returned just long enough to save her dear friend Anastasia. I hope she's at peace now.

"Let's get over to Lenore and Kristen and find Oksana. Do me a favor and reach out to Sharon, will you? Tell her it's over, that our mission for today is done. The priest is dead, whoever he was. But he was no priest," I tell her, walking across the bridge to embrace my wife and daughter. Kristen is shaking and soaking wet, but alive. Her quick thinking saved her life; she jumped from the gondola just as the priest became distracted. I see Oksana approaching us, smiling as she rubs her face with a cloth, removing some of the heavy makeup.

"I'm back. It's me, your partner. No more Anastasia … Well, the real one is safe with her family in Moscow. What a day, huh? And it's barely sunrise. How is the cappuccino? Well, we are in Italy; it has to be good, right?" she asks and laughs.

We all do.

"I don't know, Oksana. But we're about to find out. There'll be more than just cappuccino at our breakfast table this morning, a lot more."

Chapter 23

"I called Nolan. He's just landed in Budapest, and will meet us in Rome tomorrow," Sharon tells me at the breakfast table.

"How did he react? He'll deal with carabinieri at their Rome HQ, I hope?" I ask.

"He sounded OK. Not thrilled, but not angry or upset. I don't know who's harder to read, Ben Nolan or Don Pierce. Guess we'll find out tomorrow in Rome," she says, reaching for another chocolate croissant. "Are these better than the ones in Athens?"

I whisper back, out of earshot of Lenore and our daughter, "It's a toss-up, Sharon. We must all look like hungry savages to these refined Venetians. The amount of food and coffee we're consuming is probably hard for them to process. But I don't care. We did it, Sharon, against all odds. Well, it will be interesting to talk to Nolan tomorrow. I think they'll pull me out of Russia, out of the legal attaché program. But we did what was necessary to rescue Kristen, and the priest serial killer's dead."

Jennifer and Oksana are enjoying one another's company.

Kristen is also smiling and talking; that's a good sign.

"I don't see it like that, Dennis. Our methods may have been unusual and not very conventional, but it's how we roll, isn't it? We did what was necessary, what had to be done.

"Hey, the good news, my jet lag's gone. Not sure if it was the all-nighter or this Italian coffee I'm binging on, or perhaps those beers in Budapest. Doesn't matter, does it? We'll take the morning flight to Rome. For the rest of today, let's relax, sleep, enjoy Venice. Rome can wait."

"Yeah, see Rome and die. It's just an expression, Sharon, from some play or a famous poet or philosopher, I think. Lenore, Kristen and I may fly back to the States from Rome, marking the end of our own Roman holiday and the conclusion of my international FBI career.

"And as far as this diplomatic stuff, it's far beyond my pay grade. I already talked to the local carabinieri commander and gave him enough to satisfy his curiosity, but they'll have more questions, no doubt. I'm sure they're not exactly thrilled we were operational in their backyard, and they knew nothing about it. Hey, that's life. I wouldn't do anything differently.

"Thank goodness the Bureau and the director have excellent relations with the Italian authorities at the highest level. I don't think they'll arrest us. Well, I hope not, not until I've had all the cappuccinos I can take in one sitting."

I motion the waiter to bring a third cappuccino to the table.

"How is she doing? You don't think he touched her, do you?" I ask Lenore, as we sit outside on the hotel room balcony, with Kristen already sound asleep inside.

Lenore says, "She said he didn't, and I really don't think he did. She wants to see some sights in Venice later this afternoon. That's a good sign. She asked if she did the right thing, jumping out of the gondola and swimming away. I told her it was exactly the right thing to do at the right time.

"She just smiled. I have a feeling that swimming will become her new passion, perhaps even more than ballet. We'll see. It's her decision, not ours." Lenore shrugs. "How does this work? The recovery process, I mean. Do you relive this every day, your cases, dreaming about them, or does it all fade away? I never asked you about your cases and how you manage afterwards, but I'm curious now. We've gone through quite a bit these last few days."

"I'm no expert on this stuff. You just go on. Maybe better to ask Jennifer, but later, much later," I say. Lenore never did ask about my cases and how I dealt with them.

I'm too tired to discuss such things at the moment. My brain is shutting down.

"I forgot to mention something," Lenore tells me, lying on the bed. Her eyes are nearly closed. "When I got to the other side of the canal, Kristen was struggling to climb up on the pilings. There was a woman there helping her. A local, I think. She probably lived in the neighborhood and heard all the commotion. Funny thing is, she reminded me of your mother."

"Oh, how so?" I ask.

"Not from her hair color or skin tone. Your mother would fit in here, with her dark hair and olive skin. This woman dressed a lot like your mom. The way she used to dress in those photos I saw of her when she was much younger, when you and your siblings were children."

She is struggling to keep her eyes open.

"You've lost me. What are you talking about? What photos?"

She's not making sense. Perhaps she's sleep talking.

"Those sunglasses, the hair, the makeup, the clothing, the kerchief from the sixties when she looked like Catwoman from the Batman and Robin TV series. That actress, Julie Newmar, and in some photos just like Jackie O with those huge sunglasses."

"This woman was dressed like that?"

"Yeah. I mean, she differed from your mom in that this woman was blonde. Beautiful, like your mom. But her hairstyle, her clothing, her shoes, they were all from another era.

"I remember hearing that northern Italy has lots of blondes. Your mother told me that. Well, once Kristen was safely on the dock, the woman gave me a long look, scanned my body from head to toe, then smiled. She said nothing. Perhaps it's the custom of Italian women? They are always judging one another, their clothing, figures, makeup, etc. I turned to Kristen, checking her for cuts and injuries, and hugging her. By the time I turned back, the woman was gone.

"I wanted to thank her for the help, how she'd assisted our daughter like that. She probably ruined her dress, reaching across those dirty, greasy pilings."

Lenore's eyes close, and she's instantly asleep but I'm now awake.

It's probably the four cappuccinos, and what she's just told me has my mind racing, yet again.

Could it be?

Was Lenore describing none other than the mysterious Ms. Kandyse Brandt?

She said the woman was blonde, pretty, and dressed sixties' style.

Did Brandt follow us to Venice, and witness the rescue of Kristen, and the final moments of the priest? Or could she have been more than just a silent witness?

Did she play a role in the dramatic events which transpired only hours before? I thought my rounds hit the priest in his torso, but could I have missed?

Is it possible Brandt shot him instead?

There was a cacophony in those otherwise quiet, empty streets. My shots were noisy and echoing, but my focus was on the priest when I pulled the trigger.

Nothing else mattered at that moment. I attributed the loud noise to the Makarov pistol.

I lie down next to my wife and daughter, both out for the count.

There's just no point in dwelling on this possibility any longer.

My eyelids are heavy too, now. Sharon told me she'll wake us mid-afternoon, so we can enjoy some sights before we all fly to Rome tomorrow.

***

Sharon tells me on the flight from Venice to Rome, "I found a wonderful hotel for us, right next to Villa Borghese Park. It will help us decompress. Ben Nolan's already there, and he wants to talk to you and me, separately. And tonight, we're all invited to the U.S. Ambassador's residence for an informal dinner. I've never been to Rome and never been to an ambassador's residence."

Sharon sounds excited.

"You'll get over it, Sharon, believe me. It may be anti-climactic after Nolan gets through with us. I'm so sorry to have dragged you into this mess, but I'm grateful. Without you, I couldn't have done it, and I only hope your position in San José is still intact when you return. You did nothing wrong." I expect Nolan will remove me from the legal attaché program and ban Sharon from working internationally.

She replies, "We'll meet Nolan in his room after we check in. Jennifer, Oksana, Lenore and Kristen can enjoy the park. I told them we should all go to the Coliseum together before dinner at the ambassador's." She seems so relaxed, and so unconcerned about our meeting with Nolan.

Maybe she knows something more. After all, she was in regular contact with FBIHQ and Nolan until we left Budapest for Venice.

***

"Come in, take your seats," Nolan tells us as we enter his room, a junior suite with a view of Villa Borghese Park. "Let's get this over with," he tells us.

I am surprisingly relaxed and at ease, expecting my international days to soon be over. It's merely a formality, to hear the news directly from him, our Head of International Operations.

"This is on me, Ben. All of it. Sharon was just doing her job. Don't punish or censure her."

He just looks at me somewhat blankly.

Then he says, "First things first, this so-called priest. The Italians will send us and the Russians his fingerprints. I'm fairly confident it's the source Sharon identified and reported on. We've done the checking from our side, a lot. But there's still plenty we don't know and may never know. It may depend on what the Russians will be willing to share. They may prefer to—"

I interrupt. "Ben, I get all that. But what was the motive and who was directing him? Victoria's dead, so we can't ask her. The priest's dead too, the real one, Nikolai Stavros. Oh, and this maniac, the imposter priest, he's been killed too, as well as Victoria's father! His associate, Sokolov, also dead. Perhaps there's someone still alive in their secretive circle in Russia who could enlighten us, explain what was really going on—and the why, Ben."

I don't dare touch the elephant in the room, Tiffany Ames and Kyle Davenport.

If Ben Nolan doesn't mention them, I'm certainly not going to open that particular door.

Perhaps they're both clean, and the disturbing information in the sensitive Bureau databases found by Sharon has a legitimate explanation and justification.

"Ben, I appreciate we won't understand everything; it's Russia. The Russia of Churchill's timeless quote: the riddle, the mystery, and the enigma, all of it. I get that. But you sent me to Athens to investigate a murder and find a missing girl. Not just any girl.

"I almost got my daughter killed and we stopped a serial killer. Granted, I may have stepped over the line here and there, but you knew I would, didn't you, Ben? Otherwise, you would have never chosen me for this assignment. Now, you're about to pull me from Russia and from international work and send me back to California. Fine, Ben.

"But I wouldn't have done anything different, absolutely nothing. I regret nothing either, not even involving my sister—who saved the life of Legal Attaché Georgia Kaye in that parking lot, by the way—and my Russian partner Oksana Aleksandrovna who most likely saved my life at the Aphrodite nightclub in Athens. And my wife … Yeah, involving her had risks, but it was the right decision, Ben. We all did what we needed to do and got the job done, your assignment— actually, the assignment from the director. I feel no remorse, no regret."

I stop, realizing I've been rambling in a stream-of-consciousness manner.

Ben Nolan and Sharon Austin are sitting there in silence, just looking at me.

I inhale deeply and then continue, "And the Russian Detski Dom 57, the KGB institute, their DNA and cloning research, the research and manufacturing of synthetic stones; you must know something more than we do? Did the killer and Victoria have a falling out? They had a parting of ways; perhaps the killer thought he was being cut out or deceived and took revenge.

"After all, there was lots of money to be made, either by successfully developing the technology to produce quality synthetic stones that would compete with the global diamond consortium, or by eventually being bought out by them for big money.

"And just who were the investors in this elaborate scheme? Yeah, I'd like to know, Ben. I—no, we, Sharon and I—both deserve to know. You know more, Ben. You've flown all this way from Washington, perhaps to do damage control with the Italian carabinieri, but you know more.

"It's you, me, and Sharon; no one else will know. There *is* no one else. I can keep secrets, lots of them, just ask my wife."

They both smile at me. I've had enough, and intend to enjoy my last international day with the FBI in Rome with my wife and daughter.

Our son is still in New York and will be surprised, perhaps disappointed, when he learns he'll soon be flying west to California instead of east to Russia.

"Enough," Nolan says, pausing to take a deep breath. "Pierce, Don Pierce, he's a busy guy these days. Well, I take that back. He's been a busy guy for a while. Going back to your Golden ADA case, when Sharon told him Ames and Davenport were snooping around inside the case files, that's when it started, for me, at least. It ends for them both today.

"Don has been running the operation, highly sensitive as you can imagine. They will serve search warrants on Ames' and Davenport's homes later today."

I just look at him, speechless, shaking my head in disbelief.

"What? Does this surprise you, Cos? You suspected as much, didn't you? That's what you told Sharon a while ago, anyway. We've had wiretaps on their phones, both at work and at their homes and got enough to charge them. Were they directing the priest? We're not sure, but they were in close contact with him, that's confirmed. They were blindly ambitious, driven by greed, the love of money and the love of those shiny stones. They'll cooperate.

"Well, one of them will. I suspect it will be Davenport. But will we understand everything, assuming Davenport or Ames agree to cooperate? No, I very much doubt it."

"And Don Pierce, when I met him in Washington, he was already working this case?" I ask for confirmation.

"Yeah. But he couldn't tell you that. It would have been an enormous distraction for you. We needed you to be focused on your assignment, nothing else. And as far as your international work, you're going back to Russia. But it's your call, for you and your family to decide."

"And Georgia, Ben. What about her? That assault or attempted kidnapping, whatever it was, were Ames and Davenport behind that?" I ask.

"Not sure. It's possible, but our investigation is far from complete. Georgia will go back to Athens if the director decides and if Georgia wants to go back; I am pretty sure she will."

"And Adam Wheaton? He played an important role, Ben. He's going to be OK, right?" I ask.

"He's fine. I spoke with him only yesterday, as it happens. He's looking forward to working with you in the future. Guess he likes this sort of stuff, the intrigue, and mystery. Right up his alley. That's enough for now.

Get out of here and enjoy Rome. It's a beautiful, sunny day.

"Forget about this case for now. We'll all be at the dinner tonight. I'm looking forward to meeting your wife, daughter, Oksana, and your interesting sister. As Don Pierce likes to say, 'Later, dude.'"

We shake hands, and I head out to explore the sites of the eternal city of Rome.

I turn to Sharon. "See Rome and die? Well, perhaps not today."

She laughs. "No. Not today, definitely not today."

Ben Nolan is waiting outside the entrance to the ambassador's residence when we arrive in our minivan taxi. Our three-hour walking tour of some of the ancient sites of Rome gave us the chance to begin to unwind and decompress. My mind and body still feel exhausted.

I'm sure it's the same for everyone. The U.S. Ambassador, Thomas Foglietta, is a gracious and welcoming host. He tells us about his working-class upbringing in one of Philadelphia's poorest neighborhoods, and his time as a U.S. Congressman before his appointment as U.S. ambassador to Italy. It's an incredible story, breaking free of poverty to head to the U.S. Capitol, to representing his country as ambassador.

He doesn't probe us with questions about the case, letting us each speak freely, sharing some of the amusing and funny anecdotes from the past few weeks.

It feels good to joke and laugh while we savor the incredible Italian cuisine from the antipasto to the pasta dishes, then the main entrée, and finally, to the panna cotta dessert.

Nolan pulls me aside after the dinner, suggesting I take my wife and daughter to Crete for a few days of rest and to have our son join us there.

He tells me we can decide whether we want to return to Russia to continue the assignment there, or if we would rather go back to California.

Nolan then asks me and Oksana to accompany him to a separate room, down the hall from the main dining room. As he opens the door, there he is, sitting alone … Louie Freeh, FBI director.

"Sit down, relax. I don't want to disturb your dinner tonight and won't take much of your time this evening. I know you are both tired," he says.

Stunned, I just look at him, the director, here in Italy at the ambassador's residence.

I met him once before, at his FBIHQ office right before my transfer to Russia.

It was a courtesy visit, and now we are in a separate room, alone with him.

Nolan steps away as soon as we enter.

"Ben has briefed me, and I'm fairly knowledgeable about the case. Sit down, both of you. Let me start with you, Oksana," he says, turning to her.

She immediately stands up as he addresses her.

"At ease, Oksana. Please sit down. I have spoken with the MVD minister, and with Deputy Prime Minister Popov. We have offered you an appointment to the FBI National Academy in Quantico. It's an eleven-week program, very intense, but it's your decision whether to accept the appointment. Your minister and deputy prime minister support the idea," he tells her.

She doesn't smile, just looks at him. She is Russian after all.

For an American or westerner, her non-reaction may appear odd, but I understand her. She is pleased, extremely so. She reserves smiles for friends, family, and close partners.

"Oksana? At least say something," I tell her.

"Thank you. I accept," she says, evidently shocked at the meeting with the FBI director and hearing what he's just told her.

"Well, that's all, Oksana. You can join the others for coffee unless you have questions for me? Oh, I do have one favor to ask, one request. I'd like you to work with our Academy's Defensive Tactics Unit while you're there. I understand you have a certain skill, and they could learn something from you," he tells her. This time, she smiles, stands, and extends her hand.

The director stands and they shake hands, both smiling now.

"Now, for you, Special Agent Cosgrove. What am I to do with you? And your sister, for that matter. I know I didn't give you the easiest assignment, but some of your, well, your actions, weren't exactly Bureau protocol. No matter, you've completed the assignment. The Russians are pleased—very pleased—with the results. As far as the Italians, well, that's quite something else, but they know me well, so, we'll get through this," he says, and pauses as he picks up his glass of juice, or what looks to be juice of some kind.

"I apologize about that, Director … Louie," I say and pause.

I had forgotten that Director Freeh insists FBI personnel address him by his first name. It's unusual for a senior government official, the head of the FBI, to insist his subordinates refer to him by his first name, but if that's what he prefers, so be it.

He's the boss. He must have his reasons.

I make a quick mental note to address him as he wishes.

"Louie, there was a lot on the line, the life of my daughter. I accept whatever punishment or censure may be coming." At that moment, I'm certain he will order my transfer back to California. My days of working abroad for the FBI are done.

"I brought you something," the Director tells me, flipping through the folders in his weathered brown leather portfolio. He pulls out a sealed manila envelope. "It's the rest of that lead, the one from OSI if you recall. Well, the background portion that wasn't included with the original paperwork. Frankly, I sometimes don't know what to do with stuff like this when it crosses my desk. I could kick it back to D-O-J and decline, I suppose. But we're the FBI; there is no one else. I've had to deal with some strange stuff since taking this position. More than strange, things that most people would dismiss as nonsense or fantasy. UFOs, ghostly apparitions, conspiracy theorists, Nazis, you name it. But you're not most people, you and your sister, Jennifer, are you?" he asks, locking eyes with me.

I'm tempted to look away, but I lean in.

After all, I'm a Special Agent, and while it's none other than the director of the FBI talking to me, the art of the interview rules still apply. They always do.

It's no time to be looking away or breaking eye contact.

No. Instead, I lean in. Oksana certainly would do the same, and so would my sister, Jennifer. Where this is going? I do not know.

He looks intently at me. "So, are you game? You can take this lead off of my desk and deal with it later, after you get some rest in Crete or wherever. You'll need that rest, believe me, once you open the envelope and read its contents. And what am I going to do with your sister? She saved my Athens legat Georgia's life. I, Georgia, and the Bureau, we all owe her for that. Adam … That's Adam Wheaton … spoke highly of her. You can tell her we spoke. I'd like her to consider accepting a place in our next new agent training class at Quantico; she has a couple of weeks to decide. It's entirely up to her."

"I'll pass the offer to her, Louie," I say.

I reach for the envelope, stuffing it into my coat pocket. Why not? The lead can't be any more difficult than the case we just went through. Well, one never knows.

"OK. Good. Now, I need to make some phone calls. Washington is six hours behind," he says as he stands. We shake hands. "Oh, one other thing. Sharon, Sharon Austin. I understand she enjoys working with you. I've already directed her boss in San Francisco to allow her to continue to work with you as needed while you're overseas. Besides, I wouldn't want to break up such an effective partnership. The Bureau needs dedicated people like her. Good luck, Dennis," he says, turning his head as if trying to recall something more. "Oh, good hunting."

He smiles politely, sits down, and begins tapping in a number on the phone. I can only smile back politely as I walk out of the room and close the door.

"How'd it go in there?" Nolan asks as I walk down the hall to join the others.

He's no doubt curious about what the director said to me in the one-on-one setting.

"Fine, I think. The director knows a lot, far more than I thought. Guess that's OK. Well, I think I'll take you up on that offer, Ben. We'll head to Crete for a few days. Would that be OK?"

"Sure. Get some rest and enjoy the downtime. Has Louie anything else in mind for you?"

"No. Not really, Ben. Just a routine lead to cover. No big deal."

"Oh. That's good. He's hard to read sometimes. There are few people he can trust, even in the Bureau. You best stay on his good side. Let's get some coffee and hear some more of those stories from the ambassador. I really like that guy, something about him," he tells me.

"Ben, I also like him. I would have loved to fight with him when we were kids. I bet he was a good street fighter," I say.

Nolan looks at me, confused, perhaps not sure whether I'm joking.

"It's a childhood thing, Ben. Just ask my sister. No, on second thought, don't do that. Best to leave the past in the past."

Chapter 24

"So, Jen, are you up for a run? There's an interesting trail up that hill. We can go as far up as you like, enjoy the view and then walk or run back down," I tell her, gazing out at the calm Mediterranean Sea in front of us.

"OK, why not? We can talk about it at the top of that so-called hill, though it looks more like a mountain than a hill to me. It's pretty scenery dramatic here. You had to choose this place to stay in Crete, in a place called Stavros? I can't believe there's a town with this name.

"We've had enough drama for a while, no?" she asks, lacing up her running shoes.

Lenore and Kristen just look at us, shaking their heads as they walk toward the calm, clear waters for a swim.

"You know anything about the history of this beach, this setting?" I ask as we begin our run along the beach, heading for the mountain.

Jennifer looks at me momentarily as she picks up the pace on the shifting sands.

I struggle to keep up. She finally responds.

"No, nothing. But you're going to tell me, huh?"

"Zorba the Greek. The movie, starring Anthony Quinn, made in 1964. Filmed right here, on this beach. You must have heard of it and its memorable beach closing scene?" I ask.

She looks at me, clueless, shaking her head.

"Nope. Never heard of it. It wasn't a Greek tragedy, I hope?"

"No, definitely not. More like a story of redemption and rebirth, something like that," I tell her between labored breaths as we begin to ascend the steep trail. "Let's focus on the trail, and talk when we're at the top, at the entrance of that cave."

I point up the mountain toward the cave opening.

We're both breathing heavily when we reach the cave's entrance, much larger than it looked from the beach below. "Let's sit over there, on those rocks. Some view, huh," I say. She nods.

We can see far out to sea, the entire village of Stavros visible off in the distance. I can understand why Hollywood chose this dramatic setting for a film.

Jennifer looks at me, then turns her gaze toward the open sea.

"I've given it a lot of thought these past few days. Thanks for not pressuring me about it, but I'm passing on the director's offer. It's not for me, not now, anyway. I need to finish my dissertation and continue my work, my research about our grandfather, his cases, and other cases from that era as well. You may not agree with my decision, but it just feels right to me."

She looks at me as she waits for my reaction.

I slowly nod. "It's OK, Jen. Really, it's ok." Her turning down the offer to enter the new agents training program at Quantico is not so surprising.

I'm disappointed, naturally, but she's my sister and it's her decision, her life, and her career.

She turns her gaze to the open sea.

"What a sight. The ancient people of this island surely came up here and sat exactly where we are now sitting. I wonder what they thought, how they lived, those Minoans."

I say, "We'll explore some of their ruins on the island. There's a ton of history left by them and others who followed them. They left traces all around us, believe me."

I stand and begin to stretch, preparing for our descent.

"I respect your decision. I spoke with Adam Wheaton a few days back. He told me you should call him and stay in contact. I know he'll be disappointed, but perhaps you can work with him from time to time. Why not, right? You want to know something? What impressed him most was your readiness to act without hesitation, to take physical action. He really loved that.

"Don't tell him I told you. Well, regardless, I'm going to miss working with you. Honestly. After what we've been through, it will feel weird to not have you there to bounce things off of, or to tell me things that no one else would. Funny, I never imagined I'd feel this way. It's life, right? Hey, we still haven't talked about that LAX woman. You promised, didn't you, when the case was over? Well, the case is over. So, go ahead, I'm ready." I sit back down, waiting.

"LAX, yeah. I found her, exactly as I told you I would. She was strolling around those upscale shops in Carmel Valley. I watched her from a distance as she went in and out of jewelry stores and boutiques. Then, I spotted her as she jumped into her car. I jumped into mine, caught up with her and followed, far enough behind so she didn't see me."

"No, please, Jennifer. That's exactly what I told you not to do. OK, so then what happened? You obviously survived, since you're here telling me this story. Go ahead, finish your story. No more comments from my side. Promise."

"She's speeding south down PCH highway one, heading toward Big Sur, so I figure, but she makes a dramatic U-turn right after the Bixby bridge, and heads back north. I make the turn and race to catch up, staying several cars behind. It's then that I call your Monterey County Sheriff's deputy friend Vance, Vance Stevens, telling him I can use some help.

"He knew who I was right away. Well, when LAX then turns toward Carmel, I suspect she's cleaning herself or knows I'm following her. She parks and heads on foot toward the beach.

"Vance races to Carmel to meet up with me after I've given him a quick briefing by phone, trying not to freak him out too much. I mean, this woman could be dangerous, right? You told me Vance is good at tracking people, he and his tracker dog. My plan was to find this LAX woman, confront her, and end this mystery."

"OK, Jen. So, now you're both on foot, she likely realizes you're following her. You've got Vance with you, and his dog? This sounds nuts. Sorry, I can't help but comment. I'm just trying to process what you've just told me. But go ahead."

"Well, we search most of the beach for her. Nothing. Then we check to see if her car is still where she parked it. At one point, I think I spot her jogging along the beach path, and could swear she sees us, but can't say for certain. Maybe she was just playing with me, with us. I don't know. Vance and I sat together in a nearby café, where we could watch her parked car through the window in case she returned. The car never moved, not for the two or three hours we were inside that café. That's all. Vance was there and helped out, just as you told me he would.

"He even ran the license plate for me, but it came back as a rental. I told him not to contact the rental company, to leave it be. I didn't want to get him in any trouble with the Sheriff's office. As much as I wanted to know who she was, some part of me didn't. Strange, huh?"

"No, not really. She's still out there. We'll find her one day if the fates allow, right? For now, let it go. I'm glad you let it go, Jen. I needed you far more in Athens, even though I wasn't happy you were there. If you'd confronted LAX on that day, things might have taken a bad turn. Who knows? And you wouldn't have been able to travel to Greece. We wouldn't be sitting here outside of the entrance to this cave, talking about it."

"Yeah. You're right. We'll find her and solve the mystery one day."

"Jen, I've been thinking about Yelena. You think we'll see her again? Do apparitions—" I say as she cuts me off.

"What? Reappear? Follow you? It's up to them when they appear or reappear. I only know they're real. Well, for us, they are. Yelena was there when it counted most, on that fateful morning. We should be thankful to her for that and leave her be. Let her rest in peace. Will Yelena return? Will we ever see her again? Perhaps, but we don't get to decide. Hey, what's with that OSI lead? Did you open the envelope? The one that you took from your director?" she asks.

"Nope. Not yet."

"Aren't you at all curious? Perhaps it's related to your missing Fabergé egg?" she asks.

"Jennifer, no. It's not. Not everything is interconnected. The LAX woman, the missing egg, the OSI lead, and those apparitions are all separate and unrelated."

"Really? You still think like this, after all we've been through? And what about your UFOs? You believe in those, yet you've never seen one with your own eyes. What will you do if—no, when you encounter them? Tell yourself they're not real; they can't be.

"Don't fall into that trap, brother. Follow your own instincts, your own gut. You're too good an investigator to do otherwise. Sure, you may find yourself out there isolated and alone, perhaps opposed or stymied by others at times. But isn't that how you roll? Admit it, it's your preference, working alone, doing your thing, on that razor's edge. And your gifts; as I've told you more than once, you need to acknowledge them and let them speak to you. I have a sense you're going to need me, brother, sooner than you think. I have to return to the States, and you … Well, I think you're heading back to Russia. I'll be there when you need me, and you will. Now let's get off this mountain," she says as she stands, slowly stretches and begins walking down the steep path.

Concentrating on my foot placements, I proceed carefully down the rocky incline following her, trying to keep from losing my footing and tumbling down. I stop at the midway point for a short break, and to admire the view of the beach still far below for one last time.

I spot Lenore and Kristen emerging from the water.

There's a young girl standing near them. She isn't wearing swimming attire, dressed more for an evening outing than for a swim or walk along the beach on this clear sunny day.

The hair, the dress, the body shape—no, it can't be—as I rub my eyes. I'm about to call out to Jennifer already twenty meters ahead, but let it go.

It's not her, Yelena, I decide just when the girl stops, turning her gaze to the mountain.

I swear she's looking directly at me and smiling.

No. It's just my psyche playing tricks. Still, I smile back, and shift my gaze down the steep incline, my sister having paused her descent to allow me to catch up with her. I turn my head back toward the beach, to the girl. She's gone. I think about telling my sister but decide to let it go. Yelena's brief appearance on the beach was personal, only for me, her final farewell.

After all, we're in Crete on this island so full of history, drama, and mystery.

My sister hears me laughing; I can't control it. The iconic closing scene of Zorba the Greek is unfolding right before my eyes; I see them both: Anthony Quinn—Zorba —as he teaches the Sirtaki dance to his British co-star, Alan Bates as Basil. They are smiling and laughing while dancing the Sirtaki, linked together arm in arm, alone on this deserted beach.

Jennifer finally pauses her descent on the rocky foot path and looks back uphill at me.

"You ok? Let's get off this mountain, back to the beach. Not sure why you're laughing so hysterically. I can barely manage to stay upright on these slippery rocks; it's much more difficult descending than it was running up, and you're laughing?" she says, just shaking her head in disbelief, refocusing her attention on the steep winding path.

"Yeah, Jen, I was thinking about you and me, and beaches. We always seem to be heading toward or away from one. What is with that?" I've caught up with her.

We stop for a short break, standing side by side, shoulder to shoulder on the narrow trail, gazing at the distant beach far below.

I just know Zorba and Basil are out there somewhere on that sand, arm in arm, dancing.

Jennifer smiles at me, then turns her gaze back toward the beach.

"Accept it. Embrace it. The fates will decide. We're in Crete, and this is Zorba's beach, right? The beach of redemption and rebirth, so you told me."

"I'll try to remember that. Perhaps this is one of those beaches whose magic is real, not just an illusion. No matter, let's get back down there for one last swim while there's still enough light."

The sun is setting.

I need to get off this beach.

Dennis T. Cosgrove spent decades pursuing criminals and advising governments on complex security issues during and after his FBI career. His work took him across the U.S., Europe, Central Asia, and the Balkans, offering rare insight into international crime and political tensions.

His debut novel, *The Diamond Game*, is fact-based fiction drawn from real cases and operations. His second book, *Nadezhda Dies Last*, builds on those experiences, weaving a gripping story of suspense and betrayal set in Moscow and Athens.

Dennis lives in Florida with his wife. When not writing, he enjoys rugby (now touch), yoga, and open-water swimming—always chasing new challenges. A third novel in the series is currently in development.